CANDYLAND

THE BATTLE OF NAUGHTY AND NICE

THE CLAUS UNIVERSE SERIES
BOOK 12

TONY BERTAUSKI

1

he bells sound different.

He had heard bells on Christmas Eve ever since he was little. The small silver kind. The *ring-ding-a-ding* kind. And in the morning, there would be presents under the tree. And his mom would say to his dad, "Did you hear Santa's bells last night?" Only she'd whisper it loud enough for him to hear. Loud enough for him to believe. Every Christmas. Just like that.

But this year the bells sounded different.

They were far away. There were more of them, too. Thousands of them. Like the galaxy was an instrument that vibrated under his skin. In his head. His fingers and toes hurt. Like he'd forgotten to wear socks and gloves in a snowball fight. The weirdest part? He could *taste* the bells.

Peppermint.

They rang faster as the universe shrank. His legs ached; his head thumped like a marching band snare drum. He didn't like the way it felt, not at all. There was a humming unpleasantness, like recovering from anesthesia when he had his appendix removed. He wanted to get away from the sound of them. He wanted to wake up somewhere soft and warm and safe. And then he did.

But not in his bed.

HE WAS HUNCHED OVER A DESK, with his forehead planted on a notebook. A string of drool hung from his lip, a quivering line of saliva that made a dark spot on the page below. He came into the world from somewhere far away.

There was singing. Quite a few voices sang a song he'd never heard before, but one that was merry. The Christmas kind of merry. There was also the smell of nutmeg, cloves, and sugar. The smell of cookies. The aroma was thick and filled his nostrils.

All of this and he hadn't even opened his eyes.

He did so, finally. Picking his head off the desk. It was a bowling ball on his shoulders. He wiped his mouth with the back of his hand. His face strange and rubbery. His body had fallen asleep like his leg did when he sat the wrong way for too long. Pins and needles would soon savage him as feeling came back. They never did, though. The pins and needles.

He blinked a few times, rubbed the sand from his eyes. He didn't know what to think. There was a squatty Christmas tree in the corner of the room and marshmallow kabobs at the fireplace. A little desk where he was sitting—a little desk with a glass of milk and a plate of cookies on it. Peanut butter cookies with fork prints in the middle of them.

He didn't know where he was. He didn't know anything. Not the day or the year. How he got at this desk and where he was before that. He couldn't remember (and this was where real panic set in) *his name*.

Anxiety wrapped his chest with an iron grip. He couldn't remember anything, but he knew this feeling: the cold plunge in his stomach and icy flow in his legs. He was grasping for memories— anything, *something*—to get a toehold. They weren't slippery and elusive.

They just weren't there.

The only hint of familiarity (and he could be imagining it, sure) was the notebook he'd been drooling on. A sketchbook, actually. The drawings done in ink. Those were *his* drawings, he knew. He turned the pages, hoping to see a name. And then:

"What are you doing in my house?" someone said.

He hit his head on the ceiling.

The young man wasn't particularly tall (average for his age, which was early to late teens, if he had to guess). The ceiling was just too low for a ceiling. He cracked his head good and solid. Crumbs and sweet dust fell from where he hit it.

To make things worse, he accidentally kicked the desk over. The sketchbook flapped like a kite in a windstorm. He crab-walked next to the Christmas tree, watching the milk that had been on the desk slowly spread across the gritty floor. Then watched the floor soak it up like a dry cookie. He continued staring at the same spot on the floor, long after the white puddle had disappeared, to avoid looking at the figure in the doorway.

The crown of his head hurt where he'd torpedoed the ceiling. He rubbed his face. Debris from the ceiling was sweet on his lips and stung his eyes. He put his head between his knees and closed his eyes until fireworks burst in the dark. He panted like a cornered animal; quivered like a puppy.

This is a dream. Plain and simple.

"Gandy?" someone called. "Come out here, sugar."

The young man opened his eyes (that, dear reader, took more courage than you might imagine). Through blurred vision, the image of a woman stood on the other side of the room. She was the color of putty; her skin sparkled like glitter. She held reading glasses in one hand, a book in the other.

Her head was perfectly round. Just like her eyes.

The young man clenched his fists and pressed them to his eyes. That thin wall holding back hordes of panic began to shake. *Try it one more time,* he thought. *Maybe things will be different. I'll be awake. I'll be in bed. I'll remember my name and—*

The air grew thin. Fluffy panic filled his head while lead pumped into his chest cavity. He labored to fill his lungs, to keep from falling over.

"Breathe, sugar. Breathe." The woman dropped her book, took a knee in front of him. He felt her mitten-shaped hands on his knees, the coarse texture of her skin scratching the denim. "It's okay. You're safe. You just need to breathe slowly, all right? Breathe in six seconds. Come on, I'll count it out. You follow."

And she did. She counted to six—tapping his knee for each second—and he inhaled along with her. Then she counted again for the exhale, and he followed. And even though his eyes were closed, he could feel the hoofbeats of Panic recede. The room no longer a category five.

"What's this?"

Enter the second voice. This one deeper and sandier than the first. Despite the soothing pats on the knees and kindly countdowns, the young man's eyes flew open. There, across the room, holding what looked like a toasted marshmallow in a pair of scalloped tongs, wearing an apron that read *Gingers Make the World Sweeter,* was a putty-colored man. A sparkly man with a circular head. And this was the important part—the part that dumped adrenaline into his bloodstream and filled him with ice.

Their bodies are as thick as plywood.

He might be dreaming (a betting man would take those odds), but he was seeing just fine. That wasn't just a thin man across the room (and a very thin woman patting his knee). Because they weren't people. They were generic outlines. Their faces painted with icing.

They were cookies. Simple as that.

(Specifically, they were gingerbread cookies. But details like that weren't important.)

His lip began to quiver like a bedsheet on a clothesline. He hated this part of himself. He wasn't a little boy; he was a young man. Old enough to know better. But when he got scared, when

Anxiety heralded in the troops of Fear and Loathing to begin another skirmish, he could not keep the tears from his eyes or the hiccups from his throat. Resist, he might. Win the battle, he could not.

"You don't have to do anything, sugar," the Cookie Lady said. "Just keep breathing."

Well, if he could talk (which was impossible at the moment), he would tell the Cookie Lady that not moving and breathing was all he could do when smothered by Panic. The Cookie Man picked up the desk that had been kicked over. The spilt milk was gone.

Outside an open window, where pink sunlight fell through a watermelon filter, hundreds of odd voices sang a song he'd never heard before.

"Meg." The Cookie Man held up the sketchbook that had been on the desk.

She pushed glasses on her flat face. The hooked ends fastened to stiff curls that were the shape of locks of hair. She turned the pages until she got to the end. Looked at the young man.

"Arthur?" she said.

He hummed all over. The name struck him like an arrow.

Art. Yes, Art. Arthur to be official. Named after... well, no one. I was the first in the family to be named Arthur.

This revelation, however, did not uncork any more truths, like where he was or what kind of dream this was. At least he had his name. *Art.*

"Get him a cup of milk, Gandy," the Cookie Woman said.

"He don't want milk, Meg."

"Then water. Go on."

The Cookie Man, Gandy was his name, did what he was told. Meg, his wife, picked up the chair Art had knocked over and sat down to watch him with kind, round eyes painted on her flat face. It was soothing, the way she looked at him. His shoulders relaxed.

Something went springing past the window.

Gandy returned without the apron and tongs. The water was in an ugly-face coffee mug he put on the floor within Art's reach. Meg leaned forward in the chair. The way her body twisted and bent in a claymation way made Art a bit woozy.

"Do you know how you got here, sugar?" she said. "Do you know where you are?"

He gave a headshake for both answers. Her lips moved like edible ropes to match the words she was speaking. But there was no mouth between them, no throat to speak with. The lump in his throat road-blocked words from passing. *No words,* he thought. *I have no words.*

Meg looked at Gandy, her husband (*Do gingerbread cookies marry?*). Gandy sighed and shook his head.

"It's going to be all right," she said. "I know this is all strange, but you're safe here," she said. "Okay?"

He wasn't certain if he believed that and didn't feel any safer for her saying it.

"I'm Nutmeg. This is Gandy. And you're Art." She waited for him to acknowledge she had it right. "How old are you, sugar?"

Now this was a stumper. Ask any kid that question and he or she will tell you just how old they are to the month. Even an adult could get you within a few years. Art had only learned his name a few minutes ago. How was he supposed to answer that. *Sixteen? Seventeen?* He thought, however, he was older than that. For one, he had a honeycomb tattoo on his arm. So he couldn't be sixteen. He was in his twenties, probably. But when Meg asked him how old he was, he felt sixteen years old. Like he'd never grown past it no matter how many birthdays had gone by.

"Gandy, can you get him a blanket?"

Art was shivering, but he wasn't cold. Gandy brought back a handmade blanket, one that was crocheted with heavy yarn. He draped it over Art's legs. Meg watched from her seat, humming along to the unfamiliar Christmas song being sung outside. Art liked the way her presence made the room feel. He relaxed a bit under the weight of the blanket. Some of the ornaments had been knocked off the limbs of the Christmas tree. He felt a jab of guilt for the ones that were broken, their pieces scattered among the presents.

"You draw these?" Gandy said.

He showed the sketchbook to Art. Meg didn't take her eyes off Art for a moment, then nodded at her husband. He pulled a chair next to his wife and sat down. They looked through the sketchbook.

"WHERE..." Art swallowed. "Where am I?"

"You're in Candyland, son," Gandy said.

Candyland? Well, that didn't help. At all. Art covered his face. It was better when no one could see him, especially life-sized gingerbread cookies. When he was sure his chin wasn't quivering, he looked up. "What does that mean?"

"You remember anything from before?" Gandy said.

Art's mouth turned to ash. He took up the ugly mug of water and drank. It was floral and minty. Cooled his throat. He held the mug between his hands, closed his eyes in hopes his memories were done playing hide-and-seek. *Olly olly oxen free!*

He shook his head.

"It's all right," Meg said. "You don't have to remember anything. You're here, sugar. Just be here."

"How'd I get *here*?"

"This happens from time to time," Meg said. "Someone crosses."

"Crosses?"

"Crosses over," Meg said. Art's brain needed a moment to generate more words. It was like solving a crossword puzzle on a sinking ship. "Where you were born," Meg said, sensing his stalemate. "Where you're from—*your world*—you've crossed over into this one."

"Candyland," Gandy answered with hometown pride.

Art laughed nervously. Looked at the toasted floor and said: "How?"

"We don't know how it works," Meg said. "It just happens sometimes."

"What did you ask Santa for, for Christmas?" Gandy said.

This was a sharp turn. "What?"

"Did you write Santa a letter asking for, I don't know, an adventure? Inspiration?"

A memory blew through the corridors like a ghost. It was fleeting. Barely a snapshot. He was sitting at a desk, one not too different from the one he knocked over, writing in a journal. Although it wasn't a letter to Santa.

"Are you too old for Santa?" Gandy said. "Is that it?"

"That's not the problem," Meg said. "It's what you ask for. Sometimes you expect to get what you *want* from Santa. At Christmas, though—"

"You get what you *need,*" Gandy finished.

The absurdity of what was happening had become quite clear. Two gingerbread cookies were lecturing on Santa Claus's ethical approach to gift giving. Ask for what you want all day long. You'll get what you need. Like socks or underwear. A terrifying trip to Gingerbread Town, where cookies get married and drink from ugly-faced mugs

"I'm ready to wake up now," Art said.

"You're not—"

"Shh." Meg silenced her spouse. "You want to wake up. Of course. We're going to help you. Gandy, can you grab that gift for me? No, the one under the tree. It's wrapped in the red glitter paper."

Gandy did as such, crawling under the branches to reach the present with the red glitter paper. It was rectangular and flat with a shiny green bow. Gandy handed it to Meg. A smile curved on her face and struck dimples in her cheeks. She presented it to Art.

His name was written in thick, black lines. Below it was a single word. *Santa.* He remembered that handwriting; somewhere in his shrouded past he'd seen it before. That was Santa's handwriting. At least, until Art was too old for Santa.

Art sort of laughed. That abruptly stopped when he opened the gift. It slid out with ease. It was a work of art on cardstock. Someone had done it with markers and ink liners. It was of a generic man, tall and slender, holding a balloon in the shape of a red, red heart.

He stared at it, unblinking. His eyes glassy. *I drew this...*

There was a memory attached to it. A delicate little thing that danced in the fog, ducking in the shadows to avoid the light. Art sat patiently, giving it time and space to dip into view. He had made this for someone. The closer he came to remembering—the blurry contour of a face, a vague memory of a fragrance—the more he shook.

It felt like the key to everything. Where he was, how he got here. *Who* he was.

Then he went too far, and his entire body flash-fried with hot-wired thoughts. A river of emotions poured through him. A river he did not have room for. He did what he always did when he didn't have room.

Run! the signal word blared. *Get out! Get away or be drowned!*

That was the general sense of it. Art never stuck around to work out the details. He heeded the warning whirring in his head without argument. He scrambled onto his hands and knees, scraped his head on the ceiling when he tried to stand, and was nearly to a doorway. Conflicting emotions of longing and sadness, disappointment and love, safety and loneliness clung to his backside like teeth. They were enormous. He was so small.

So vulnerable in a big, big world.

"Wait! Please wait!" Meg jumped in front of him. He tried to get around her and could've if he wanted. She just felt so warm, and the sound of her voice so sincere. Even though she was a cookie. "You're not alone," she said. "I promise you you're not. Life goes so fast, I know, and it feels like you can't keep up, and some days you can hardly breathe. I know how that feels."

Art wanted to crawl out of his skin. She was on point. A little too on point.

"You don't need to stay here with us. In fact, you shouldn't. It's out there you need to be. But you came *here* for a reason. You came to our house. That's not a mistake."

"She's right. We have your back." Gandy joined her at the doorway. "But you can't go out looking like that."

Art was in blue jeans and a T-shirt with a pocket on the chest. Pretty ordinary, he thought.

"You're going to get too much attention," Meg pointed out.

"Crossers always do," Gandy said.

"You didn't come here to be a celebrity."

Art fell on his bottom. The floor was soft where the milk had spilled. A little sticky. He locked his arms around his shins. The demand to flee had passed. He sighed long and loud. With it came a wave of relief so great he wanted to weep. Instead, he said: "*Why* am I here?"

"Only you can find out," Meg said. "I know who can help."

"To the castle," Gandy announced.

"*Not* to the castle," she said.

"Because that's where—I'm sorry. What did you say, love?"

"He's not going to the castle, Gandy."

"It's in the manual. 'If you meet a crosser...' It's on page one, Meg."

"I know what the manual says. But Arthur needs real help. Can you bring him something to eat? And also, the sheet from our bed." She tucked the cardstock gift from Santa in Art's shirt pocket. "I know exactly who he needs to see."

2

"Watch your head. And don't break the door. It's new and, that's right, turn to the side... like that. Hold it right there."

Candied silver beads popped out of Gandy's forehead like drops of perspiration. They dribbled like BBs and rolled across the floor. Meg handed a brown paper bag to her husband. It was rolled at the top like a sack lunch. Their thin lips puckered up, and the two of them pressed their round faces together. Art couldn't look away.

He was rigid with Anxiety and Fear (and so many more Emotions were coming to visit), but took comfort in watching this gingerbread couple embrace, the way they whispered to each other, how their arms were flexible enough to pull each other closer. In the time that he'd been there, their warmth and honesty kept him from diving out the window. He trusted them, for better or worse.

"Don't let the world beat you down, sugar. Remember, we got your back. So many of us do." Meg pulled the string tight under Art's chin. The hood cinched over his eyes. "And don't forget these words: *Keep your stocking hung and your chimney open.* They're wiser words than ya think." She patted his face. A trace of ginger root remained on his cheek. "Off with you, then. Don't forget the snacks."

Gandy shook the brown bag. "I'll step out first, right? When I wave, you follow. And don't forget, watch your head."

He did just that, turning sideways to slip through the narrow doorway. Plenty of room for him, seeing he was only six inches thick. He was quickly engaged in conversation. The longer he went on, the stiffer Art felt. He was cagey when Meg held his hand between both of her hands. They were warm and crispy. Her eyes—blobs of white icing—were somehow gentle.

"Be nice," she said.

She meant something by that and not the obvious. She meant be *Nice*. Capital *N*.

"Eh-hem." Gandy was waving.

It made no sense, waking up in a fantasy world where he felt adopted by gingerbread cookies. Cookies he trusted. Cookies he wanted to hug. But dreams were like that. That was why he wanted to hug her. Good thing he didn't. His hugs were world-class hugs. Not something a cookie would survive.

"Merry, merry," she said, and shoved him through the doorway like a quarter in a vending machine.

HE DUCKED JUST IN TIME. The house was made of gingerbread, and he'd already put dents in the ceiling. With Meg's motherly shove, he skidded sideways through the slot and across the sidewalk. Gandy caught him before he tumbled into the street.

Meg had fashioned a bright red bedsheet into a hooded cape. If not for the knot she'd tied under his chin, the peppermint breeze would have blown it off his back. Gandy pulled the hood down to hide Art's face while at the same time waving and wishing a soccer ball bouncing down the road a merry, merry.

"Take your time," Gandy said. "It's better to soak it in before we start. Yeah? That's page two in the manual. 'Let crossers adjust to Candyland. Don't rush them. Things are very different here.' So, you know, look around—Tomkins, yes. Merry, merry to you. How's Tippy and Turny?"

Art snuck a peek from under his cowl. Gandy was talking to what looked like a plastic turtle standing on back legs. Gandy was a cookie, but somehow a plastic turtle felt more surreal. *Familiarization,* he thought. *The bizarre normalizes with time.* He'd learned that somewhere. Sometime. A crumb of memory that decided to bob close enough to the surface to be remembered. *We drink milk from a cow. But milk from a human is gross.* At least, that was how he remembered it.

Gandy engaged with the passersby. He was a friendly sort, and it seemed natural to him. He was also working the attention off Red Riding Hood. Art avoided any wayward glances. When the turtle moved closer, Art looked up.

The sky is pink.

It was a lovely color. Soothing and delicious all at once. A childhood color. Puffs of cotton candy hovered in its depth like tasty flotsam, none going in the same direction. They moved at different speeds, ignoring the peppermint breeze ruffling the red cape on Art's back.

The walls of the buildings were baked and held together with icing and strings of licorice. The road was paved with blocks of fudge, and things walked on it and rolled on it, bounced and danced on it. Exotic things. The most amazing things. Beyond imagination things. Toys of every stripe and concoction—dolls and soldiers and dancers and fighters and thugs and trolls and *who-knows* and *is-that-even-a-toy?*

But then forget the toys. Food strolled down Fudgy Lane. Pickled eggs and chocolate eggs and hard-boiled ones, too. Giant apples with caramel toppings; pears with bows on the stem. A family of sugar plums stained the pavement wherever they bounced.

There were also pigs. Three of them wearing different hats. Walking upright. Arms around each other, singing a merry song. Behind them sheep and a dainty young lady with a long shepherd's crook. *Is that Bo Peep?*

Unbelievable. Overwhelming. Someone Art's age (sixteen, he was sure of it; maybe seventeen) might run away and hide or freak out. Because this was real. All of it, right in front of him, real as his left hand. But the thing that kept him on his feet, that kept him upright and conscious, that turned the corner of his mouth—just a tiny smile on his face—wasn't visible at all. It was in the air.

The air was electric.

It wasn't positive or negative, didn't come from an outlet or a battery. It was a feeling that passed through space like a silent wave. It filled his stomach and blossomed in his chest. It was everywhere. It was everything.

Christmas spirit, he thought.

Although he couldn't remember his grandmother's face or the way she sounded, he knew she'd said it sometime, somewhen. This was the feeling of Christmas. Some called it spirit.

She called it *Pure Joy.*

"Are your legs rubber?" Gandy said.

"What?"

"Can you walk? Or is this too much?" He waved his arms at an orange plastic locomotive puttering down the fudgy brick road. The face of it was smiling. It had cheekbones. "We can squeeze back into the breadbox if you need some time. Meg means well and all, but I'd wager she wouldn't mind you staying a few chimes or even a ring longer."

Art's legs were slightly rubber. Roughly half his body didn't have feeling. It was coming back in pins and needles now. This was happening. Whatever this was, it was happening right now. There was a reason for how and why. An explanation. He didn't know it, might never know it. There were great mysteries that never got solved. This certainly qualified as one. Until he woke up, the only thing to do was float downstream until something made sense.

"Where's everyone going?"

"To the market," Gandy said. "It's a Christmas thing. It's what we do."

"That's where we're going?"

"Yeah." Gandy pulled a paper hat onto his head (it resembled something a chef would wear). The line of icing that served as a mouth turned upward in a smile. Then he said: "S'ven."

Art waited for more. When there wasn't more, he said: "S'ven what?"

"You're going to see him."

"Why?"

"If anyone can help a crosser, it's S'ven."

Gandy hopped onto the brown, chunky road and joined the crusade of stranger things. *Misfits.* But there was only one thing here that didn't belong. He was hiding in a red bedsheet. Art caught up to Gandy, who was swinging his arms like he owned the road. (By the way, the fudgy pavers felt good to walk on. Like flexible plastic that emitted sweet, syrupy smells.)

"Merry, merry!" Gandy called and waved. "Merry, merry!"

A band of hopping cowboys bounced past, their plastic lassoes twirling over them like antennas. Their round bottoms sounded like popping bubbles when they hit the road. Art pulled his hood down and looked the other way when a yellow buckaroo snuck a peek at him.

"Merry, merry!" Gandy shouted. Then to Art: "Just a word, and no offense, but around here when someone says 'merry, merry,' you say it back. Just something we do. When in Candyland, do as the Landers do."

"Landers?"

"Never mind. It's just—oh, hey. Yes. Merry, merry!"

This time a pair of glazed donuts was followed by a dozen donut holes. "Merry, merry!" they chimed.

"Merry, merry," Art muttered.

It felt weird to say that. To donuts.

He kept his head down and eyes on the road. It was better this way. Too many distractions. Too much stimulation. Pretty much too much. Then a black rope of licorice slithered between his feet and looked into Art's hood. Art closed his eyes and kept walking.

"Meg wanted me to tell you to breathe, son. Remember to breathe, she said." Gandy skipped to keep up with Art. "Does that help?"

"What?"

"Breathing."

Art shook his head. Nothing slowed down the Panic train when its engine was hot. All he could do was wait for it to run out of steam. It didn't matter if he was breathing into a paper bag or standing on his head. The air in his lungs was thin, and his chest magically turned to lead. Hands in pockets, head hung too heavy, he walked. He breathed.

"Strange," Gandy said. "She said it would help."

"What?"

"Breathing. She specifically said, 'Tell him to count to six when he goes in. And count to six when he goes out." He held up his flattened mitt as if he'd raised a finger to make his point. "Are you counting?"

"Do you breathe?" Art asked.

"Not like you. And I don't understand the whole air thing. Sounds exhausting. I mean, does it ever stop?"

Gandy had obviously thought about breathing. His case against breathing was, as he put it, *airtight*. (Art didn't understand why he would be *against* breathing.) This conversation, Art imagined, was not what Meg had in mind. This was just laying more track for the Panic train to gather momentum. Art buried his hands as deep as they'd go in his pockets. Gandy switched to the topic Landers never slept. Crossers insisted on it. It didn't make sense at all. Why would anyone lie down for eight to ten chimes with their eyes closed? It was an insult to evolutionary—

"What do you do, then?" Art said.

Gandy was jolted from his speech. Apparently, Meg never stopped him when he was on a roll because he stumbled on the pavers and looked around, gathering his wits. It looked like he'd just been yanked from a nap. "Wh—um, what do I do?"

"You said earlier, when I asked if you breathe, you said *not like you*. What does that mean?"

Gandy thought a moment. Then shrugged. "You caught me, son. Crispy-handed." He sighed, shook his head, and looked into the pink sky like someone was keeping score. "I told a square one, I did. Four corners with a hole in the middle of it, yeah."

"I'm not—"

"I lied. Okay? There, I said it. I was just trying to make you feel better, making it sound like I do something like breathing when the truth is I don't do anything like that at all. No one does. No one except a crosser." Only he said it like *cross-uh*. It had a little weight to it. Not particularly unkind, but maybe just a little.

"How do you know I breathe, then?"

"I don't." Gandy swatted his chest. Bits of crumb chipped from the edges of his hand. "Meg's the expert. She's a memorizer, she is. That woman loves to know things and tell others about them. Like count to six on the inhale and whatever. None of that's important, ask me. Nope. Just two questions is all you need to answer, and that's—ah, merry, merry!"

He nudged Art closer to the curb. A sward of mops swaddled past them. (A group of mops is a sward, Gandy told him later.) Art didn't look at them. When they were far enough ahead that their wet tracks were drying, Gandy leaned against Art.

"Two things, right? Why are you here, and where are you going? That's what the manual says, page four. And if I'm being completely honest, I don't even think the first one matters. *Why?* Who cares why? You're already here. *Where*, now there's a question. Let's answer *that*."

He dug a rounded elbow into Art's hip and launched into Gandy's philosophy of living.

"Who wrote the manual?" Art interrupted.

"What?"

"You said it's in the manual. Who wrote the manual?"

Gandy reorganized his thoughts, then replied: "*They.* Like they, you know. Everyone knows who *they* are."

"I don't."

"It's not important. We're taught about crossers." *Cross-uhs.* "It's like we live for crossers. You know, things like you. From another world. *To be of service,* that's what the manual says. Because if you're here, you're here for a reason. And that's why we're here. That and to celebrate Christmas. Merry, merry!"

"There's others like me?"

"Don't get excited. The last crosser was a disaster."

"What happened?"

Gandy walked in silence. Finally, he said: "Misunderstanding is what happened. The root of all problems, yeah? Misunder—whoa!"

Gandy came off the road. Art caught him before he went stumbling. *Would he break in two if he fell? Could I just paste him together?* Art didn't have to answer that question. His hood fell back, exposing loops of hair hanging over his eyes. He yanked the hood back over his face.

"Merry, merry," called a sweet voice.

She was as tall as Art. He didn't look up, but he could feel her staring at him. Her legs were bare and plastic from the hem of a ballet skirt. Toes permanently pointed, she walked as if her legs were stilts that didn't bend. *Tap-tap-tap* they went.

"Ah, merry, merry!" Gandy recovered with a hop and a bounce. "Nice to see you, Dixie. Looking fit today, you are. All snappy and curious. On the way to the market on this—what is it, *twenty*?"

"Twenty-one rings," she said.

"Twenty-one? I'm always losing count. Meg can tell you how many ticks to Santa's coming."

"Of course she can. How is Meggy?"

"Well, she's good. In fact, she's great." Gandy explained how Meg was baking a new wall for the house. Going to make another room, you know, just in case a little one came out of the oven. Dixie the Dancer faked interest in the story. Art recognized a faker. Maybe she wasn't uncomfortable with small talk the way he was, but she was distracted.

She was sneaking peeks under the hood.

"Anyways, good seeing you," Gandy said, stepping between her and Art. "I'll send Meg your best. Merry, merry to you and—"

"Red Riding Hood?" She ducked down. "Are you mad at me? I thought we—"

"Who, this? Haha. No, no. Sorry. This is, uh, my baker."

"Your *baker*?" She sounded hurt. "This isn't—"

"No, it isn't. Look at his feet. Red Riding Hood doesn't have feet like that."

Dixie the Dancer took a long look at Art's dirty boots and faded blue jeans. She tried to look under the hood one more time.

"He's shy," Gandy said. "And to be honest, not used to crowds. So—"

"What happened to Chef Shelly?"

"Oh! Oh, no, no, no. Chef Shelly, she's good. She's great! Better than great. She's like *greeeeeat!* Heh-heh. No, this here, he's not *my* baker. He's *aaaaa* baker."

"Does he have a name?" *Tap-tap-tap.*

"He does, he does. This is, uh, Ar-Ar-Ar... Arfy the Cooker. From Bonbon Town."

Dixie the Dancer's laughter sounded like bubbles in her throat. Her feet twittered with a little hop and a leap, then a twirl. There was a definite whirring sound coming from her, like a string had been pulled on her back. Art caught the sparkle of her eyes like jewels pressed into a perfectly smooth face.

"Are you strong, Arfy the Cooker?" she asked.

"He doesn't talk," Gandy said. "All he does is cook."

"I could use a thrower, if he ever gets tired of—"

"He never gets tired. He cooks, that's all. He loves to cook all the time, always."

Art's legs were getting weaker. He didn't like the hiding and the dishonesty. Lies were heavy. When carried long enough, they spoiled to shame. At least they did for him. He just wanted to crawl inside his red cape and go to sleep.

"Okay, Dixie," Gandy said. "Bye-bye. Merry, merry. Maybe we'll see you at the market. Arfy can throw you across the lake or something."

She attempted one more look. *Tap-tap-tap.* Gandy threw himself in front of Art like a shepherd guarding his flock. Then a host of tapping plastic toes and stiff ankles came down the road, followed by bubbly giggles and twittering steps. Dixie was swept up in a herd of her kind. (*That's a swatch*, Gandy later said.)

Gandy pushed Art between two buildings.

"That way, Arfy."

THE ALLEY WAS narrow and tall and smelled like cinnamon toast; the walls flaked with blackened bits that fell when Art squeezed between them. The sky—as pink as a puppy's belly—was all he could see above them.

Singing echoed down the long enclosure. It was sloppy and cheerful, merry in a different sort of way. They passed under a sign that read *Toasted.* The smell coming from the open window was delicious. It looked like a sports pub. Televisions blared above rows of syrup bottles. At the tables were puffy, white marshmallows sitting with spongy yellow ducks. The marshmallows were tanned on the edges and the size of basketballs. They sang along to a Christmas song and swayed against each other. One fell off a stool and bounced across the floor.

"Wrong way."

Art didn't see the bike until it was almost too late. No one was riding it. It coasted toward them, pedals slowly churning. The silver handlebars waggled around, the front tire swaying in a relatively straight line. Streamers hung from the rubber grips.

Art threw his back to the wall, put his hands on the opposite wall, and sucked in his gut. A pair of eyes was pasted to the handlebars.

They lazily rolled toward him. One of the handle grips poked him in the stomach.

"Merry, merry," the bike muttered.

Art shuffled after Gandy, passing through different smells from windows above them: maple syrup, powdered sugar, caramel. And singing. Always singing.

Gandy stopped at an intersection. He looked right, then turned to the left and waved Art to follow. A sign waved on pretzel links strung between the buildings. *Kettle Korn Trail.* It made sense, although it wasn't a trail. No rocks or dirt; no roots from trees. It was cobblestones. Big, spongy cobblestones lacquered in a crispy coating.

"Watch your step," Gandy called. "Gets a little, uh, unpredictable. At least we won't run into anyone this way. Not till the market, anyhow."

Kettle Korn Trail was a wide alley that went several blocks with no one in sight. A back door here and there with garbage piled up— broken cinnamon sticks, clumps of cookie dough. Spilled bags of flour. Flies and gnats zipped and hovered from one heap to another. Art waved them out of his face.

Gandy reacted to the flies and gnats. Not annoyed. He seemed a bit more... surprised. Then worried.

"Why are we hiding?" Art's voice quivered. He hated when it sounded like that. His emotions were billboards for everyone to read.

"You're not in danger, son. It's the total opposite. Everyone—and I mean *everyone*—will want to talk to you. You saw Dixie back there. She could smell the crosser on you. Surprised we got away from that one. Arfy... I panicked on that one. Sorry." He shook his head. "It's just easier if we get to S'ven without notice. Straight there with no interruptions. Meg was right; she always is. Forget the manual," he whispered. "There's a reason you're here. We just need to get— watch it."

A geyser of popcorn burst from the middle of the alley like a relief valve opened. Softball-sized kernels rained down. Art picked one up. It was warm and sticky. Fresh from the kettle, somehow. If kettles were under the cobblestones. A rubber-toothed leaf rake extended from a window. Big, fabric hands were on a long handle, sweeping the loose kernels into piles. Art threw the one he'd picked up onto one of them.

"I don't want to be here."

"You're always *here*." Gandy rubbed a spot on his chest. *Is that supposed to be his heart?*

The gnats were gathered near a trash can overflowing with banana peels. They got in Art's face. He pulled down his hood, holding his breath until they were past.

"Is S'ven a crosser?"

"Yep. He's from your world, I assume. I think. I don't know, come to think of it. They're rumors he looked like you when he first dropped in, but he don't look like you anymore. He's been here many o' bells. Ever since the Nutcracker."

"Nutcracker?"

Gandy twisted his flat head around. "You know her?"

"No."

"Too bad. She made a lot of changes to this place. Not good at first. But everything turned out better."

"What'd she do?"

He waved his hand. "Another story. Best we keep our head in this one. S'ven, he'll know what to do."

"So he is a crosser?"

"That's what I said."

Up ahead, another supply of kettle corn erupted. Rakes extended. Flies and gnats descended. Gandy skipped around the harvesters. Art kept his head down. When he caught up to Gandy, he said: "Then why is he still here?"

"What do you mean?"

"Meg said crossers come here sometimes. Do they go back home?"

"Um, I mean... you know, if Meg were here, she would say—"

"Did the Nutcracker go back?"

"Oh, yeah. She went back with a bang. Took a bunch of us with her. That was a toot, let me say. We got sucked into her world and then came back. Meg and I were dizzy almost till next Christmas. Woo-wee! Merry, merry."

"So why didn't S'ven go back?"

Gandy stopped in the middle of the alley. He raised a round hand. A ring of icing formed on his face, but no words came out of it. Art was fascinated by how his expressions changed. It was claymation in real life. Gandy shrugged.

"I don't know. He stayed for a reason, I guess." He patted Art's arm. "Like you."

It sounded like an excuse, but Gandy really believed it. Like maybe this S'ven stayed in Candyland because he was waiting for something or had a job to do. Art didn't care why he was here. If S'ven could wake him up from this borderline nightmare, nothing else mattered.

Art swatted at the gnats and flies. They avoided his hand. They were buzzing, but it wasn't their wings. They were whispering. Of course they were. Art wasn't surprised. What he didn't expect, when he swiped at them one last time, just before they swirled up toward the underbelly sky, was the little, teeny uniforms they were wearing.

Military uniforms.

"Stay here." Gandy held up his mitt, then waved Art back. "I'll be right back."

It was noisy around the corner. Drums were beating, and people (or toys or food or whatever Art was supposed to call them... *things?*) were singing and dancing, laughing and shouting. Gandy's head twisted on his shoulders, ears perking on the sides of his flat head when someone started up a flute. From where he stood, Art couldn't see the party. The only things in view were awnings and signs.

Above the sidewalk, hanging from a peppermint stick on a gingerbread wall, was a flag. The edges were frayed, the fabric faded. *King Cheese* was written across a sigil of gold crowns.

"How do you know he's here?" Art said.

A stiff shrug, followed by: "Landers just... we know things about each other."

"Just, like, gossip?" Now Art shrugged. *So what?*

"It's more than that, son. Thoughts around here are butterflies. You know, in the wind." When Art didn't respond, he added: "Like music."

The flute bubbled inside Art. He could feel it. Could *taste* it. It was like fizzy lemonade in his ears. He shook his head, feeling a rush in his legs.

"You-you can read thoughts? Like what I'm thinking right now?"

This alarmed the pants off Art. The thoughts that ran through his head were not for public consumption. They were embarrassing. Sometimes dark and mean. Really mean. So mean they left trails of shame.

"Ah, no. It doesn't work like that. You want me to see your thoughts?"

Art shook his head and pressed his back against the wall. He didn't want anyone inside his head. *Thoughts are like butterflies.* That was the truth. He couldn't remember how he got here (*where are dreams, anyway?*), but there were wisps of memories that had no form, only flavors. Art's thoughts didn't just have their own mind. They *lived* inside him. There were parts of him that were cruel. He didn't want anyone knowing what they said. Even if it was to himself.

"Oh, hey." Gandy looked in both directions. "I know it never works to tell someone to relax. But relax. Yeah? Everything is the way it is. I don't know what that means, but Meg says it. And remember, just breathe. Count to twenty or whatever. And act natural."

Act natural?

"If you get hungry, eat what's in the sack. It'll make Meg happy. And stay here; don't move. I'll run, run as fast as I can."

The icing on his face winked. Then he was gone, like that. Around the corner and into a door beneath the King Cheese flag. He would find S'ven in there. And S'ven would tell Art how to wake up, and this would all be over. All he had to do was wait.

TIME was funny in CANDYLAND. It was flexible. Sometimes it stretched like taffy. Like it buzzed in Art's head, this deep humming sound that wasn't unpleasant. And then minutes passed instead of seconds. Or maybe it was hours. It's hard to tell when your head feels like a blender.

The music suddenly felt different. The noise, louder. More people, more dancing than just a few seconds ago. The sound of it crawled under his skin, made him twitch and itch. Anxiety did a jig on his chest and stomped on his pulse. He imagined bodies out there packed together. Sticky bodies, smelly bodies.

How do they do it? Art could pretend like he was having fun, but people had no idea what it was like for him on the inside. The doubt. The fear. They were anchors he carried. One on each shoulder. Gandy didn't have to worry. He wasn't leaving the alley.

Chocolate.

The smell was suddenly overwhelming. Like a river flooding the street. A memory as faded and torn as the King Cheese flag waved through his mind. The smell of hot chocolate in front of a fireplace. Christmas music on speakers. Someone in the other room singing along to it. The feeling of a warm blanket. He liked the way it felt. It felt like—

"Rey Rida Hood."

Art jumped at the sound of the voice. Someone was in the alley— the most human-looking person yet. A wiry boy about half Art's height. Pointy ears poked out of looping, brown curls. Black sunglasses wrapped around his face.

"Yaw anna choc'lat?"

The imp's delicate fingers unfurled. A chocolate wafer sat square in his palm. Unmelted with sharp corners. The smell of it tantalizing. Promising to melt down his throat and drop the anchors off his shoulders. Even if only for a few minutes.

"Wass inja sack, hey?" He pointed at the paper sack. The paper brown and soft and damp in Art's hand. "Issa cookees inder? Trade jaw, line up."

A blocky-tooth smile spread across the lower part of the imp's face. He held the block of chocolate like a coin. Art put the sack behind his back. He hadn't the slightest interest in opening it (he didn't know if there were *cookees* in there or not), but didn't want to give it away. Meg had made them.

"Ee stingin' yo mops? Idda play a differen' song on tha' one, peebie."

He leaned in for a look inside Art's hood. The smile started to fade. He dropped his hand to his side. The chocolate landed on the bumpy surface of Kettle Korn Trail. He took a step closer. The smile returned in full bloom. Every tooth square and white and cartoonish.

"Ey, nop. I'ssa think yew makin' for—"

"Aye, Rude!"

The imp was snatched out of the alley by a taller version of himself. Another skinny boy wearing muted colors and flat-soled sneakers with black glasses over his eyes. This one's hair long and straight, fluttering like tails on a kite. He had the imp by the licorice arm, yanked him off his feet.

"Low-low," the taller one muttered. "Fresh now."

The imp ducked his head. He'd already forgotten about Art. The chocolate, too. Art picked it up. It was wrapped in gold foil and stamped with two initials. *KC.*

The imps hopped toward the market. Art followed them around the corner and watched them disappear into a crowd, slipping between bodies like eels through seaweed. They had something strapped on their backs. They looked like spongy noodles. The kind used in swimming pools.

THE GOLD FOIL had torn from the corner. It smelled bitter, like healthy chocolate. Art took a nibble. It didn't taste any better than it smelled, but it melted on his tongue.

He took another small bite, following the imps with the foam boards on their backs into the best or worst costume party in the world. Art couldn't decide which. They were toys. They were animals. *Things.*

Bouncy balls with googly eyes.

Dancers with dagger toes.

Boxers with square heads and wrecking-ball fists.

Clowns made of wire.

Chefs made of felt.

Dwarves with sacks, rocks wearing hats, pogo sticks laughing, and teddy bears singing.

They milled about in all directions, weaving like starlings. Some playing instruments, like fiddles and horns and pipes. The music chaotic, but sometimes it would fall into rhythm, and the crowd would sway with it. And then back to melodic noise. And no one seemed to notice. Or care.

They spoke like they knew each other, like good friends who grew up together. And when they bumped into each other—which was often—they tipped a hat or bent a knee, wishing each other a merry, merry before swimming back into the flow. Sometimes they took each other for a spin and a dip. With a quick shuffle, they bowed and went on their way.

A bell went off. The sort that was enormous and heavy.

The vibrations passed through the crowd like a sonic wave. Art felt it in his chest and cheeks. His teeth tingled.

All at once, like a sporting event witnessing a last-second win, the crowd of misfits and strange things raised their arms and sticks and strings and mitts. They leaped and they bounced and they swirled on the street.

"*Huzzah!*" they cried. "*Huzzah!*"

They embraced and swayed. A song rose up, one well-rehearsed. For the random instruments played together. The voices in harmony, they were. Along with squeaks and honks that, somehow, were lovely. It was intoxicating.

Art was pulled toward the crowd like a fish on a hook. He went willingly, unknowingly. When the bell went off again and fresh sonic waves rattled his eyelids, he plunged into the thick of it and didn't hesitate.

Huzzah!

It was the song that did it. Not the way it sounded. The way it felt.

It was the sweetest feeling of all. It bypassed the lips and tongue and went straight to his stomach. It swirled around. Starry fumes crackled in his chest. A childish smile spread on his face. He was smelling firewood and marshmallows. Heard the crunch of wrapping paper torn from presents. The bubble of laughter.

The crowd swallowed him like a merry, greedy thing.

They didn't notice the gangly young man in the red riding hood cape. For they were intoxicated with song, as well. *Christmas spirit* flowed like spring water. From them, through them. In them. Into him.

He was two feet taller than most of them. The crowd went as far as he could see in both directions, swaying like a hive of insects.

Huzzah!

A row of storefronts was on his left. Traders and barkers (busy singing at the moment) stood by their carts or under their tents, by their tables of fruited candies, buckets of knick-knacks, and bowls of sugar and spice.

To his right, there was nothing of the sort. To the right was something Art had never seen. Never in his life. It was in the distance, but so close it seemed like he could reach out and touch it. A castle so big and so tall that it scratched the pink sky and snagged clouds with gleaming turrets that sprouted from its sides like branches. It sparkled and shined.

To call it beautiful was an insult.

When the bell rang, ripples raced over the rose-colored lake surrounding it. The vibrations flooded his senses. They lifted him off his feet. For a moment, Art didn't feel the cobbled road. It seemed he would float into the sky along with the others, a million balloons, all happy and singing with foolish smiles.

"Huzzah!" Art shouted.

Pumped his fist. Showed his teeth. All his teeth.

He might even have danced. He'd been known to get loose when the spirit was right. And it was right, all right. It was everywhere. He wobbled his knees and shook his hips with his eyes on the castle that breathed through open windows, that sang from its walls. Beat a pulse through the ground.

The castle called again.

The rosy lake so smooth and still. Tinted glass and bottomless and pristine. No fallen leaves or floating sticks. No dust, no bugs. No reflection at all. As flawless as the castle it surrounded. Art was certain he could walk across it.

At the very top of the castle, from the highest spire of them all, a small light winked.

He felt it before it he saw it. The castle saw him, who he truly was. That light—that pinprick of light—picked him out of the crowd and urged him to walk across the water. *Come to the castle,* it said. *Stay awhile.*

He was a step from the shore, held up by a ring of dancing frogs wearing tuxedos. Their wet tongues going up and down and slapping against him, leaving sticky tracks he didn't mind or even notice. He was one step from the perfect, rose-petal water.

"Whoa, whoa there, my red-caped friend. Easy does it, now."

Art was yanked back into his senses. His body pleasantly numb. Head buzzing. Eyes jiggling in their sockets. The very thin man between him and the red water was all that was stopping him. Not a man, really. But that didn't register.

Art's eyes drifted up the length of the slender castle—a beautiful dagger stuck in the earth, pointing at the pink sky. The tiny light all those thousands of feet up its shiny wall winked out.

"Down here, my boy. There you go. Look me right in the dollop."

The very thin man's name came back to Art. Gandy, it was. Then everything else returned. A dizzy world of impossibilities on anxious waves. The gingerbread man pointed at the dolloped eye on his round face.

"Turn around, come with me. Yes, yes, yes. This way, nothing to see." The crowd took them back without notice. "Merry, merry to you. And to you. As well as you."

Gandy nodded at his neighbors, bowed when they bowed, and twirled when they twirled. Keeping his gritty hand on the small of Art's back, guiding him to the narrow opening of Kettle Korn Trail.

"I should've warned you," Gandy said. "Of course you peeked. Why wouldn't you? But it took me longer than I thought it would, and now here you are about to go swimming. No one seemed to notice, I think."

He gave a look at the bustling crowd, which was back to the business of the day now that the bells stopped thrumming. No more huzzahs.

"What was that?" Art asked.

"The market. It's more of a, uh, a social thing, really. No one buys much. It's an excuse to—"

"No, the thing." Art raised his hand above his head, searching for a simple word. Then found it. "*Castle.*"

"Ah, that. Yes. Not important. What is important is S'ven. Apparently, he..."

Art wasn't listening. *Not important?* How could something like that, something so tall and elegant and shiny and-and-and... *not important?*

"Art. Hoo-hoo? Down here, son. In the dollop. We don't have much time."

"It's a castle?"

Gandy sighed a puff of sugar. "Yes, yes. That's it. That's exactly it. But right now, it's not important. S'ven is. And he's gone."

Art shook his head. Everything had been knocked out of it. Replaced with feelings for the castle. He wanted those feelings back. And he wanted the anxiety that was wringing his stomach like a dishrag to go away.

"S'ven?"

"Let me start over," Gandy said. "We're here to find S'ven. He will help you on your journey."

"He's gone?"

"Well, he's not there."

"So gone?"

"They weren't very merry about it, either. Seems he's been gone quite some time."

A glimmer of hope fluttered in Art's chest. "You mean he went back home?"

"No, no. I don't know. They said he was gone, that's all. I don't think he went back like you mean he went back. What do you have there?"

Gandy nabbed Art's hand. It was balled into a fist. It looked like mud squeezed between his fingers. When he opened it, a ball of gold foil was all that was left of the chocolate square.

"Where'd you get that? Never mind. Here." Gandy began wiping Art's palm with the bottom of the red cape. "Don't eat that, son. Don't ever eat it. Never, ever, ever, swear on the spirit of Christmas."

"It's chocolate."

"Trust me on this, will ya? Promise you won't even taste a King Chocolate while you're here."

King Chocolate. "I don't—"

"Promise!"

The tone that came out of the gingerbread man was unexpected. Loaded with fear and loathing. It shook Art like he'd missed a step and was falling. He nodded at the gingerbread man furiously cleaning his hand.

"I have another idea. She's a little odd. Well, not a little. Grimjoy knows things others don't. Sort of a last resort thing. You know the type?"

"Her name's Grimjoy?"

"She's blocks from here, near the border. I don't like getting that close, but you know what they say—when candy's cooking, there's no time to wait."

"What's the border?"

Gandy was done wiping Art's hand. He kicked the balled wrapper past the corner. "It isn't all *nice* here, son. Now, let's not burn our hands on the kettle. Off we go, back the way we came and—"

Gandy stopped short. Arm out.

"On second thought, we'll take the market. No one noticed when you walked right through the middle of it. They won't notice now. Hood up!"

He herded Art back into the open. Poked him in the back.

Art caught a glance of what Gandy had seen down Kettle Korn Trail. There were two of them marching with tall hats. And bright-colored jackets.

And he thought—he could've sworn—there were swords on their belts.

3

He was a large man in a large chair. A throne, if you will. A big, boxy, gaudy thing with rock candy embedded in dark brown leather (it wasn't really leather). It looked like milk chocolate blasted with a shotgun of jewels. No real design to it. Just lots of shiny things. And if he was hungry, he'd pluck one from the armrest and suck on it till he got some real food.

Chocolate.

The throne could sit two normal-sized men quite comfortably. You could squeeze a third in between them, in a pinch. The man living in the throne filled it from armrest to armrest. As if he were poured into it. The only thing he moved was his hand. And that was to put something in his mouth.

King Chocolate was his name. His friends called him Choco. He had no friends. So King Chocolate.

His legs looked like overcooked noodles glued to a stomach. They didn't reach the floor, almost ever, and constantly kicked the threshold to an imaginary song. Nothing upbeat or Christmassy. No beat at all, really. It sounded like someone dropping hammers on a cutting board. The beat got particularly loud when he was excited. And you might guess what excited him most.

At this very moment, a small wooden puppet had walked into the room, holding a rectangular tray. Upon the tray were five stacks of chocolate wafers. Each stack was numbered and came with a short glass of milk.

The puppet was the size of a toddler. His arms and legs were no bigger than kindling. The tray shook in his hands. The tray was heavy, of course. But the closer he got to the massive load of royalty, the more the tray quaked. Milk splashed over the sides.

Rivulets of drool ran down three chins to King Chocolate's neck.

His eyes were on the chocolate wafers, not the white puddles of milk racing around them. In fact, he hadn't noticed the puppet at all, even when the puppet stood in front of him, locking the tray between the throne's armrests. It wasn't till a glass tipped over. King Chocolate looked up.

His eyes looked like marbles pushed into a tray of fudge. They were brown, almost black.

"Who are you?" His words slurred into each other.

"I'm Poko."

The puppet removed the Alpine hat. The white feather fluttered in the band. He bowed. Then he turned his head and, with a smile, waved at the jolly fat man standing on the other side of the room. The jolly fat man wearing the red coat waved back.

"Don't wave at him!" King Chocolate blurted. It wasn't clear whom he was addressing. "Where's Jelly?"

"I-I-I don't know," Poko answered.

"Then why are you here?"

"Because she told me to bring you the recent harvest from the south fields. They're numbered so you know which ones—"

"Get out."

He was unconcerned with the spilt milk. To get wafer replacements would take too long. And Poko would just spill the next tray. King Chocolate shoved two wafers from pile one into his mouth. The chocolate thawed like his tongue was an overworked furnace. His eyes rolled back and disappeared.

Poko smiled at the jolly fat man in the red coat and started to say: "Merry, mer—"

"No!" A chocolate shower of spittle stained Poko's Alpine hat. "Not in here, you don't. Blah-blah. It's blah-blah. Do I have to send another memo? *Blah-blah!* If I hear one more merry, I will throw you and everyone in Fudgy Lake."

He could do that. The giant Sweet Tooth would do whatever he said. The unmerry citizens were slow to catch on. Change was hard. Everyone in Candyland said merry, merry at this time of year. King Chocolate had had enough of that. There was nothing merry about it, so why did they say it?

No one knew.

"Say it," he insisted.

"Blah-blah," Poko whispered.

"Louder."

"Blah-blah," Poko said.

The rivers of drool had turned muddy. He inserted one more wafer from pile one and raised his finger. "One more time, or you get dipped."

"BLAH-BLAH!"

Poko shuddered. His joints creaked. He hated the way those words felt. Despite living in the shadow of the Naughty Side, he *wanted* to be merry. He liked the way it felt. They all did. Everyone except maybe the chocolate-eating machine filling the throne.

"Merry Christmas," the jolly fat man wearing the red coat said.

Poko smiled. He couldn't help it. He shuffled out of the room as fast as his wooden shoes would go, clobbering his way through the door, and then looked back. Mouthed the words without a sound so King Chocolate wouldn't hear him.

Merry Christmas, Santa.

"WHY?" King Chocolate groaned. "Did you not hear the blah-blah part? Not merry, merry, not merry Christmas, not happy holidays. Blah-blah. It's so easy. Rolls off the tongue."

He waved his hands and sang.

"*We wish you a blah-blah blah-blah. We wish you a blah-blah blah-blah*. See?" He pointed at a wafer from the second pile. Stack one was decimated. "Now you try it."

"Throw me in Fudgy Lake," Santa said.

"You wish."

He devoured stack two like an industrial vacuum. The chewing sounded like animals stuck in a tar pit. The rolls across his belly burped like a boiling vat of goo. King Chocolate savored the flavor, letting it slide down his throat. He tipped his head back and poured a glass of milk in it like he was watering a potted plant.

He wiped his face with the back of his fleshy arm, plucked a wafer from the third stack, pointed it at Santa before throwing it into his mouth.

"So the big day in twenty rings. You must be excited. Making your lists, putting names on them, checking them off. Deciding who gets toys or coal."

"You know what you're getting," Santa said.

"I already have everything." He narrowed his eyes. "You know, those elves making the toys... I don't think that's right. You don't pay them, do you. There's something wrong with that. I'm sure it's breaking laws."

"They do it for love."

"Love of the game, sure. Keep telling yourself that. They make the toys; you get the glory."

King Chocolate paused to jot down a note concerning the wafers in the third stack. There was something unique about them. Not particularly good or bad. He'd pass his notes on to Jelly, who would make his wishes come true.

"I'm just going to say it," King Chocolate said. Pointed. "Egomaniac."

"Are we done?" Santa said flatly.

"A true friend tells the truth. And I'm telling you you're full of yourself. No judgment. Think about it. There are people in shopping malls who dress up like you. Kids get on their laps—crying, I might add—to get their picture. There are jillions of dollars made on that face of yours. A jillion."

"That's not a word."

"You're everywhere, fat man. Admit it. *Everywhere.* And you only work one day a year. Must be nice." King Chocolate nibbled the last wafer from stack number three. "You know who you're bigger than?"

"Don't say it."

"Elvis." He smacked his hands. "You thought I was going to say God."

"I'm not enjoying this conversation. If you could just..." Santa flipped an imaginary light switch.

"It's constructive criticism. You won't get that over there in Sunnyville. You get honesty over here. Truth bombs." He walloped his belly. "I've been blowing up phonies since before I existed."

"That doesn't make sense."

"Is that right? But a fat man in a sleigh that's pulled by magic flying reindeer, that makes sense?" Laughter gurgled in his throat. Then he called between his hands: "*Free presents if you're nice! Free presents if you're good!* How about authentic, huh? What does being real get me, a dull rock?"

"Authentic?" Santa held his round belly and laughed and kept laughing. "Delusional much?"

"See, right there. Look at that. *Mean.* You're mean. Calling me delusional. Welcome to the Naughty Side. How does it feel?"

"Are you serious? You're talking to a—"

"Yeah, I know. I know who I'm talking to. I'm aware. And that makes me *undelusional.*"

Santa rolled his eyes. King Chocolate felt this argument slipping away. He had the jolly fat man cornered for a minute. He was a slippery one.

"Flying reindeer," King Chocolate said. "Am I wrong about that being impossible?"

"There are stranger things in the universe."

"Name one."

The large man in the red coat sighed. The extra, extra-large man on the throne bore down on him. There were plenty of strange things in the universe. Start with mating rituals. Grown men crying over a sports team. Free presents delivered by a fat man who shimmies down the chimney was another. But flying reindeer? That was number one, and Santa Claus knew it.

King Chocolate waited.

Santa stared back.

And then he had something. He raised his finger and said it with complete and total confidence. This was the answer. This was the strangest thing in the universe according to Santa.

He said: "Quilting."

There was a long pause. King Chocolate leaned back in the throne. Not taking his eyes off Santa. The two men bore down on each other. The four corners of the room seemed to shrink. A bead of sweat worked its way down the rolls of King Chocolate's neck. A rash broke out on his back. He narrowed his eyes. A puff of laughter escaped his sloppy lips. Then another. Santa covered his mouth. Tears welled up in his eyes. He tried not to break.

King Chocolate broke first. "Hahahahahaha-HAHAHA-HAHAHAHA!"

They both fell to pieces. Tears mixed with spit and sweat. Guffaws tearing them open. The laughter nearly strangled King Chocolate. His face was as red as gift wrapping. He slammed his fists on the armrests.

"I can't breathe..." he wheezed. "*Quilting!*"

They'd had an argument some time ago. Santa was a big fan of the craft. King Chocolate insisted it was just sewing squares together. He'd never sewed in his life, but he was certain—one hundred percent positive—he could quilt tomorrow. It was needle and thread. Come on.

He tried to scratch an itch marching down his back. That wasn't something he could do without a stick. He leaned forward, tears plopping into an empty glass on the tray, and snuck a wafer from the fourth stack.

"Quilting," King Chocolate gasped.

He popped the wafer into his mouth, leaned back to let it slide down his throat and soothe the pain in his sides. Then suddenly lunged forward. A fountain of chocolate spattered the floor.

"Number four, number four!"

King Chocolate rinsed his mouth with the remaining milk and spit it on the floor. It dribbled down his dark brown robe. A dark patch bloomed on the shirt beneath. He shouted for Poko to bring him more milk. The puppet never returned. That little fire starter would go for a swim in Fudgy Lake.

Blah-blah.

"Show me the, uh, the sector where this came from."

He held up the card with number four written on it, showed it to the room. The walls, previously plain white with no shelving or photos or decorations, flickered to life. An image surrounded him. As if he were floating over a large hillside. Below, a scrubland of chocolate canes sprouted from the ground. There were long strips taken from it. A cloud of white sugar puffed from the bottom of the mountain. If he looked close enough, he'd see the machine chopping them down one cane at a time.

"That's number four?" he asked. "Send the crew to Sweet Tooth's nest. Have them clean it for a week. See if that keeps this from happening again."

He threw the wafers from stack number four. They stuck to the wall with an ugly splat.

"That's a bit harsh," Santa said. "They were only doing what you said to do."

"I never said make me barf chocolate. Not once. Never even thought it."

"You said be creative. Try something new."

"What should I do, put coal in their stockings? Oh, wait a sec. You already got that covered. Why don't you just keep babying the Nice Side and let me take care of the naughties, okay, fatty?"

He shifted on the throne, leaned back, and wiggled around. The itch was getting worse. And the taste of stack number four was still on his tongue. It was acidic. Like a smoothie of fermented cabbage. And his gut still hurt from laughing. And his face hurt from laughing.

There was one wafer left from the third stack. He reached for it. Felt the itch run up his back. Felt it pinch the jelly rolls on the back of his neck. The wafer was between his fingers when he felt the brush of fur on his cheek. He looked at his shoulder.

A pair of beady, black eyes looked back.

"Ahhhhh!"

The fright punched him forward. He leaned with such force that his momentum carried him over the armrest. The structural reinforcement groaned. King Chocolate's mass, however, rolled over then around the armrest like a bag of soup. His chicken legs hit the floor like faulty kickstands. He landed like a violent wave in the ocean. The air whooshed from him like a bellows.

The tray clattered on the floor. The wafer from stack number three landed near him.

The mouse, sitting on its hind legs, perched on the back of the throne, rubbed its front paws together, and gave a squeak. A twitch. If you would've asked King Chocolate at that moment, he would've said the little vermin laughed at him. It did no such thing.

"Get it!" He pointed his meaty finger at the mouse. "That! That! That! Get it OUT OF HERE!"

A long, mechanical arm unfolded from the ceiling. It plucked the mouse up by the tail and carried it across the room, depositing it in a hole that opened in the floor. Squeaking as it went. Smiling, if you asked King Chocolate.

"Tell the queen." His fingers crawled toward the last wafer. "Tell her another one was up here. Tell her to do something, or I will. Tell her I mean it."

Santa squatted next to him. He attempted to pick up the wafer that was just out of King Chocolate's reach. His fingers, however, passed right through it.

"Useless," King Chocolate muttered. Then to the ceiling: "Get that."

The mechanical arm returned.

"Not you! A different one. Do you think I want a disease?"

A different arm—one that had not just handled a mouse—extended from the ceiling. It nudged the wafer into King Chocolate's hand. He quickly threw it in his mouth, rolled onto his back, and chewed.

That's better.

Poko clambered into the room and immediately began to quake. It sounded like tree trunks tumbling off a logging truck. King Chocolate, still out of breath, still chewing, looked at the timid puppet holding his Alpine hat with the white feather in the band.

"If Jelly isn't here in five minutes, I will use you to build a fire. I'll start with your legs and work my way up."

Poko nodded. His hinged jaw clattered.

"And bring more wafers. The ones from stack three. Not the pukey ones." Poko flashed a brief smile at Santa and turned. "And milk!"

Santa, still squatting next to the king, tilted his head. He wasn't hiding a smile in his white, curly beard. Nor was there a twinkle in his eyes. He was serious.

"Are you unhappy?"

"What, are you my therapist now? Of course I'm unhappy. I'm the king of the naughties, you bag of farts. Unhappiness is our birthright. Haven't you heard the song? Let me play it for you. It's all horn section."

King Chocolate rolled to one side long enough to pass gas. No one was there to suffer the consequences. Santa looked at the helpless king licking chocolate off his lips like a starving animal. He looked like something coughed up by the ocean.

"You're out of breath," Santa said.

"You're judging me?"

"Simply an observation."

King Chocolate attempted to roll onto his side and, from there, possibly prop himself up on one elbow. From there, maybe, pull himself onto the throne. With confidence, he swung his arm. Felt a sharp pain in his shoulder. And unintentionally punched himself on the chin. The second roll absorbed the blow. It didn't hurt. He accepted his fate.

"You know," he gasped at Santa, "for a nicie, you're a bit naughty."

"We all are, Casey."

Santa looked down at him. The twinkle was back. His eyes shined. He wasn't going to deny it. Santa Claus was both naughty and nice. He proved it every time King Chocolate was with him. Santa opened his mouth to laugh his annoying ho-ho-ho. Then he flickered.

He was gone. Vanished. Turned off.

"Living out childhood dreams again?" someone said.

"I DIDN'T SAY you could turn him off," King Chocolate said.

The roly-poly elf waddled over to him. "Were you tired of sitting on the throne?"

"I'm admiring the ceiling." He gestured to the chocolate splatters on the ceiling tiles. "Looks like someone had an accident."

Jelly leaned back to observe and nearly rolled over. A disgusting stain was all over the ceiling. No one had ever bothered to look up because it took such effort. But when lying flat on the floor, it was hard not to notice.

"So, you've fallen and can't get up," Jelly said.

"Enough jokes. Get the picker."

"The engine lift?"

"How about the royal lift. And shut up."

He wanted to tell her to shut her *fat face*. But that was mean. She was a weather balloon balanced on two paddles shaped like feet. As plump as a blueberry. Never smiled, not once. And always stroking that braid of hair coming off the back of her head.

But she was always there for him. Almost always.

"Where have you been?" he said once he settled into the throne. "The samples were disgusting. They tasted like feet. I'm embarrassed to have my initials on them."

"They must have been horrible." Jelly picked up the empty tray.

"The last one was gross. Have that crew fired and sent to the rock-candy mines."

"We don't pay them, Your Excellency. And the mines are shut down."

"First of all, not a fan of the sarcasm. I get enough from St. Fatty. Second, you think of something to make them learn."

"Why should they learn if they're fired?"

"It's a lesson! Word will get out. I'm teaching the next generation. You'd make a terrible king, you know that. What do I pay you for?"

"You don't pay me."

"How about I pay you to shut up. How's that? Now where were you? Mr. Pencil Face brought me the samples and spilled the milk. And he said merry, merry when I *specifically* said not to. See what you did?"

"Sounds awful." Jelly scraped the chocolate wafers off the wall. "I was in the other room."

"Which room? There's a thousand of them."

"Newsroom."

"Oh, goody. The news. Tell me Christmas got cancelled."

"There's a new crosser."

"It's not like anyone around here would miss the fat—I'm sorry, what did you say?"

Jelly repeated it with slow confidence bordering on arrogance. Her eyes half-lidded. Complete boredom possessing her face. It was the only thing that kept her in King Chocolate's good graces. He'd thrown everyone else in Fudgy Lake except her. She'd learned early on his one critical weakness, something he couldn't stand to admit.

He wanted to be liked. He was addicted to it. If she was bored, he would do backflips (figuratively, of course) to entertain her.

Who's the awful leader in the room?

"A crosser?" he said.

"A crosser."

"From another world."

"Is there another kind?"

Stunned silence. King Chocolate looked like a wax replica of himself. He didn't blink or lick his lips or twitch. It was eerie. Jelly didn't know he could be so still.

"Did you die?" she asked.

"Shut up a second. I'm thinking."

Thinking, indeed. He hadn't thought about a crosser in a very, very long time. He chose to forget. His queen had taught him how to do that. *Compartmentalization,* she called it. Lock the bad memories up. Now Jelly was prying open one of those compartments. There hadn't been a crosser since—

"Is it a nutcracker?" he asked.

"No."

"What is it?"

"A boy."

"A wooden boy?"

"A regular one."

"You're sure? Positive?"

"Yes. And yes. Generals Fly and Gnat confirmed it."

King Chocolate scoffed. Spittle flew down his chins. He didn't bother wiping it. "Gnat Brain and Fly Poop. Those two morons could talk to a statue. May as well ask a magic ball, even though magic isn't real. Or ask a ghost. Even though ghosts weren't—"

"The Lost Boys saw him, too."

"Okay." He started nodding. "What did those noodle heads say?"

"He's with Gandy."

"The ginger?"

"They were looking for S'ven."

"Hahaha." King Chocolate pounded his chest. It felt good to laugh the appropriate amount. "Good luck finding that rodent. Did they find him?" He leaned forward, anticipating the answer. He flopped back in the throne when Jelly said no. "Good. He's a loon. Kids still saying that? Loon?"

"They never did."

"*Loon*... I'm bringing it back. Send the memo out. Loon is cool again. And let the crosser be Macey's problem. Maybe he'll wreck the castle again. That would be sweet." He snorted. "The loon. Hey, where's Poko? I ordered chocolate and milk, like, two chimes ago."

"You might want to reconsider."

"I'm starving."

"I mean the crosser." Jelly shuffled closer. It was hard to get the king's attention when food entered the conversation. His skinny legs were thumping a mad rhythm on the throne. He drew a breath and was about to scream when Jelly said: "His name is Arthur."

"I'll bet." He laughed. "Artie-fartie."

"You know why that's important?"

"Because it's funny?" He looked up, then back to Jelly. Legs shaking. "What?"

She pulled a snapshot from a pocket. Generals Fly and Gnat had taken it in Kettle Korn Trail. The photo was fuzzy, since she had to blow up the one they gave her (the original was a speck of pepper). King Chocolate took it from her, held it to the light. He struggled to make sense out of it, like it was an X-ray, and he wasn't a doctor. So she explained. Those were drawings in the crosser's pocket. A sketchbook. That meant he was an artist.

"He's a creator," she said. "You know what that means?"

"Of course." He gave back the photo. "What does it mean?"

"Whoever has him wins the war."

King Chocolate let that soak in. *Win the war?* He hadn't entertained the idea since he couldn't remember. The border hadn't moved an inch in one direction or the other in forever. What was the point of fighting if it never moved?

But now.

If this was true. If this crosser could hand him victory, if he could cover all of Candyland in darkness, then that was something better than food (for now). Just once he wanted King Macey and all those singing *loons* to know what it felt like to live in oppressive darkness. They didn't know. And they judged King Chocolate and all his residents for it. They blamed them for who they were, what they felt like. If they walked a tick in naughty shoes, they would know.

And King Chocolate would taste victory sweeter than all the wafers in Candyland.

"Send the Lost Boys! Now! Before Macey figures it out. Go-go-go! I don't want to see your fat little face until you bring the, uh... what's his name?"

"Arthur."

"Him! Bring him!"

He needed to burn some of this excitement. He flipped open a control panel on the right side of the armrest. There were buttons and controls. He thumbed a small joystick. The throne started sliding like a Zamboni machine. He whirled around the room. Maybe he'd race down the halls for a bit.

"Tell the queen we're going to *win!*"

"Would you like her to join you for dinner?" Jelly asked.

"God no! Just tell her the winning part. And the mouse part. One of her mice was up here, and I didn't hurt it. The next one goes straight in the lake. Tell her that."

"I'm not telling her that."

He didn't hear Jelly say that. Victory bells were ringing in his ears.

4

Gandy peeked into the market. He looked in one direction, then the other. Back and forth he went, and when he was satisfied, he turned back to Art and pulled the hood over his eyes.

"Follow me. No need to look around, yeah?"

No one paid attention to the gingerbread man and the Red Riding Hood poseur entering from the alley. Art kept his head down and eyes on the back of Gandy, whose flat legs scurried ahead, cutting through the crowd, calling out as he went.

"Merry, merry," he said. "Merry, merry to you. And to you."

Above the crowd, the castle soared into the pink sky. It didn't feel magical anymore. The castle was lovely and all, but without the chiming bell, that sensation of oneness, the way it stripped away the illusion of separation, was gone. It was a mob of individual things bouncing and dancing and running in circles, wishing each other a merry, merry.

The speck of light was winking at the top of the castle. Like an antenna warning low-flying planes to stay away. Although there was nothing in the sky but cotton-candy clouds. Not even birds.

Art had an urge to eat more chocolate. He didn't know why. It didn't taste good. But it felt good.

The hood came down over his eyes. "No peeking," Gandy said.

There was barking laughter, hoots and hollers, music and song and stamping of feet and hooves and whatever else was in the market. There was plenty of merry, merry and bubbles, too. Big bubbles and small bubbles drifting in the air. One stuck to Art's sleeve, the soapy film iridescent and smelling like strawberries.

It popped when Gandy yanked him beneath a tarp propped up with pretzel logs.

They passed carts full of candied apples and cardboard shacks stacked with balls of yarn. There were shipping containers loaded with glass furniture that smelled like grape juice, carriages piled with nuts. They passed a tent that smelled like a county fair. There were self-winding yo-yos and jack-in-the-boxes that told jokes. There was one thing that everyone and everything seemed to have in common.

Freedom.

They were who they were, and no one or no thing held them back. No judgment to fear. Like the essence of joy was the air they breathed. It was the ground they walked on.

Gandy stopped.

Art nearly knocked him over. Gandy clutched a handful (a fistful? a pawful?) of the red cloak.

"This way, yeah? I think we should go this way. A better way."

They did a one-eighty and were now going back the way they came, toward Kettle Korn Trail. Gandy walked like a frightened animal, bumping into things without an "excuse me" or even a "merry, merry." Art couldn't keep up with the zigging and zagging. He fell behind two yarn dolls swaggering arm in arm—their corded red hair falling over their shoulders—and could no longer see the gingerbread man.

A wave of anxiety stomped on his chest.

He looked around, unconcerned someone would notice a crosser in their midst. How they would mob him, paw at him for attention.

Want to know who he was, where he came from. Why he was here. All the things he didn't know—

"Over here." Gandy pulled him into a dim shadow. "Pull down the hood and stand still. Crouch down a little, you know. Bend the knees."

Art did that. He would've done anything he was told, feeling relief that Gandy knew where they were and where they were going. Gandy was looking left and right, that flat head twisting back and forth. The eyes big circles that weren't moving.

"What are we—"

"Just wait," Gandy said. "Give it a minute."

Gandy stopped panning the crowd. His face locked onto something like a satellite dish finding its target. A tall hat slid through the crowd like the fin of a shark. It was fuzzy and black and moved steadily, pausing every now and then. Turning this way and that before continuing. Like a bear catching wind of a meal somewhere in the trees.

"Don't. Move," Gandy said.

For the first time, he looked like a cookie made to eat. Not one who was married and had a house and an apron he wore when he cooked.

Art didn't move. Not a twitch.

Another hat cut through the crowd from the left. This one moved fast and smooth. A third one came from the right. No one was bothered by the swarm of tall hats except a petrified gingerbread cookie. Art wanted to run. Wanted to crawl out of his skin. Wanted a nibble of chocolate.

"Merry, merry, Gingerman," someone said behind them. "To you as well, Red Riding Hood."

A TENT WAS SANDWICHED between a metal shack filled with birdhouses and a wooden stall selling balls of dough. The flap was thrown open. Red and green lights twinkled inside.

The plump head of a bushy-browed young man peeked out of the two-person tent. An elfish smile spread wide and deep into fleshy, brown cheeks. Black hair pulled into a tight ponytail that swished over his shoulder.

Above the entrance, tied with twine, a banner was hung. The words were sloppy and painted in red, sparkling with glitter thrown on the paint before it dried.

Keepers of the Lost.

"Now, if you don't mind, move yourselves along. You're making quite the wall in front of our humble abode."

Peeps and chirps came from the humble abode. Along with the smell of a county fair.

"Ah, yes." Gandy looked around. "Could we come inside?"

"For a gander or a keep?" the plump, smiling face said.

"We won't know till we peek." Gandy looked at the crowd. "We're in a bit of a hurry, if you don't mind."

Something neighed. It sounded like a horse, but even a mini wouldn't fit inside a tent that size. The smile drooped a little. Then the face disappeared into the depths of the two-person tent entirely. The flap closed, and the red and green lights disappeared.

That was that.

Gandy turned back to the circling hats coming closer. His eyes growing bigger. He was as inanimate as a cookie fresh from the oven. Art knew that feeling well. Fear had taken hold of the gingerbread man. Fear so pure it paralyzed the body. Tasted like cold steel.

It was a boulder that ran you over, that flattened out thoughts and squeezed out breath. It was a thief ransacking the house, leaving it empty and hollow. Whatever the hats were, they were shepherding Fear closer. Gandy and Art could only watch.

"It appears we've had a cancellation." The tent flap whooshed open. "It seems we can spare a few ticks for a couple of curious lads."

❄

GANDY DUCKED inside without hesitation and was greeted with: "Gandy, old friend, it's been quite some time. How is Meg these days?"

Art followed, having to drop to his knees to squeeze through the opening. He crawled into a humid odor of damp fur and bird droppings. There was a hint of a large aquarium. The hood of his cloak hung over his head. His hands were on a dirt floor scattered with hay. And feathers. And scales.

"Stand up, lad. You're not in a barn."

An odd thing to say, given the smell and the sounds of the place. The host, it seemed, didn't know the meaning of the word *barn*. Or they used that word entirely different in these parts. Because it *was* an enormous, round barn.

There were stalls all around and cages stacked on top. There were three levels with more enclosures above. Things were flapping wings and sharpened claws, things staring down with gold-ringed eyes. There were aquariums, just like he thought. Only little mermaids were inside, no bigger than trout. Add to that glass cubicles decorated like miniature condos with bats sitting on sofas and worms watching TV. A salamander in a tuxedo held binoculars to get a better look at him. Gophers with hard hats building walls. Ants painting a landscape with watercolors.

There was one normal thing. A cat was on the third level, staring with lazy boredom as cats do. Then Art blinked, and the cat was gone. *Maybe not so normal.*

"My name is Herkle. And this is my brother, Derkle."

The hand that helped Art to his feet was thick. The hair on the back of it was coarse and straight. As black as ink. It hoisted Art up as if he were as light as a scarecrow. Art found his balance and then stumbled into Gandy, who kept him from falling over and crawling back out the flapped doorway.

Derkle, who had helped him stand, looked as strong as a horse. From his feet to his shoulders, he bulged with muscle. The problem was from the shoulders up. There was a long muzzle and rubbery lips. Pointed ears that turned. A flowing mane as coarse as the hair on his hands.

"Well, well, what do we have here?"

It wasn't Derkle the horse-headed farmer who said it. It was Herkle, who had introduced himself and his brother. He was standing on the other side of a Christmas tree in the middle of the round pen. Standing, of course, on four legs. Because Herkle was a horse. From the waist down. A plump-face man from the waist up. A shiny ponytail slung over his shoulder. He spoke with a churlish grin that was wide and wet.

"Gandy? Would you mind introducing us to your friend?"

"Of-of course," he stammered. "He's not from around here, I'm afraid. Down from Bonbon Town. Believe it or not, he's never been to the market."

Herkle and his brother exchanged looks. Derkle sighed noisily, lips flapping. It was almost a neigh. Herkle nodded.

"Well, then, that would explain his fascination with all this." Herkle gestured to the three-story barn. The cat was now on the shelf right behind him, blinking heavily at Art. "Does he not understand expansion, Gandy?"

"You'll have to ask him."

Gandy shook his head at Art. It was a signal. A signal Art totally didn't understand. *Expansion?* If he was talking about how a two-person tent could house a circus, then the answer was no. He did not understand expansion.

"You're a long way from home, aren't you, lad?" Herkle said. "Remove your hood, please. I would like to see your original face."

"He's shy," Gandy said. "Let him be. Your place is enough to give anyone the fits."

Once again, Herkle nodded. But not in a way of agreement. He studied the length and width of the red-cloaked stranger, clopping his wide hooves on the ground. Circling Art. Puffs of dust hovered off the ground.

"There's nothing to—" Gandy started.

Derkle held up his hand, then crossed his bulging arms. The

horse head tilted with curiosity. Black eyes big and shiny. Art could see a dash of red reflected in them. Derkle finally sighed (this time it was a neigh). Herkle nodded to his brother in agreement.

"My brother smells a fib like a rotten apple." Herkle offered a joyless smile. "Oh dear, Gandy. That's a naughty strike on you. And so close to Christmas. What will the jolly fat man put in your stocking this time?"

Gandy began to stutter. How many fibs could one tell before the jolly fat man backed the coal truck up to the chimney?

Art couldn't stand to see Gandy quiver that way. He pulled the hood off his head and showed his original face. Herkle's smile was a spotlight not a birthday candle. It beamed with fascination that exceeded what Art had felt when he crawled into the tent.

"My, my, my." The heavy hooves danced in place. "A cross-uh."

He whispered the last part. Derkle let out a whinny that stirred the entire barn. Feathers drifted from cages. The worms looked away from their TV. The fancy salamander dropped the binoculars. The cat had disappeared again.

"It's been quite some time since we had one. What would you say, Derkle? Twenty bells, maybe?" The horse head whinnied softly. "Thirty-three? That is a long time. It seems our friend Gandy is hiding him." He clicked his tongue. "That's a naughty the fat man won't forgive, my gingerbread friend."

"I am not hiding him. Besides, it wouldn't be a naughty if I was. Which I'm not. This is simply help, nothing more. You know how Landers are. If they knew there was a crosser, they would get... *excited*." The pause sounded like a swallow. The kind hiding a fib. "I was taking him to S'ven."

"S'ven is gone," Herkle said.

"I know. Where is he?"

Herkle's eyebrows were as thick as scouring pads. As coarse as steel wool. They rose and lowered. "Mystic Mountain, Lemonade River, Gooey Gully... who knows. He's a complicated one."

Herkle studied Art. Derkle hadn't even shuffled his boots. Only the wide nostrils on the end of the shiny muzzle flared, exhaling like exhaust pipes.

"My brother would like to know your name," Herkle asked.

Derkle raised his hand before Gandy could protest. Art cleared his throat. Said his name without hesitation.

"Art?" Herkle looked at his brother and back. "And what are you doing in our lovely world, Art?"

Art shook his head. Anyone's guess.

"You're lost, then? Then there's only one reason you're here, lad. The greatest Christmas gift of all. You're here to be found!"

Derkle threw back his head and let loose a full-throated whinny that shook the vaulted ceiling. The animals and things cheeped and sang and growled and barked with him. Stamping their tiny feet and flapping their feathered or scaly wings.

"He wants to go home," Gandy said. "He wants to wake up."

"And you, gingerbread man, are not helping!" Herkle shouted.

Derkle thrust a finger in Gandy's direction. Even from ten feet away, Art could feel the power of the horse-head man. Gandy felt it, too. Stumbling just a bit.

"Going home and waking up are two different things, my delectable friend. You mean well, Gandy. You do. But you're interfering with the lad's journey. It is his to take."

"I'm a guide, Herkle. Look it up in the big book. *Should a crosser seek assistance, we will provide that no matter the inconvenience.*"

He'd never quoted the big book to Art. In fact, he'd always called it the manual. Maybe they were different things. Herkle smirked and let that sour smile open wide. "And what chapter is that from, Gandy?"

"He landed in our house for a reason. You can't deny that, Herkle. You either, Derkle. *A reason.* We were chosen to guide him."

That swayed the brothers, who exchanged glances. Derkle shrugged. Something in the big book agreed with that. After all, why did Art land in their house and not somewhere else?

"A guide you seek," Herkle said. "Well, you've come to the right place."

"Hold on a ding-dong. Just hooooooold your ringer. We didn't come in here to adopt one of *these.*"

Derkle whinnied. It was disapproving. No horse whisperer needed. He raked his boot across the dirt floor like a bull seeing red. Gandy took one step in Art's direction. He hadn't said anything wrong. It was the way he said what he said about the animals in this place. *One of these.*

Herkle held a hand up in his brother's direction. Perhaps the only thing keeping him from charging. He laced his fingers. Wet his lips.

"Let's try again, my dear cookie." Herkle cleared his throat. In a flat, dangerous tone, he said: "If our young cross-uh here landed in your house for a reason, then he must have entered our domain for one as well. Don't you think?"

"*We're* here for a reason," Gandy muttered. But not exactly in agreement.

"We are home for the homeless. Love for the loveless. All the forgotten are remembered, and the lost are seen." Herkle trotted in a circle, hands raised toward cages and stalls and boxes. "They are not misfits, if that's what you think. Perish the thought. For one who doesn't fit isn't broken, only trying to be something they're not. Look around, lad. What does your heart see? What do your eyes feel?"

It wasn't the first time Herkle had given such a speech. Certainly not the last time it would inspire. Gooseflesh sprang up Art's arms. It felt like the horse-man was talking to *him.* Because he felt that way.

Lost. Forgotten and unseen.

There was a reason he was here. These were his people. Well, not his *people.* They were kindred. They were family. Misfits. *Like me.*

"Most kind," Gandy said, "but a travel companion is not what we came for."

"Companion!" Herkle stamped the floor. Derkle clapped his hands. "That's a better word, cookie man. Who would be your *companion,* lad? Your friend. Always at your back, mmm? Would it be Mr. Jimmy here. Our slaggo friend fell asleep on a cargo bunk and woke up on the wrong side of the border. When he tried to go back home, the family wouldn't let him. A tight bunch, slaggos are. Short memories."

What Herkle called a slaggo was, apparently, a chameleon. Because one waved through a glass box. He was wearing Bermuda shorts and rubber flip-flops strung between his toes. He held a tiny book in one hand.

"How about something more exotic, mmm? Sort of a cross-uh, this one. From a story world much like this one. Skin like leather and the tail of a serpent. You've never seen anything like this, lad. Wandering alone in Gooey Gulch, afraid and lonely. Once he was lost, but now he is found, the one and only and uniquely gifted... *grimmet!*"

Tiny applause came from several cages. Herkle threw out his arms. Three stories up, through a wire-mesh enclosure, a bright red bat hovered on small wings. Somehow it stayed airborne with a belly as round as a baseball. The whiplike tail slithered beneath it. It wiggled tiny fingers at Art.

Impossibly cute.

Endearing.

How could anyone say no to—what did he call it? A *grimmet*.

Art might have walked out with the grimmet had it fluttered down to his shoulder. Herkle, though, introduced five more companions, each with more potential than the one before. Gandy protested louder with each one. Herkle didn't care. He was on fire. In his element. Top performance gear for a reluctant crowd.

Derkle watched Art with those big black eyes.

All this was interesting, in the weird sort of way Gandy was a walkie, talkie. And somehow that was no longer surreal. But Art didn't want a pet. Not something to care for, to be responsible for. He struggled to care for himself. *I don't even know where I am or where I'm going!*

Silence.

Herkle stopped mid-sentence while describing the merits of a baby warthog snoring in a hammock. He clopped his hooves and frowned in concentration. He nodded at his horse-headed brother.

Derkle approached Art like a stray dog. A hungry one backed into a corner. His nostrils flared as he neared. The exhales were warm and laced with alfalfa. Art didn't move as Derkle moved his muzzle up his arm, the long hairs on his trembling chin tickling the honeycomb tattoo on Art's forearm. The nostrils soft and wet.

Derkle took Art's hand.

Turned it over. Examined the heavy calluses on his palm, the kind that developed on the handle of a shovel. His eyes rolled toward his brother.

"You tasted the chocolate," Herkle said.

"He didn't know what he was doing," Gandy said. "Someone in the market—"

"Who?"

Gandy stuttered. All the attention was on Art, who shrugged. Then he described what the imp looked like. Said the imp's name was Rude. That didn't ring a recognition with the horse brothers. But when Art mentioned the things strapped on their backs, the foam-board-like pool noodles, Herkle and Derkle looked at each other.

"Lost Boys," Herkle muttered.

"I-I doubt that," Gandy said. "Not this far over the—"

Herkle stopped him. Derkle traced the creases with his finger. Put his hand on Art's chest. Heart beating against it. Thumping. Running.

Running. Running.

Derkle looked into his eyes. Staring and seeing deep inside. Art's warped reflection in the depths of those black pupils. The red cape over his shoulders. Shaggy mop of hair.

"Interesting," Herkle said.

"Interesting? What's interesting?" Gandy said. "I'm sorry, Herkle. I haven't been honest with you. It's not exactly a fib, just... well, the reason we're in here is because—"

"Shhhh." Herkle pressed a finger on Gandy's mouth. The icing smudged and clotted. "Are you certain?" he said to his brother.

His brother whinnied.

"Very well, then." Herkle looked at Art. "We found your companion, lad."

"STAND RIGHT OVER THERE. A few more steps, that's it. Thank you very much."

Art stood next to the doorway. Gandy seemed unsure what to do, his head twisting left, then right. The candied outline of his mouth (still smeared) formed a perfect O. At one point he started toward the exit, but Herkle clicked his tongue like a dog trainer.

"Not yet, my cookie friend."

Derkle had something long and flexible. It looked like he was preparing to pole vault. There was no hook on the end—which was what Art figured it was for. It reached the third story. Maybe he was going to knock one of the doors open and let a rainbow mini-dinosaur parachute to the ground.

He pulled some switches embedded on the pole. A few clicks and the pole split longways. Rungs snapped between the two pieces. Herkle swung the ladder into place. There was nothing trustworthy about the way it swayed. Herkle, though, didn't hesitate: he scaled to the very top of the ladder and climbed into a dark space between a cargo box stamped *Merry, Merry* and a net full of seashells.

"He should be to the left," Herkle shouted. "Behind the counter." Then to Art he said: "Daryl plays hide-and-seek when there's company. He's here; he's there, then fits himself in this tiny little space behind a kitchen counter up there. Don't know how he does it. This one is rare and special, lad. Derkle, though, he says there's an indelible connection between the two of ya. And Derkle's never wrong. You'll see what I mean—careful!"

The horse-headed brother returned to the ladder with a duffel bag in one hand. The ladder twisted and bowed. Derkle descended as if he were sliding down a fire pole. He leaped off the last rung and landed with a puff of dust. Bits of hay floated in the hazy air.

The bag looked nine months pregnant. The way it squirmed.

"Ah, here we go." Herkle pulled the zipper and reached inside. "Hold your breath, lads. It's about to be taken away."

A load of fur cuddled against Herkle's chest. Long whiskers and triangular ears.

"We found this one on Two-Face Mountain. It was after the battle. I think he helped the hussars win. No scars." He ran his fingers through the fur and over the generous belly. Derkle whinnied. "That's right. My brother said no scars we can see, but he's wounded, this one. We think he might be a crosser. Hard to say. Just never seen one like him in the Land."

"What were you doing on Two-Face Mountain?" Gandy said.

"Looking for lost ones."

Gandy seemed to forget about his hurry. He drifted away from the exit as if Herkle had hypnotized him with a fat, furry animal. The tail swished like a feather duster. Gandy reached out.

"I wouldn't, my cookie friend. He's temperamental. You know, fussy when it comes to strangers. I'd be worried what might happen. Look at the teeth. How sharp they are. Could puncture a balloon. And little knives in his feet, look." He pushed on the paws. A hooked claw sprang out. "Retractable."

Gandy backed up. His eyes round. "What's that sound? Is that coming from him?"

They leaned closer. Except for Art. He knew what they were hearing. It was the sound the animal made when it was cradled in someone's arms. They looked at each other, the three of them. Herkle biting his lip. Derkle nodding that big horse head. Gandy holding his chest.

"It's a cat," Art blurted.

And that was it. Your garden-variety tabby. Long fluffy tail. Sprigs of whiskers bunched around a pink nose. The belly, though, looked like he preferred beer over milk, spending his days soaking up sun in a windowsill instead of hunting game.

"Cat?" Gandy said.

"Yeah. A cat."

"Are *cats* rare?"

Art laughed. He still didn't know where he'd come from or what home looked like, but he knew cats were everywhere. You couldn't give them away.

"They're not... no, they're not rare. Not where I come from."

"You remember?" Gandy said.

Art shrugged. "I just... no. But I don't think cats are rare."

"He's a cross-uh, then. Like you." Herkle rubbed the cat's belly. The purring grew louder. "We don't call him *cat*."

"What do you call it?" Gandy asked.

Before Herkle could answer, Art blurted out a word. It was a name that came from faraway. One as familiar as the tattoo on his arm.

"Daryl."

Herkle and Derkle exchanged a long glance. "That's right, lad. He's a Daryl. How did you know?"

Even Gandy was nodding. Like they were sort of surprised Art had guessed it.

Art couldn't explain how he knew his name. Like the word came through a speaker planted inside his head. It came on a purr. He could feel the warmth, feel the cat lying on his bed in the mornings. Greeting him at the door when he got home. Flopping on the floor to get that fat belly rubbed. This cat came to the sound of plastic bags rubbed together.

Daryl locked those vertical pupils on him now and didn't waver.

Art was dying to hold him. Begging to feel the fur. The warmth. *The purr.*

"Do cats scratch furniture?" Herkle asked. "Do they poop in sand boxes?"

"Yeah. They chase lasers, too."

"Hmm." Herkle nodded at his brother. Derkle took ten steps back. He pulled a tin of animal food out of his pocket, hooked his finger in the pull ring. "And cats do this?"

When the lid cracked and the seal broke, before the meaty smell of wet food wafted out, there was a vibration in the air. An electrical current Art felt in his teeth and down in his bones.

It tingled.

He didn't blink, though.

He didn't look away, not even for a second.

One second, Daryl was curled up in Herkle's arms. And the next he was crouched on Derkle's shoulder, watching him peel the lid from the can. Licking his whiskers. Showing his teeth when he meowed.

Derkle held up the can. Daryl went to town.

"Can they…"

Teleport? No. No, they can't do that.

The little bit of foundation he'd felt under him, however small that fragment had been, was now gone. The familiarity of seeing a cat had put him at ease. He knew the cat's name, after all. He probably knew the cat from where he came from, he was sure of it. And if he was honest, it was more than that.

He *loved* that cat.

But cats didn't cross a room without moving. They didn't disappear and reappear when hungry. *And cookies don't talk, and horses don't wear bib overalls.*

Herkle flashed a self-satisfied smile.

Art didn't know what to think of that. He just wanted to hold the cat. To feel him. To cuddle with him when the world felt dark and heavy. Daryl was almost done eating, his long tongue reaching for the whiskers. His eyes were on Art. He was going to do that thing again. The air took on that sharp, electric edge again.

Then something clamped around Art's arm.

He was yanked through the tent's exit and pulled into the market.

PRESSURE FILLED HIS HEAD. It was a balloon on the verge of bursting.

Art covered his ears. Hooked at the elbow by a white-gloved hand, pulled into the peppermint air of the market, he stumbled off the curb. His knees skidded on the soft stones. The hood fell back.

"Crosser," someone muttered.

"Crosser," someone answered. "Look at the eyes!"

And then a third someone connected the dots and shouted for all to hear: "CROSSER!"

The road thundered beneath Art. His head was down, but he felt the walls close in around him. Bodies pressing closer, squealing and laughing and gasping and clapping. A ring of black boots surrounded him. Boots made for marching, not singing in the rain.

Art followed the boots up starched pant legs, past shiny belt buckles and stiff jackets.

Tufts of chin hair.

Square mouths with hard jaws.

A ring of tall-hatted soldiers surrounded him. Shoulder to shoulder, eyes staring ahead. Pressure coming down, a weighty vapor filled Art's brain. Made the street rock on stormy waters.

"This isn't necessary!" Gandy turned sideways and slipped between the guards like an envelope through a mail slot. "You're making a scene, all of you!"

The heavy air pulsed. Art felt it push behind his eyes.

"No, no," Gandy answered (although Art didn't hear a reply for him to answer). "I *was* bringing him to the castle and avoiding attention doing it. Look at the mess *you've* made. Just look!"

The full-sized nutcrackers didn't flinch.

"How dare you accuse me of avoiding you!" Gandy shouted. "The boy wanted to see the animals. There's nothing in the rules that prohibits such a thing *on the way to the castle!* It's in the manual; look it up! I'll be sending a complaint straight to King Macey, count on that. On all of you."

Art got to one knee. He staggered and leaned into one of the soldiers. A tight hand clamped around his arm. He jerked free and shoved the nutcracker (who barely moved). With a couple of steps, he could break through like a game of Red Rover. He would've, too. If not for the firm, gingery hand on his chest.

"Don't," Gandy whispered.

"Am I in trouble?"

Gandy shook his head. "Of course not. They are peacemakers. It's all right, I promise."

The pressure lifted from the crown of Art's head.

He inhaled clean, crisp air to cleanse his lungs and mind.

In unison, the nutcrackers saluted. It looked like they were saluting Art—and maybe they were—then they abruptly did an about-face. They moved in unison, boots clopping the road in time with each other and through the crowd like a bubble in a stream.

"We're walking. We're walking." Gandy pulled the hood over Art's face. "No pictures, please. We ask for privacy, thank you. He's just like us."

Flashes went off.

Screams of joy exploded.

"Where am I going?" Art asked.

Gandy stopped. The soldiers kept marching. Gandy was waving when the nutcrackers ejected him from the circle, keeping Art trapped inside as they marched. Gandy's voice, somehow, rang in Art's head like a dinner bell. The words as sharp as the peppermint breeze.

"Your journey, son."

5

The boat drifted like a wafer through a pool of rose tea.

It wasn't so much a boat as it was a floating panel. A miniature barge with no cargo. Well, none except for the young man wearing a red cape. And the soldiers posted around the perimeter with only a red whip of licorice keeping them from going over the edge.

There was no sound of a motor or whine of an electric troller. If there was, it was drowned out by the cheers from shore. More bodies had flooded the market once word of a crosser was out. Toys and puppets and muppets and things all getting a look at the awkward young man standing on the floating stage, the size of it a bit much. But it was the only boat in sight.

Slowly, the cheers faded.

Slowly, they drifted toward the great spike in the sky. It felt like he was moving into the shadow of the castle—the way it felt, the drop in temperature, the gloom—but there was no shadow.

No sun.

Only a pink sky. Only cotton-candy clouds.

The closer they got, the more the castle looked like it had been carved from a stalagmite of gold and not quite finished. Still, it was stunning—the arching windows and pointy turrets. The way the golden walls glittered. Just the size of the thing insisted on being worshipped. Art followed its rise into the sky. It felt good being near it. Felt better the closer they got.

He went to the end of the boat (not a boat, but whatever). The nutcrackers didn't stop him.

The water was still. Unbroken. Not a ripple in their wake. As if they weren't moving. Not even touching the water. It didn't seem real. Because when he leaned over the edge, he wasn't in the reflection. Only the clouds. Only the sky.

Only the castle.

He could swim back to shore. It wasn't too late. It wasn't too far. The crowd would greet him, maul him. Take pictures. Maybe hide him. But he didn't. And for one silly reason.

He didn't want to. Because the castle felt good.

"Hey." He said it to the nearest soldier. "What's in the castle?"

The nutcracker's head turned toward him. Then Art's head rang with pressure. Like a tuning fork jammed between the eyes.

A GATE LOWERED an inch at a time.

Giant links in a chain that could heel a dragon. Giant links the color of breakfast cereal. The kind with artificial flavors and loads of sugar. The good kind.

It landed with a boom. Art felt it in his chest.

The boat eased up to it. The nutcrackers stepped over the licorice whip at the front of the boat. In two lines, parallel with each other, they marched into the castle. Swallowed by the darkness inside. Boots thumping on the wooden door on their way.

Leaving Art alone.

Like they'd forgotten him.

He followed the height of the castle until his neck hurt. It pointed into the pink heavens. The details of the thing—the windows and turrets, the staircases that circled the perimeter connecting balconies and doorways—were dizzying. It was daunting and alluring. Pulling him toward it and pushing him away. Left him with a knot in his belly.

He took a step.

A cheer rose from the distant shore. They were quite small now. A mob of color. Their enthusiasm went up a notch when he took another step. And the same for the next.

He stopped at the edge of the entrance. Peered into the darkness. It was black, keeping its secrets hidden. The price was total commitment. The breath of the castle sweet and damp. Like moist cake. He turned toward the market. Lifted his hand and waved.

They lost their minds.

IT WASN'T DARK. Once he was inside. Dim, maybe.

His eyes adjusted within seconds. The corridor was long and empty. The nutcrackers were somewhere up ahead. Their bootsteps echoed. There was nowhere for them to hide. But he couldn't see them.

"Hello?"

His voice ricocheted down the arched ceiling.

Funny. He couldn't hear the cheers anymore. Even though the gate was open. He could see them quite clearly, just as before. Only nothing but his own *hello* running the length of the hallway and back.

The castle didn't feel dangerous. It smelled good. Had a vibe like the walls were smiling.

A candle caught flame when he neared it. Tendrils of black smoke slithered past a painting in a golden frame. It was a two-story house. White with green shutters. An old-looking thing with rotting steps leading to the front porch. He stood for a moment, thinking. Wondering.

Then went on.

Another candle. Another painting.

This one a snow hill with kids in snowsuits speeding down on sleds. Adults at the bottom drinking from steamy thermoses. Wrapped in scarves, wearing puffy coats, with leaky red noses.

Next was a vacation beach.

A snowball fight.

A skateboard park.

They meant something. He couldn't tell you what. Like a story you might have heard once upon a time, but you're not sure if you imagined it.

The last one was not a painting. It was a photo. A man in a red suit and a bushy white beard. Black boots and a wide belt to match. A lumpy sack thrown over his shoulder. A clutter of toys and dolls and things around him. Following him. A rather large crowd. Larger than the one at the market.

Art leaned closer.

He recognized some of them.

Meg and Gandy. Their eyes were big circles of excitement. Their mouths just as round. There could be more than one gingerbread couple in this world. But it felt like them. One fact was most certain and indisputable. And he thought with a smile and a laugh puffed from his throat, *The jolly fat man they were all excited to see... that's Santa.*

THE NUTCRACKERS WERE SUDDENLY on both sides of him.

They stood in two lines, one on each side of the corridor. Backs as straight as lumber.

They must have stepped out of secret panels on the walls. Art had hardly blinked. He'd been so absorbed by Santa Claus he didn't notice. Or hear their boots (which seemed highly unlikely).

"Where'd you come from?" he asked.

No answer. He didn't expect one. Although a slight headache pinged between his eyes.

The red-coated soldiers with the ridiculously tall black hats marched deeper into the castle. Art fell into step with them, letting his boots hit the ground when theirs did. It pulled him along. No more candles or paintings of ordinary things or jolly fat men. Just stepping. Just marching.

A spiral staircase soon appeared.

It was the center of the castle, he assumed, since a perpendicular cross hall went in opposite directions. Where X marked the spot.

A titanic corkscrew twisted into the misty heights. Bits of pink snow wandered down and stuck to the metal treads that would undoubtedly clang with each step. Beads of moisture clung to the railing that coiled around and around.

The nutcrackers marched around it. Stood in a circle facing in. That was it. Nothing more. No pressure in Art's head. No nudging him toward the first step. One look up that climb was all it took. It would take days to make it to the top. If that was where they wanted him to go.

"What now?"

They stamped the floor. He felt it.

"Yeah, I'm not—"

A balloon rose out of the floor. It was red and the size of a pickle barrel. It bounced through the center of the spiral steps, squeaked when it rubbed against the railing. A hefty rope was tied to a knot the size of a cowboy's fist. It pulled something out of the floor.

A one-person hot-air balloon basket hovered in front of him.

The gate opened on its own. The hinges needed oil.

Art looked at the nutcrackers. But like before, they moved without Art seeing them move. Now they were behind him. In a row. Shoulders as square as their jaws.

Pretty clear what they wanted.

Art didn't move. They didn't make him. He stood between them and the basket and counted his options. There were quite a few. In the end, he decided no matter what he did, he was going to end up here again. His journey would take him to the top of the castle. Whether he took the long way or not.

May as well do it now.

THERE WAS HARDLY room in the basket.

It cracked and settled under his feet when he stepped in. Like an old wicker chair. Fibers peeled from the rail. Paint chips stuck to his palms. To be honest, he really didn't think this thing was going to work. The balloon wasn't *that* big—not big enough to lift him. And that, if he got down to the truth of it, was why he climbed into the warped basket.

And then it went up.

His heart bellyflopped into his stomach. The railing crunched in his hands.

It didn't float off the floor. It soared. Like wind-on-his-cheeks soared. Like tears-in-his-eyes soared. The balloon didn't get any bigger. It wavered in the column of space, occasionally bouncing off the spinning staircase.

He closed his eyes. It didn't ease the growing nausea.

He tried dropping to the floor, but his knees buckled against the side of the basket. Every movement made the balloon wobble. Every thought was dark and doomed. Like if the balloon popped. Like if the bottom of the basket rotted out.

The air became denser. Heavier.

The balloon smaller. It didn't slow down, though. Just the opposite.

The stairs were a blurring corkscrew. *Is that frost on the railing?*

His hands ached. Fingers numb. He tried to slow his breath, like Meg had told him to do, but the frigid air froze his legs. He choked on each breath. Wind whistled through his ears, pulling tears down his raw cheeks on a ride that was never going to end. When it did, his dark thoughts insisted, he would crash through the top of the castle like a rocket shooting into space.

That, he thought, *might be the way home.* It was a wishful thought quickly stamped out by another dark thought. *You wish.*

Something crashed and rang. The inside of his head vibrated. Everything went dark. He hadn't closed his eyes, though. Moments later, the rushing stairs were back. It happened again. This time he recognized the sound of it. The way it felt. The good tidings that chased away the dark thoughts.

The bell!

He was inside the castle when it rang, the sound of it deafening. The vibrations dissolved his fears and worry, replacing them with a surefire sense of goodness. Okayness. Like things were perfect just the way they were. He melted on this strange balloon ride, closing his eyes and feeling layers of anxiety peel away and fall a thousand stories. Or however far down it was.

The minty air stung his nostrils. An evergreen scent mixed with it: the smell of freshly cut limbs from pine or spruce. It became over-powering. Intoxicating. Squeezing the past from that lost treasure of memories he couldn't find.

A tree in the corner of a room.

Decorations heavy on its limbs. A star crammed on top. Presents stacked below.

Songs on the radio. And cookies in the next room. The cheer of good feelings.

When he opened his eyes, he was no longer moving. The balloon detached and wobbled toward a domed and icy ceiling far above. The basket he was in sat firmly in a bank of pink snow, as if it had been gently placed there the night before. And all around him were trees.

A forest of Christmas trees.

NOT JUST ANY CHRISTMAS TREES. Although they were uncut and, as far as he could tell, rooted into the ground (or was there a floor beneath the pink snow?). They were decorated, one and all. Big ones and small ones. Fat and skinny with droopy limbs or pokey needles. Some reached high above, some short and squatty.

Stalactites pointed down. The balloon looked like a red kick ball bouncing between them.

Footsteps pocked the pink snow. They were wide and shallow.

Someone in snowshoes had been through, going in this direction and then the other. No one way to follow. Or avoid.

Strands of tinsel grew from the branches like silver hair. The ornaments were curious. Orbs clung to the limbs. They varied in size and shine and color. No hook or wire attached. As if they grew from the tree. A sort of fruit made of glass.

That's impossible, he thought. And then laughed. *Impossible?*

He reached for a bright red orb. It was dense and heavy, weighing on the pendulous limb. He lifted and twisted. It was attached, all right. Attached by a thick stem that refused to break. The ornament wasn't glass, or at least it didn't feel like it. It was soft, almost mushy. Like an overripe melon wrapped in plastic.

BAP!

He stumbled into the tree. At first, he thought someone had punched him in the back. A direct hit between the shoulder blades. A wet thud. But no one was behind him or anywhere near him. And snow was stuck to the back of his shirt.

He listened.

"Hello? Someone there?"

The wind blew somewhere nearby. It howled and whistled. The Christmas trees, however, didn't shake or shimmy. They were as still as deadwood.

Something shuffled. A scamper to his right. A flash of color through the trees.

Art scooped pink snow and packed it into a tight ball. It was all he could think to do. And he followed. Reluctant and slow. Snow pushing up to his knees in some places. He peeked around a wide tree with a tiny star on top (it was dull and unfinished) and stopped to listen. Only the sound of his heavy breathing reported back. He sounded like a desperate animal.

"Who's there?"

The answer came. It was *BAP!*

The snowball hit exactly where the first one did, square between the shoulders. This one knocked him on his face. He stumbled and ate a pink snowdrift. He wiped his face and spun around. That was when he heard it. A sound he would never forget.

Laughter.

A giggle and a snort. A rapid-fire chuckle that jiggled the belly. A contagious chortle that spread a smile on his face.

"Okay. All right." He molded another snowball. "Is that the game? I hear you. Let's do this."

Art went after it, and he went hard. Cutting corners. Slogged through drifts. Ornaments rang when he brushed a tree.

The Christmas forest was endless and winding. The footsteps everywhere. Whoever he was chasing was nimble in snowshoes that barely dented the snow. The laughter always ahead of him. Just around a corner or the other side of a tree. Catching a flash of color or a dashing escape. It sounded like a child, sometimes. Laughing just out of reach.

Art was gaining. He thought.

Sucking the wintery, peppermint air into his lungs, snot running from his nose. The snowball numbed his hand. One more turn and he'd launch it through the branches. Ducking below a pendulous spruce branch, he planted his foot on the ground and cut through a small opening, sure to cut off whoever it was and—

No more trees.

A wide track of snow, the width of a two-lane highway, cut through the forest. There were trees on the other side, just as dense and just as shiny. The road between the two was smooth and pink. On one end, the wall was obscured by a haze. It was blue and rocky and slightly curved where it soared toward the arching ceiling.

There was a building in the other direction. And not far.

He walked close to the trees.

The building extended the full width of the road. Going from tree line to tree line. A slanted roof with cedar shingles. Daggers of ice clung to the eaves. (Strange. With all the ice and snow, Art wasn't cold in a T-shirt.) The walls were bright red. The trim forest green. He didn't recognize it until he was close enough to see the broad door.

A barn.

The farm kind for horses and tractors.

He could smell hay or grass. At least he thought he did. It was easy to imagine big bales in the loft.

Puffs of smoke billowed from a chimney behind the barn.

Art stayed near the trees, going around the barn to find a cottage attached to it. A rather small one with a low thatched roof and cobblestone walls. The windows were round and flickering with orange light. He waited for something to move. When nothing did, he peeked through the window to see a blazing fireplace shedding warm light on recliners and books and tables.

He considered knocking, even made a fist and held it before the thick oak door, but looked across a short stretch of snow. The end of this room (or cavern or whatever it was) was within reach. The bluish wall curved upward. It was rough and scarred, as if carved from inside the castle or a dense patch of ice. In the middle, the exact distance between the tree lines, was a round window like a portal on a ship.

Beyond it, pink sky.

Cotton-candy clouds.

THE SNOWDRIFTS WERE past his waist on his way to the hole in the wall. It wasn't a big hole. Didn't let much light in. (Which, by the way, couldn't explain how the Christmas forest wasn't dark. It was *inside*, after all. This was a giant room that was, somehow, well lit. And not from this tire-sized window.) Barely large enough to stick his head through it. When he tried, he hit a windowpane of some sort. Not glass or plastic. It didn't look like anything was there. His hand, though, hit an invisible field.

He could see through it, though.

The rosy lake of tea surrounded the castle. The market at the shore. Rows of gingerbread houses and lines of gummy paved roads. A giant Ferris wheel was far to the right. Waterfalls of lemonade were to the left. Rivers of fudge in between.

The light was strange. It lay like a luminous blanket, all cheery and bright. Then halfway across the land, it ended abruptly.

Beyond was shadow, of sorts. Not darkness or night. It was a dimness that lay on the other side of Candyland. There wasn't much to see over there. One thing, though, he couldn't miss. It was far away and outlined in the gloom. A dark spike that reached into the gray swirl of clouds. A castle just like this one.

In between, he thought, *is the border.* That was where Gandy wanted to go, to find Grimjoy the fortune teller. *Where light meets dark.*

Between the castles and on the border was a mountain shaped like a child's crayon version of a volcano. Cone-shaped. Broad at the bottom. The top disappeared into a dense wad of cottony clouds. It was enormous and mysterious.

Then a third snowball exploded above his head.

It popped against the wall like a paper bag filled with air and showered down his neck. His heart slamdanced against his chest. He spun around to get eyes on his opponent. All he saw were footprints.

Super-wide footprints.

THE TRACKS WENT to the cottage. The door was open.

A shaggy doormat had been shoveled and dusted off. *In or Out,* it read. Below that: *Either way, close the door.*

A rectangular mailbox was nailed to the doorframe. (*Did someone deliver mail?*) It was red and sparkly. *Belly* was traced through the glitter.

He ducked his head beneath the low-arching doorway. "Hello?"

Silly thing to say. It was all he could think of.

The cottage was one room. And he could see it all from the doorway. It was warm and toasty inside. Firelight orange. The smell of spice and smoke. Of sweet things soaked in sugar. Holding the doorknob (brassy and frigid in his hand), he looked outside for someone. Maybe this was a trap. It felt like a trap.

The warmth, though. He couldn't resist.

He pulled the door closed behind him, like the doormat said to do. He kept his knees slightly bent. The top of his head brushed the ceiling. A silver mug was resting on the floor in front of a blazing fireplace. The light danced on jewels set in the cup's handle.

He crouched in front of a fully reclined lounger (too small for him to sit in) and warmed his hands at the fire. The heat stung his fingers and brought back sensation in pokes and pricks. He leaned over, peered into the silver mug, sniffed what was in it. Sweet, it was. And sour. Gold flakes glittered at the bottom, or maybe that was just the light.

He ignored the drink. For now.

Even though he was thirsty. Very thirsty.

He hadn't had a swallow of anything since waking up in this world. That was how he'd come to think of it. *Waking up.* It felt like days since he woke at that desk in the gingerbread house. And nothing had changed. Just one long day. Nighttime might never come, and he was no closer to going home. Unless you counted sitting in a tower that reached into the sky. If home was up there—out there—then maybe he was closer.

It was a hoarder's paradise. Books, there were plenty. Old ones with fading titles and fraying spines, but none he recognized (not that he was a reader; he could read; he just didn't want to). Rocks and cups in cabinets and toys and shoes on shelves; walking sticks in tin cylinders; tangled balls of yarn in baskets and leaning stacks of paper on the floor; bowls of pinecones by the door. Knitting needles on a tiny couch. A half-assembled puzzle on a three-legged table.

No coat on a rack or boots by the door.

He got up, rubbing his hands, checking for a door to a back room he might have missed. Looked out the window to see if someone was coming home. Went back to the fireplace and sat on the floor.

Stomach twisting.

Mouth watering.

He picked up the silver mug. Sniffed. Wet his lips on the rim of it. He didn't know the proper amount of time required to test if something was poison. It definitely wasn't ten minutes. That was all he lasted before taking his first swallow.

It warmed his belly. Slaked a thirst he didn't know was there.

It fizzed in his throat. Pulled at his cheeks.

He tipped the mug for the very last drop. Letting those golden flakes (turns out it was gold) fall on his tongue.

So good. So, so good.

He leaned against the recliner, completely thawed inside and out. Melting on the circular rug where he sat. Feeling light and relaxed. He'd danced in the market. Had been to the Keepers of the Lost. Walked down Kettle Korn Trail. Was cared for by a lovely couple of gingerbread cookies.

Beyond that, he couldn't remember a thing. Not where he came from. Not how he got here. Most importantly, why he was here. He closed his eyes to think of a reason. That fire, though. It felt good.

He didn't hear the door open.

6

"What now?" King Chocolate whined.

Dark spittle shot from his lips. A plate of chocolate wafers tumbled to the floor when the carriage lurched to one side. He'd been sampling a batch of dark chocolate. He hated dark chocolate. Yet couldn't stop eating it. It was a curse to love something so vile. Like blue cheese dressing. Like chicken liver.

"Pothole."

Jelly sank into a beanbag on the other side of the carriage, filing her toenails. The swatches of red hair on her toes made King Chocolate want to look away. You could scrub pots with those things.

"What's the point of having roads?" King Chocolate mused.

Then he pointed at the floor. It had been quite some time since he'd been able to bend over. Jelly pretended not to notice. He cleared his throat, to give her a chance. She sighed and, with great effort, picked up the spilled wafers. Having to roll on her stomach to do so. When she was back on her enormous, hairy feet, King Chocolate had his mouth open like a baby bird.

She flipped the wafers into his mouth like coins tossed into a wishing well.

He hardly chewed. Chocolate made everything better. Even if it was dark.

The carriage interior was crimson velvet with detailed stitching. Something Jelly designed and he couldn't care less about. But this was cool. He flipped a switch on the armrest of his throne. The roof folded back. The dim sky fell on them like fog. Another switch and the throne began to rise. Slowly, he was lifted out of the fancy carriage, and insect song greeted him. The little buggers were synchronized and playing a merry tune he didn't hate. If he wasn't mistaken, they were singing "We wish you a blah-blah Christmas."

Trees were on both sides of the road. Their branches heavy with dark ornaments. The cinnamon trunks were peeling. On the road in front of him, a crew of grumpies were laying slabs of peanut brittle over deep holes. The humpbacked grumpies looked like softshell beetles with a bad case of warts. They smelled like bread mold.

There were five more potholes in the shape of a foot. As deep as wedding cakes.

"What's the story?" Jelly said with the enthusiasm of a third grader at an abstract art show.

"Once upon a time," King Chocolate said, "you walked the rest of the way. The end."

She didn't like that story. But where they were going wasn't far. He could see the door against a wall of yellow light.

The carriage split like a plastic Easter egg. The throne was placed on the road. A joystick popped out of each armrest. King Chocolate sped forward like a county fair bumper car, hovering a few inches above the ground, weaving around the potholes. Jelly made no effort to keep up.

He shaded his eyes.

The glare from the light was painful. It was like being punched with a sixteen-ounce boxing glove. He squinted through paper-thin slits. A rectangle was ahead. It was, very likely, the door he wanted. At this rate, it would take twenty ticks for his eyes to adjust to the brightness.

He stopped the throne and closed his eyes. Jelly could figure it out when she caught up. The bug song was accompanied by giant apple spiders plucking the threads of their webs like strings on a cello. The creatures on this side of the border slithered and creeped. They snuck and spied, slurped nectar from wild sugar flowers, munched spines from a darkling cactus plant.

It was beautiful. Like blue-cheese dressing. Like chicken liver.

"You get stuck?" Jelly said.

King Chocolate peeked down at his side. His roly-poly assistant had no problem with the glare. Black sunglasses wrapped around her eyes. They were pointy and shaped like teardrops.

"Where'd you get those?"

"My pocket."

"Where's my glasses?"

"Where you left them."

He snatched the sunglasses and shoved them over his face. The hinges squealed as they spread apart. He could see. Oh, thank Santa and all his reindeer. The sunglasses had dimmed the bright light closer to normal. He could see butterflies fluttering over there and bluebirds in their nests. Squirrels dancing hand in hand, carrying bags full of honey-glazed acorns. Dragonflies bathing on sunflowers.

The Nice Side.

Disgust rolled in his gluttonous belly. The urge to vomit hadn't been this strong since he ate a bag of fermented cheese curds. The Nice Side with their perfect smiles and their merry, merrys. The fake phonies with their beautiful toys and good girls and boys. It made him sick-sick-sick. They had no idea how the world worked. What it took to keep them alive.

King Chocolate did.

It was dirty work to keep the order of things. Unsavory things. Things they couldn't think about, let alone do. If it weren't for the Naughty Side, say goodbye to the light. Spoiled brats.

Blah-blah.

"Well?" Jelly said.

King Chocolate was squeezing the armrests on his throne. There were indentations where the tips of his fingers clawed into the cheap metal frame. He opened his mouth. Jelly knew what that meant, unveiling a hidden stash of wafers in her sleeve. She frisbeed them one at a time into his gaping maw.

The chocolate melted in the back of his throat. Slid into his stomach.

A subtle haze of euphoria rose like a column of vapor.

It lifted his spirits. Uncorked a vicious smile.

"Better?" Jelly asked.

"Much."

IT WAS JUST a door with a crescent moon hung on it. An outhouse straddling the border. A sharp line rode down the middle of it: one side light, the other dim. This close to the border, King Chocolate could smell the peppermint breeze. He preferred the dank bitterness of Naughty Side air. Chocolate in its purest, richest form.

Jelly opened the door.

King Chocolate steered the throne up to it. The doorframe caught the armrests. He'd upgraded since last Christmas. The model he was driving (called a Royale Primo Deluxe) was wider and sturdier. Twice the add-ons and ten times the power.

He backed up. Backed up some more. Then rammed it home.

Wood splintered off the doorframe. The metal squealed like forks on a China plate. He winced and threw his weight forward. The throne popped out the other side like a champagne cork. Jelly was trying to close the door, but the door jamb was gone. Deep gouges were carved into the sides of the throne.

"Bill them for that," King Chocolate said.

He spun the throne around. There was no toilet inside. Nothing of the kind. It was an expanded dining hall, of sorts. One side brightly lit. The other dipped in shadows. To the right was a grand fireplace, where a fire burned on the light side. To the left, an over-sized Christmas tree. Only half of it was alive with ornaments. And in the middle, a table was set longways. It was shiny on one side, dull on the other.

"Sorry I'm late," King Chocolate announced. "Potholes in the road. Sweet Tooth gets restless at this time of year."

The royal couple sat on the other side of the table, bathed in light, and watched him drive toward the table. His super-cool throne was twice the size of theirs. He swung around and approached the empty thrones on his side of the table, snowplowed them out of the way. They twisted and raked the floor, tipped over and crashed. The headboard on one of them cracked.

"There we go," he sang. "All set."

He sighed with a grin. The royal couple sat with rigid postures. Their faces were still and unmoving. They wore robes laced in gold trim and ornate crowns studded with candied jewels. The sickening smell of peppermint oil was strong. Pretty rude. King Chocolate wore a stained tunic and a chef's hat. He smelled like sugar farts.

"Macey," he said to the king. Then to the queen: "Lydia, you look... like you."

Her beauty taunted him. Like waving a cake under a starving man's nose.

"Merry, merry," she said. "You look well, Casey."

"Do I?" He smiled at Jelly. It was hard to see her through the dark lenses. But he wasn't going to take them off. "You both still doing Pilates and pumping iron? I can see the veins in your arms. It's gross."

"You're late, brother," King Macey said.

"Yeah, I said that."

"And dressed for the occasion."

"Never satisfied, are you, brother." He turned to the queen. "Is he like this at home?"

Lydia smiled. It looked authentic and, he hated to admit it, lit a warm flame in his enormous belly.

"Jelly," she said, "merry, merry."

"Blah-blah."

They cringed at Jelly's reply. King Chocolate smiled. And that was genuine. "It's what we say now," he said. "Where's Belly?"

"She's attending to chores," the queen said.

He didn't like the sound of that, not with the crosser somewhere on their side. Belly was always at the meet. "What chores? Is there something new? Tell me."

He bit his lower lip before he blurted out all his worries.

"Preparations for Christmas Day, is all," she said. "Shall we wait for the queen?"

"What? Oh, no. She's not coming."

"I hope she's all right."

"She'll be fine. Stuck on the toilet all morning. Ate a bad pork rind. Big party last night. *Huuuge.* Anyway, I brought you something." On cue, Jelly threw a box on the table. It slid into the light. "Finest batch of the year. Verified and stamped. Eat those and you'll have joy running out your ears."

They eyed the gift like a box of spiders. "You know how we feel about that, Casey," she said.

He gripped the throne. The hypocrites. They ate sugar on everything because they liked it. It made them feel good. But a box of chocolates from the Naughty Side wasn't good enough, was that it? Everyone knew he made the best. Both sides agreed. Eat a wafer and your world got right. Eat a wafer and you became your best you. Eat a wafer and all your worries went away. No more this side and that side. All one side. All Candyland.

But no. Just not good enough for them. *It was too good.*

"Let's get this over with," he grumbled. "I've got a bathroom date. You don't want me to be late."

KING MACEY STRAIGHTENED a stack of papers and pushed them across the table. They rested halfway between both sides.

"Fifteen rings till Christmas," he started.

They went on, the two of them. Taking turns to deliver their boring speeches. It was the same thing every year. A pointless meeting. King Chocolate stared at Lydia the whole time, his eyes cloaked in the dark lenses. That was the only reason he kept coming, to see her. He didn't need to see a skinnier version of himself. His brother wasn't exactly skinny with the gut and white beard. But he was skinnier than King Chocolate. By a mile.

King Chocolate slumped in the throne as they droned on about a parade and decorations and surprises and then how awesome their Christmas tree would be. (King Chocolate had cut his Christmas trees down; the sap was the secret ingredient in his special-edition wafers. Then he'd burned the trees to make little briquettes.)

Then King Macey would dress up as Santa and greet all the nicies, hug them, take pictures with them. Hand out presents. The royal lovebirds were laughing and remembering funny things that had happened at previous events. Recalling the parade to the town square where he climbed onto a big chair to talk to every single one of the nicies and kissed all the little babies and merry-married his way into their hearts.

And here's the thing: the nicies thought he was Santa. The real one. Is it stupidity or willful dumbness? And is there a difference?

King Chocolate was melting into a pile of boredom and contempt.

"I'd like to propose something new," King Macey said.

A second pile of papers was delivered halfway over the line. King Chocolate shoved them at Jelly. Way too many words to read. Like hundreds.

"We've prepared treats and gifts for the Naughty Side," the queen said. "To fill their stockings and place under their trees."

"We don't do trees." King Chocolate yawned.

She continued. The Nice Side would send an envoy (whatever that was) to decorate Christmas trees and deliver stockings to hang above fireplaces. It was pretty clear what she was getting at. Like crystal. King Chocolate wasn't the smartest Lander on either side of the border, but when it came to underhanded, shady, backstabbing schemes... he was a genius.

"Santa would visit," King Macey said.

"Visit where?"

"The Naughty Side."

"You mean *you* would visit," King Chocolate said. "In your costume."

"Of course," he whispered. Even in the privacy of this exclusive dumphouse, he couldn't say it above a whisper. "I have a route planned already. It'll bring joy to the Naughty Side. And when—"

"Terrible," King Chocolate said.

"What?"

"What you're saying. It's terrible."

"I-I..." He looked at his wife. She wasn't surprised. "How can this be a bad thing, brother? The naughties have been overlooked every Christmas. They can't even—"

"I'm not talking about that, you royal dingdong. It's you. The dressing up, the pretending. Don't you get it?" He looked back and forth. "YOU'RE LYING! Santa Claus isn't flying into your castle. He's not coming down to deliver presents in person. IT'S YOU! You tell them not to lie, to tell the truth, that honesty is the best policy, and what do you do?"

"It's pretend," King Macey said. "It's fun to pretend."

"IT'S A LIE!"

"Do you really not believe Santa Claus is real, Casey?" the queen said.

"Here we go." King Chocolate slumped in the throne. Why did he even start this? It always ended like this. He waved his hand. "Go on."

"What we do is for fun. But Santa Claus delivers gifts all over the universe—"

"In one night," King Chocolate added flatly.

"How do you think our stockings get stuffed?"

"Gee. I don't know. Tell me, please."

"Why is there coal in your stocking, Casey?" she asked gently.

King Chocolate's puffy hat began to smolder. All the angry words were locked behind his lips and beginning to boil. It was only going to make things worse if they escaped. *And you want to give us gifts, that's your plan? If Santa Claus is smarter than smart, why does he punish us with coal? We hate him even more. Coal! On top of everything else that's gone wrong, he gives us coal? I'm not saying we deserve an award. Just a little understanding would be nice. The naughties aren't that bad.*

King Chocolate was truly naughty. To the core. Worse than spoiled milk. He deserved coal. But the rest of the naughties? That was why he didn't believe. A real Santa wouldn't put coal in stockings.

"Please consider our offer," Lydia said. She waved at a fly buzzing over her head. "It's a kind gesture, that's all. We don't like the coal, either. Candyland is one. We're brothers and sisters. You, Casey, you get to be the hero. You can help bring us all together."

King Chocolate forced himself to keep eye contact with the queen. They hadn't noticed the fly landing on Jelly's shoulder.

KING CHOCOLATE NODDED, even smiled a little. Encouraged them to keep talking until he felt a tickle on his ear.

The fly crawled up his earlobe.

He clutched the armrests. Quivered in stillness.

The insect settled into the pocket of his ear. Then it began to whisper. King Chocolate listened to what it had to say while staring through the queen. He was shaking now. Rivulets of sweat ran down his back, soaked his shirt. It sounded like bacon fat frying in a skillet.

The phonies.

The two fake phonies smiling and promising Candyland is one. He didn't fall for it.

This wasn't about the good of the land. They didn't care about coal and the naughties and fairness. They had a plan. This was just a distraction, to keep him looking the other way. They wanted the same thing he wanted. The same as always.

To win.

Silence stretched out. King Chocolate didn't know how long. They were waiting for a reply. He hadn't heard the question. He had to beat them at their own game. They wanted deception? They were messing with a master.

A smile grew on his face. He showed his dingy teeth. "Let's do it!"

"Really?" King Macey didn't see that coming.

"Really, really. It's worth a try, why not? It could bring world peace. We could sing songs and scratch each other's backs. Who wants a shoulder rub? I know I do."

Jelly looked at him.

King Chocolate stuck out his hand. His brother clasped it. One cold and clammy. The other soft and warm. (You can guess whose was whose.)

"It's been too long, brother," King Macey said.

"I know a brilliant idea when I hear one. You'll bring all the presents to us, then, yeah?"

"It's all in the document." King Macey pointed at the stack of papers. "Let's meet back here in seven rings to confirm. This will be historic!"

"Yay!" King Chocolate shook his fists. "History!"

"Thank you, brother."

"No, thank you, Macey. Thank you, Lydia. Thank you Santa and Cupid and Cuspid and Molar and…"

He threw out more random names. He stopped after twenty or so, which, he felt, was too many. The king and queen splayed their hands over their hearts.

"Merry, merry, Casey," they said. And said it with enough sincerity to make King Chocolate gag.

"Yes." He swallowed a lump of bile. "Merry, merry."

He spun the throne around before they began weeping tears of disgusting joy. He got a running start at the doorway and jammed his way through. Shards of wood sprayed the ground. The grumpies had finished patching the potholes. He steered right through them and nearly hit a few.

When he got close to the split carriage, a lift panel lowered to the ground. He drove on top of it. As the carriage closed around him like a clamshell, he hollered: "Go, now!"

He didn't wait for Jelly, who was running to catch up. (That was the first time he'd ever seen her move that fast.) Before Jelly could crack wise, King Chocolate filled her in on the news General Fly had whispered into his ear. Jelly wasn't surprised. She'd heard the report, also.

It just felt better if he said it out loud.

"They got the boy!"

7

A great shadow passed over Art. It had no form, no shape. He couldn't see it, but he could feel its cool wings spread over the planet. There was nowhere to run, no way to escape.

It blocked out the sunlight.

He could feel its sweet breath tickle his nose.

Art opened his eyes before opening his mouth to cry out. Colors bled into the shadow. Details sharpened its face. Icy blue eyes stared down from beneath shaggy brows. The cheeks were fair and smooth. Smelled like pine sap and candy corn.

The lips parted.

"Look at you." Chubby fingers pinched his cheek. "All scrummy in front of the fire."

Art's wits got in line. He rolled to the side, scrambled against the tiny couch. His heart pumped too much blood into his brain. He rubbed the sleep from his eyes.

She was still there. Still blocking the fireplace.

As round and wide as she was tall. At full height, she barely reached the mantel. She wore baggy pants and a thin shirt that stretched over her stomach. A thick braid was slung over her shoulder. It looked like a rope used to pull over trees. Her pointy ears were tucked under silver hair.

She looked in the mug sitting on the floor.

"You like?" Her voice was a song. It made words feel beautiful. Like each one was happy. "The jewel fruit wasn't quite ripe when I pressed it. Was afraid it would come out a little bitter, you see? I added extra twinkles at the bottom." She winked at him and whispered, "Shook them from a short star."

She ran a stubby finger around the inside of the silver mug and popped it in her mouth.

"It warms the insides, you see? When the inside is warm, the outside is, too."

A long deep sigh escaped her. She looked at him adoringly. A smile bloomed on her face like a flower in full sun, stretching her doughy cheeks to their limits.

"You hungry? I have much to eat, you see. Spiced pecan pie bars with pecans from nutcrackers." She said *pee-cans*. "Also chocolate gingerbread cookies from the market, made fresh. Also, overripe fruitcake with dried mango and orange slices. One piece left in the cupboard of that. Also, almond snowballs. My favorite, you probably know." She covered a wry smile and winked. Then said: "Also, fudge."

She paused. Waited.

"You are shy, you see. Don't want to make trouble. But I know, Ms. Belly knows, you have not eaten since crossing. You are hungry and don't know it."

She shook a chubby finger at him. Then started for the kitchenette in the corner.

That was when he noticed the feet.

The size of them. The width. They didn't look real. They were feet for a giant on this incredibly short body. Her shoes—if she wore them—would be size 100. They were living snowshoes that scratched the hardwood like industrial sandpaper. Those hadn't been snowshoe tracks he was following in the snow.

They were footprints!

"I am sorry for the snowballs, you see. I think I throw a bit too hard and did not mean to. I missed on purpose the last time, if that makes you forgive me. I left the cider for you and door open while I go to harvest more jewel fruit. Do you forgive me?"

She turned her head. The hair fell away from her ear. The top of it was pointed.

"How did you know?" he said.

"To throw snowballs? It's what we do. Snow and ice are my—"

"No, I mean… how'd you know I haven't eaten?"

"Oh. Well, there are no secrets on Nice Side. All whispers reach the castle. We see everything up here."

She pulled something from a cupboard. A plate from a shelf. The sound of cutlery was sharp and loud on the countertop.

"You will love it here. I will raise the ceilings so you do not bump your head. You will get better at snowballing. I will teach you. King and queen will love you, too. I just know it. Now, it is time to put meat on your bones!"

She turned with a pizza platter of food. She placed it in front of the fireplace, went back to the kitchenette for napkins.

"Eat!" she bellowed. "You need a winter coat, you see!"

She slapped her belly. It jiggled in waves. Her face lit up. Her laughter was contagious. He felt a smile growing. Then she did it again, more serious this time.

"EAAAAT!"

She didn't wait for him to volunteer, scooping a mess of ice cream on a graham cracker and holding it in front of his face. He opened his mouth like a baby. She brightened another degree.

"King and queen?" he said, chewing.

"They are away now. But they will be back soon, very soon. As the nutcrackers say, *Huzzah!*"

Art grabbed a sugary chip and a scoop of vanilla-bean ice cream. She was right. He was starving. All it took was one bite to wake up his appetite. Next, he ate a pancake soaked in maple syrup, folded it around a peanut butter cookie.

"Did you hear them say *huzzah* when they escorted you?"

He shook his head, said with a stuffed mouth, "De dint say anthin'."

She scratched at the second roll of flesh beneath the hint of a chin. Then pointed and said: "Did your head perhaps hurt when they look at you?"

He nodded.

"That is why. No frequency yet. It is up here you will hear." She tapped the side of her head. Just above the point of her ear. "It is how they talk. Well, lots of Landers do as well. You will learn. Once you are settled. This becomes home. Now eat!"

His head had hurt when he was around the nutcrackers. So, they had been thinking at him. That was how Gandy had been talking to them.

She's an elf! was his next thought.

But those thoughts were quickly washed away by something she said. He stopped chewing. Felt his appetite wither like autumn leaves. He was holding a warm donut. Jelly dripping from the side of it.

"I want to go home," he said.

"You are home."

"I want to go back from where I came."

"Where you came from is not as important as where you are."

"Yeah, it is."

Her broad smile dimmed a few degrees. "That's how I see it. And you will, too."

And then she broke into song. Like they were onstage with the world watching.

Her voice was good. Like opera good. Her arms going side to side, head thrown back. A long note filled the room. His ears rattled like overworked amplifiers. He held the sides of his head and could still hear her.

"It doesn't matter now," she sang. Her words punchy. "It doesn't matter now where you came from. It only matters now. It only matters where... *you... ARE!*"

She popped up on her hairy toes—her head almost touching the ceiling—and held the last note. He closed his eyes until it stopped. Then softly she sang on her way to the kitchenette, swiping a cup of cider off the shelf and spinning around the room. The song continued.

"You're here, with me. I'm here, with you. This place is fine; I know you'll dine. With me, right now. As we, count cows."

Art cringed. *Cows? Did she say count cows?* He smiled, dropping his hands to hear a bit more, but holding them close to his ears in case she took it to the house again. It was the most absurd thing he'd ever seen or heard. That included waking up to gingerbread cookies. She was on her toes now. Ballerina style. The soles of her feet were coarse. Scaley. Literal scales. Like fish scales overlapping toward the heel.

Cider sloshed from the cup.

She poured it into her open mouth. Gargled, sang, and swallowed.

"It's winter. It's winter. Santa's here in winter. In winter. Arriving on his sleigh from a long ride. On a long ride."

Art moved away from the fire. Sweat was breaking out on his brow. His shirt damp with perspiration. She was twirling like a top. Cider slung against the walls. Splattered on his cheeks. She spun in front of the couch.

"You're on the *right* side." She jabbed her finger at him.

Behind her, sitting on the couch with its legs curled beneath its generous belly, was the tabby from Herkle and Derkle's Keepers of the Lost. Daryl was his name. His tail swayed like a charmed snake. Staring at Art. Not blinking. Not twitching a whisker.

Belly, meanwhile, tossed those squatty arms out. Chest swelling in one long inhalation. Art was ready for it. She delivered the last note like a runaway train.

"On the niiiice SIIIIIIIIIIIIIII!" She wasn't finished. One more breath and—"IIIIIIIIIIIIIIIIIIIIIIIIIIIDE!"

She fell onto the recliner. The legs buckled and squealed. Her arms out to the sides, gasping for breath, she picked up her head and smiled at him.

"You're on the Nice Side."

And dumped the remains of the cider in his mouth.

"You have a cat?" Art said.

"A what?"

He pointed at the tiny couch. There was a slight indentation on the cushion. Maybe the cat just looked like Daryl. Tabbies all looked the same. Although Daryl had a beer belly that was hard to miss. Whoever the cat was, he was gone. That last note had scared him off. Or blew him up. Art looked behind the couch, out the window. The Christmas tree forest was too far away for the cat to hide outside.

"A cat."

"A cat, uh-huh. Of course." She licked the gold flakes from the rim of the cup. "What's a cat?"

"It's an animal. Four legs, long tail. Furry. It's a pet. He was sitting right there two seconds ago."

"Ooooooh," she wheezed. "That's impossible, my Artie. You have an imagination, and a good one. It's why the king and queen will be so happy to see you. Ooooooh," she wheezed again. "No pets in the Christmas Wood. It's just you and me and what you see."

The cup fell from her hand. It rolled against a tangle of dead lights.

"They're the only true Christmas trees left... *anywhere!*" She swiped her arm over her belly. It jiggled and danced. "I mean anywhere. Your world, this world, that world, another world. Whatever world. These are the last of them. *THE LAST!*"

Her words were slowing down.

Her eyes closed for a second. Then two. They popped open.

"When the tinsel is in bloom, the countdown begins."

"Countdown to what?"

"When the sugar pollen drops, we're covered head to toe in gold." Her head rolled side to side. "You're going to love it here, Artie. My Artie. When the ornaments are ripe, you can hear the trees sing. It means he's on the way. When the stars unfold their last leg, he's almost here."

She picked her head up, looked past him and out the window.

The Christmas trees were shiny with ornaments. At the very tops of them, there were dim clutching stars. Like flowers before a bloom.

"He's fifteen rings away."

"Who? The king?"

She closed her eyes. A few deep breaths later, they opened halfway. The blue-blue eyes slid toward him. She whispered: "The Big Man."

That wasn't an answer. It told him nothing. Her laughter rolled from her belly into her throat. Slowly it ran out of steam and transformed into snoring.

He looked out the window.

The cat was sitting in the pink snow. Looking back at him. Tail waving.

He had his hand on the doorknob. Turned it and pulled. It cracked open. The last words sputtered from Belly's fat, smiling lips.

"It's soooo nice here," she said. "You'll see."

8

Artie stood in the doorway, letting the heat escape the cottage while Belly ripped snores like a leaf blower. Maybe the cat had burrowed beneath the pink snow. Art walked farther out, occasionally stopping, listening. When he reached the very spot where the cat had been sitting, there were no holes dug, no network of tunnels.

Just an indention. A wide one.

There were no paw prints leading away. None coming toward it. Like the cat dropped from the ceiling.

Or just appeared.

THE BARN DOORS WERE OPEN, and nothing surprising was inside: leather harnesses and pitchforks, buckets and stalls. Troughs for water. A winter coat hung on a wooden peg. It was forest green with fuzzy cuffs and a giant hood.

He pulled it down. Tried it on.

It was twice his size. His fingertips barely cleared the cuffs. But it was thick and warm. He kept it on, wandered out to the clearing where the air was brisk and clean. More evergreen than peppermint. Two hundred yards away, or maybe three, the road ended at the other wall. The air was clearer now, and he could see a giant door down there. The kind of door found on a space station, one that slid open and sealed shut. Big enough to let a commercial jet inside. Although the road was too short to land a plane. Besides, it was covered in snow.

The cat was nowhere to be found.

He put his hands in the coat pockets, found a furry hat. It was red with gray fuzz on the hem (probably white at one time). He put it on and wandered into the Christmas Wood in search of the elevator that had brought him up. Or one of those emergency stairwells.

An exit sign would help.

TREES, trees, trees.

All smothered in pink frosting with shiny orbs and silver strands of tinsel. Some so tall they scratched the ceiling. It wasn't long before he stopped looking for a way out and just wandered about. Hands in pockets, strolling this way and that, feeling the Christmas vibe radiate from the trees like radio waves. Happy radio waves. Warm and bubbly waves.

What was it Belly said? *It only matters where you are.*

He walked to the perimeter of the room (or cave or whatever this was), where a pink hue leaked through a portal. This one had a magnifying effect. If he turned his head and didn't get too close, the view zoomed into focus like a telescope. The market was still crowded. So many of them facing the castle. A banner read *We Heart Crossers.*

The barge was back at the dock. The nutcrackers nowhere to be seen.

He looked over the valley, where light met dark. There were so many waterfalls—grape ones and watermelon foam, sparkling rainbows beaming from mist—that he'd lost count. The border divided the volcano in half. He couldn't see much beyond the border, only lumps and dull forms. A sooty land, it seemed.

He would've rambled through the Christmas Wood for hours, maybe even days or weeks, lost in the evergreen scent and lovely hum, had his head not started to hurt. A brain freeze spiked between his eyes and began to swell. His brain felt like a size ten stuffed into a size nine cranium.

Then the buzz.

Carbonated thoughts went *pop-pop-pop* in his head.

He closed his eyes, listened to the sound of static. Then ringing. Like bells only he could hear. And something else. A distant sound inside his head. It *felt* far away, sending a chill beneath the oversized green coat.

It was purring.

IT WAS like trying to locate a cricket. The sound was everywhere.

He thumped the side of his head like he'd just gone swimming. The pressure between his eyes faded. He was hearing it as clear as a radio. The volume changed when he turned one way or the other.

He wandered into the Christmas Wood, hands over his ears, changing direction when the purring grew softer. His temples started to pulse. Maybe this was just a side effect of the cider. *When did I drink that? Yesterday? Or was that an hour ago?*

Time was stretchy.

The light hadn't changed. He hadn't seen the sun move across the sky. Hadn't even seen the sun. The day was endlessly the same. Same temperature. Same light.

He closed his eyes and started walking. He could feel the purring out there. He hit a branch or two on the way, but never stopped to look. Pressure buzzed on his forehead. When he turned his head, it shifted above his right ear like his head was a radar dish.

When the sound was so loud he couldn't take it any longer, he opened his eyes. He was surrounded by trees, looking directly at one of the biggest ones in the forest. The limbs heavy with ornaments. Snow had not fallen in the dark shade beneath it. A gift rested on the ground below the tree limbs. As if it had fallen out of the tree.

Scritch. Scritch. Crack.

Bark crumbled off the trunk, revealing a reddish hue where it had been pulled off. The cat sauntered out of the great tree's shadow, tail swishing above him. Art let Daryl approach (as any good cat person would tell you to do). He stopped at the edge of the snow. Parked it where the ground was still bare. Stared up with forest green eyes.

Art didn't move. Then said: "Did you follow me up here?"

It wasn't strange talking to a cat. People do it all the time. They didn't expect the cat to answer, though. Not where he came from. But this was Candyland. The purring stopped, and Art heard two words as clearly as if the cat had opened his mouth and spoken them.

Of course.

After all he'd seen, it took a lot to surprise Art. This qualified.

He was suddenly dizzy. His stomach churned. He fell forward and dry-heaved on all fours. Nothing came out, but he felt better when the purring started again. The furry tail brushed his face. The cat had stepped in the snow and now leaned against his arm.

"Was that... *you*?" Art babbled.

The cat nodded in response. No imagining that. The feline moved his head up and down. Perhaps even a curl of a smile as the whiskers twitched. Daryl crossed the snow to Art's other arm, arching his back into it.

"What's your name?"

Art didn't know why he asked that. He knew the cat's name, and the cat didn't answer him, not with his name, at least. Daryl said something much more important. The words, once again, swelling in his head. Splashing white in his vision.

Don't trust her.

"THERE YOU ARE!" Belly called. "Did you get lost?"

Art swatted the snow beneath him, threw it under the branches to cover any tracks the cat had made. He didn't think about what he was doing or why. It was instinct.

Don't trust her.

There were no paw prints in the snow. Either he'd done a fine job covering them up, or there were none there to begin with. Because the cat was gone. Not in the tree or behind it. Just gone.

"The trees aren't for climbing." Belly wagged a playful finger. "You're not trying to climb 'em, you see?"

She giggled that infectious laugh. Waves cascading beneath her T-shirt. Her nose and cheeks as pink as the snow. The joke (if that was what it was) went over Art's head.

"I thought I heard something."

"You probably heard the trees. It's about time they started whispering. When the glowers start to glow, that's when they sing." She flicked one of the shiny orbs dangling from a tree limb. "It's a natural cathedral in here. A sound chamber. And you've never heard anything till you hear the Christmas Wood on Christmas Eve. I've heard it a *thousand* times. Cry every time."

She wiped her eyes.

"I'm crying now!"

Art didn't hear the whispering she was talking about. If it felt anything like the words the cat put in his head, he'd be crying for different reasons. The cat's voice was loud enough. If all the trees were doing it? He didn't want to think about that, got up, brushed himself off.

"Look!" she screamed, then fanned her blushing cheeks. "It's the first one, Artie. The first one!"

He didn't know what that meant. She bounced on her toes and waggled her finger at the bottom of the tree. He took a knee to look, hoping she wasn't talking about Daryl. All he saw was a present. He reached for it.

"Don't touch it!" she screamed again. This time in panic. "I'm sorry. I'm so sorry, Artie. Did I scare you?"

He shook his head. "I don't know what's going on."

"Of course you don't. How could you? You just got here. That's the first gift of the season. Oooooh, it's so exciting. I got gooseflesh, look." She showed him her arm while dancing.

"Where did it come from?"

"These are Christmas trees. Get it? *Christmas* trees."

"I don't... get it."

"Where are my manners? This is a teachable moment." She cleared her throat. "All those presents Santa brings, right? Where do they come from?"

"Um. The... elves?"

"Right! But wrong! I mean, some do. But the elven can't make that many presents. Most of the presents come from *Christmas* trees. It's why the trees are special. They make *presents*."

Art had the image of a chicken laying an egg. "What?"

"I'll say it's magic, even though the king says it's not. Magic is just science we don't understand. But it *feels* like magic, doesn't it?"

No need to convince Art. *Everything about this feels like magic.* "Can I open it?"

"Is it Christmas?"

Art shrugged. "I have no idea."

"It's not. So, no. We'll leave that there for now. Just before the Big Man comes, we'll scoop them all up for him. How do you like the sound of that?"

Like, all the trees? If they were all *Christmas* trees, there would be thousands of presents. And that was if a tree only laid one present. "This place... it's so big."

"It takes a lot of space to keep the Christmas Wood safe."

He shook his head. He didn't have to ask the question. It was on his face. At least he hoped it was and she didn't somehow hear him thinking it. There were thoughts he didn't want her to hear.

Don't trust her.

"Space is a dimension." She pulled her hands apart like she was making taffy. "It can be expanded. It's how Santa gets down chimneys, you see. And you can thank elven technology for that."

That explained it, sort of. It was how there was a barn inside

Herkle and Derkle's tent. But it didn't sound like science or technology. Still magic.

"The last crosser wrecked the castle, you see. Tore the top right off the place. We built all of this since then."

"Are you talking about the nutcracker?"

"That's it!" She snapped her fingers, but they didn't make a sound. "I see you were in the barn."

She tugged on the green coat he was wearing. Belly stood on her toes—which raised her up almost two feet—and swatted at the floppy hat. The fuzzy ball went twirling around his head.

"Big man's coat doesn't fit you. Wouldn't fit anyone, I don't think. Specially you. All bones and skin. I'll fix that. You can count on Belly to get you winterized. You'll have your *own* winter coat." She slapped her stomach, and laughter came out in waves. "Come on, let's eat."

"We just ate."

Her smile never seemed to stop. She pointed at him, then buzzed her finger around and around. It came toward him like feeding a baby. She rose up on her toes and tweaked his nose with a giggle and a snort.

"Time's a funny thing, Artie. By my clock, you've been gone thirty chimes. I've eaten twice since you wandered off. I'm pretty sure it's time—"

She froze. Her eyebrows rolled like caterpillars escaping a bird. She lifted her nose, sampled the air. Then squatted on the ground. (She didn't have to go far with legs that short.) Art shuffled out of her way, intentionally stepping where Daryl had been.

Belly snuffled the snow like a truffle-hunting pig.

Art moved to the side. Blocking a direct view of the scratched-up trunk.

"What are chimes?" he asked.

"Huh?"

"You said I was gone thirty chimes. Is that, like, thirty hours?"

She scooted through the snow. Looked like a penguin sliding on her belly. Her short arms like flightless wings paddling toward him. She put her nose against his shin and snorted. He jumped back.

"You smell funny," she said.

"This whole place smells funny."

She rocked back onto her feet. Quite nimble, really. She looked around. Nodding. Nodding some more. Then gave her belly a slap and walked away.

"A chime is a chime." She shrugged. "It's a piece of time."

"Like hours?"

"What's an hour?"

"It's, uh..." Now he thought about it. *What is an hour?* "It's a piece of time," he said.

"Exactly." Snap, no sound.

"A chime is smaller than a ring?"

"I knew you were smart. The king was right about you."

"Right about what?"

"Artie the Smartie. That's what we should call you."

"No. We shouldn't. It was just, you said I was gone for thirty chimes and Santa was coming in twenty rings, so I figured a ring must be a day, and a bell, like, that must be a—"

"Fifteen. He'll be here in fifteen rings."

"Okay, fifteen rings. Is that like days?"

"It's *rings*," she blurted. "I don't know how else to put it. It's so simple."

"I know. But..." He didn't know how else to say it. He said it anyway. "So one ring is when the sun comes up and goes down. It's not really going up. It looks like it, but it's the world that's turning that makes it look like it's going—"

She stopped suddenly.

He nearly tumbled over her.

She looked at him with a grim smile and said: "What's a sun?"

"What?"

"A sun, what is it? Point at it."

He didn't see the sun to point at. He hadn't seen it yet. There was just pink sky out there. In here, in this unexplainable cavern, there wasn't even a light source. There was just light.

"Then how do you know when its Christmas?" he asked.

Solid question. She acknowledged it with a nod. Then rushed ahead.

Her feet treaded over snowdrifts like a dune buggy in the desert. Art tried to keep up, plowing through the snowdrifts in a straight line. She climbed to the very top of a steep snowdrift that was almost as tall as one of the shortest Christmas trees in the wood. She was eye level with a yellow wad of paper stuck on the terminal bud.

"See that?" She was whispering. He had no idea why she whispered and could barely hear her. His breath wheezed in and out. She pointed at the yellow ball on the tippy-top of the tree. "Three of the five have unfolded."

Without paddle-sized feet, Art couldn't scale the snowdrift. But he saw what she was pointing at. Three of the five legs had begun to open like petals on a flower. A golden glow was deep in the heart of it. It wasn't a yellow wad of paper.

It's a star. A blooming star.

"That's how we know when he's coming," she said.

"In fifteen rings."

"In fifteen rings," she repeated.

"Right. And how many chimes are in a ring?"

"As many as it takes."

She didn't even smile when she said that. Like it was a legit answer. *Because time is funny here.* Then she skied down the snowdrift on those snowboard feet, and off she went.

ART TORE the hat off his head and stuffed it in the coat pocket. Sweat rolled down the side of his face. When he caught up to her, she was standing at the edge of the long snow-covered road.

Her nostrils flaring.

Art's ears were ringing. His chest had a minty burn in it. A stitch in his side, eyes watering. He unbuttoned the coat to let the cold air in. It was frigid and good. He put his hands on his knees, turned his head.

"What is it?" he asked.

But he knew what she was smelling.

He couldn't see Daryl. But he was around. He could feel him. *So can she.*

"Don't get that dirty." She tugged on his coat sleeve. "Big Man won't be happy."

"It's already dirty." And it smelled like horses, but he didn't say that. "Who's the Big Man?"

"Who do you think?"

Art's head was buzzing. Too much exercise and too many voices inside his head made his brain fuzzy. He shook his head.

"Do I have to spell it out?" she asked.

"I guess so."

"Starts with an *S*."

"I don't know. Sam?"

"Right. You're right. It's Sammy Claus."

It came out dry, but she was smiling.

She waddled off, her fat scaly feet making scrunchy sounds as they compressed the snow. Art didn't have the energy to keep up. His legs were dead sponges. At least she wouldn't call him Artie the Smartie anymore. He put his hands around his mouth and shouted, "I thought he wore a red coat!"

"He's got more than one coat, Artie."

Belly sniffed the air on her way to the cottage, where they would fill their stomachs. He could feel her smile. Felt it in his belly. He watched her trundle down the snowy road. This place was nice. And she was right; he was a little hungry. This story would have a different ending if not for the cat and those little thoughts he gave Art. Because Art was content in the Christmas Wood. He liked how nice things felt.

This was the Nice Side.

Did it matter why he was there as long as he felt good?

Daryl didn't think so.

Following Belly's wide footsteps, the cat's voice returned. It was lazy and rough. Filled with smoke that was warm and true.

Ask about the war.

BELLY THREW OPEN the barn doors. Diffuse light cut through the dark, illuminating chaff floating in the air like diamond dust. It smelled dry and grassy. Sweet.

Belly rolled a wheelbarrow into a stall.

There were bales to stack and buckets to clean. Bags of food to get ready. Repairs, which were minor, needed to be made, such as a broken buckle. Nothing urgent. Still fifteen rings to go.

"The reindeer don't eat much." Belly handed him a pitchfork. "I mean, they hardly eat any of this, but we got to be ready, you see. Just in case."

She got to work stacking and sweeping and moving. Art stood in a stall with both hands on a pitchfork. Staring out the open door. He felt lazy and full. He'd napped after three helpings of porridge with maple syrup, followed by three draughts of cider (with the gold flakes). He ate again after he woke up. Then he walked to the portal window to look out over Candyland.

Did I take another nap?

Now he was slightly numb, standing there while Belly whistled while she worked. It went on like that for quite some time (half a chime, maybe?) while he stared at the pink haze obscuring the long road.

"That works better if ya move it, you see," Belly said. Balancing three bales of hay on her head.

"What's at the other end?"

"Oh, you'll see in a ring or two. We'll need to make sure it's working."

Art didn't expect to get an answer. Belly was a magician at avoiding direct answers. Her explanations had a way of washing over him, satisfying him until he thought about it later. And then it was too late.

Belly piled the bales of hay against the wall.

She returned with a bag of feed over each shoulder. Paused outside the stall. Art was still there. She dropped the bags on the floor. A cloud of dust whooshed into the light.

"Artie."

He turned. She was wearing a kind smile that was warm and understanding. The kind of smile that felt like a hug. Behind her, Daryl watched from a shelf in the breezeway, swinging his tail around. Art could feel the purring inside his head.

"You're going to love this place," she said. "There's a change of seasons up here, did I tell you that? It's the coldest it'll ever be right now, but springtime? Oh, lovely. Smells like flowers. And the pollen tastes like honey."

She smacked her lips.

"And you're going to be on a first-name basis with the Big Man. That might not sound all that great until the king tells you what Santa said. You just might faint. I did. I rolled right over and down the hill."

"You don't see Santa?"

"Only the king sees him. The Big Man wants it that way. But the king tells us everything! And one time," she whispered, "I snuck a peek when I wasn't supposed to and saw Santa standing right out there. Oh, oh, the chills, Artie. I know that's a bit naughty, peeking like that, but ooooooh, the chills!"

"I want to go home, Belly."

"Of course you do. And you will. You absolutely will find yourself at home."

Of course, she gave a sweet smile with those slippery words. *Find yourself at home.* Art found the nuance in that one. If he stayed there long enough, this would be home. And he would find himself there.

"What about the war?"

She flinched and teetered on those giant feet. A second later, she slipped him a nice, sweet smile. The words came out like pieces of tinfoil.

"War?" she said. "Where'd you hear that?"

You heard a lot of things, Daryl whispered in his head. *About S'ven.*

Art repeated what the cat said. Even though he'd heard almost nothing about S'ven other than he was gone. It was enough to get a response, though.

Belly took the pitchfork from him.

She began filling the wheelbarrow with hay.

"And what have you heard about S'ven?" she sang.

Nothing about S'ven until she tells you about the war.

"Tell me about the war. I'll tell you what I know."

Very good, the cat said. Art was a quick study, answering Belly with deceptive truths. He'd tell her everything he knew about S'ven. Honestly and truly.

"A game of scritch and scratch, is that it?" she said. "Once chores are done, we can play that."

ART'S MUSCLES ACHED. He'd lost count of the bales he'd stacked and bags he'd moved. The stalls (there were nine of them) were clean and ready. Not a speck of hay on the floors or pellet of alfalfa in the corners.

He fell asleep in the cottage, sitting in front of the fireplace, leaning on the tiny couch.

He woke with a plate of food on the floor and Belly snoring in the recliner. There were no clocks anywhere. Could he make sense of one if there was? Belly seemed to announce chimes and rings based on some internal clock, as far as he could tell.

The cat was on the couch.

Art ate the food and waited for Belly to wake up. It was hard to tell how long it was before she said something.

"I feel you staring," she said, without opening her eyes.

Belly sat up and rubbed her eyes and smacked her lips. She

plucked a sardine off his plate (it was drowning in honey, and he wasn't going to eat it) and threw it in her mouth, chewing on her way to the kitchenette. She returned with two mugs of cider. Passed one to him and fell into the chair.

Art stared at the gold glitter at the bottom.

She drank half of her mug. Released a long sigh.

"It's not a war, Artie. Some call it that, and I get it, but that's not what it is. It's more of a conflict of nature. Opposites, you see. Light and dark, good and bad. Naughty and nice. It's all out in the open; nothing to hide. You have the good fortune of being on the Nice Side."

With that, she gave him a fizzy burp. Sardine oil glistened on her lips.

"Why are they fighting?"

"It's not a fight, Artie. It's opposites. Like ends of a magnet, you see? They need each other even though they push each other away. It's built into their nature. They *think* they can win, but they can't. They can't stop the other from being there, but that doesn't stop them from trying. It's in their nature. There's a line down the middle they're always going to push. It's not a war, Artie. It's who they are."

The cat appeared in the corner.

Belly scrunched her nose.

The cat disappeared. This time Arthur saw it happen. *Poof!* He was gone. There and then not.

What does the war have to do with you?

"What's that got to do with me?" Art asked.

"It's got *nothing* to do with you," Belly said, looking into her mug.

"You said the king was going to be happy I'm here. There's a reason I'm here."

It has something to do with the war, the cat added.

Art followed the cat's lead and repeated it. Belly swished the contents in her mug. She swallowed the rest in one gulp. She was considering how much truth to tell. When she spoke, it was heartfelt.

"We need you. The Nice Side needs you. *That's* why you're here."

"But I don't *want* to be here. That's not very nice."

"Being nice isn't always nice. You see?"

She was admitting to something. That was a first. But not to everything.

"Why do you need me?"

"I don't know, Artie."

She knows, the cat said. "You know, Belly."

She shrugged. Then: "You're here because we need you, Artie. And I like you. That's the truth of it. You can trust me on that."

The cat appeared. This time on the bookshelf between a crumpled leather boot and a jar of pinecones. He was satisfied, the way cats always seem to be. Blinking lazily. Art didn't need any more of Belly's answers. He'd heard plenty. It felt nice being here with her. Content.

There's a way out, the cat said.

Art nodded.

Do you trust me?

Art looked at Belly. They locked eyes. A hopeful smile rested on her chin.

He said: "I trust you."

Art was patient.

Belly taught him how to make the perfect snowball. They had three snowball fights. Belly won all three, but Art did manage to hit her once. She let him, he was certain. They repaired harnesses and sewed mittens and patched holes in the Big Man's coat. They picked a few ornaments off the Christmas trees. They cracked open like glass eggs, spilling a sugary yolk that tasted like French toast.

She decided to start gift harvesting to get ahead of schedule. Art dragged the sled, and Belly plucked the presents that appeared below the trees. This went on and on. Art lost count of how many sleeps he'd taken. Then Belly announced it was fourteen rings till Christmas. Which made him doubt a ring as a day. But time was funny.

It's time to go.

Daryl was nowhere in sight when Art heard it. He was more than ready to follow. Even if it meant jumping out the window. Only a ring had passed, and it felt like a month. There was only so much nice he could take.

"GOOD NEWS!" Belly announced. "The king and queen are on their way. They were delayed by some unexpected business, but they'll be here in a chime. You're going to love them, Artie. They are so *nice!*"

"Can't wait," Art said. "Don't we have to get ready for Santa's landing?"

The cat didn't tell him what to say. He only told him what they needed to do. Art figured out how to do it. Although he didn't understand how they were going to escape.

"We do!" She snapped her fingers without a sound. "That's something we *can* do. Otherwise, we'll sit around waiting for the king and queen, and you know what that's like. Time gets stretchy with nothing to do. Let's *gooooo!*"

He followed her through the barn and onto the roadway between the trees. The pink snow was falling thicker and deeper. It was up to his knees. Belly bounced over the top of the snowfall.

There was a spring in her step.

The Christmas Wood was jingling. *Singing,* Belly called it. When the trees were happy and the Christmas spirit flowed in the sap, a lovely melody sprang from their branches. The sound was hard to explain. As if bells had voices was the closest he could come.

"This is the Big Man's last stop," she said. "That's what makes this so special and our job so important, Artie. They're exhausted when they arrive. The reindeer have been pulling the sleigh and the Big Man sliding down chimneys in all the worlds throughout existence. Everywhere, Artie. We have to make sure everything goes smoothly, you see?"

"He's been delivering presents all night."

Art still didn't believe Santa *actually* delivered presents or that flying reindeer pulled his sleigh. Maybe in Candyland. Because in Candyland, gingerbread cookies lived in townhouses and warmed themselves in front of a fire.

"Where does he go after that?" Art wanted to hear this.

"Well, after a plate of special Christmas Wood cookies, a glass or two of milk, he takes all the gifts we harvest from the trees down to the market. That's where all the boys and toys and girls and whirls sit on his lap and get a hug. It's... *joyous*."

She clapped her hands to her ruddy, round cheeks.

"Do we go to the market to meet him?" Art said.

"Of course we do!"

Belly bounced ahead of him. He had to dig his way through the drifting snow to catch up. Pink snow packed into his boots and froze his ankles. *Of course we do!* At first, he was filled with hope. A second later, he knew it wasn't true. He could smell the fib, even smothered in niceness. They weren't leaving the top of the castle. *Being nice isn't always nice.*

"We'll have to make sure the barn is ready," Belly said.

"It is."

"We'll have to harvest presents until the last minute."

"We will."

"And the food will have to be ready." She sounded worried. "Did we leave the stove on? Maybe we should go back and—"

"It was off. We should do this now." He pointed. The end of the road was coming into view. That was exactly where Daryl wanted them to go. "If not now, then when?"

"Artie the Smartie."

The bouncy steps were back. Halfway there, they passed the cat watching from a tree.

THE WALL at the end of the road was curved and frozen. The ice looked like clumps of pink frosting on two pairs of enormous knuckles protruding from the wall. A line was faintly visible. As they approached, he could see it was in the shape of a rectangle as tall as a two-story house. As wide as a commercial airliner. It looked like a drive-in movie screen.

"This is it," she said. "This is where the Big Man flies in."

"It's a door," he muttered.

A door that hadn't been opened in forever. Or since last Christmas. Whenever that was. She rested her hands on her belly. Her T-shirt was thin and worn with *I heart Christmas* printed across the front of it.

Ask if she's going to open it, the cat said.

He was nowhere in sight. His voice, though, sounded like he was on Art's shoulder. A stampede of gooseflesh trampled up his arms.

"Are we going to open it?" Art said. Trying not to sound nervous.

"Oh, yes, yes, yes. That's why we're here. Need to make sure all is working." She searched pockets that were buried under her generous belly, pushing her hands into various spots like she was digging for treasure. "Ah. There we go."

It looked like a phone. Not a phone Art could recall. The screen lit up.

She poked at it with her index finger. Slid a few things around the screen. Pointed it at the door.

"Stand by," she said. "Christmas in the hole."

There was a loud crack, followed by three more. The first one made Art jump. It sounded like a frozen I-beam snapping in half. The sound went through the ground. The Christmas Wood shivered, throwing a cloud of pink snow off their branches.

Ice fragments fell from the lumpy knuckles, revealing hinges as large as economy cars. The rectangular outline popped outward. Steam hissed from outside as warm air rushed in. The salmon sky was showing.

"Good so far," Belly said. "Now for this."

The rectangle split down the middle. A line appeared between the two halves and began to widen. The wall shuddered. Snow came down from the ceiling in clumps. A mystery, Art would wonder at a much later time, that would never be solved. *How is it snowing inside?*

Candyland was a beautiful mystery not to be solved. Only experienced.

The wind came through like the exhaust of a jet engine. Snow whipped from the ground and swirled overhead. The trees swayed back and forth, ornaments breaking off a few limbs and rolling down the runway.

Art covered his face.

The snowstorm quickly passed as the doors opened wide, mechanically rumbling like an enormous machine.

"It's so big!" Art shouted.

"It has to be! It's so windy up here. Sometimes the reindeer are tired. One year the weather was awful. Not here, of course. It's always perfect here. Just somewhere along the way it was terrible. The reindeer had to work harder than usual to deliver presents before they finally got here."

I believe in you. The cat was talking to Art this time.

"Oh, it broke my heart to see them limping through the air. Poor Ronin dragging the others with him. The sleigh sagged like it was full of coal."

The doors rumbled to the halfway point and began moving faster. The vibrations under his feet began to quiet. The limbs of the Christmas Wood were bare after having shaken the snow off.

"You should've seen it, Artie."

Do you trust me? the cat said.

"I trust you," Art answered.

"If the door were any smaller," Belly shouted, "I'm afraid they wouldn't have made it through."

Step forward.

Art hesitated. The wind had cleared the snow from the ground. A runway of green grass led to the widening edge where the doors were pulling apart. It was a straight shot. He took half a step in that direction. There must be a ladder or, more likely, an elevator on the outside of the castle. That was how they would escape.

"The Big Man thought I was being overly cautious to make it this big, but you can't be too safe when it comes to Christmas, I said. That's when I told him—Artie, what're you doing?"

"I just want a closer look."

His voice was thin and reedy. The cat's presence was heavy. For a moment, he thought the cat was on his shoulders. Art closed his eyes and took a normal step. Then another. His legs were colder than usual.

"That's close enough, Artie. There aren't safety nets out there."

He wished she hadn't said that. *No safety nets.* There probably wasn't an elevator, then. Just a ladder to climb down. How long was it going to take to climb to the bottom of the castle? A chorus of paranoid thoughts rose up and questioned whether the cat was even real. Had he been imagining it this entire time? A cat doesn't disappear like that. It also can't talk inside his head. Maybe those were just paranoid thoughts pretending to be a cat. A cat he so desperately wanted to be real. A cat he thought he knew.

He took half a step. He would've stopped completely had he known what Daryl wanted him to do.

"What's that?" Belly shouted. "Artie, get back! Get away from that... that... *CAT!*"

Art's eyes snapped open. Daryl was in front of him.

Belly saw him, too. Because he was there. Daryl was real. And so was his voice.

Do you trust me?

Art nodded.

Then run!

The cat stretched its four legs and started sprinting like a cheetah on the open plain. Its fat beer belly bounced and swayed and dragged on the ground. Art didn't think. He leaned forward and started after him. Pumping his arms, raising his knees. Feeling the frosted grass crunch under his boots.

"Artie? Artie!"

If the deep snow had remained between them and the door, Belly would have easily outraced him with those snowshoe feet. On bare ground, she waddled like a stuffed penguin.

KA-CLUNK! KA-CLUNK!

The doors stopped in their tracks. A moment later, they reversed direction. Slowly moving toward each other. Belly was shouting, but Art could no longer hear her. The wind ached in his ear. The cold minty air burned his lungs. The cat looked back.

Art thought he saw a smile.

A few steps later, he watched the cat—without hesitation—leap off the edge. Legs outstretched. Beer belly extended.

Daryl dropped from the pink sky. Out of sight.

The doors closed in. The escape narrowed.

Art closed his eyes and figured (despite what Belly had just said) there must be a net. He kept running. He ran until he no longer felt the ground under him. His stomach slithered into his throat. He took one long stride before stepping off the ledge to find out Belly wasn't fibbing.

There was no safety net.

9

"How much longer?" King Chocolate called.

He'd been wearing a blindfold for half a chime by now. He didn't care much for the dark. Even when he closed his eyes. Made him nervous. Bothered him not knowing what was out there. There were voices speaking a strange language. Didn't like that, either, not knowing what they were saying. They could be talking about him, like how stupid he looked with that blindfold on.

"Jelly?"

He began to fidget. Claustrophobia beginning to squeeze. The vest they'd put on him (the ones speaking the funny language) was tight and heavy. Made him sweat BBs.

"Jelly!" He reached for the blindfold.

"Just a few more ticks," Jelly said from somewhere on his left. "Be still. Almost ready."

"This thing is heavy."

"No, it's not. I wore it."

"Yeah, it is." He scratched his head. They'd put a hat on him after the blindfold. "My head's cooking."

"Your head is fine."

"I don't like it."

"What *do* you like?"

Pretty good question, that one. He liked chocolate. What else?

He had a good think on that. He liked his throne. The castle, too. Yeah. Not much else, though. Except one thing. An emotion doctor had made him aware of it. She'd come to the castle for a visit, just the one time. Jelly thought she could help him relax. Totally didn't work. But she did one thing good. He discovered something he loved.

King Chocolate *loooooved* to hate.

He hated most people and most places. Ideas, too. He hated them almost as much as things. It was his hobby. His passion. His super-power. He was strong when he hated. It felt so good to be right about the stupid and ugly. The arrogant. The crazy. Fat ones and skinny ones. He wasn't prejudiced. He hated them all.

"I like not waiting," he grumbled.

"Good one," Jelly said. Then she went, "Choo-choo!"

King Chocolate knew what that meant. He opened his mouth. A chocolate wafer slid onto his tongue and made everything better.

I hate Christmas.

It was such a tease, having to wait. He liked to get stuff now, not ten rings later. *Now.* There was power in now. *Patience is weakness* was his motto. So was: *See it. Get it. Eat it.*

He was done waiting.

"Way-way-wait." Jelly stopped him from peeling off the blindfold. Then: "All right, *now.*"

King Chocolate flung the blindfold against the wall.

All the anticipation and nothing had changed. The royal room was off-white. The throne was still a throne. Jelly a lump of general unhappiness. Only the Triad was new. And he wasn't happy about that.

That was what they called themselves: the Triad. Like they didn't have names. Three plastics with arms and legs no wider than soda straws. They were sort of flat (flattish, they said), like they'd been sorted with a rolling pin. They came in funky colors—blue, red and green—with clothes permanently stamped on their bodies. Their color was their name.

Hate.

King Chocolate was looking down at what he was wearing. It looked like a bedsheet with a hole cut out for his head. It was bright red. The jacket, however, was silky and shiny. Slick and fine. Dark brown with fuzzy white cuffs. He almost forgot about the tight-fitting something underneath it all. If it was a girdle, it wasn't working.

Blue pushed thick square glasses up a beak of a nose. "Do *not* touch ya *head.*"

King Chocolate hated the way they spoke. Emphasizing odd words in a sentence made his head hurt. And he wouldn't have touched his head if Blue hadn't said anything. Now he wanted to touch his head.

Blue looked at Green and Red and said something in their Triad language. King Chocolate didn't speak the language, but he understood snooty. The way they laughed and looked at him.

"Please *stand,*" Red shouted and flipped his flat wrist.

"I don't stand," King Chocolate said.

Red whispered to Jelly. Jelly said, "Just try."

"These legs ain't made for walking." He kicked the throne like an infant. "I will fall. I will hurt myself. I will be in a very bad *mood.* And you, you little... whatever you're called—"

"Triad," Jelly said.

"Whatever! I am not standing. Next question."

There was no next question. Only whispering and snickering. Eye rolls.

"I saw that." King Chocolate pointed at Green. "You'd better not be talking about my legs. Are they talking about my legs? I got a deficiency. I'm handicapped."

That ain't nice, he was about to say. In fact, it was naughty. Which would explain why they were there.

"They look *like* match*sticks,*" Green said.

They were either idiots or geniuses. Because that right there, what Green said, lit King Chocolate's fuse, and it wasn't going out. He shoved the joystick on the armrest forward, aiming to plow over them like a bull elephant. They'd look like linguini when he was done pressing them into the floor.

So fired up, he leaned forward to throw all his weight into the throne's acceleration. When it didn't move (Jelly had turned off the throne when the blindfold was up), King Chocolate's momentum tipped like a building with a cracked foundation. He was going to squash the triad and have to dry-clean them off his brand-new, silk jacket.

The girdle snapped tighter. Squeezed. He wheezed like a dog toy.

Something clicked. Whirred. Followed by a high-pitched whine. A magnetic sensation hummed along his spine.

An invisible hand had reached under the bedsheet and kept him from falling. He bobbed like a buoy. His matchstick legs dragged across the floor, the hard soles tapping against it. He was a marionette without strings. A balloon over a parade.

"I'm standing," he muttered. "I'm standing!"

"You're floating." Jelly explained the Triad had outfitted him with an antigravity vest, which was currently squeezing his guts like a tube of toothpaste.

"How does it work?"

"Magnets? I don't know."

The Triad explained, and King Chocolate didn't understand a word. Or care. He was floating. He looked like a strange ghost, the way his clothing dragged on the floor. It wasn't a shirt he was wearing. Not a dress, either. More of a muumuu.

The floating was intuitive. Leaning was all he had to do. He decided not to throw the flattish threesome into Fudgy Lake after all. Even if the vest was giving him a wedgy—*worth it.*

The Triad followed him around the room, pulling at the jacket, grabbing the muumuu. They chattered in their Triad-speak. Blue was not happy with the fit of the jacket, King Chocolate guessed by the way he was yanking on the sleeve. Red was doing the same thing to the muumuu. King Chocolate dragged them along like tin cans on a wedding car.

"*Arms* out," Green demanded.

King Chocolate didn't like the tone, but he was still high on this new mode of transportation. He held out his arms, scarecrow fashion. The off-white walls flickered and shimmered. Then turned into reflections. He saw himself from every angle. He liked what he saw. The muumuu hid his freakishly small legs. The jacket was sharp enough to cut someone. He didn't hate the color. Brown was his favorite.

The hat on his head was floppy with a white fuzzy ball.

"It's a merk," Jelly said over the Triad's argument. "The thing you're wearing, in case you're wondering. It's not a dress. It's a merk."

"What's a merk?" King Chocolate said, spinning to see his back side.

"It's that. It's loose fitting for comfort. Fuzzy cuffs for style. The jacket for a night out. All the fabric is sweat-wicking and odor-killing."

"I don't stink."

"Not with that, you won't," Jelly said. "You're Naughty Claus is what you are. You'll deliver the presents that Santa won't bring."

And then King Chocolate understood why Jelly had insisted the Triad come to the castle. The Santa hat. The Santa jacket. With one twist.

"It's chocolate brown," he said.

"They call it doo-doo brown," Jelly said. "Same thing. Santa Claus hasn't changed his outfit in forever. You're bringing style back to Christmas. Cutting-edge fashion. Everyone will want to dress like you. They'll talk about you on the Nice Side. They'll want to be like you."

This was big. This was bigger than big. This was a major swing in the battle. Even without that crosser, that Artie the Fartie, he could win the hearts of the nicies. He could bring them across the border. Flip them to the Naughty Side.

King Chocolate wanted to hug someone.

"Hello?" a voice called.

King Chocolate instinctively covered his body as if he were naked. He leaned too far and zoomed toward the corner. He jerked his head back before colliding with the wall, overcorrected in the opposite direction, and hit the Triad like bowling pins.

Right. Left. Up. Up again. Down.

He looked like a mechanical bull.

The room was a blur. The Triad was arguing. Someone kept calling hello.

Jelly watched the balloon rocket around the room, ducking to avoid a collision. Then, out of sheer luck, King Chocolate slammed into the throne. It tipped back and groaned. The magnets or whatever levitated the throne went into overdrive. It righted like a rotating cup. Sweat was wicking through the merk like a dishrag on a wet floor.

He was panting. Melting. Heart kicking its way out.

Then Jelly spoke. And things somehow got worse.

"The queen wants to see you."

"What does she want?"

"She wants to come up."

"What? Gross, no."

"She can hear you."

King Chocolate's eyes widened. "I'm talking to them, you three. Gross, I hate the way this looks." But he was shaking his head at the Triad, mouthing *I love it.* "Now go, get out of here before I throw you in Fudgy Lake. Uh, hello? You still there?"

"Hello, Casey?" the voice responded all around the room.

"What do you want?"

"I'd like to come up. I don't remember the last time I saw you."

"No reason, I haven't changed. Gained a few pounds, maybe. Besides, I'm not decent. Just trying on something new, nothing special."

"Then video me in. I don't like looking at a blank screen."

"How about a picture?"

"Casey, please."

He grumbled. Time spent with her was like driving over a cliff. "Just a second!"

Off with the floppy Naughty Claus hat. It was hot anyway. His hair was impossible. It had enough static electricity to light a small building on fire. He gave out orders, and Jelly followed them. His reflection was on the walls. He didn't want her to see everything, only from the neck up. Truth was he'd lost weight since he'd seen her last. He couldn't remember when that was. It didn't matter.

He practiced a smile. His teeth deeply coffee stained. Almost matching the color of the merk.

"All right," he said.

The image on the walls shifted and reorganized into rows of bright candy sticks of emerald green, cinnamon red and orangey orange. They glittered with dew in the dusky dimness. The queen was on her hands and knees, pulling rascal weeds from the ground. They cried when she dropped them and then ran away on thick white roots.

"Quick, quick," King Chocolate whispered. "Do the thing."

Before the queen lifted her head and showed her face, Jelly did something to the image. The queen shapeshifted on the wall into a much more pleasing thing to look at, as far as King Chocolate was concerned.

"Can you see me?" she called. "I'm in the garden."

"I see you all right. See you perfect."

Her waist shrank and hips curved. Her hair was short and black and almost as silky as his jacket. Her lips full and wet and brown, blending beautifully with the blueberry shade of her skin. Eyes as big as pocket watches.

Sometimes when he did that, he fell in love with her again. One time he almost invited her up. But she didn't look or sound like what was on the walls. He would get nauseous if she didn't.

"We're harvesting candy crystals," she said. "For the kids in Dirty Downs. A new community garden is opening at the school there." She held out a basket. A toy tractor dumped a load of watermelon crystals into it. "Thank you, Tracky," she said.

"Great," King Chocolate said dully. "So much fun."

She rinsed her hands in a puddle of nectar dripping from a voodoo lily, then sat on a three-legged stool. She sipped from a glass of sparkling lemonade, the crown tilting on her head. Always with the crown. If she would just lose it, he could maybe get everyone to believe she wasn't the queen. He'd tried to have it stolen once, but it never left her sight.

"Why wasn't I invited to the meeting with Macey and Lydia?" She sounded hurt.

"It was a, uh, last minute thing."

He was going to say it was cancelled, but she would know. She always knew.

"And what about the time before that? And the time before that? I told you I wanted to go."

"Why didn't you tell me the queen wanted to go, Jelly? You're awful. A terrible assistant. I'll have her punished."

Never did she laugh at anything he said. Not that he said anything funny anymore, but it wouldn't hurt for her to fake it once in a while. "I wanted to tell you that their idea of you giving gifts to the Naughty Side is wonderful."

"How did you know about that?"

"Really, Casey. Who do you think sent the Triad to you?"

Jelly shrugged when he looked down. He'd assumed she was the one who brought them up.

"I helped them design your outfit," the queen said. "Do you like it?"

"You? Well, it's... I don't know. Good. The colors are okay. The doo-doo brown is—"

"Doo-doo brown?"

"You know what, I hate it. I didn't want to say it, but you made me. I hate all of this—the hat, the muumuu, this stupid jacket. They're going to the bottom of Fudgy Lake as soon as I burn them. Does that make you happy?"

She laughed, amused. Nothing he said bothered her anymore. Or maybe she knew he was lying. There was no way he was burning these clothes. They felt great and looked even better. He would have Jelly spread rumors that he designed it.

A mouse hopped through the grass. She lowered her arm, and it climbed up to her shoulder, nuzzling against her ear. The tail whipping around her neck.

"Give it a chance, Casey. I think you'll like it."

"Too late," he lied. "Listen, I've got ruling to do, so just don't call me—"

"I heard the crosser is looking for S'ven."

What is the point of locking her up on an island? Those little vermin were gross little spies, that was it. He was this close to exterminating them. Sweet Tooth was too slow to squash them, and no one else cared.

"That's a ruuu-mor," he sang.

"It's not a rumor. What's he want with S'ven?"

"What do you think he wants?"

This was her only sore spot, as far as he could tell. The sensitive part he could grind his heel into. *S'ven.* That thief had left a long, long, loooong time ago. Even her furry little spies didn't know where he was.

"S'ven didn't cross back," she said.

"You don't know that. But if he did, you can *foooollow*," he sang. *Why do I always sing at her?*

"No. I can't."

"Yes. You can. I want you to. Total permission. Pack your bags and *whooooosh!*"

He didn't know if she could cross back to where she came from. S'ven probably did and left her behind. She deserved that. She would admit it.

"He's still here." She held the mouse in her cupped hands. "I can feel it."

"Good for you. So, I got to go do king stuff. It's been—"

"Do you know the boy's name?"

That was the thing with her. She couldn't take a hint. That was why he never ever wanted to talk to her. Because of this. Unless he was going to be horribly rude, he'd be staring at this fake woman on his wall playing with a disgusting little mouse until he starved. It was why he'd sent her to an island. Why he never let her visit.

"Biff. Bart. Steve. I don't know."

"It's Arthur," she said. "Art."

"I was close. He crossed from your world, I'll bet. You know him?"

"Of seven billion people?"

A long pause. She put the mouse down. It hopped through the crystal garden. She leaned on her knees and stared at him with moon-pie eyes. And he said: "Soooo... no?"

"He's special, Casey. I can feel it. It's not like when S'ven and I came over. He's here for a different reason."

"First of all, I'm tired of your *feelings.*" She was almost always right, and he hated that. "Second, special how?"

She shook her head, looking down at her beautiful blue feet. Perfectly shaped with bright red and green polish on the toenails. Which, by the way, looked nothing like the queen's actual feet. He would never forget what those monstrosities looked like. They were branded into his memory.

"He's lost," she said. "Lonely. He's not supposed to be here."

"I thought he was *here for a reason.*" He air-quoted the last half of that sentence.

"His imagination brought him here." She looked up suddenly. "He's going to change everything."

"So I hear."

"Do you know where he is?"

"I absolutely do not."

"My little chickens know where he is."

He didn't like the sound of that. Gave Jelly a look, and she was out the door. The boy was in King Macey's castle on the Nice Side. King Chocolate was hatching a plan to break him out. Then he shivered. It happened whenever the queen called her vermin chickens. Something gross about that.

"Let's have dinner, Casey."

"I'm busy."

"I understand." She nodded. Then added: "I'm sorry."

"Bye."

The walls went blank. He had to do it. Once she started talking about dinner, the clock was ticking. And then the apologies from the Apology Queen. Sorry this, sorry that. She meant it, too. It came from this deep well of shame and regret. He used to love to hear it, but then her apologies started to change. Like she was sorry for what she'd done. And, strangely, sorry for what *he'd* done.

She was trying to pave her way to the Nice Side with apologies and good deeds. It was so obvious. And disgusting. She didn't want to be on the Naughty Side, didn't want to be by his side or anywhere near him. And that was the deep dark secret of why he hated her.

She can't accept who she is. That she's rotten at the core. Naughty in her blood.

She needed to embrace that ugly scar, just like he did. That was where freedom lived.

He put the hat back on his head. He was going to keep it, the entire outfit. It was too good to throw away. Even if the queen designed it.

"Eh-hem." Jelly had returned. "I've got good news and bad."

His smile was delicious and gross. "Start with the bad."

10

Arthur woke next to a short dock.

He was clutching the muddy shore, awakened by a feathery tickle across his face and remnants of freefall in his stomach. He dragged himself out of the raspberry tea of Rose Lake and flopped onto dry grass. When he closed his eyes, his stomach began to freefall all over again. He opened his eyes, staring at the castle spearing the pink sky.

Impossible.

There was no way he fell from up there. The top wasn't even visible, cloaked in cushiony clouds and pink mist. But the memories of that endless tumble were freshly tattooed on his stomach.

The panic. The terror.

Complete loss of control.

The last wisps of memory before waking on the shore were that of not crashing into Rose Lake, but rather the soft and kindly embrace of its waters in a red mist lullaby. And here he was, soaking wet and in one piece. He pulled himself farther up the shore, his hand landing on a pile of clothing: a pair of burlap shorts with a belt of hemp cord and a dry T-shirt with a cartoon pig on the front and a curly tail rump on the back.

In the distance, a crowd roared.

He ducked behind the dock and waded into the lake to hide. The water filled his boots and rose up to his knees. He peered over the wooden planks. The market was on the far side of the lake. The cheers carried across as if he were over there.

A bit suspicious standing there.

The thought rang in Art's head. He nearly went underwater at the sound of it, bobbing with the surface at his shoulders. Sitting on the pig shirt and burlap shorts, the cat waved his tail. Art crawled toward him, keeping low to the ground and hidden from sight. Daryl didn't flinch.

"Why didn't you tell me I was jumping out of the castle?" Art hissed.

Would you have followed if I did?

Art looked over his shoulder, his eyes running up the never-ending totem. Art wouldn't have jumped even if he had a parachute.

"How am I not dead?"

Because nothing ever dies, Arthur. Like it was common knowledge that nothing ever died. The cat made biscuits on the T-shirt. *There was only one way to escape, and that was it.*

"Why would Belly lie?"

She wasn't lying. She believed every word she told you. It comes from innocent ignorance. They had you, Arthur. That is not where you want to be.

"And where do I want to be?"

Back home. You've made it quite clear. And there's only one way to do that. You have to find the truth, Arthur. And the truth is not in a nice, comfy tower on the Nice Side.

"Where is it, then?"

Get out of those clothes. They're wet, and someone will recognize you.

It wasn't the clothes they would recognize, but the lean young man in them. He was, however, soaking wet. Daryl stepped off the pile. Art held up the pig shirt.

"Where'd you get these?"

They're on loan.

There was a narrow road cobbled with multicolored triangles of candy corn. On the other side were three-story rowhouses with postage-stamp front yards and deep porches to sit and gaze at the castle. There were decorations in the yards, some sculptures and flashing lights, ornaments hanging from the gutters. Laundry hung on swooping cords in front of three narrow homes, which were made of curious materials.

One of brick. One of sticks. And the third made of straw.

Art ducked behind the bulkhead wall.

Not to worry. They're at the market like everyone else. Daryl leaped onto the wall and swaggered toward the three little pig homes. *If only they knew you were stealing their clothes.*

"I'm not—"

The cat didn't wait. Art had no idea if his thoughts or words were in Daryl's head. He gathered the clothes in a ball and climbed over the wall, hunching his shoulders like he was dodging bullets. Nothing suspicious at all. Candy boxes were stacked in the three little pigs' front yards. Bees hovered around them.

"Merry, merry!" they cried in unison.

Art waved on his way by.

Daryl sprinted into the alley that ran behind the three little pig rowhouses. There were buildings all around, three stories tall with balconies looking down. Daryl nosed open the door of a storage shed. It was dim inside. Smelled earthy and sweet. Light filtered through a window yellowed with pollen (more likely it was sugar).

Art's heart leaped. He backed into a tool rack. Rakes and shovels clattered on a workbench.

Someone was in the shed. Someone looked right at him.

He held his breath. Daryl leaped onto the workbench. *It's a mirror.*

Art's heart rate would not return to normal for twenty ticks. Which, on Art's world, would be twenty minutes. Give or take.

"You stole these?" He shook the clothes at Daryl. The absurdity of talking to a cat was, for a brief moment, staggering. It was like that for quite some time, but always dispelled when the cat talked back.

Borrowed.

"You're on the Nice Side. *Borrowing* isn't nice."

I'm not from here, Arthur.

"So Herkle was right. You're a crosser."

Right now, I'm from here. That answer joined the long list of things that didn't make sense. Art had learned to ignore them. They only slowed things down. *Now, get dressed. Leave your wet clothes here. They'll be worth more than what you took off their lines. You being a crosser and all.*

"*You* took them. Not me."

Art stripped off his wet clothes and threw them in a bucket. The three little pigs were not so little. Their clothes were big on him. The burlap shorts were itchy, but at least there was room.

Nice tattoo.

Art turned toward the mirror as he put on the shirt. The fresh outline of three clouds was above his right shoulder blade. He paused, searching for a faint and distant memory of a needle delivering ink into his flesh. He was young to have a tattoo.

Put those on, too. Including the hat.

Daryl had leaped onto a shelf where a thin, white suit hung from a hook. A netted veil was next to it. It seemed unlikely bees would sting anyone. This was the Nice Side. Wouldn't they just share their honey?

Art slipped on the lightweight coveralls. The veil was much too big. Obviously made for the round head of a pig.

"Where we going?"

Your gingerbread friend was right. Grimjoy will have the answers you need.

"Okay."

The border is a long way off. I'm afraid someone will find you out before we get there, even wearing that. If you're caught, you'll go back to rooming

*with Belly in the tower. King Macey will lock the doors this time and—
don't forget the drawings, Arthur.*

The sketchbook in his shirt pocket had fallen on the floor. How it didn't sink to the bottom of Rose Lake was shocking. Art tucked it into a pocket on the coveralls.

"So how do we not get caught?"

We *don't have a problem.* You *do.*

Daryl hopped across the shed and looked through the yellowed window. For a beer-bellied cat, he was quite graceful. Over the rhythmic purring, Art heard celebrating among things banging on the ground. A small group was playing a vaguely familiar game not too far from the three little pig rowhouses.

They were gathered on the grand steps of what looked like a courthouse wrapped in glittery paper with a bow on top. It was the imps. Only from the shed, they looked like boys. They were the ones at the market, the ones with the chocolates and swimming noodles strapped across their backs. Only they were riding the noodles.

A short, fat boy rode across the edge of a planter box, knocking flowers out of the dirt as he slid to the end. The noodle fell away from his bare feet before he landed. The boy bailed on the trick and rolled like a lead tumbleweed into the road. The boys laughed. One of them looked like he was filming the trick.

Art put his hand on the window.

He could feel what they were doing. Could feel it in his stomach. The way they moved their feet to pop the noodles off the ground. The way they bent their knees, leaned into the turns, shoved their back foot to get speed.

He imagined the clatter of wooden boards on concrete. The hum of plastic wheels on his feet.

His hands clenched unconsciously. Ached to feel a board in his grip.

I think we have an answer.

"What?"

Pretty obvious.

"Those things? You want me to ride one of those things?"

The cat waved his tail above his arching back. The pupils narrowed to vertical slits. The whiskers twitched.

And then he was gone. No poof or wisp of smoke.

Just gone.

ONE OF THE boys landed a rail slide down the entire flight of steps. It was his tenth attempt, and he landed it. The boys banged their noodles on the ground, threw them into the air, and piled on top of the boy in celebration.

Art had no idea where Daryl went. Until one of the abandoned noodles started moving on its own. It slid behind a row of popcorn bushes.

No one noticed.

JUST FOLLOW ME.

Daryl explained how he'd appear where Art needed to go. There was a lot of turns to make, and the crowd at the market was going to get bored soon, so they needed to hurry.

"Wait!" Art caught him before he disappeared up the road. "I don't know how to ride one of these."

Yes. You do.

"How would I know? I've never seen one."

That much was true. The noodle wasn't a noodle once it had been taken off a boy's back. It flattened out like a short and narrow snowboard. Only nowhere to lock in his feet. The top side was grippy and soft. The bottom was an undulating plank of tiny tentacles that were leathery and slimy.

A dull pain spread between Art's eyes. Someone was trying to talk to him. He dropped the noodle.

"Is it *alive*?"

Everything's alive, Arthur. Take off your shoes and step on. We don't have time for this.

The boys had been barefoot. They had been riding the noodles hard. Art had to stop calling this thing a noodle. It didn't look like one anymore.

It's called a beam.

"Wait. Can you hear my thoughts?"

They were on your face. Then Daryl disappeared.

Art was afraid of this. Daryl expected him to ride this thing all the way to the border? He needed some time to figure it out. No one just jumps on a bike and rides it the first time. Failing was part of the process. The cat was being unreasonable.

To prove it, Art took off his shoes.

Gently, he put his right foot on the back of the beam. The surface molded around his heel and squeezed between his toes like warm goo. He leaned onto it, felt the beam absorb his weight. Good so far. Until he put his left foot on it.

The beam zipped out from under him. He flipped onto the ground. The beam came to a stop several feet away. It was shuddering. And giggles echoed in Art's head.

The boys suddenly grew loud. They were shouting.

Daryl appeared next to the beam.

"See what I mean?" Art pointed. "I don't know how to ride it."

The cat's tail waved behind him. A smug look grew on his furry face. An angry mob was getting louder. Art got off the ground, took a step toward the corner. The boys were getting closer.

"Where'd you just go?"

The Cheshire grin was in full bloom. *I applied a little heat.*

THE FIRST BOY came flying around the corner.

He was leaning into the curve, the beam tilted on the edge, riding smoothly over the candy corn cobbles. His weight pressing forward. The look on his face was as hard as the fists at his sides.

Art's insides flash froze. His legs turned liquid and dissolved his thoughts.

Instinct kicked in.

He was in full stride when he leaped onto the beam. The surface snapped around his feet and between his toes. He leaned with forward momentum. A storm was in his ears. His hair whipped his face. Clutching a wet boot in each hand, he went flying down the street.

The feeling of freedom humming in his chest.

Vibrating in his legs. Warming his stomach.

He didn't turn to see if the mob was gaining on him. He couldn't hear them over the wind, but he could feel them back there. Feel them receding. This was the first time he'd ever been on a beam. But he knew how to do it.

The skills were baked in. Balance as instinctual as a bird leaving the nest. Every fiber of his body knew what to do.

Daryl sat in an intersection up ahead. Calmly, he strode to the left. Art felt the beam respond to a slight change of balance, the subtle twist of his ankles. He went into a sweeping turn, feeling the beam grip the road and carve the turn.

It was beautiful. Delicious.

And the board said, *WEEEEEEEEE!*

And Art thought: *This is who I am.*

HE NEVER SLOWED DOWN, riding over spongy marshmallow paths, over bumpy pretzel bridges, and down slushy roads of icing.

Down narrow alleys.

Up flights of stairs.

Ollying over obstacles and grinding edges, he no longer thought about being followed. Filled with the joy of riding obliterated his thoughts, calmed the emotional turmoil. Troubles fell away like discarded snakeskin. Anxiety evaporated like water in the desert. He was one with the wind in his ears, in his eyes. In harmony with the ground running under him.

Daryl waited at the edge of a forest, where a path opened in the candy-cane-striped tree trunks.

Art trusted his guide, jetting into the shadows, taking the turns like an Olympic skier. His legs started to jelly. Ankles slow burning. He dodged bright ornaments dangling from branches, popping back out into the light beneath the pink sky, where rolling hills of dewy grass sparkled. A chocolate waterfall roared in the distance.

Art wiped the tears from his cheeks.

The air was cooler. It was humid and smelled of mold and fermentation. The dampness of an approaching storm took the form of a shadowy film up ahead. Like a dark curtain cut the sky in half, separating one side of Candyland from another. That curtain ran the length of the land and to the top of the volcano.

Sitting alone on top of a grassy knoll, nestled into the shadowy border, was a small building.

ART KICKED the back end of the beam. The front end popped off the ground, and he caught it, slinging the beam across his shoulders. The ground felt rock solid beneath him. He approached the little building in sloshy wet boots.

It was a cottage made of striped tree trunks. A stone chimney puffed from the right side of it. A granular path led to a door on the bright side (the Nice Side) facing him. His boots sank in the candied granules, which were reds and blues and greens and yellows. Pocket gardens bloomed along the wall. A merry little statuary of Santa and elves mingled with polka-dotted flowers and vivid stems. Christmas lights hung from the eave and drooped over a window to the left of the door.

It was all quite cheery.

The door was tall and wide. Round on top. Strands of garland were welcoming, but a sign was posted that said otherwise.

EXIT ONLY! GO THAT WAY.

An arrow pointed to the left. He left the candy gravel path, put his hands to the window. There was nothing inside. Nothing at all. Not a chair or ceiling or even a wall.

Daryl was waiting for him around the corner. *So, you* can *ride.*

"Yeah."

Think of all the things you have yet to do.

Art wasn't in the mood to talk about potential, about his future and where he saw himself in five years. He didn't want any more fires being lit beneath him, either. He'd admit what Daryl did—having the boys chase him—had worked, but he needed a break.

The cat sat in front of a pair of double doors. The kind that would swing when pushed. The border ran along the seam between them. And right down the middle of Daryl—half of him in the light, the other half in the dark, his tail swishing from naughty to nice. One word was painted above the door.

GRIMJOY.

GRIM was in the shadows. The red paint flaking in long streaks where the striped logs were weathered and tinted green with algae. Clumps of lichen clung to the door.

Art stepped over the border like passing through a wet membrane. The shadowy air was cool and humid. Heavy. It weighed on him like a tropical depression. The grassy fields turned to rolling hills of ferns. A tropical forest in the distance. Sadness weaved into its beauty.

He returned to the light side, where JOY was written in vibrant red letters. Where the walls were clean, and the door freshly painted the color of sunshine.

This was the place.

With a hand on each door, he pushed. They didn't budge. He looked for a hidden handle or sunken doorknob. When he tried the doors again, two voices blared from the other side.

❅

"WHAT'D YOU WANT?" said the first one.

"May I help you?" said the second.

You can imagine what they sounded like and you'd be spot on. Gruff impatience versus sweet compassion. Grimjoy wasn't a person or a thing. It was two persons or things. And not hard to guess which one was Grim.

"I'm here to see Grimjoy."

"What've you *got*?" said Grim.

"What can you offer?" said Joy.

Art stepped back. No one had said anything about payment. He looked around, but his furry guide with the buddha belly was no longer there.

"Daryl?" he whispered. "Hey, what—"

"*Daryl*?" Grim said. "What's a *Daryl*?"

"Um, he's a cat. He's the one who—"

"You're offering a *cat*?" Grim shouted.

"No. No, he brought me here."

Art twisted his fingers together. A thing he did when silence stretched out uncomfortably long. Maybe they were thinking it over, but Art wasn't giving them Daryl. The cat wouldn't let him if he tried. Maybe that was why he bailed.

"What do you want?" Art answered.

"What do you *have*?" Grim said.

Art wished he could talk to Joy. "I didn't bring anything."

"Oh, *great*. That's just great. Another charity case, you hear that? Santa ain't here, beggar. These presents ain't free."

"I'm not begging. I'm a..." He swallowed nervously. "I'm a crosser."

More silence. Then: "*So?*"

"Countless travelers cross through our land," Joy said sweetly. "They don't stay long."

"Because they're not *lost*!" Grim blurted at him.

"You know about me?" Art said.

"We know about *everything*! That's why you're here. Empty-handed and on your knees."

"Not everything, darling," Joy said. "But we can help. What do you have to offer?"

Back to square one. "I didn't know I needed to bring something."

Joy answered, "What is that you're holding?"

"This? It's a, uh, it's called a beam."

"Okay," Grim said. "Now we're getting *somewhere*."

"But I can't give it to you."

"Why *not*?"

"It's not mine."

"Why do *you* have it?"

"I borrowed it."

Pause. "Yeah, you *stole* it. It's all over your sad little face. Welcome to the Naughty Side, kid. Step over the line, and someone will be along with a gift basket."

"I didn't steal it."

He wasn't going to drag Daryl into it. And to be honest, Art had rode off with it instead of giving it back when the boys came for it. At this point, it was as good as stolen.

So that was it. He had nothing to give. He couldn't sing or dance or write poetry (not that he was going to offer that). He couldn't give them the clothes he was wearing because they weren't his, either.

"Daryl!" he shouted.

"We don't want the *cat*!"

"I don't have anything to give you!"

Art threw the beam down. It bounced against the doors. The outburst seemed to please the first voice. It spoke bitterly with an edge of pleasure.

"Then go back where you came from and leave us *alone*."

"That's what I want! I want to go back. I don't want to be here anymore."

"Well, boo-hoo in a bowl of *stew*. You're already here, and life doesn't care what you want. There's some free advice, beggar. Now pick up your stupid ripstick and go find something we want." Then Grim said, a bit more seriously: "I don't mind the litter, just not in front of the door. We have a business to run. Now scram."

Fine. Art didn't want to be there anymore, anyway. Although he had no idea where to go. Daryl had brought him into the middle of nowhere and left him. If only he could get back to Gandy and Nutmeg's house. That felt more like home than anything. It was warm; it smelled good. They were nice and not fake nice. Like genuinely good people. Or cookies. He could get back there in disguise, hide in their house until he figured out what Grimjoy wanted.

He bent down to pick up the beam. His sketchbook fell out of his pocket.

"*Wait!*" Grim shouted. "What are *those!*"

"Yes, what *are* those?" Joy said.

Art was confused. They sounded amazed by something, and he wasn't sure what they were talking about. The only thing around was the sketchbook, which contained simple designs. Abstract drawings and nothing else. He flipped the pages.

"*Closer*," Grim said.

Art took a step forward and let them get a good look. Then said: "One for each of you."

Long silence. This time Art didn't twist his fingers. He didn't flinch or fidget or think of leaving. The hook was set. He was going to reel them in slowly.

Then the doors opened.

THE INSIDE WAS NORMAL SIZED. Not the *expanded space* thing he'd seen at Herkle and Derkle's or the top of the castle. Just a regular-sized room with very irregular decorations.

There was a round table with three chairs. Not so strange. The dome-shaped fruitcake sitting in the middle of the table was odd, but not crazy. A velvet curtain had been drawn across the room, the kind at a theater before plays begin. This one was held up by a clothesline, nothing fancy. None of that seemed too unusual.

It was the line down the middle of the room that couldn't be ignored or explained.

The border was unaffected by roof and walls. It went through the table and across the floor. To the right, Christmas was bright and shiny. String lights and garland, bowls of fruit and plates of cookies. A tree hung with ornaments with presents beneath its limbs. Train tracks circled an elaborate town covered in fake snow with little vehicles and tiny figurines. *Choo-choo* went the train as it rounded the corner, loaded with itty-bitty gifts for the teeny-weeny townsfolk.

To the left... well, very different. It was steeped in dank shadows, for one. There was a tree in the corner, brown needles sprayed on the floor beneath barren limbs. Ornaments broken and dusty. A plastic baby doll sitting on a chair, her face graffitied with permanent markers. A plate of moldy cookies beneath the dark window. A fly circling a glass of spoiled milk.

"Payment on the *table*," Grim said, standing just on the other side of the curtain. "Now."

Art did exactly that, ripped two cards out of the book, and slid them next to the round fruitcake. Two arms darted through a closed part in the curtains, one slender and fine and pale blue; the other arm was hard to describe. It was hairy.

"Thank you," Joy said.

The curtain bulged. An elbow here, a hip there. There was muttering and hissing. A deep growl that made Art second-guess being there. Someone wanted to switch cards because it wasn't fair.

"Two *more*." The hairy arm shot out between the curtains. The palm, also hairy, opened in the shadows. "For *payment*."

"No," Art said. "The deal was two cards."

"*FINE!*"

Another argument, although Grim was the only one Art could hear. It looked like bears wrestling behind the curtain. The frayed clothesline bounced and twanged between the walls. And then it stopped.

"Sit *down*."

Art pulled out the chair on his side of the table. It was perfect for a first grader. He squatted with his legs awkwardly folded in front of him, his knees too tall to fit under the table. One half of him was in the light, the other in the shadows. He could feel the opposing elements pulling at him. It was disquieting. Uncomfortable.

He was naughty *and* nice.

The curtain suddenly jerked open; the curtain rings at the top slid noisily on the clothesline. Two figures were exposed. The one on the left, bathed in dimness, threw her arms out and shouted, "You *flinched!* You owe us another picture." She pulled a stained white T-shirt over a protruding belly. "Out with it, on the *table*."

"Silly-billy. Do no such thing, darling." This from the woman in the light. Her delicate arms held out to the sides, she curtsied. "Pleasure to meet you."

She was hairless all over. Bald with no eyebrows or eyelashes. Yet stunning. Art couldn't stop staring. The lips full and dark blue as if she'd just eaten a bowl of blueberries. Her teeth were spotlights, and her skin as smooth as a newborn and the color of a clear blue sky. Cheeks dashed with glitter. Her dress sparkled new off the rack.

"Oh, sure. Don't get *up*. Whatever you do," said Grim.

She was, perhaps, the twin sister. Identical in height, but that was it. She was covered in matted hair that had never seen a brush or bottle of shampoo. Yellowy eyes stared out from bushy pockets. Teeth that were crooked and stained from a lifetime of hot chocolates, wearing the same T-shirt to catch the dribs and drabs of drink that escaped her greedy mouth.

Art started to rise.

"No, no. It's all right." Joy motioned for him to stay seated. Her plum-painted fingernails were polished and shiny. "Thank you for joining us. What's your name?"

"Art."

"Art. A name with creative roots for a handsome, young man. Don't you think, Grim?"

"Uh, *no*. After you, Joy." She gestured for her sister to sit first, then scrambled into her chair before Joy could adjust her dress. "Too *slow*."

"Merry, merry," Joy said to Art and then to Grim.

"Blah-blah," Grim replied.

Joy settled onto her chair. Grim leaned her elbows on the table. The hair was coarse and tangled and smelled like cheese. It was hard to tell in the dimness, but it looked tangled with algae.

"They call you Grimjoy at the market," Art said.

"Yes, well, my sister and I were never separated at birth," Joy said.

That was puzzling. They were two individuals about half Art's height. Sensing his confusion, she tried to lean away from her sister. As she did, Grim was pulled toward her, as if invisible strings were connecting them. Grim's face pushed against the border of light but didn't pass through it. She let out a growl and yanked away from it. Joy was jerked toward her, and the same thing happened: Joy's creamy blue cheek was mashed against the shadowy border.

"Okay, okay." Joy held up her hands. "My apologies. I should've asked your permission before demonstrating."

"I thought you were one person," Art said. "Grimjoy."

"Is that really what you want to *know*, if we're one person?" Grim relaxed, and Joy smoothed the wrinkles on her blouse. Grim leaned over the table. "You traveled aaaaaalll that way on your dumb little stick to waste a question on *that*?"

"It-it wasn't a question," Art said.

"It wasn't," Joy added.

"I distinctly heard you say with these two ears"—the ears were pointed and, of course, hairy—"are we one person? Did you or did you not say *that*?"

"No, I didn't."

"You're calling me a *liar*?"

Art looked at Joy glowing with innocence. Grim weighed down with shadows. "You are on the Naughty Side," was all Art said.

"Point!" Joy declared with glee.

Grim leaned back in her little chair and crossed her arms. Bugs crawled through the hairs on her forearms. "You disgust *me*. Both of you. Your judgment is offensive, and you smell."

"Very well," Joy tittered. "You have bargained for three questions, Sir Arthur. And three answers we will provide. You may take your time to think about—"

"How do I get back home?" Art blurted.

It surprised the sisters, how quickly he asked it. Grim yipped, and Joy jumped a little in her seat. Laughing with surprise, Joy patted her cheeks, which had flushed with strawberry patches. Grim coughed up a hairball.

A red light lit up on a scoreboard just beyond the parted curtains.

"Very good," Joy said. "Pick a fruit from the cake and pass it to my sister."

The fruitcake was the size of a spare tire and weighed about the same. It glistened in the light, looked wet in the shade. Jellied fruits (which contained no fruit) studded the surface. Art wasn't certain he was doing it right, but neither one of them objected when he plucked a green glob from it.

"There you *go*," Grim said, low and smoky.

She leaned forward. Her tongue unrolled like a slimy, red carpet. A putrid fog of dead fish leaked out. Art tried not to wince.

"That's right," Joy said sweetly. "On the tongue."

It was at this moment Art became acutely aware of what he was doing. Yet he did exactly what the blue-faced princess asked him to do. What choice did he have? He put that congealed blob of green sugar on Grim's tongue.

A smile crept into her hairy cheeks.

The tongue folded once, then twice. Then disappeared behind the snapping gate of chocolate-stained teeth. She chewed slowly, eyes closing in deep satisfaction. Her throat bobbed, and her mouth opened to emit a fetid breeze.

"Aaaahhh."

Art turned away. And just as he did so, Joy began to convulse. She smelled the dead fish breath, too. But the convulsions sounded more like a dog who had eaten from the trash can. It was deep and dark. Grim watched with wide eyes and a cruel grin. Joy started moving her head like a chicken, jutting her chin out farther and farther with each contraction.

Five times it happened.

On the fifth, something slid from between her lips. She reached up and pulled a strip of paper out of her mouth. Showed it to her sister. Then slid it across the table. It looked like a fortune-cookie message. It read:

YOU CAN'T GO BACK. ONLY FORWARD.

"Can't go back? Why can't I—wait, that's not my question."

Grim pointed at the scoreboard. A second light came on.

"Too *late.*"

She was happy. So, so happy.

ART REFUSED to feed fruitcake to Grim. He hadn't been asking a question. Just talking out loud.

It didn't matter.

Grim pinched off a chunk and tucked it into her cheek like a dip of tobacco. Staring at Art with a wicked grin. Joy spit out the answer. Grim didn't bother reading it before she passed it over.

YOU ARE ALREADY HOME.

"What does that even—" Art stopped. "That wasn't a question."

"It *sounded* like a question," Grim said.

"No. It wasn't."

"A *little* bit." She held her finger and thumb so close. "Let's go to the judges. Survey says!"

She pointed at the scoreboard. A long dramatic pause. *Bing.* The third light.

"That's not fair," Art said.

"I mean, you *said* it."

"No, I didn't."

"You *thought* it. You want to pick?"

Art was thinking *What does that even mean?* But he didn't *say* it. It shouldn't count. He thumped his fists against his legs. Delight crept over Grim's scruffy cheeks and into those jaundiced eyes. Joy seemed to wilt with disappointment.

Grim ate a piece. Joy produced the answer.

YOU ARE HERE.

He threw the scrap of paper. "What does *that* mean?"

"I'm so sorry, darling," Joy said. "We only provide the answer. They are one hundred percent guaranteed."

"And guess who's *out* of questions?" Grim stood up and threw her arms out to the sides. Loose skin gathered around the elbows. "Thanks for playing. Hope you enjoyed your stay as much as we did. It's been real. It's been fun. You know how the rest of it goes, so *bye-bye.*"

The tufts of hair twittered at the ends of her fingers.

"*Unless...*"

"We would be open to three more questions," Joy said. "For a pair of your delightful drawings."

"But *we* get to pick!" Grim slammed a fist on the table. "Lay them out, sonny boy!"

Art thought long on it. The first three answers were no help. They were worse than generic horoscopes. The odds of the same kind of answers were one hundred percent guaranteed. And that smelly smile on that snaggled face wasn't helping. But the drawings didn't matter. He could make them again.

And he couldn't leave now, not yet. Where would he go?

He opened the book on the table. Joy glanced over them and picked one without a fuss. Grim hopped like a child in need of the bathroom. Little squeaks and squawks that might have been laughter or gagging. She balled her fists to her cheeks.

"So many *choices*! I can't pick. I can't pick! I WANT THEM ALL. Ooooh, this is torture. I hate this, hate this, hate this." She held her breath, grunting until her eyes turned the color of mustard. "I love them so *much.*"

Even if the next three questions were as useless as the last three, her dilemma was worth the price. Art watched her squirm and doubt and spin circles of frustration. It was delicious. And it was only getting better.

"Did you make these?" Joy said.

"I can't answer that," Art said. "You didn't purchase questions from me."

"Oh." A wave of fresh glitter sparkled on Joy's cheeks. "What would you like?"

"I want to go home."

"Kid, look." Grim groaned. "We've been *over* this. The answer is right there." She pointed at the first answer Joy puked up. "And I don't care one spit if you made these. I don't, I really don't. I just want them, and I'm going to have them—"

"Then I want three more questions for payment," Art said.

"Will you just shut up for a second and let me *concentrate* so I can—"

"He's right," Joy said abruptly. "I asked a question before payment was rendered, Grim. He gets to name his price."

"What?" Grim deadpanned.

"Three questions," Art said. "That's my price."

"That's not going to *happen.*"

"I'm afraid he's right." Joy put her card back on the table. "We can't draw payment from him."

"*What?*"

"I'm sorry, sister. I wasn't thinking clearly. The drawings are so captivating, I lost focus."

An unexpected surprise was unfolding. Steam began rising from the knotted hair on Grim's head. Her eyes narrowed to darkened slits, the vertical pupils sliding from Art to Joy to Art to Joy.

Art tried not to grin. But not very hard.

"*WHAT?*"

Grim hammered the table with both fists. The sketchbook jumped, and the fruitcake jiggled. Joy backed away from her sister. What was coming, Art guessed, had happened before. The room smelled like roasting fur. The odor filled Art's nostrils and fouled his sinuses. It didn't spoil the satisfaction or the smile he no longer tried to hide.

"No. No, no, no, no—*NOOOO!*"

Grim bit the curtain with her teeth and shook it like a dog with a chew toy, the heavy fabric clogging the animal screams in her throat. She pulled it down and wadded it into a ball, fired it into the fireplace. It went up like newspaper. She destroyed the table with the glass of spoiled milk and stale cookies. Flies buzzed around (there were quite a bit more in the room).

She stomped the cookies into little bits.

Strangled the dead Christmas tree with both hands, squashing the sad ornaments that fell with her fat, fuzzy feet. Broke off limbs and snapped them over her knees. Threw them into the walls like ax handles.

Fell on her knees, seething.

Huffing. Puffing. And smoking.

She returned to the table and took the last bit of frustration out on the hairball she'd spit up, chucking it into the fireplace with the flaming curtain. She crossed her arms and bit her lower lip, staring icicles at Art. Joy nodded at her sister, then turned to Art.

"Ask your first question."

"Where's S'ven?"

Before Joy could tell him to pluck a gummy fruit from the cake, Grim dug out a handful and crammed it in her mouth. Moist crumbs got stuck in the matted fur sticking out of her T-shirt. She chewed without taking her eyes off Art.

Joy gagged.

It was a big bite her sister took. Payback for asking the question prematurely.

A strip of paper inched its way from between her lips. She passed it directly to Art this time.

ON HIS JOURNEY.

Well, he wasn't disappointed. The vagary met his expectations. "This is no help," Art said.

"When the student is ready," Joy said, "the teacher will appear."

Art didn't utter a word in response. But his eyebrow did rise in an arching manner. A questioning manner. And one Grim did not miss.

"Aha!" She reached across the table, finger waggling in his face, a tuft of hair tickling his nose. "Gotcha! GOTCHA!"

She swung her arm at the scoreboard.

"Survey says!"

Bing went the second light.

The scuffle of her feet was like sandpaper on a sea wall.

Art didn't argue this time. He hardly cared. What was the point of asking questions when the answers were vague nonsense? Grim bent down and bit from the fruitcake like a dog eating from a bowl. The chewing was loud and wet and sloppy. Bits shot across the table when she barked laughter.

The answer arrived.

THE ANSWERS ARE WITHIN.

Great, he thought, shooing the flies divebombing the crumbs shooting from Grim's caked lips. *When the student is ready, the teacher will appear means the answers are within. Got it.*

"What's your last question, *genius*?" Grim teased. "Why is the sky pink? Dogs bark? Is that air you're breathing?" A frown crashed down on her face. "That's *rhetorical!*"

She was shouting at some unseen judge lighting up the scoreboard. Art didn't want any more questions. So far these oddball oracles had told him he couldn't go back home, and the answers were within. It made no sense, what they were saying. If the answers were inside him, what was the point of a journey? And more importantly, *where were they inside him?*

It was pointless. All of this.

"Why even search?"

He didn't care if the question made sense. A part of him hoped it didn't. Maybe Grimjoy would feel a hint of the depression filling him.

Grim scooped two handfuls of fruitcake and mashed them into her mouth.

Chewing with loud satisfaction, nearly choking.

A bit of paper started crawling from Joy. It continued, curling like a long, flat tongue. She pulled it out, and it kept coming until it finally ended. She handed him twenty-four inches of paper.

Even Grim was curious. "Read *it*. Out loud, *read it*."

Art read it to them. He said, "Is the mighty redwood in the seed? Is the pearl inside the oyster? The search is the water and the light. It is the grit. Without these, they are only seed and oyster with no treasure."

Art read it again, this time silently. His lips moving.

Grim was laughing. Mouth wide open, attracting flies to the fetid odor and slimy teeth.

It didn't bother Art at all. It wasn't the answer he was looking for. He was numb and lost. But something peaceful was in the unknowing. He'd stopped grasping for concrete answers. He'd been so desperate to find out how he'd gotten to this place and where it was and why he was there that he couldn't think of anything else.

None of that mattered now.

He was on a journey to somewhere. If he couldn't go back home, then he would go wherever it took him. He didn't know where. Maybe not home, but somewhere he belonged. He couldn't conceive of where that was because he'd never been there. That was how discoveries were made. Journeys into new and uncharted parts of life were mysteries. There was no way he could know where he was going.

And he was sort of okay with that now.

Trust would take him there. Just like Daryl had had him leap from the castle into Rose Lake.

Where nothing ever dies.

Flies had gathered on the remains of the fruitcake. It looked like feral hogs had been through it. Grim was licking her furry fingers, staring with fiery eyes and a snarl. Art pulled the cards out of the sketchbook and wiped them off. He pulled them all out. There were twenty of them. He threw two stacks of ten on the table.

"Three more questions?" Joy asked, surprised.

"No. Merry, merry." He pushed one of the stacks toward Grim. "Blah-blah."

"You can't leave," Joy said.

Art had turned toward the double doors, Christmas spirit bubbling through him. He stopped abruptly, concerned what she meant by that. Grim was hugging the cards to her chest, rocking back and forth with a smile.

"Not the way you entered," Joy added. "You'll have to go this way or that."

She gestured to the door on her side of the room, the one that led to the candy-crush walkway he'd seen when he first arrived. There was a twin door on Grim's side of the room that led to the Naughty Side.

"Do I have to choose?" he said, flinching as he asked. Knowing she might not answer unless he paid for the question.

"One or the other."

He looked back and forth. One side was a dark disaster where Grim had thrown her tantrum. There was beauty in the field of ferns and shady tropicals, but that was just the beginning. The other side was bright and shiny and promised goodies. But he'd been there, and part of him didn't want to go back.

"It's an easy decision, darling." Joy batted her hairless eyelids. Her plastic smile stretched and glistened.

"Oh, is *it*?" Grim sneered. Then to Art: "Want to have *fun*, kid? Don't be nice."

"Hahahaha... oooh, you silly goose. We have the *most* fun. All we *do* is have fun."

"Sure, sure. If doing *chores* and following the *rules* is fun, you'll have a blast. Want to be merry, kid? Like really merry?" Grim clicked her tongue. "Red Rover, Red Rover... send Artie right over."

"We have respect and honor," Joy said.

"So do *we*."

"Fibbing is neither, sister."

Grim started to laugh. It started as a rumble and picked up steam. She stuffed the cards inside her stained T-shirt and clutched the lower half of her exposed belly. It jiggled and quaked. Rusty tears squeezed from her eyes, staining her face. Her nose started to leak. She covered one nostril with her thumb and cleared the other one on the floor.

"Oooooh, that's *rich*." Grim waved the flies away. "Everyone lies, you spoiled brat. You tell people they look nice when they *don't*! That's a lie!"

"It's an opinion. Arthur, choose a door."

The window on the Nice Side was growing dim. The Naughty Side was pitch black. There was nothing to see out there. Flies were now buzzing around Joy, and she didn't like it. The very first frown creased her face.

"Look at *her*," Grim said. "Trying to kill an innocent fly. That's *nice*."

"If you didn't leave food out, they wouldn't be here."

"I don't want Santa to *starve*. Do you?"

"Santa won't drink spoiled milk." She waved the cards at the circling insects. "Choose, Arthur."

"They're attracted to the stink of *fakeness*," Grim spouted with devilish glee. "You know why she wears perfume, kid? Because she smells like an armpit."

"I do not!"

"You *do*! Like a grody armpit! And that, my sister, is *not* a lie. *You* are *lying* about your smell, covering it up so no one knows who you *really* are."

"Choose, Arthur." Joy stiffened. "Naughty or nice."

"And those *gorgeous* eyes? Contacts! I seen her put contacts in *those* eyes so they're *that* color. The glitter on her cheeks? Lies! Lies, lies, LIES!"

"Arthur, please—"

"I am the *TRUTH*!" Grim bellowed. "Like me or not, you see who I *am*. I am *real*!"

Art stepped back. The room was vibrating with little flying things. Someone needed to open a window or turn on a fan. Art wanted to be on his way, but he didn't want to choose a side.

"What you *see* is what you *get!*" Grim threw handfuls of fruitcake across the room. They stuck like mud on the walls. Flies swarmed over them. "Choose, kid! You want to be fake? Then we don't want you. You want to be who you are, no judgment, accepted with all your faults and shortcomings? Come to the—"

A coughing fit overwhelmed her. Bent over with a string of drool on her lip, she gagged and spit. Joy fanned her face with both hands, no longer opening her mouth to say anything. Grim stood up and gave one last pitch.

"COME TO THE NAUGHTY SIDE!"

THE DOOR on the Naughty Side burst open. A black cloud swarmed into the room. The roar of tiny wings blotted out all sound. Grim and Joy faded into a swirling cloud. Art turned to escape, unsure what direction he was going. First door he found, he was taking. But tiny whispers floated inside the swarm.

Secure the arms!

Art's right arm was pinned to his side, the elbow grinding into his ribs. His left arm followed. Bugs crawled on his face, tickled his nose and ears. He closed his eyes and walked carefully to avoid hitting a wall.

Take the legs!

His ankles popped together, pain flaring in his feet. His momentum continued forward. He braced for impact, turning his shoulder to avoid faceplanting on the floor. But the crash never came. Something slowed his descent and lowered him gently. He thrashed like an animal in a trap.

Incapacitate!

Bindings whipped around and around until he was encased in a cocoon. He didn't dare open his eyes, but then it didn't matter when a blindfold was dropped over them.

Hitch lines, ready!

The cocoon shrank and took his breath away.

Right flank! HEAVE!

In the chaos and confusion, the blackness of the blindfold and silence of the noise, Art felt a sudden wave of peace fill him. He was snug in its grip, floating off the ground. He surrendered to the helplessness.

One of the doors opened.

11

"Incoming!"

The voice was tiny but brash. A sharp voice that cut through buzzing static. It was followed by three blasts from a horn. The kind of horn that warned large ships. Something large and wet was released. It sounded like cold slush sliding from the metal bed of a dump truck.

A new smell hit Art in the nose.

He turned his head. His ear grinding into the grit beneath him. His head the only thing he could move. His body trapped under criss-crossed bindings pinning him to the ground. Filling him with panic.

A bit of light slipped through the bottom of the blindfold. Sharp white lines suggested he wasn't on the Naughty Side after all. But the wet sucking sounds, things writhing in a pool of something foul. The *smell* stung his nostrils and corrupted his sinuses. The kind of smell beyond an expiration date. A smell that seeped into pores.

He started to gag.

Convulsions knotted his gut. He couldn't move, couldn't cover his face or see where he was. The urge rose on a wave of terror.

"Raise the fold!"

The voice was closer this time. A cloud passed over him, cutting past the light sneaking under the blindfold. Teams of tiny wings orbited his face. One by one, they landed in his hair. On his ears. Little membranous wings tickling his cheeks. He shook his head, tried to blow them off.

"Easy there, crossa," he heard. "Be still a moment. We helpin' not hurtin'."

This was someone new. Still far away, sounding deeply Southern and relaxed. Art did his best not to move. Pins and needles poked at his face. The wings went into another gear. A slight breeze on his face and the blindfold began to slide. The light grew whiter. And then punched through his eyes and into his brain.

He turned his head. A maroon afterglow hovered in his vision.

He wanted to raise his hands, rub his eyes. Even his fingers were immobilized. There was nowhere to turn, no way to escape the smells or sights. The tide of panic still rising.

"Easy goes it now," the voice drawled. "Breathe through your mouth and crack your lids a li'l at a time. C'mo now. You can do it."

Art pursed his lips and breathed through an imaginary straw, one that delivered fresh air. It was enough to open his eyes. Just enough to see blurry forms. It looked like a giant Christmas tree in the distance. The way it was shaped. The way it glistened.

There were banks of light above him. The kind that lit stadiums. They beamed down on wide leaves dripping with condensation and dangling roots. Glass panels were above the lights, hexagonal in shape, interconnecting a giant biodome. And beyond that was the dim sky.

Little black specks zigzagged through the lights. Flies. Tens of thousands of them. Maybe millions.

"Well done, ladies. Off ya go, now."

Art couldn't see who said it. There was movement on the ground. Insects not more than a few feet from his nose. It was mostly houseflies. The odd thing was they weren't moving all that much. A hundred or so were in formation—two blocks—and they weren't standing. They were sitting. Art's eyes were burning from the rank odors inside the biodome, but he could swear they were seated in itty-bitty chairs. An audience watching a movie on Art's face.

Two toothpicks were anchored in a stained wine cork between the blocks of insects. Wee little flags hung from them, one red and the other green. Without a breeze, the emblems were hidden in the folds.

A horsefly stood out front. It was twice the size of the houseflies. The multifaceted compound eyes aimed at Art. "Ya hear me, son?" it said. Although it wasn't an *it*. The horsefly was more like a *he*. "Nod if ya do."

Art blinked. It was all he could do. The stress of being tied to the ground with bugs all around was dreadful. Add to that a contingent of insects watching over him and one of them talking like a Southern general.

"Why don't he answer?"

The horsefly addressed a bug standing off to the side. It was a fly (they were all flies), but this one shimmered green as it scurried over. It spoke softly. Art could barely hear it.

"He might be in shock, sir."

"Shock? I don't imagine he seen worse. He's been here long enough to wrap his head around us. Let me get a close-up and talk him down."

The green fly bolted from the ground. It was a few minutes before it returned (Art decided that wasn't a Christmas tree on the far side of the biodome). A black box was lowered next to the horsefly by a swarm of flies. It looked like helicopters delivering a care package. The green fly crawled over the box.

A round fisheye lens unfolded like a switchblade.

It dropped in front of the horsefly. Art really wished it hadn't.

It wasn't just a horsefly standing on hindlegs. He was wearing a uniform. The kind with medals and a scabbard on a belt. And the green fly, he was wearing a uniform, too. So were the houseflies sitting in their chairs in organized lines. And wearing uniforms, you bet.

Art began to laugh. What else could he do? *When will I wake up?*

When he opened his eyes, they were still there. The air was still rank and full of insects, and the glistening mountain shaped like a Christmas tree still glistened.

The green fly fixed something on the horsefly's coat. "Try again, sir."

"Hm-mm." The horsefly cleared his throat. The sound was amplified. In that deep, Southern accent, he said, "Son, can ya hear me?"

Art nodded.

The audience of houseflies threw up their arms (or legs, if you please) and cheered. It sounded like the tiny voices of cartoon chipmunks. It went on for a full minute. When it died down, leaving only the background buzz of airborne bugs, the horsefly leaned into the fisheye lens. The bulbous eyes were the size of quarters.

"I'm General Fly. General Gnat won't be joinin' us. He just might make it back before you're gone, but no matter."

Before I'm gone? That could be really good news or the total opposite.

"In the meantime, you are in our custody. This ain't an act of war, you bein' a crossa from another world an' all. It is written in the Candy Code that should a crossa be identified, they will be detained in safe keepin'. At present, that is what you are, son. Detained and safe. Am I makin' myself clear?"

Art nodded.

The general covered the thing that amplified his voice and muttered something to the green fly assistant. They conferred on something. When the general returned to the fisheye, he puffed out his chest, put the medals on full display.

"We have a bit of a problem, son. You are not a citizen and have not declared allegiance to Naughty or Nice. Is this true? That's what I thought. I am goin' to have to read you your rights, ya understand?" The general cleared his throat. Art could see the mouthparts working. "You have the right to remain merry. Anything you sing will not be ridiculed or judged in anger. If you have needs, they will be attended to to the best of our ability. You have a right to an understandin'. Should you request an explanation, a representative will be assigned to give one. Do you understand these rights? Say yes or nod your head."

Art nodded.

"Good. Now, do you have any needs that need attendin' at present?"

"I-I-I need to get loose. I can hardly breathe."

"I'm afraid I can't do that right this second. Shortly, though. Count on it."

Art closed his eyes. Panic that had receded in the shock of awareness was starting to catch a second wind. A sheen of sweat broke on his forehead.

"You look thirsty, son. We got eggnog only a day old in the pantry. Seal ain't even broken. No? You sure?"

"Water," Art whispered.

"Plant drink?" There was a ripple of tiny laughter. "Why in Candyland would you want that? Son, we got flat soda, warm ginger ale, hot corn syrup, and spicy cider. None of it more than a week old."

Art repeated his request.

He kept his eyes closed. He didn't want to see the team that would deliver his drink. He stayed that way, breathing as slowly as possible, until the tip of a straw knocked on his lips. He drank with greed. The water was warm and slightly sweet. He drank until it was gone and the straw pulled from his mouth.

"You like the plant drink, then, all right. How about somethin' to eat? No? Didn't think so. This ain't your kind of food, I imagine." A ripple of laughter from the gallery. "Okay, well, I want to start by thankin' you for comin' along peaceful an all. No swattin' or sprayin' saved us some trouble, and none of the ladies were hurt during your translocation. For that, I am grateful."

A smattering of applause. Art peeked to see them clapping their legs.

"Merry, merry to you, son," the general said.

"Blah-blah," Green Fly Assistant corrected.

"I ain't sayin' that. It's merry, merry and always will be. That's what time it is, to be merry. Now, despite what's around you, we made every effort to make you comfortable. Are you comfortable?"

Art shook his head. "Get me loose, please."

"Soon. Very soon, I promise. Hold tight for me, son. You with me?"

He looked at Green Fly Assistant, who replied, "Two ticks."

"In about two ticks, all right? In the meantime, I want to fulfill your right to an explanation. Is that okay with you? Okay. All around you is home to the finest regiment this side of the border. We live by a code of honor and are the first in line to defend our side. When we are called to protect, then by golly we shall. We were ordered to capture a crossa. That crossa is you, son.

"Now, you ain't a threat. Anyone can see that. You ain't nothin' like the last one who come stompin' through the Nice Side and destroyin' the castle. You're a special one, I reckon. I don't know why that is and no offense. Whatever it is that makes you special, I'm just glad you didn't side with the Nice. They're a good lot. Nothin' against them. They mean well, just not our kind of folken, you could say. They ain't all shallow and naïve, but a good bit are, if you know what I mean. Now—"

A fly dropped out of nowhere and handed the general something far too small to see. The general muttered his thanks. Then he stopped Green Fly Assistant from turning off his amplifier.

"The boy should hear it," General Fly said. "It's about him, after all." The general spoke into something he was holding. "General Fly present. Yes, sir, that is correct. We have the crossa in custody. He is immobilized and has been read his rights. He has refused food and—right, right."

A long pause while he listened to a voice Art could not hear.

"I'm afraid we cannot deliver him, sir. No, sir, that's right. Troops were taxed getting him to Fly Dome. Correct, sir. He weighs an awful lot. Okay, yes. Yes. That would be fine. We'll have him ready and... oh, no, sir. No, a medal is not necessary. It was our duty. Although a gesture for the hardworking ladies who made this acquisition happen would be more than enough. A delivery of chocolate sludge?"

He turned to the contingent behind him. They erupted with cheers, embracing each other, throwing tiny hats in the air. The general ended the call and celebrated with a few of the nearest ladies. When they returned to their seats, stirring with giddiness, he stood in front of the fisheye once again.

"Your transfer will arrive soon. We'll get you out of the bindings in no time. Now, where was I? The Nice Side, right. They think we lack respect and honor. That's what the twin said, the one named Joy. There are many who dwell here in the shadows who do lack such respect and honor. *But not flies!*"

"Hoo-ah! Hoo-ah! Hoo-ah!" the regiment chanted.

"The Nice Side thinks they're better than us. They think—"

He was interrupted by the foghorn. Three short blasts announced the next payload. This one a special delivery of chocolate sludge. Art turned toward the glistening mountain in time to see a chunky land-slide pour out of a chute. It spilled a load of dark slime from the ceil-ing. It tumbled down the sides of the pyramidal mountain. Bits of trash were buried in the side of it. Candy wrappers and plastic toys and rotten food and broken playthings, fish bones and loose fur.

The new delivery set off a landslide. The enormous, putrefied pile teetered on a round platform. And when globs of gray stuff rolled over the edge, it plopped into a soupy basin where white larva squirmed among bits of discarded candy and mushy cookies.

Panic arrived with a head of steam and broke something inside Art. He opened his mouth to let it all out.

"CUT HIM LOOSE!"

Art heard the general cry out the order in between screams. Art thrashed his head side to side, as that was the only thing he could move. Claustrophobia had taken over. He might as well be in a box, tied down the way he was. The smells piling on top.

"Sir," Green Fly Assistant objected, "I don't think—"

"He's havin' a panic attack. I seen it before. Start cuttin', ladies!"

A swarm went airborne and blocked out the light from overhead. They divebombed in formation like fighter jets on a mission. Buzzing past Art's ears, over his open mouth, down to the ground where the thin ropes were anchored.

Plink!

The bindings snapped like guitar strings playing an awful tune. Houseflies were flying in small squadrons, clipping the wires in midair. The bindings flew off in bunches. Art wiggled his fingers, then his arms.

Plinkplink!

He bent his knees and turned his hips. Rolled onto his side. He'd stopped screaming by now but couldn't slow his breathing. Hyperventilating short, choppy breaths. He began kicking his legs and flailing his arms. He had to get away and out of this rotten meat locker. Had to—

PLINKPLINKPLINK!

He rolled across the ground, crashed into the nearest hedge. Sticky drops of dew rained down on him. He crawled out of the bushes and shook like a dog, wiping down his arms and legs and face as if the heebie-jeebies were something he could wash off. He pulled his shirt over his nose.

The chocolate sludge slowly slid down the slag heap where bits of wrapping paper and soggy boxes were trapped. Apple cores and orange peels, pineapple slices and carrot tops. Cookies and cakes, things that could break were swallowed in the fudgy landslide that dripped like fermented icing with bits of corn and beans and hard candy. They oozed from the round tabletop into the writhing cesspool below.

"This way!" The general's voice went buzzing past.

The wall of Fly Dome was twenty feet away. One of the hexagonal panels was open. Art could feel the hint of fresh air. He staggered toward it, throwing all his momentum at it before it closed. He burst into humid air with sweat cooling his cheeks and forehead, dropping to his hands and knees, taking in long draughts of clean air—clean, humid air! Spitting the lingering taste onto the mossy ground.

The panel behind him closed with a muffled impact. A latch fell into place. The nuclear sound of a million beating wings went silent. The putrid odors vanquished. Outside the biodome, crickets sang and frogs chirped.

Condensation fell from one leaf to another.

Art leaned against a striped tree trunk, pulled his knees to his chest. Never would he take fresh air for granted again. He rubbed his arms where the bindings had left crisscrossing marks. The urge to weep was rising toward his eyes. The runaway Panic Attack began to flutter. He remembered someone telling him what to do when this happened, to breathe slower.

He laid his head between his knees. And began to count.

"YA DID GOOD, SON."

General Fly tickled the hairs on his arm as he scurried up it. Art didn't lift his head.

"You were looking gray in the gills for a tick, though. But ya held it together. Proud of ya. Now take a nibble. It does the boys a bit of good when they ain't feelin' right. Brings them around right side."

Art could smell it before he lifted his head. A square of chocolate was on the ground. He didn't ask how it got there or how many flies had walked on it. It was crisp, not slimy, and newly unwrapped. He put the whole thing in his mouth. It melted on his tongue, washed away foul odors still hanging around. A chocolatey explosion filled his stomach.

The jitters evaporated.

Anxiety went bye-bye.

"There ya are," General Fly called. "Just like the boys. They can't live without the stuff."

Whatever was in that wafer lifted him out of the funk to a level that was bright and shiny, new and exciting. It stripped away the heaviness, the sadness, and the worry. Escorted Panic and Anxiety out the door. He was still sore and hot and in need of a shower. But he didn't care anymore. He was better.

This is who I am, he thought. The chocolate made him feel like himself.

The world was right. And he was talking to a fly. A little fly in a military uniform with tiny medals on it. Art wanted to hug the general and would've if it wouldn't have crushed the delicate wings.

"Thank you."

"Don't thank me. We dragged you here; just glad you made it. The boys will be here to take ya on the way."

Art laid his head back on the tree and smiled. He paid no attention to what the general was saying. Didn't care about any boys or where they were going to take him. "It smells bad in there. No offense."

"None taken. It's all perspective, son. Change how you see things and you change the world."

"Right." Art chuckled. *Change how you see things...* that was deep.

"You might call that a heap of garbage in there. I call it dinner. Where do you think all those fish bones and broken toys and whatever else comes out of that chute come from? That's straight from the Nice Side, son. All the things they don't want, they send right over. They can't be troubled with lookin' old and dirty, so down the chute it goes. They have to keep up appearances. They got to look nice, know what I mean?"

The general buzzed in a circle and dropped on the back of Art's hand. Standing on hind legs, he puffed up with his medals on display.

"You smell death in there? I smell life. A heap teeming with microscopic life. Billions and trillions of bacteria and things is what that is. Does their size make life less important? Am I less important than you?"

Art shook his head. The general was almost an inch tall and felt like a giant.

"What would happen if it weren't for us? Or the bacteria in there?

We're every bit as important. We ain't less than, son. That land needs us."

Fly Dome beamed white light from inside, casting sharp shadows into the trees. Art could feel the ground hum with life. Maybe he just imagined it. Beneath all the rightness of the chocolatey goodness running through him, he felt the gouge of worthlessness somewhere inside himself. It didn't bother him, but it was there. It was deep. That he didn't matter.

"I never made a difference," he mumbled.

"Maybe so. But I can tell you this. There's life ahead of you. And this life you got, the pain you feel and the blues that drag behind you might feel impossible. But there will come a moment, maybe far away from here, that you make a difference in one person's life. Just *one*. And you're the only one who can make it. You'll look back at all this sufferin' and ask yourself if it's all worth it. Was it worth the price to help the one person? You'll know the answer. Deep down, you'll know."

A truly amused chuckle came out. "Doubt it."

"My eyes are better than yours." Light reflected off the many lenses in the general's compound eyes. "It's why I accepted the mission to go get you."

Art nodded. "You have any more chocolate?"

The general didn't get a chance to answer.

It happened all at once. From all directions.

Branches snapping. Leaves sweeping off the ground.

The boys were all around Art, still sitting on his bottom, leaning against the tree. General Fly watched from his forearm, head twitching left and right. Art didn't recognize them; they were going so fast and in so many directions. What they were riding, though, he knew what those were.

Long, skinny boards that cut the air.

The boys slalomed between striped trees, careened off Fly Dome with heavy hollow *thumps*. Their lean bodies tilted into the turns, pressing the boards forward. Their shirts soaked. Skin glistening with sweat.

Art didn't move.

He watched the show play out with a slight smile, resting in the euphoric state called *Chocolate Brain*. And he liked it there. It felt right. The world was okay. He was more than okay. Even the chaos felt more like a dance than a threat.

"All right, boys." General Fly's voice was on the amplifier again. Art's forearm was his stage. "Take it down a notch before ya break somethin'. Take the young man where he's going, straight to it. No sidetrackin', now. And be careful. He's been through a lot."

Art felt the general pat his arm. Or he imagined it. The things that happened in Chocolate Brain didn't always happen.

The boys slowed their dance, kicking up their beams and slinging them over their backs. A gang of pointy-eared troublemakers, the same crew that tried to catch him on the way to the border. The same crew he'd *borrowed* from. Although they weren't wearing sunglasses anymore. Their eyes were swallowed in pupils with thin rings of color. Eyes that cut through the Chocolate Brain and gave Art the shivers.

The last of them rode up.

Two of them were on one beam. The boy on the back clutched the shirt of the boy steering from the front. They slid to a stop, splashing leaves and dirt against Fly Dome. The one on the back got off. Art recognized this one. It was the imp from the market, the one who found him hiding in the alley and gave him the chocolate stamped *KC*.

Rude, the other boy had called him, the boy who yanked him out of the alley. Then Art thought with a shadowy smile, *Rude Boy.*

"Ee's a lot mo' comin'," Rude Boy blurted. "Snacked muh beam and ee'll make change for it."

Art had yet to move or understand a single thing the imp said. He was stomping toward him, boney chest puffed up, sharp elbows thrown back. General Fly translated for Art.

"You stole his beam."

"No. I didn't steal anything."

"Ee run it four lines and a half. Two in the ki'chen." Rude Boy stood over Art, long fingers curled into fists. "Mind ee to beam, have you? Aye have it on back or thump it from your gourd."

"Your friend here," General Fly said, "wants to know where you learned to beam. And he also wants it back."

"I left it at Grimjoy's."

The boys snickered at the name. All except Rude Boy, whose knuckles went white. "Oh two dingies. It's bad as gone, then. Ee owe me."

Rude Boy took another step. Art rolled off the tree and got to his feet before he got any closer. Everyone shuffled toward him and around him. A loose circle formed, cutting off any thoughts of escape.

"Settle it with the king," General Fly announced. "Best get on your way, boys."

"Ee'll settle on point, buzzy. Back to your slop and mind your maggots."

The words triggered an alarm, one Art didn't hear. In seconds, the trees shivered. Flies hovered and zipped and crawled. One of them couldn't hurt the boys. A million of them, though?

"You boys had best behave," the general's voice bellowed. Art couldn't see where the highly decorated horsefly had gone. "I'll have you strung in the trees like Christmas lights and dip you in the pool. You understand, now?"

The boys understood. They were as still as tree trunks. Big black pupils dialed on Art, not moving.

General Fly landed on Art's shoulder. He buzzed quietly in his ear. "Did you steal the beam, son?"

"I didn't mean to. But, yeah. I stole it."

"Fair enough," the general said. Then loudly proclaimed: "Settle it quick, boys. Or the king will send you for a swim. Keep it fair, though. Just the two of you. A race out to the swamp and back would do ya, far as I'm concerned."

"Nah, buzzy," Rude Boy said. "Skin on bone 'ill do it."

Art didn't need a translation. The look in those big black eyes spoke clearly enough. Art didn't get a sense he knew how to fight. There was no hidden instinct for it like there was when he rode the beam.

"What's that going to prove?" Art said.

"Steal on me, wrecker, and ee give up a piece for pay."

Art got the gist of it. He apologized. No point in explaining it was a cat who stole it. Art had had a good reason to ride off on it, not one they'd care to hear. If this was about the beam, they could go back to the border and find it. But it wasn't about that.

"It's for honor, son," the general whispered. "What little he has, he's got to save."

Art backed away from Fly Dome. The air vibrated with the beating of countless wings. He felt safe with the flies watching over him. He wasn't scared of the boys. Even with Rude Boy closing in on him. In an odd way, Art felt drawn to the boys. They were outcasts. He wanted to ride with them, follow them through the trees, feel the wind on his face. Jump down the steps and slam a beam on the concrete.

Because they were his people. He could feel it. *Lost Boys.*

"Sorree don't git a beam on my soles," Rude Boy said.

"Neither does fighting."

"Ee'll feel flighty though."

The boys laughed at that. *I'll feel better,* Art translated. Or something like that.

Rude Boy jumped up and down and wagged his arms. He entertained the Lost Boys with a wild dance. Like a chimp establishing rank. He took a foil-wrapped coin from his hip pack and made a show of peeling it open, biting it in half like a hyena ripping open prey. Chewing it loudly, smacking his lips and smearing his teeth.

Art's mouth watered. He spoke without thinking.

"Will ee nick of snap for me?" Art said.

He had no idea where the words came from. He knew what they meant, though. And so did the Lost Boys, who looked at each other with startled delight. They roared with laughter, doubled over and pointing not at Art, but at Rude Boy, who found it not funny at all. The very opposite.

All Art wanted was a bite of chocolate. He stole the spotlight, instead.

"Enough show, boys," General Fly. "Time is tickin', and the king is waitin'. Settle up and get on your way."

Rude Boy was all for it.

Art's plan was to pull him to the ground and wrap his arms and legs around the pointy-eared lost boy and hang on as long as he could. Rude Boy circled around. Art bent his knees, bounced on the balls of his feet. He flinched when Rude Boy feigned a charge. The sharp edge of stress cut through the cottony comfort of Chocolate Brain. Art just wanted to get it over with. He was going to make the first move.

Then fruit fell from a tree.

A BIG SHINY orb thumped on the ground and burst open, spilling juicy flesh full of sparkling seeds. Then another fell. And another.

Then all the trees started dumping fruit.

It sounded like drums. Like an oversized hailstorm.

Everyone covered their heads. The flies were stirred into flight. The general flew circles around Art. The ground trembled. A mild earthquake sent the army of flies inside the dome. Art's knees were weak. And then a voice spread throughout the land. It was childlike and enormous.

It said: "*YUM!*"

The Lost Boys jumped on their beams and scattered. They circled in figure-eights, falling into some unspoken formation like birds in flight.

"HOLD!" General Fly ordered. "Not without the boy!"

One of the boys broke out of line and zipped past Art, snatching him by the piggly-wiggly shirt (also stolen) and dragging him onto the back of the beam. Art grabbed the boy's back and quickly found his balance. They were at the back of the line, heading into the trees.

General Fly zipped in front of Art and saluted.

Art felt the next tremor. It shook the trees and the ground and the sky above. Everyone slowed down. A few of the boys fell off their beams. Art held on tightly as they banked into a turn. One of the riderless beams hit a tree and bounced into the canopy. Art leaped into the tree and climbed up to reach it, pulling it down. He was riding it before he hit the ground, cutting through the undergrowth. The one who lost the beam held up his arm. Art slowed down, locking arms and heaving him onto the back of the beam.

"YUM! YUM!"

The boy held onto Art's shirt with both hands. They followed the Lost Boys through the bush, over fallen logs and between boulders, down a mossy trail toward a fizzy stream that smelled like cherry soda.

Art's heart hissed with adrenaline.

Steady tears streamed across his temples.

This was what he wanted. This feeling. This freedom. This wild, untethered freedom that sang in his veins and bloomed on his cheeks. This lovely chaos spoke to him. It was his song.

And then branches above him broke.

He was pulled off the beam and into the dim sky above and away from where his heart felt at home. Just like that, he was lost again. Truly.

"YUM!"

12

The stagecoach jostled King Chocolate like a mixed drink.

The roads were rough this far out. How far the Naughty Side went, no one really knew. King Chocolate had sent explorers over the mountains. They always came back with no memory of what they saw. Just a jolly good time. The idiots.

King Chocolate wasn't going that far out. Just into the Cacao Wildwoods, where the ground was bitter and the trees were dense. How bitter and dense, he had no idea. Shades had been installed over the window of the new stagecoach, and he hadn't seen a thing since leaving his castle. Just the two dingdongs sitting across from him.

"Close your eyes," Jelly said when the stagecoach began to slow.

"I'm not closing my eyes," King Chocolate said.

"It's a surprise. Close your eyes."

"I'm not a *child*!" He shifted in the throne. His bum was sore from all the bumps in the road. "And I hate surprises."

"You do not."

"I just told you I do."

"You specifically said when we started the project *I would love this to be a surprise.*"

"You did," Santa Claus said. "I heard it."

"No one asked you." King Chocolate harrumphed. Then added: "You're not even real."

He probably had said it. He'd totally said it. But he didn't want to be surprised now. He just wanted to get what he wanted. It had been a long ride, and he was overstimulated. Also, he had high expectations for this project. Jelly had warned him about expectations. *Future disappointments*, she had said.

Not if they do their jobs they're not.

The stagecoach was barely moving now. They settled in their seats. Santa Claus didn't jitter.

"Can you not look at me like that?" King Chocolate turned to Jelly slumped against the padded bench. "Why is he programmed like that anyway?"

"Like what?"

"All judgy! Look at him, taking my inventory with his eyes. I don't like it."

"You wanted Santa Claus."

"You don't know what he's like. He could be an angry fat man who doesn't like to shave, with horrible taste in winter wear. And *not* judgy."

"If he's angry, he'd be judgy."

"That's a mean thing to say, Casey," Santa added.

"No, it's not. Those are facts. And theories. Something I heard someone say. Besides, I'm not mean. You are."

"You are," Jelly said. "A li'l bit."

"You can shut up, too. I put you—"

"HERE!" the driver shouted from above.

The stagecoach came to a complete stop. Butterflies took flight and fluttered throughout the generous space of King Chocolate's stomach. It felt like Christmas morning, all antsy pantsy to see what was under the tree. He'd explode if he waited any longer.

The levitating hoversuit gripped and hummed. Squeezed the breath out of him. Like a girdle from a magical torture chamber, it lifted him out of the throne. His twiggy legs twittered beneath him.

"Open the door," he said. "Open it. OPEN IT!"

The side of the stagecoach popped open like the lid on a jack-in-the-box. Stairs unfolded. He floated down, pretending to walk on them. The curly toes of his designer shoes (*Flockeby Manor shoes are very expensive*, the Triad had told him) clunked on the treads.

His smile faded to neutral confusion. Followed by annoyance. Bordering on rage.

Nothing but blackened trees. The bark smooth and shiny, almost glassy. Hard as diamonds. Not one of them had been cut down.

A welcome party was on the side of the rutted road.

A patched-up stuffed doggy, a dirty teddy bear. And a wrinkled lump of something with two googly eyes. While waving triangular pennants on wooden sticks, they put their fingers to their mouths and kissed them.

"What's this?" King Chocolate said flatly.

"Your fan club," Jelly said. "I think they want autographs."

On cue, they held out the pennants. King Chocolate spit on them. Coffee-colored spots stained the stiff fabric. The wrinkly lump was the most excited to get the king's autograph.

"What are you?" King Chocolate asked.

"He's a prune," Jelly said.

It looked nothing like a prune, bouncing up and down like a rotten soccer ball.

"Beat it." King Chocolate turned to Jelly and sipped a long breath of air. The rage was ready for duty. "What am I looking at? And don't say trees."

The stagecoach slowly pulled away. Jelly waited for it to be out of the way, then pointed across the road and started to answer. King Chocolate cut her off.

"What I should be looking at is a stage, you helpless batbrain. I should be seeing a mosh pit and spotlights and drums and those things you walk on, the things overhead that are skinny and—"

"Catwalks," Jelly said.

"NOT TREES! I didn't bruise my delicate cushions just to see—" King Chocolate looked at what Jelly was pointing at. "You little stinker," he said. "I should sit on you."

"You love surprises."

"I do."

She knew him so well.

THEY CROSSED the road to a lighted boardwalk.

King Chocolate's long, flowing Christmas coat dragged along, giving the impression he was floating. Which he was. His shoes could be heard dragging across every board.

The boardwalk journeyed between trees and over stumps, down a long winding slope. Gorilla workers wearing dented hardhats and holding deep-toothed saws stopped what they were doing when he passed, kissing their fingers like the welcoming party had done.

"The ticket booth is over there." Jelly pointed to a tunnel. "It'll send everyone through the gift shop and then the concession stands. General seating will be to the left, standing room in front of the stage. VIP booths on the right. Corporate skyboxes up there."

Treehouses were lit with string lights.

"Attendance is required. Every Naughty has been notified it is not an option. Anyone or anything will be fined if they don't purchase a ticket. There are affordable ones way in the back. Anyone who doesn't buy a ticket gets one of *them* knocking on their door."

Them were the gorilla workers.

"Commemorative shirts are not included in the ticket price, but all attendees are required to purchase one. If they don't—"

"I don't like this." Santa Claus walked alongside them, his black galoshes treading silently. "Christmas is not about profit."

King Chocolate came to a halt. Jelly did, too.

Santa went three more steps. He turned around. Stunned silence swelled between the three of them. Jelly looked up at King Chocolate. He looked down at her. They looked at Santa Claus.

Laughter went off like party favors.

Hysterical whining and hitching of breath. Tears literally squirting from their eyes. Jelly hung onto King Chocolate's coat to keep from falling over. King Chocolate veered to the edge of the boardwalk and almost went over.

"I can't breathe! I can't breathe!" King Chocolate bellowed between breathless guffaws.

Jelly punched her chest as if her heart had stopped.

When the hysterics faded to giggles and gulps, the king and Jelly attempting to hug each other for support, King Chocolate blurted to Santa (who had yet to smile):

"Christmas... not for... profit? What world... do you *live in*?" More laughter. Jelly fell on the boardwalk and almost rolled off. "You really are Santa," King Chocolate said. "Oh, oh. I think I tore a lung."

Santa Claus walked away. He wouldn't get far since Jelly had the projector in her pocket.

THE STAGE WAS MASSIVE. The width of a football field with those walky things over it. *Catwalks.* Movie screens as tall as stadiums on both ends. Banks of lighting anchored in the trees. The brightness was worse than the Nice Side. Hundreds of workers wore black sunglasses. Sawing trees and turning bolts and pounding nails. It smelled like fame.

"The green room's on that side." Jelly pointed to a giant box behind the stage. "You'll be projected onto the screens the entire time."

"Whoa, whoa. I didn't sign up for *that*."

"It won't be live. It'll be put together with AI." Jelly winked. "No one will know the difference. You'll be in the green room, sipping chocolate syrup from a hose. And then, just before Christmas, you come onstage."

"Hang on—"

"They'll want to see you in the flesh. And you'll want to strut around in your new hoversuit. Right? Right?" Jelly held her hands to her mouth. "*Choc-late! Choc-late! Choc-late!*"

He didn't hate the idea. He shouldn't deprive them of their king.

Jelly climbed the steps leading up to the stage. King Chocolate floated behind her. Santa behind him. Mop-top roadies were working on an elevated platform, assembling a thirty-piece drum kit with four bass drums. A lanky orange octopus was tuning the snare drums. They all gestured when they saw the king. Fingers to their lips.

He would never get tired of that.

THE TRIAD WAS CENTER STAGE.

The fashion waifs were holding rolled plans, pointing at spotlights and arguing with a mop-top roadie. They dropped the plans when King Chocolate arrived. Their eyes swelling and jaws dropping. They swarmed around him, plucking at the overcoat they designed, fawning over the way it hung on him, how he floated over the stage. A vision of grace and power.

"And that there." The green one twirled his finger. "What is that?"

King Chocolate dug the gold chain from the inside of his coat, displayed the medallion in his sweaty palm. The letters *KC* raised on the center. He braced for their reaction. The chain wasn't their idea, so they would probably hate it.

"I love it, I love it," the green one said. "I *looooooove* it."

"Really?"

"Oh, yes-yes-yes," the red one said. "It radiates power and strength. Wealth." The red one made a fist. "*I am the king, and this is my necklace!*"

"It's not too much?"

"My dear," the blue one said, "can anything be *too much*?"

The three of them laughed. King Chocolate did, too. He wasn't certain why or convinced they really liked the necklace. The downside to wielding power. If they told the truth, he'd throw them in Fudgy Lake.

"It's good you're here now," the green one said. "We're discussing the exit play. I think you will like. Come, come."

The Triad came together like magnets. They swayed when they

walked. It made King Chocolate a little motion sick watching them. At the far side of the stage, a polka-dotted tarp was covering a large object. King Chocolate smiled. He couldn't remember telling Jelly that he'd always wanted a monster truck, but what else could it be?

Several roadies were called over. They attached ropes to eyehooks at the edge of the tarp.

"Ready?" the red one asked.

King Chocolate quaked with anticipation. When the tarp was lifted to the catwalks, his expectations were dashed. No monster truck. It was a photo. A giant photo.

A photo!

Imagine wanting a monster truck for Christmas and getting a photo of one instead. And worse, it wasn't even a monster truck!

It had golden rails and torpedo rocket boosters. A slick, aerodynamic chassis with a bucket seat and a dashboard of buttons and switches and doodads. It was brown and gold and silver. A long lead of chains was attached to the front of it. He was speechless. He didn't know what it was. He didn't know whom to drop in Fudgy Lake first.

"After the ceremony is over," the green one said, "you will fly off into the night in your brand-new—"

"SLEIGH!" the three of them screamed.

King Chocolate ground his teeth. Jelly patted his arm. She could feel the storm coming. Patting his arm was her way of calming him down. To wait and listen. He could be hasty. Like the time he threw the plumber in the lake for not using gold pipes on the royal toilet.

"A sleigh?" King Chocolate said through gritted teeth.

"Yes, yes." The green one gestured. "Like Santa."

"Pulled by reindeer?"

"No, no, no," the blue one said. "Pulled by those."

Over by the trees, just past the blackened stumps that had not been shredded and buried, yellow flames danced from a trash can. Several wolves stood around it, some with their paws over the fire. Others were on all fours, playing a game that involved dice. From a distance, their rough laughter could be heard.

"Is that the Big Bad Wolf?" Jelly said.

"It is," the red one said.

"Oh my God, oh my God. My niece is *dying* to get his autograph. I'll be right back."

"No, you won't," King Chocolate said. "Not yet. First of all, wolves don't fly."

"Neither do reindeer, darling," the blue one said.

"Yes, they do," Santa said.

"You're not real," the blue one said. "Santa Claus uses boosters, like the ones in the photo. Although they will not work, either. They don't have to. You will not fly for real. You will be hoisted up with clear cables that no one will see. Then they will see an amazing projection of you and your sleigh in the sky going all over the Naughty Side. And when they get back to their homes—because they will all be here—there will be presents waiting for them. From you!"

"Full credit goes to you," the green one said. "King Chocolate."

He didn't hate this idea, either. These triplets were a little annoying, but they were on their game. He hated that the queen had sent them. This was *exactly* what he wanted. Like it could not be more perfect.

All the credit. And he does nothing to deserve it.

"Great," he said. "Now, just explain how I'm going to fly off with a picture and we'll be cool. Go on."

And they did. They told him exactly how he would make a rocket sleigh. It sounded like bunko. How could they even know that? But they weren't wrong so far. And if they were wrong about this, he'd enjoy dunking them into the lake. *So, winning.*

"What's with the box?" King Chocolate asked.

They were on their way to the green room when something fell from the sky. A roadie had dropped a roll of tape from the catwalk. It nearly hit King Chocolate. Naturally, he looked up to see who had tried to hurt him. (Santa was a prime suspect. The real one. After all, he knows when you've been bad or good. Not much of a secret in Candyland.)

A box was dangling on a heavyweight chain. It was a wooden crate.

Swinging in a light breeze.

"Oh. Oh no." The green one covered his face. "I told them to cover it. I told them, I told them."

The Triad gathered in a consoling hug, rocking back and forth. Whispering. It went on for quite a while. The hoots and cackles from the wolf pack filled the awkward moment.

"What's happening?" King Chocolate muttered. Jelly shrugged.

The Triad held still now, humming to each other. They let go and wiped each other's tears away. The green one faced King Chocolate, who was, quite frankly, a little worried what was in the box. Now he *had* to know.

"It was a surprise," the green one said. "Now it is ruined."

"I don't like surprises."

"Yes, you do," Jelly said.

The green one hung his head. "Just before you are hoisted away in the sleigh, the box will be lowered. It will be wrapped, of course. A beautiful silver wrapping with a red glitter dusting and satin bow. It will come down right after your speech."

"Speech? What speech?"

The red one let out a wail. They took their surprises seriously. For a moment, King Chocolate didn't care about the box. Speeches were not in his nature. Waving to crowds, sure. Throwing presents at little ones, okay. There would be no sitting on his lap (yuck) or whispering what anyone wanted from him. Definitely no speeches.

"We'll talk later," Jelly said.

"No, we won't. No speech. *What's in the box?*"

The Triad waved their arms. Someone got the message. The box trembled. It dropped a little and shook. King Chocolate backed up. If a wild animal jumped out, he was putting everyone in the lake. Including the Big Bad Wolf.

Clack-clack-clack.

The box descended one link at a time until one corner touched the stage. When all four corners settled, the box remained still. King Chocolate moved behind Jelly. She would make a fine snack.

The blue one pulled a lever on the side of the box.

The wood cracked. The wall lowered like a castle gate and thudded on the stage.

There was a cage inside. Cold metal bars running top to bottom. He took his hands away from his face to see what was inside the cage. He had visions of snakes or lizards (he hated lizards more than snakes; they were snakes *with* legs). No one else had moved. And now the box was open, and they were staring.

Empty. It was empty. The box was empty. The cage inside it was saving him from nothing.

"Is this a joke?" he bristled. "I don't like jokes."

"Yes, you do," Jelly said.

"It's not a joke," the red one said. "It's for the boy."

"Boy?" King Chocolate said. "What boy?"

"The *boy*," Jelly said. Her eyes widened. King Chocolate didn't get it. Her eyes widened more. Like how many boys really matter? *There's only one.*

"We were waiting on the Lost Boys," the blue one said. "When they arrive with the crosser, we're going to give him to you as a gift. Jelly knew."

"You knew?"

"Yep."

"You were going to put the boy in there?" King Chocolate pointed at the box.

"Not for long," the red one said. "We'd feed him, of course."

"Of course," the other two said.

King Chocolate thought about it. With all the excitement—the concert and the rocket sleigh—he hadn't thought about using the boy as a prop. The crowd would want to see him. And this way it would make the king look good. *Genius. Absolute genius.* The king was now certain they were right about getting the rocket sleigh made.

"You are *not* putting the boy in a cage," Santa said.

"Of course not," King Chocolate said. Then winked at the Triad.

The idea needed tweaking. But it was as solid as a bar of virgin cacao. The boy didn't have to go in the cage as soon as he was delivered, but he was totally going in there. First, he'd come to the castle and do his thing. Then in the box. That was that, and no one would change his mind.

"Casey, please," Santa said.

"*What* did you call me?" King Chocolate ground his teeth. This was not a first-name crowd and Santa knew it.

"I know what you do at Christmas." Santa had a voice that carried. Even the wolves looked at the stage. "You sit by the window on Christmas Eve, watching the sky, looking for my sleigh to come streaking toward your house."

"Um, it's a castle. And *that* never happened. And you're not real."

"You listen to reports of an *unidentified flying object* coming closer. You pull up a chair and imagine where I am and how fast my reindeer are flying. You put milk and cookies out for me. Chocolate chip. The chocolate still soft and melty. You leave me three cookies."

"I don't even know what he's talking about! He's not real, you know. He's not even—"

"And carrots, too. You insist on leaving carrots for the reindeer. They *so* appreciate that, I promise you. Then you make sure the fireplace is open—very kind of you—and curl up on your favorite chair, where you pop your thumb in your mouth and suck it till morning."

"What?! This is crazy talk. Shut him off, Jelly!"

"And then you run down to the big Christmas tree where I leave the presents and begin ripping them open. I'll never forget your all-time favorite gift. It was a Chef Hoobie Cookie Oven. A light bulb would do the baking. It would take all day before the cookies were ready. You would sit and wait and suck your thumb—"

"I DID NOT SUCK MY THUMB!"

"Until the batter was warm. Then you'd take your thumb out of your mouth and—"

King Chocolate lifted Jelly with one hand and rifled through her clothing like a clumsy pickpocket. He found what he was looking for and snatched the projector from her pocket. It was a silver orb no bigger than a golf ball. All he had to do was hold it in his palm and say *off* and the Santa Claus program would turn off, and this big fat liar would go bye-bye. So he held it in his palm, lifted it above his head. And chucked it onto the stage.

It bounced like a stone.

He made Jelly fetch it and hand it back. He did it again. And again. Each throw harder until the stage was dimpled with divots.

"He's a liar! Santa Claus is a liar!"

Bang!

"A BIG—"

Bang!

"FAT—"

Bang!

"LIAR!"

King Chocolate was out of breath, with a sharp pain piercing his chest. His arm was tired, so he made Jelly throw it for him. Told her not to stop until that thing cracked like an egg. King Chocolate raised his fist.

"Santa is a liar! Santa is a liar!"

It caught on with the wolves, howling as they joined the chant. The mop-top roadies followed. The octopus climbed behind the drum kit and laid down a beat. Gorilla workers were coming out of the trees. Listening at first. Then fists rose. The air quivered with the chant.

Santa is a liar!

King Chocolate called one of the gorillas over and told him to stand right there. Not to move. Then looked out at the gathering workers—the apes and the wolves and mop-tops and octopus. "You deserve better than that!" King Chocolate shouted. "You deserve more than that fat liar!"

SANTA IS A LIAR!

The stage was shaking. Pine cones fell from the trees. The chants took on a life. Wolves howling. Gorillas jumping. The energy sizzled. King Chocolate pointed at the gorilla standing next to him. Jelly dropped the silver orb responsible for projecting the Santa Claus program. The king made a fist. The gorilla raised his leg and held it there. Waiting as the chant continued.

SANTA IS A LIAR!

Santa shook his head with disappointment in his eyes.

The king nodded with a cruel twinkle in his.

The gorilla brought all his weight down on the orb. It shattered like an antique timepiece. Metal shards and springs and circuits sprayed over the stage. Ravenous cheers went up, and the chant continued. When it reached a fevered pitch, the king answered.

"You… deserve…" he said, "*ME!*"

King Chocolate threw out his arms.

He soaked it in. Soaked it all in.

Maybe I will give that speech.

WINGED MONKEYS WERE WORKING on the green room. Their wings slowly flapped when they concentrated, sped up when they were excited. Wilted when they were tired. They pretty much did everything except fly. They were, however, extremely creepy looking.

"Out," King Chocolate said. "Leave us."

They dropped their tools and scrambled out of the room, the tips of their furry wings curling under. King Chocolate drifted into the green room, dragging his tired feet. He'd barely touched the ground and couldn't wait to get these clothes off. The hoversuit was slick with sweat and chafing his many rolls of flesh. A rancid odor wafted out from under it. It had the smell of soured fudge. Not bad, really.

He hovered straight at the throne, hit it hard enough to ram the back of it into the wall. Flat chunks of wood fell from the ceiling. King Chocolate collapsed into the seat and began to melt.

"Air!" he cried. "It's a thousand degrees in here."

It was not. In fact, it was cool enough to store meat. Jelly pretended to adjust the thermostat. A three-tiered fountain splashed chocolate milk in the corner next to a soft-serve ice-cream machine (chocolate only). Gourmet bottles of syrup and muffins and cookies were on a table. King Chocolate laid his head back, panting. He opened his mouth like a baby bird.

Jelly handed him the end of a long tube on a jointed mechanical arm that was attached to the ceiling. It looked like something at a dentist's office. Something to rinse and spit. King Chocolate put it in his mouth and began to suck. An icebox began to hum and pump. Dark liquid slithered through the tube and gushed into his mouth. The chocolatey goodness filled his belly with sweet love.

There was a tiny knock at the door.

"Hmm-mphm," was the sound that came out of him.

Jelly had been to enough feedings to understand what he said. "It's the Conflict Advisors."

"Wah?"

"You told them to be here."

King Chocolate sucked so hard the tube collapsed, choking off the flow. The machine started to chug.

"Take a breath," Jelly said. "Let it come to you. I'm going to let them in while you digest."

He closed his eyes and relaxed his lips. The sugar stream spilled over his tongue. He let it fill his mouth until it overflowed his lips and ran over his chins, soaking into his stylish overcoat. With one gulp, he choked it down and let it start again.

He had no memory of calling this meeting. Things like that sometimes disappeared in a food haze. *Starving amnesia,* he called it. A mixture of hunger and hurt feelings. So he sometimes sucked his thumb. No big deal. Everyone had a thumb; everyone had a mouth.

But King Chocolate had an extra layer of shame added to it. He'd heard the rumors of what the naughties were saying about him. What they were calling him. Sometimes he'd put lemon juice on it so he would stop, but he'd suck right through that. He just loved it too much. There was only one thing he loved more.

He grabbed muffins off the table and plugged them into his mouth. Shoved cookies in after them. Poured milk on his face. He coughed and sputtered. Soggy crumbs rifled across the room and stuck to the wall.

He mopped his face with a towel. Threw the towel over his shoulder. Then belched like a truck without a muffler.

"All better?" Jelly asked.

"Much. Now…" He leaned forward with a groan, drool hanging from his lip. "Advise me."

He was talking to twelve-inch soldiers. Three of them standing at attention. Plastic-molded clothing and solid hairdos. Kung fu grips for holding weapons or punching through walls. The one in the middle had permanent marker scribbled over his face and down the front of his plastic coat. He stepped forward and snapped his arms to his sides.

"Last report, the Lost Boys arrived at Fly Dome. The crosser should be in their possession by now and en route to the castle."

"General Fly deserves a medal." This was the soldier with a missing left arm. All that remained was a hole in his shoulder where a new arm (should he ever get one) would snap into place. "His team executed a flawless extraction."

"He didn't want a medal," King Chocolate said. "Wanted chocolate slop instead. To feed those squirmy babies, I guess." He nibbled on a cookie that was stuck to his jacket. "Is that all?"

"We'll have a full report when the crosser arrives," Scribble Face barked. "An evaluation will need to conclude to—"

"All right, all right. Go impress someone else." King Chocolate waved the syrup feeder like a scepter. Then: "What do you think of the box idea?"

The Conflict Advisors exchanged stiff looks. Jelly summarized the gift idea, of keeping the boy in a cage to present to King Chocolate on Christmas Eve. The scarred and marred soldiers didn't react with expressions, mainly because the plastic forms from which they were molded didn't move. But they shuffled. And the more they heard, the more they shuffled.

When Jelly was done, King Chocolate took a pull on the tube. "Well?"

"I strongly advise against it," the third soldier said. He was the most normal and unaltered of the three (except for the eye patch that hid whatever atrocity was under it).

"And why is that?"

"The boy has experienced trauma."

"So?"

"It is in your best interest to make the boy as comfortable as possible. Weapons such as him should be kept clean and well-oiled."

"Is that what he is?" King Chocolate said. "A weapon?"

"He's whatever you want him to be."

Whatever I want? He liked the sound of that. "What does he do... *exactly*?"

"He's a creative," Eye Patch announced. King Chocolate didn't like the tone.

"I know, I know. But what does that *mean*? Do you even know? Like he draws pictures. Oooo... scary. Every degenerate on the Naughty Side can draw. Like this sack of dough." He pointed the scepter at Jelly. "She draws stick figures. Don't you?"

Jelly shook her head. King Chocolate laughed with the tube between his teeth.

The Conflict Advisors conferred.

They mumbled. They nodded. King Chocolate was about to throw them out when Scribble Face spoke up.

"You remember the Nutcracker?"

For some reason, this hit the king on the wrong side. He pulled the tube out of his mouth, aimed it at the mini-soldiers and pressed the button. A burst of chocolate syrup burped from the end of it. It hit Scribble Face in the chest. Dripped from his kung fu grip.

"OF COURSE I DO! You think I'm an idiot?" He aimed the tube at the other two with his thumb hovering over the trigger. "What about it?"

Righty spoke up, waving his one and only arm. "She crossed over from another world and *manifested* her subconscious."

"All right. Good." King Chocolate didn't know what *manifested* meant. But after hosing down Scribble Face, he didn't want to admit it. "Tell me more."

"What she was thinking and feeling... it came true in Candyland."

King Chocolate sank in the throne to give this a good think. There was a theory about Candyland, what it really was and why it existed. How people could *cross* into it from other worlds. Candyland wasn't exactly a dream, but sort of. What was it Jelly told him once? *If a dreamer wakes up inside the dream... anything is possible.*

He propped his elbows on his knees. All his weight slid to the front.

His dark chocolatey eyes aimed at Righty.

"What're you saying?"

"He can change things." The soldier didn't flinch. "You just have to guide him."

King Chocolate laughed the rumbly laugh of no-good. The kind of laugh that made children cry. Dogs whine. Jelly rolled her eyes. He was overdoing it for no one but his own entertainment. He paddled a quick rhythm on his belly and squirted chocolate syrup at the ceiling. It rained down on his head, over the folds of his belly. He licked it off his sausage fingers.

He got it. He finally got it.

The boy was important. That was what everyone was telling him. But for the first time, he knew why.

He can change things. The boy is a creative. He has an imagination that can change things. The Triad was right! A rocket sleigh is just the beginning of what the boy can do.

King Chocolate was going to use him. He was going to win. All those citizens on the Nice Side would feel the burden of being naughty. They would get coal in *their* stockings when he was done.

They would make King Chocolate statues when this was over.

They would rename Two-Face Mountain and carve his face on it. It would be One-Face Mountain when the boy was done.

They would bow and give *him* gifts. Not the boy. The king, he would get the gifts because he would be the one driving the boy.

He cried chocolate tears of joy and apologized to Scribble Face for the syrup bath. Jelly wiped him clean with his towel. King Chocolate closed his eyes and bathed in the expectations of complete and total victory. It tasted like the purest, sweetest chocolate in all of Candyland. He didn't notice the fly enter the green room and whisper in Jelly's ear.

13

Art tumbled like a bingo ball in a basket weaved from tree trunks. Instead of numbered Ping-Pong balls, a mess of empty nutshells and gooey seed pits dusted him with crumbs. He smelled like a spoiled sponge cake.

The basket tipped one way and then the other, rolling the contents like a wave machine filled with marbles. A meaty hand gripped the handle. The fingernails—painted red and green and blue —were jagged at the ends. Occasionally, when the basket swung just right, he'd catch a glimpse of the arm and follow it to a big, round face. Strawberry hair and orange cheeks.

And one square tooth. Latched over the bottom lip.

A lip stained purple.

Tooth as square as a box. Made for cracking nuts. Or other things.

Art had to get out of the basket before it was too late. Each time he went tumbling to one end of the basket, he slammed into the pine lumber before rolling to the other end. He was sick and dizzy with no way of knowing which way was sideways when, as luck would have it, his boot wedged between weaved tree trunks. He hung suspended from one end as the spent shells and gooey pits rolled to the other. And came crashing back seconds later.

He got a handhold in a knothole and pulled himself up. The gap where his boot was stuck wasn't big enough to squeeze through, but enough to see where he was going. The basket swung higher. His stomach parachuted into his socks. He closed his eyes and hung on.

Water splashed into the basket and shot through the gaps.

It soaked his hair. Tasted like sweet tea with a scoop of molasses.

Outside the basket, footsteps plunged deeper in water. The air grew cool and humid. The basket went higher.

Long hot wind exhaled from above, streaming from nostrils like hotrod exhaust. It was warm and sweet like yeast rolls fresh from the oven and buttered with cinnamon. Water churned below in deep eddies; then the steps became shallower. The sound of soft mud sucking them down, not wanting to let go. Advancing to hard thumping land and the sound of gravel. Then grass.

And then no more steps.

The basket teetered. Art worked his boot loose with an eye on the hand above him. If it came sweeping through the basket for him, he'd be ready to climb for it. When he freed his boot, he scaled the basket like a wall in a log cabin. There was no hesitation. He raced to the top and was about to throw his leg over the edge when the world shivered like an enormous dog. Lake water rained into the basket, sweet drops of black tea running down the sides. Its commotion knocked Art back inside.

"*Yum!*" went a deep voice.

The braided handle creaked. The dim sky was blotted out by an orange face. The face of a moon made of circus peanuts with eggplant lips smacking a bulletin-board tooth. The nostrils flared. Art held onto a branch poking out the side. The endless inhalation gurgled. Curly hairs inside the nostrils filtered out debris.

Art's grip slipped on the wet branch. He wondered, as his fingernails etched the bark from the branch, if being hoovered into a giant's sinuses was worse than being swallowed. *Depends if the giant chews her food.*

Then it stopped.

Art thought he heard something. A tiny voice. The orange face looked up. A smile as wide as a house spread into the pumpkin cheeks. The voice called again, although Art couldn't understand it. The giant did.

"*Yum!*"

The basket tipped upright. A landslide of shells and seeds spilled over the side. Art hung on until the giant gave the basket a good shake. He went crashing into the pile. And thank goodness he did. He sank halfway down and, without half a thought, dug to the bottom, where he hit ground.

HE WAS LOOKING AT A FOOT. A bare foot as big as a toolshed. As orange as a tangerine.

Cracks ran from callused soles that had never felt the inside of a shoe (no store carried such a size). Toenails, long and jagged, were the colors of the fingernails. Art wondered if they were painted at all. Maybe they were just those colors. He knew nothing of giants, after all.

When that foot rose off the ground, it came down like a pile driver and rattled the shells and seeds. The second footfall spread the pile further. Several more and Art was barely able to hide.

The giant was across a green clearing, holding the basket under a pipe. An avalanche of colored rocks wrapped in blankets of crinkly cellophane (if Art assumed it to be hard candy, he would've assumed right) spilled from the oversized faucet like a slot machine jackpot.

"*Yum! Yum!*"

She cracked one open with that giant tooth and hopped up and down. Earthquakes rattled the world. Then she leaned over, put her face near the ground. Art thought she was vacuuming something into her nostrils, but something moved. A faint shadow. He couldn't quite see what it was—that part of Candyland was more dim than dark, like a full moon on a cloudless night (although there was no moon)—but it hugged the giant's nose.

The giant sighed with pleasure. "Yum."

Then she strode back the way she came, down the rocky bank and into the blackwater tea. She held the basket of goodies above her head as the water rose to her waist. The water rippled around her, but she never slowed down, carving her way to the other side. Climbing onto dry land and shaking like a dog before pushing through the trees. Her footsteps were collisions that slowly faded.

Until they were gone.

Until there were just frogs singing night songs and cicadas joining in. The air pulsed with the fluorescent signs of fireflies.

Stillness wrapped around him.

He embraced it. Became part of the scenery. Hardly breathing. His eyes moving back and forth, taking in the unknown. There was so much he couldn't see. He'd have to turn his head, and he wasn't ready to move. Not yet. Not until it was safe.

Someone or something had honked that giant's nose. He or she was out there. Maybe they were watching, so Art blended into the pile. Became one with it. He'd lie like that for as many ticks or rings or bells as needed. Last thing he wanted was another pair of giant fingers tossing him into a basket.

He wanted to rest. That lasted a few ticks.

In other words, not long.

Something was scratching around him.

It was sniffing the ground. Little fingers or claws dug through the soil. Not close to him. But close enough.

A shell tumbled off the pile. Another one followed.

Padded footsteps ran off, and it was quiet again. Until the scratching returned. This time a handful of shells cascaded off the pile. More footsteps followed. And then something else.

Squeak!

Like a trigger had been pulled, Art exploded from the pile of shells and seeds and ran for the shore. He went down a slope, over jagged ground until his hands hit water. He spun around, eyes just above a speckled boulder. Scanning the pile he'd just blown up.

They were little lumps at first. A train of little, long-tailed lumps running to the scattered shells and seeds and then back to a grassy meadow surrounded by a split rail fence. It reminded him of ants finding food. Only ants the size of work boots. Ants with tails. And fur.

They weren't ants.

He knew what they were and didn't want to admit it. He might make a sound he would regret if he did.

There were so many of them, each of them grabbing a shell or a seed and marching it to the meadow. The pile receding piece by piece.

Art backed into the water.

THE PILE that the giant had emptied from the basket was nearly gone. The long-tailed harvesters (or were they thieves?) rooted around for the last pieces.

Rats. No question about it, Art finally admitted it. Big ole hoppy rats. Or mice. He didn't know the difference. *Vermin.*

They cleaned up the mess, and Art wondered if the giant had left it behind on purpose. The way the vermin lined up for it didn't seem to be an accident. He didn't know what they were doing with it. Only saw them carry the spilled treasure down a narrow trail carved through swards of blooming weeds and under a split-rail fence.

Art stopped caring about the rats. They weren't interested in him, even when he'd jumped out of the pile like a birthday surprise. The water was getting chilly. He crawled out and sat on a rounded boulder. The sounds of night were all around—things splashing in the water behind him, frogs synchronizing their beats.

There were no stars in the night sky, but a galaxy of glowing lights hovered just above the ground. Fireflies signaled to each other with long pulses of phosphorescent light. Art heard faint whispers from the ones near him. It was mostly laughter. They didn't fly over the water, staying mostly above land. And mostly around what he thought was a giant tree.

He had mistaken it for a tree because that was what it was shaped like. The width of its pendulous branches was the size of a public swimming pool. It was three stories tall and as still as stone. Because that was what it was: an enormous sculpture rooted in the earth.

In the dim light and eerie glow of firefly fannies, he could see bright colors painted on the branches. Random circles of warm light began flickering on its surface. At the top, a three-dimensional star had been carved. Smoke streamed from the five points.

The swamp water behind him was black and sticky. Sweet on his lips. He could probably swim across, disappear into the trees like the giant had done. He was certain he could swim that far, although there were things churning the glassy surface. Big things that sometimes exposed large scales or cutting fins.

This is the Naughty Side, he thought. *Those aren't friendly fish.*

He started walking along the shore, gravel grinding under his boots. The rats had all gone beyond the split-rail fence now that the mess was cleaned up. Art climbed onto the lawn. The grass soft under his squishy boots.

There were more fences and gardens. No tomatoes or peppers or rows of corn. Branches of some bushy plants hung heavy with red-and-white-striped peppermints. It looked like clusters of crystals sprouting from raised beds. Some had been harvested and packed into boxes.

Art walked past the pipe where the giant had filled her basket. It was larger than a sewer pipe and shaped like a spigot. The grass around it was worn down to speckled granite. Just beyond it, light spilled from the stone Christmas tree, tossing long shadows across the grass. Art went back to the shore, crawled over a jagged outcropping and into a thicket of trees. Only a few feet in and he had to turn sideways to squeeze between them.

This was a good hiding spot. For him. Probably for other things, too. Rats, for one.

He walked back out and crouched on the shore. Fireflies descended on him. Whispering, giggling. *Merry, merry,* they said.

He could swim for it, although that was still the worst idea. But it was on the list. He could leave this area (maybe it was an island) and find a bridge or something better. A zipline. A door that took him back home. Anything was possible.

Then a shadow stepped into the light.

A doorway had been cut into the bottom of the stone Christmas tree. Orange light flickered around a ball of fur licking an extended back leg. When Art saw him, the cat stretched. Turned. And walked inside.

The door stayed open.

"Daryl!" Art half whispered.

Daryl didn't hear him or didn't care. Art hadn't seen him since the House of Grimjoy. And that felt so long ago. Time was a funny thing. *Sometimes it stretches like taffy.*

It was Daryl, though. He was sure of it.

No other cat had a belly like that. It nearly dragged on the ground as he strode deeper into the concrete tree. Tail raised. Tail waving.

Art was rooted to the ground. *Why didn't he say something?*

There was a simple answer for that. Daryl was a cat. And cats were mostly interested in a warm lap. Still, he'd helped Art escape the castle. He'd taken that beam and led him to Grimjoy.

Now he's here.

If Daryl was here, Art was in the right place, or so he thought. He stood up. Looked around. Nothing but fireflies noticed him. *Merry, merry,* they whispered. He crept closer, put his hand on the stone Christmas tree (gritty sandstone cool to touch), and peeked inside the doorway.

A long corridor went straight ahead. Longer than he would have guessed, but he'd grown accustomed to the elasticity of space. Colorful murals decorated the walls, wintery scenes with toboggans and snowmen, reindeer, and elves. Flickering light from the end.

He took a step inside. The floor was gritty and made a grinding sound under his heel. Warm air that was humid smelled of sweet smoke and floral incense. Made him feel safe. Made him take another step. He dragged his hand along the wall, felt the rough-hewn surface on his fingertips, as if it had been carved with crude tools. He looked back every two or three steps, the doorway still open. After several stops, he quit looking. It was too far to do anything about it. He was in too deep.

He stopped when he could see what was beyond the end.

He held still and watched.

It was hazy. The air undulating in waves. Someone was sitting on the floor. Her back to him. Nothing else that he could see. He waited for a sign, a signal to move in one direction or the other. Daryl's voice to tell him what to do. There was nothing.

He went forward. Carefully.

The sweet smell of incense tickled his nose. Water pooled in his eyes. He wiped them with the heels of his hands. The woman on the floor wore a patchwork robe that puddled around her. White hair spread over her shoulders.

The room was magnificent and simple: an enormous cone with three fires equidistant in the circular space. Each fire burned inside a metal cylinder on an ornate pedestal. Smoke crawled along the walls, leaving sooty trails to the very top, where they snaked out the legs of a star sitting on top of the tree. Circular skylights, the size of dinner plates, were randomly sunk through the walls.

In constant slow motion, a mobile of silver objects turned above them. As intricate as it was enormous. Anchored on thin wires. Chiming as they rotated in the fires' thermal draft. He was transfixed by the timeless movement, like birds in the sky or playful stars dancing to the universe's song, and hadn't noticed the woman turn her head slightly.

"Join us."

Her voice effortlessly carried. It was raspy. Kind. Art jumped back a step, hanging onto the wall. She didn't seem alarmed or hurt by the reluctance. As if endless patience and acceptance were sitting with her. That wasn't enough to get him to move. But the sound that followed helped. The lapping of drink taken from a bowl.

The sight of a fluffed tail swishing in pleasure.

Art moved inside the room, careful not to step on the thousands of tiny gifts stacked at the perimeter, until he saw Daryl was hunched over a dish.

"Daryl?" The word bounced around the room even though he whispered it.

There was no response. Then a hum spread between his eyes. And he heard that lazy voice. *Have a seat, Arthur.*

There was a small bench opposite the old woman. A bench only a foot tall and twice as wide. It was on the edge of a circular rug. Daryl was in the middle of it, his tongue working a steady rhythm. White flecks of milk lighting his whiskers and tufted chin.

"He followed you the entire way. Even when you couldn't see him," the old woman said. "I knew he would."

She watched Daryl. Spoke without looking up.

Art only needed to see the side of her face to know that she wasn't an old woman. A triangular ear poked through her hair. A tiny gold loop pierced the end of it. Her face jutted forward, covered in white fur. A pink nose surrounded by sprouts of stiff whiskers. A tiny smile curled at the end of her black lips, reaching the eyes. The human eyes. Brown. The color of good dirt.

Art walked the perimeter of the round rug, stood behind the small bench. He assumed she was sitting on something similar, her lower half buried beneath the checkered robe, her hands folded under a knitted blanket on her lap. Under that robe and blanket, he assumed there was a long, leathery tail.

"He's *your* cat," she said.

Daryl stopped drinking. Looked up with white droplets clinging to his chin. He blinked heavily.

"My apologies." The rat woman put her long-fingered, knobby

hand on her chest. "Old habits, I'm afraid. I'm reminded animals aren't objects and don't *belong* to anyone. You and he have been *friends* for quite some time, I'm told. He crossed not long after you." She scratched Daryl's back with a long, pink finger. "And yes, we know each other quite well. That's the thing with crossers: we're all connected."

Cold filled Art's legs. He locked his knees to keep from folding.

What she said.

He wasn't sure he heard it right.

She looked up for the first time. When her eyes landed on him, it felt like a beam of sunlight went through him and warmed him from the inside out. He opened like a flower promised spring rain and summer sun. She tipped her head to one side, hummed (it sounded a bit like a purr, but Art was too gobsmacked to notice), and looked into him. She saw all of him, read him like a script. And he let her, so welcoming was her presence. So accepting. She saw who he truly was, even if he didn't.

He was naked and exposed to her. Vulnerable.

To the side of her, sitting on the floor, was a little bell. She gave it a shake. The melody drifted around the room. The shiny bits of the mobile seemed to answer. A tick later, a rat (this one normal-sized) came across the room. It was anything but normal, wearing tiny, tailored clothing and carrying a silver tray on its back. A teapot shook; teacups rattled. But not a drop was spilled.

He placed it next to the dish of milk. Daryl didn't miss a beat, still going at the milk (the bottom of the bowl was starting to show).

"Thank you, Harley," she said.

The servant rat (slightly bigger than most rats, Art guessed) nodded at the rat woman. Standing upright, he turned to Art and waited. Art tensed up. He'd never been stared down by a rat before. Not that he could remember.

"He wants to know if there's anything you need," Rat Woman said.

Art stammered. Then spoke directly to the little rat and said, "Chocolate."

Harley bowed his head. It was more of deference than acknowledgment.

Rat Woman filled a cup with tea. She held a saucer with one hand. The teacup with the other. Waved it under her pink nose. Those oddly human eyes closed as her whiskers twitched. She sipped it delicately.

"We do not use chocolate here," she said.

An odd way to put it. Who *uses* chocolate? Art was a touch hungry. He also wanted to take the edge off the anxious jitter in his knees, the invisible hand clutching his chest. The apple in his throat. He wanted to smooth out the discomfort with a quick nibble before he unzipped his skin to crawl out of it.

Harley hopped across the room, jumping into one of a hundred holes that were punched into the wall. Rat Woman went back to basking in the aroma of tea, undisturbed by the young man standing across from her. Daryl had finished the milk and was now licking white specks off his fur.

"ARE YOU A CROSSER?" Art blurted. "The way you said it, I thought maybe you meant you were. And Daryl, too."

"Please."

She gestured to the empty bench with her skeletal fingers. Art was happy to sit down before his knees buckled. He squatted on the bench, propped his arms onto his knees. She poured another cup of tea, spun the tray so that it was in front of him. He didn't like tea, but picked it up, not to be rude. It was warm and smelled spicy, like chai. He was tempted to wave it under his nose.

There was a white scar on her cheek where fur didn't grow.

"Have you heard about the nutcracker?" she asked.

"A little bit."

"She was my niece. My sister's child. A young woman when she arrived in Candyland. I followed her here. That was many bells ago. So many I've lost count."

She sipped her tea, lost in thought.

"She was about your age. She was misunderstood. Grief festered inside her and turned to rage when it couldn't breathe. Transformed her into the very thing she hid from herself. This place can do that, especially to crossers."

"Do what?"

"Manifest your thoughts. Make them tangible. Change you from the outside in." She spoke like time didn't exist. There was only this endless moment. "At least, that's what happened to my niece when she was here. Candyland showed her who she really was. It exposed what terrified her most, made her look at it. Embrace it. Accept it."

Another long pause stretched out the silence. Only the sound of crackling flames in the firepits and a cat licking himself clean.

"Where is she now?" Art asked.

"She went home long ago."

"She left?"

The rat woman nodded. "Back where you and I come from."

Art frowned. What he'd been told suddenly went off the rails. "Yeah, but... there aren't giant rats back home. Not ones who talk and, and drink tea."

He couldn't be sure of that since he didn't remember much about home. But something in his gut said there wasn't. She smiled at this and even laughed out loud. It was charming, the way she laughed. From the gut and not at his expense.

"I didn't arrive like this. I became this," she said. "And I'm not a *rat*, dear. I'm a *mouse*."

He didn't see the difference or why that mattered. What did matter was something else she said. He leaned forward. "You know how you got here?"

"There are as many ways to cross over as there are reasons to. It depends on *why* you're here. Many don't remember *how* they got here or anything before they woke up."

She offered a comforting smile.

"But *you* remember," he said.

"Like yester-*ring*." A grandmotherly grin and smart twinkle in her eye. "Yester*day* makes more sense to you, I suppose. Yes. Back in my *day,* a door opened in the pink sky. It was the way in and out. But not anymore. The door hasn't opened since I arrived."

Daryl arched his back and rubbed against Art's leg. When Art didn't give him what he wanted, Daryl went over to the rat woman (*mouse lady, I suppose*) and crawled onto the knitted blanket. She kneaded him with those bony (*and, quite frankly, creepy*) fingers. Purring filled the tall room.

"And what exactly *is* this place?" Art said.

"Haha!" The mouse lady tipped her head back and sent laughter to the tippy-top of the room. "Only a crosser would think to ask that. I used to think I knew what Candyland was, something as simple as a box that contained a magic land. But this place... it has moved on from that."

She shook her head and sighed. Art pondered the strangeness of that. This didn't feel like a box. It didn't matter, according to her. *This place has moved on.*

She scratched Daryl and watched thoughts drift through her mind. Ones she'd been contemplating for quite a few bells. "Candyland," she said with blunt laughter. "The Christmas spirit flows here like sap through a maple tree. It's where naughty and nice take form. A way station, of sorts. Where visitors come and sometimes go."

"Sometimes?"

He didn't like the way she looked at him now. It hid some truth she possessed. A truth with a sharp edge he wasn't ready to touch. A truth she let him know was there. And when he was ready, he would see it, and it would free him. Or hurt him. *Or both.*

Harley returned.

Bouncing across the room, he scaled the loose patchwork robe, climbed onto her shoulder, and whispered into her ear. She answered with squeaks and squeals and strange whispers that Harley understood. He leaped from her shoulder and scrambled across the room, squealing as he went.

Little red dots appeared in the holes in the wall. They came in pairs, reflecting the firelight.

Harley ran the perimeter of the room. The squeals echoed to the top and back to the bottom. The little red dots emerged from the holes, preceded by twitching pink noses. Then they came out of the walls by the hundreds. Maybe more.

"Would you care for a walk?" the mouse lady asked.

DARYL CLIMBED OFF HER LAP, slightly annoyed. He stretched and yawned, completely uninterested in the hundreds of mice zigzagging around the room. There was some order to the chaos, like a swarm of starlings moves through the sky.

She pulled her legs out from under her. Art saw how her legs had been resting under the bench. She rubbed her knees, which, oddly, seemed more like human knees beneath her clothing.

"Candyland is a funny place," she said. "Some things never age. While the rest of us keep getting older."

He didn't know what that meant. By the sounds she made, she was in the latter group. She put her hands on the floor and prepared to stand up.

Arthur, Daryl said, not too kindly.

Art was caught watching this old mouse struggle to climb off the floor, wondering if those were normal legs under the robe. He jumped at the sound of Daryl's voice and offered his hand. The mouse lady looked up.

"Thank you, dear."

Her palm was dry and cool. Leathery.

The long fingers wrapped around his hand.

She patted his grip with her free hand. Took his arm. Pointed to the exit, where the mice were flooding out. The tea set rattled behind them. A cadre of mice raced off with the cups and pot and tray. The rest of them moved aside to avoid being stepped on or tripping the old mouse.

The outside flashed with fireflies. The mouse lady held onto his arm with both hands, stopping to inhale the cool, humid air. With the help of several mice, Harley brought a cane outside. She took it and thanked them, poked the ground with it. Then patted Art's arm, and off to the right she went.

They entered a dense grove of trees. A meandering seashell path was softly lit by downlights anchored in the canopies, simulating moonlight to guide their way. Mice were tending pocket gardens here and there where glittering crystals sprouted and bushy plants dropped candy corn on the ground. There were baskets full of harvest and, he was quite sure, some of the spent shells from the giant's basket.

The anxiety gripping his chest had relaxed. The knot in his throat dissolved. He'd forgotten about chocolate, happy to walk in the company of this human-size mouse who seemed pleased just to breathe the air and hear frogs sing.

"You want to know how to get back." She squeezed his arm. "You want to go home."

"I do."

"Hmm." The metal tip of her cane spiked into the path. They walked for several minutes. Art thought she wasn't going to answer. Then she finally said: "My husband left me here. It was before I came to this little island. He should have left long before that."

"Where did he go?"

"Climbing!" she said with a laugh. "I didn't deserve his company. I didn't want to be here, you see. Always watching the sky for the door to open. Waiting and waiting and waiting. Never here, you know. Never here. Now look at me, still here after all these bells."

She patted his arm and laughed.

"Has anyone explained *bells* to you? Daryl, why haven't you told him?"

Daryl apparently answered her because she laughed. Art knew what bells meant. But his confusion was apparent.

"You can't measure time without the sun or moon, dear. And Christmas is all that matters here. There are twelve bells between them. *Months,* you might say. Although it's been quite a long time since I've used that word."

Art nodded along.

"It's nighttime on this side," she said. "But there's beauty in darkness, Arthur. Without it, we don't see the light."

They walked without talking, again. The sound of their footsteps punctuated by the tip of the cane was all that disrupted the frogs and cicadas. The darkness accented the soft light beaming down from the trees.

"Light is the Christmas spirit, we say in Candyland," she finally said. "The joy of life."

THE MOUSE LADY turned off the seashell path, onto an uphill climb. It seemed like an awful idea. The way she was hunched over; the way her arm shook. But she did it.

One step at a time.

They emerged from the trees and were rewarded with a view.

She'd been up here before and quite a bit, judging by the narrow rut trampled into the grass. She led him to a bench weaved of saplings and vines. Looked a lot like the giant's basket. It was a bit close to a ledge. Not a far drop—twenty feet, maybe. But it was enough. She nestled onto the bench with a sigh and a grin.

Art sat next to her.

They settled into the stillness of the night. The water was an infinite pool of blackness, reflecting the flashing bugs tracing random paths in the air. Beyond was a field of green grass where moths fluttered and bats flapped.

The frogs chirruped. The cicadas whined.

The air cool and moist. A spicy texture that reminded him of hot cinnamon cider.

Daryl hopped onto his lap and curled up. His purrs were comforting and warm. Harley climbed onto the mouse lady's lap and did the same. Minus the purring. Sleep fell on Art like a blanket. Then she spoke in a rough whisper that didn't disturb the peace.

"I was sentenced here for not eating chocolate, you know."

"Sentenced?"

She shrugged. "I'm not supposed to leave. Which is fine. I've grown very fond of this island. And truth be told, I've grown too old to want anything else. They don't tell you that about aging, not when you're eighteen years old. You find joy in simple things. Like sitting down to listen."

Her laughter wheezed in her throat, then came out in croaks. She squinted. Art didn't see the humor, but he smiled just the same. Watching her.

"Why do you not eat chocolate?" he asked.

The laughter faded. She sighed and gazed across the water, thrumming her fingers on the bench between them. Then answered: "I wanted to see the beauty."

Art didn't understand. Chocolate was good. It tasted good. It *felt* good. When he ate it, the feelings that haunted him simply went away. He felt like who he was meant to be. Why would she not want that?

"I was tired of hiding," she mused. "I'd done that all my life. It's why I came to Candyland. Why I never left. Hiding from parts of my self. My *monsters*. Same reason my niece came here. She was smarter than me, got to the point quicker. I had a lot more garbage to sort through to get to my self, and I wasn't going to do it hiding in the chocolate."

"It's just *chocolate*." He chuckled.

She nodded along, never taking her gaze from the distance. Then turned to him with kindness in her eyes.

"You know, you can't be a prisoner if this is where you *want* to be. I suppose I could return to where I came from, back through the door in the sky if it ever opened again. But I came here for a reason. We all do."

They sat for a spell of silence. He didn't feel privileged to break it. In fact, he preferred to rest in it. The beauty of the night.

"Sometimes I imagine my husband sitting next to me. Him coming back and not saying a word. Just taking a seat next to me. We would share a cup of tea and watch the fireflies. And then dance like we did when we were young."

"Is that why you had the giant bring me here?"

It seemed obvious now. The giant had snatched him away from the Lost Boys, and she'd filled up the giant's basket in return. Maybe she wanted the company because her husband was off climbing. The mouse lady looked at him with a sly smile.

"Sweet Tooth? Oh, she's a dear, isn't she? A big colorful teddy who will do anything for a handful of goodies." She patted his hand as it lay between them. "You aren't staying on the island, dear, as much as I'd like the company. You have more important things to do. I just wanted to see you."

Her eyes glittered with a glassy reflection.

"And I do."

ART FELT CHILLED and strangely honored, the way she was looking at him. Through him and into him. Seeing with an openness that was vulnerable. Loving. This big mouse was the most human thing he'd met since waking up in Candyland.

It felt okay to be with her. To be here. Just here.

"I can't go back," he said. "Can I."

"The only way to leave Candyland is to change. And if you change, you won't go back. It's a conundrum. You can return, but you won't go back."

"Because I'm here for a reason." He was sick of hearing that.

"Reason?" She laughed herself into a coughing fit. "Humans are always looking for reasons when there are none. It gives them purpose. And if they don't have one, they invent one. And that's all right." She squeezed his hand (a small part of him didn't want her to let go). "You're here because you're here, dear. And that's a good enough reason."

He nodded and understood hardly any of it. But it felt good. He just had simple questions that needed simple answers.

"I am here because I'm a weapon, someone said."

"Power isn't always a weapon."

He laughed. "I'm not powerful."

She didn't refute that. The way he meant it was true. He wasn't a strong man or a tough guy. But that wasn't what she meant by power, either.

"So if I want to go back—I mean, go home... how do I do it?"

She nodded the all-knowing nod. Let the quiet between them stretch out. Looking out as if searching for something in the pasture.

"What do you see?" she asked.

Art followed her gaze. Maybe the way back was on the other side of the water. That was why she'd brought him up here. He described to her what he saw. The water. The bugs. The field and the trees beyond. She listened, and when he was done, she said it again.

"What do you see, Arthur?"

He used more detail to describe it this time. The colors and textures. The way the fireflies created the illusion of space in the water. The way the leaves on the trees shimmered. When he checked for her approval, her eyes were closed. Without opening them, she said:

"Look again. Look deeply."

He was lost. When she didn't open her eyes, he closed his eyes. If that was what she meant, he'd go along with it. They were embraced by the night. The sounds and smells. The touch. Her hand found his and grasped it lightly.

"When you see *your* light, you will never be lost."

Well, there it was. His answer. Clear as fog. You'd think he'd be used to answers like that after Grimjoy. He wasn't.

He was hoping for something more concrete, something he could put his hands around. A button to push or a door to open. A pill that would wake him up from this never-ending dream. But no—*see the light* was the answer.

What he didn't want to do was spend a thousand years or bells or whatever before he saw his light. Just show him where it was. It was pretty simple.

They returned to quiet.

He was grateful to not be talking. No more nonsense answers that made his head hurt. Just sitting there, letting peace settle like sand in water. Watching the lights. Smelling the smells. He hoped it would stay like that forever.

And then he heard the horn.

It was a long, baleful howl that came from far away.

HARLEY LEAPED off her lap and scrambled down the path. Daryl stood up and stretched. The mouse lady had not opened her eyes. She remained in silent repose even after the second and third horn called out.

There was something on the far side of the field.

A dark box emerged from the trees. It wobbled on big, skinny wheels. Too far to see what it was, but it was coming straight for them.

"The king has arrived," she said. "You will go with him to the castle."

The peace that had settled inside him petrified. The words struck him like a hammer that shattered what little peace was left. It crumbled inside him. Sharp points poking and sticking. He'd already escaped the castle once. Daryl said if he went back, he wasn't going to escape again.

"Why do I have to go?"

"Because that's why you're here."

"But I'm not here for a reason. You *said*."

She grabbed his hand. This time he hated it. It felt coarse and cold. A long-fingered claw. He pulled away from her. She wasn't hurt by the reaction. Instead, folding her hands on her lap.

Harley returned.

He lugged something with the help of three mice. A large ring of sorts. Art wasn't paying attention to what it was. He was watching the carriage get closer, inching its way across the field. A sick feeling spread across his stomach like a slick of oil.

"What am I supposed to do?" he muttered.

She reached for what Harley had brought her and fixed it upon her head. When Art turned to face her, he saw what the ring was. It surprised him, to put it mildly. Not at all what he expected her to be wearing.

"Shine, dear," she said. "You shine."

14

The crown nestled into the silver-white hair on her head. *A queen,* Art thought. *She's a queen.*

It wasn't an impressive crown. Where jewels might have once been seated now were empty sockets. There was a sense of duty attached to it. Yet she looked slightly embarrassed to put it on.

The queen whispered something to Harley. The rat scuttled away.

A minute later, a song played loud enough to carry over the water and through the trees. A song any child would know from summer. One that blared from a cheap speaker on a colorful truck that stopped at the curb to dole out ice cream to kiddos holding crinkled dollar bills in their dirty hands.

The queen stepped to the edge of the rocky outcropping. She raised her cane and waved. A heavy thump sent ripples over the water. Firefly reflections wavered. Something whumped on the shore; then a giant roll of plastic foam began to unspool. The kind of mat high school wrestlers battled on.

A team of mice gathered behind it. More came out of the rocks and underbrush. Little by little, they pushed it toward the lake. It splashed into the water and unrolled like a giant wheel, getting smaller as it rode to the other side. Bobbing on the surface. The end of it fell in front of the carriage.

The ice-cream-truck song continued its endless loop.

The carriage rolled onto the floating bridge. The narrow wheels sank into the foam surface. Water pooled around them but didn't impede it. Fireflies swarmed around the fat little elf sitting on top, with reins in his hands but no horses to steer. He was nothing more than a grumpy hood ornament, waving off the bugs flashing in his face. When the carriage reached the island, it parked in an open space. There were no roads for it to go any farther.

The ground shook. The entire island shivered.

Waves appeared in the black water. The floating bridge rocked side to side. The carriage would have gone for a drink if it were still on it. The ice-cream song stopped playing on the cheap speaker. The queen held out her arm.

"Shall we?"

Art took her frail arm. It wasn't terribly far to reach their guest, but the hillside was steep without a path. It would be a challenge for him to get down. The queen didn't stand a chance.

The ground shook again.

Art could smell what was coming. It smelled like breakfast cereal. The frosted kind.

From around the corner, Sweet Tooth appeared. Her big bare feet crashing on the ground. Water dripping from her elbows. She stomped toward the carriage. One misstep and she could turn it into kindling. The grumpy elf looked up but didn't climb down.

Sweet Tooth bent over. Looked into the blackened windows.

She looked up the hill at the queen. A smile spread across the giant's face. The one tooth as big as a billboard.

"*Yum!*"

She cupped her hands. The colorful fingernails rested in front of the queen. Art helped her step onto them. They were soft and sweet. Smelled like buttered French toast. Very carefully, Sweet Tooth lowered them. The fireflies bunched around them, whispering as they went.

Merry, merry.

Merry, merry.

Merry, merry.

"Merry, merry, my dears," the queen said. "What a lovely night it is. Thank you for lighting it for us."

The fireflies flashed brighter.

The queen strobed and glowed in the radiance of their iridescent bottoms.

The grumpy elf watched them arrive. He made no effort to dismount. Held the limp reins that connected to nothing. A dour look pulled the corners of his mouth below his chin. Daryl appeared at Art's feet, arching his back against his shins. Purring like the carriage was nothing more than a decoration and not a harbinger of doom.

The queen was unperturbed. Amused, even.

The stagecoach elf tipped his frumpy hat. She returned his gesture with a nod. The corner of his mouth twitched, attempting a smile. But the weight of his mood was too heavy to raise it.

Finally, the door on the carriage swung open. Out stepped an enormous foot, followed by a round body.

Art recognized the elf. He knew her name, but there was something different about her. She looked like Belly, from her feet to her stubby nose. The expression, though. The deadness of it wasn't friendly. This elf waddled over, grunting with each step. Sweet Tooth bent over and sniffed the round elf, ruffling her long overcoat dragging on the ground. When Sweet Tooth was satisfied (*Yum!*), the elf placed one hand over her swollen belly and sort of bowed.

"Lady Mouserinks."

"Jelly," the queen answered. "Merry, merry to you, dear."

"Blah-blah."

"Not on my island, blah-blah." But the queen seemed pleased to see the elf and said: "You've gained weight."

"Thank you. Switched to eggnog in the mornings."

"I like it. Very wintery."

Jelly stared through suspicious slits. The queen introduced Art. And Daryl. Jelly didn't acknowledge them. Art looked away. The elf kept staring. Studying him. Art picked up Daryl. The comforting ball of fur warded off the judgy stares from Jelly and the stagecoach driver.

The queen spoke with an edge of impatience. "Is he coming out?"

"I think so," Jelly said. "You know how he is."

"Does he need a pep talk?"

Jelly smirked. "He can hear you."

"I know," she whispered. "Go on and fetch him. It'll be Christmas if we wait for him."

The elf waddled back to the carriage and rapped on the door. "She's here, Your Majesty." The sarcasm was thick enough to butter toast. "So's the boy."

A voice muttered from inside the carriage. Jelly put her ear to the door and nodded. Then looked at the queen and shrugged.

"Tell him we'll be inside, then," the queen said. "We have tea to finish. Sweet Tooth will come for us when he's ready to come out. She'll be happy to—"

The door slammed against the carriage, nearly swatting Jelly into the water. Mechanical sounds hissed and whined. The carriage rocked side to side. Something squeezed through the doorway. It looked like a balloon dressed in a theater curtain. The balloon turned toward the queen. Tiny legs twittered beneath the swollen body. The hard soles scraping the gritty soil.

What is that? Art thought.

He'd thought he'd seen everything. But this was most unusual. It was a massive figure draped in a ton of heavy fabric. The cheeks and chins folded around dark purple lips as thick as rope. Two brown eyes were pushed deep into the flesh. And sitting on his head was a crown only a child would draw—a gaudy thing three feet tall and dipped in chocolate and rolled in gemstones.

"*Yum!*" Sweet Tooth announced.

"No! It's too late for forgiveness. Eat these and shut up." The king threw a handful of gold coins at the giant. Sweet Tooth ate them without taking off the wrappings. "Don't be greedy," the king said when Sweet Tooth sniffed the ground for more.

The mountainous king floated closer with a hum and hiss. The legs were disturbing, the way they twittered like useless appendages. He floated higher and looked down at the queen. Jelly stepped aside, gnawing on a hangnail.

"Looking gray," he said to the queen. "Tail still super long, I see."

"Merry, merry, Casey. I like your tailor. The hoversuit is working good, yes?"

"It feels good to walk again." He clicked his puppet heels, then rotated toward Art. "You're the boy, I assume. I'm the king. Call me that."

He snapped his fingers. Jelly tossed him a chocolate wafer. The king didn't catch it and snapped his fingers again. He kept snapping until Jelly fetched it. She put it in the king's open hand. The king threw it to Art.

"I got a never-ending supply," the king said. "Only game in town, boy. So you're welcome." It was the same chocolate wafer Rude Boy had given him in the market. "Now, to business. What did she say? About me, specifically. Out with it. Go."

Art shook his head. "Nothing."

"She didn't say nothing? Bah! Lies flow from her like Lemonade Falls."

"I never heard of you."

The king flinched. That wasn't what he wanted to hear. Not at all. He swung at the fireflies hovering around him and snarled at the cat cradled in Art's arms. Daryl was asleep.

"Good catching up with you," he said to the queen. "Let's not do it so soon. Come on, boy. There's plenty of room. Climb aboard."

The king spun like a top and teetered like a balloon in a gust of wind. When the hoversuit rebalanced, he floated to the carriage. Art tried not to look at the legs. The king started to shove his way through the doorway. He turned his head like a turret on a tank.

To Jelly, he said: "Did he not hear me?"

"I believe he did."

They looked at Art. "I'm not going," Art said.

"I didn't ask." The king offered a smile full of brown teeth. "I am the king. That's how this works."

"He doesn't want to go with you, Casey," the queen added.

"Stay out of this!" He bounced like a kickball and sounded like one, too. "You stole him from me. You sent the Sweet Tooth after him. Then you filled his brain with lies. I can smell the fibs on him like dog farts."

He spun toward Art.

"She's a liar, Arty. She tell you she's a mouse? Yeah, I bet she did. Ever see a mouse that big? No, you haven't because she's a rat. Look at her. The tail and the fur and the... *ick.*"

"You sent the Lost Boys for him," she said.

"They're fine lads."

"They're scrappers."

"So? That's how they do it. It's in their blood. The boy is like them. Ask him yourself. You're a lost boy, ain't you?"

Art didn't answer. But he knew what the king was getting at. Art felt the draw to ride a beam, to fly through the trees.

"He would be at the castle by now if it weren't for you," the king said. "In his own room. Now look at him. He's hungry. He's tired. You poisoned his brain, and I'll have to fix that."

His hands flailed about innocently. Then he spun on Sweet Tooth.

"And you! The next time you betray me, the king—*your* king... I'm cutting you off. No more chocolate. You hear me? Go fend for yourself in the jungle. And you'd better not raid my fields, or it'll get worse. I can do that. I can make your life not yummy. Trust me, you clown."

"*Yum?*" Sweet Tooth looked at the queen.

"Don't look at her. I'm number one. She's number two. Actually, she's number one *thousand.* I rule. You get it? Now you, get in the carriage," he said to Art. "Now!"

The king whistled like he was a dog. He threw gold-wrapped coins of chocolate at him. He clicked his tongue.

Art did not move. Not even when Sweet Tooth snuffled up the chocolate coins.

"This is not how you want to do this," the queen said.

The king ignored her. He muttered to Jelly and turned the color of a ripe plum, whining like an overworked fuel pump.

"Fine! What do you want?"

"Ask Art," the queen said.

"Great. What do you want, Art? Huh? You want chocolate? Done. A foot massage? I'll make it happen. What do I have to do to get you in my sweet ride?"

"I want to go home."

"No. What? You can't go home. Didn't someone tell him that already?"

Art wasn't getting in that carriage. In fact, he didn't plan to leave the island. This was the first time he felt at home since waking up in this nightmare. The king could feel it, too. So did Jelly.

"Lady Mouserinks will come with us," Jelly said.

"What?" The king laughed. It was a bit maniacal. "That's crazy talk. She doesn't want to go anyway. She loves it on this rock. Don't you, Rinksie. You love it. I tell you what. Where's my..."

He pretended to search his pockets. Jelly knew what he was doing. Perhaps they'd done this act before. She handed an instant camera to him.

"Say cheese."

The king pulled the photo out and fanned it. He held up a shot of the queen and Art.

"Look at you two," he said. "It's good. You closed your eyes, Rinks, but we can fix that. We'll frame it, put it on the wall. Your own bedroom, Arty. What's your favorite food? Chocolate pudding? It'll be on tap. You won't even have to get up. Oh, how about a beam tube? We have a whole park you can ride without those Lost Boys getting in your hair. You smelling what I'm stepping in, son?"

He hovered closer. The smell of salty dough grew stronger.

"You get in that carriage and it's whatever you want."

"I want the queen."

Art wasn't sure why he blurted that out. He meant it, of course. He wasn't going anywhere without her. She listened to him. She heard him. *She saw him.* But he didn't want to go anywhere, really. He also knew this floating blob was going to get his way. Art was going to go with him one way or the other. And Art knew, he just knew the king didn't want the queen to come, also.

The color he turned meant Art was right.

The king gagged on his anger. Thumped his sides and twittered his twiggy legs.

Without a word, he spun around a dozen times before zooming to the carriage. He shoved himself inside, getting stuck for a moment. Jelly waited. They all did. And then the king popped his meaty face out the door.

"You," he said to the queen. "You ride in the back. I don't want anyone seeing you. No waving back if they do. And no rats, either. Not one! No touching me, either. Like ever. And no eye contact."

"That's not nice," Art said, bristling at the way he spoke to her.

"Son, I'm the king of the Naughty Side. What do you expect?"

THE CARRIAGE WAS a big box on wheels. With the king inside, Art very much doubted there was room for anyone else.

Wrong.

A twenty-foot ceiling. Shag carpet. Loungers and recliners.

Art and the queen settled into a velvet couch. Daryl curled up on Art's lap. Harley wasn't along for the ride, per the king's orders. Jelly climbed into a plastic bucket seat and spun it toward the chocolate king filling a throne at the far end, poured into it like melted flesh wearing a crown. His robe could house a Boy Scout troop.

The king was eating an ice-cream cone. Chocolate dripped over his knuckles and wet his purple lips. It sounded like eels fighting. His tongue darting over the melting globs, he reached back with a fist and hammered the wall.

"Let's go!"

The room jerked and leaned. The chandelier chattered on the ceiling, swinging to one side and then the other. Shutters dropped on the walls and slid back from the ceiling. A panoramic view of the sky opened. It was projections of the other side, Art assumed, since he didn't see the grumpy elf sitting on top. They sat in awkward quiet, watching the trees jostle past, listening to the king snorkel through a bowl of pudding.

The rats did not follow. Neither did Sweet Tooth.

"So how have you been, Jelly?" the queen asked. "I've missed you."

The elf looked at the king, who wasn't watching or couldn't possibly have heard her over the sounds he was making. Jelly spun the chair and half-whispered. Told her how things had been since she'd gone. It sounded like she hadn't been in the castle for quite some time. Twenty bells, Art guessed. Maybe longer. Art couldn't follow their conversation. But one thing was clear. Jelly missed the queen, too.

"I met your sister," Art said. "I think."

"I know," Jelly said. "How is she?"

Arthur shrugged. "Nice."

"Of course she's nice. So nice you jumped out of the castle."

"I was tricked." Art pointed at the sleeping cat.

"You regret it, then?"

He did not. If he hadn't jumped, he would be drowning in sweet nothings. He liked the Nice Side. The way it felt. The air was warmer. Sweeter. The songs uplifting. And he missed the residents, most of them anyway. The Gingerbreads, for sure.

But there was something about the Naughty Side that felt like home.

THE TREES WENT by with decorations around their trunks and fruited ornaments on their limbs. Once on the main road, pedestrians got out of the way and kissed their fingers and waved at the carriage like a limousine full of celebrities.

The sky didn't change. The dimness remained uniform and starless.

They passed through another small forest and emerged to views of hills and valleys, crossing over an arching bridge that spanned the Lemonade River. The current fizzy and loud. The second stream was much smaller. The horseless carriage passed through the Orange Brook without a bridge or even a plank. The smell of orange soda filled the carriage and made the king thirsty. He chugged a gallon of chocolate milk before they made it to the other side of the brook.

"Aw! Lookee there." The king twisted in the throne to look at the mountains behind him. "The chocolate fields are in view. Aren't they lovely?"

The king explained the operations between ice-cream sandwiches and pitchers of milkshakes. The mountains rose on the horizon. None quite so high as the Two-Face Mountain—the volcano-shaped mountain straddling the Nice and Naughty Sides. But they were plenty high. Art could see the harvesters the king described by the plumes of chaff floating like smog. And the shipping containers that rode ziplines down to transporters that took the harvest to processing plants.

Great erector sets trolled the fields with long spidery legs and blue electric arcs. The king didn't say what they did. But he did say with a very full mouth: "It's mine. All of it's mine."

"It's a blight," the queen said. "An unsustainable operation. Nothing survives and nothing grows where you harvest."

"She's jealous." He unleashed a wet burp into his fist. Then shouted at the ceiling: "How much longer?"

"Fudgy Lake up ahead," Jelly said.

"Oh, yay."

The king was elated. The floating boosters whined beneath his clothing, lifting him slightly out of the throne, enough for him to turn around and see the bubbling tar pits at the bottom of the road. Fumes hovered over the viscous surface. The air thick and warped. Nothing grew along the shoreline. There was no beach. Just black muck.

There was a structure, though. It looked like a lifeguard tower with a short plank at the top. Too short for a diving board. Too stiff to bounce. It was more for walking off. A rank smell filled the carriage as they neared it. Anaerobic pluff mud at low tide mixed with burnt sugar and boiled syrup.

The queen turned away. It was the result of harvesting, no doubt. A cesspool of greed.

As they started up the final hill, the sky grew darker and bruised. The tip of a dagger appeared just over the top of the slope. It absorbed what little light there was and continued to grow as they got closer, a monolith of sharp edges hacked away from a spire of obsidian. It was a deformed tombstone of the land. The light around it dreary and depressed.

When they breached the hill, tiny specks of light became visible.

The carriage paused. A long and winding road lay below them, winding its way to the base of that dead fang, crossing over a bridge that spanned a lake of tar surrounding the castle. Strands of Christmas lights swung in the trees, half of them blinking or not working at all.

The chocolate king settled into his throne. A sloppy, brown smile opened on his cheeky face. A coughing fit wet with phlegm and ice cream shook all his chins. Then he delivered chilling words.

"Welcome home, boy."

<h1 style="text-align:center">15</h1>

The catapult was made from a jawbreaker tree. The frame carved from its heartwood, giving it an amber hue. The wheels were peppermint patties. The spring coiled licorice.

It was a prototype. Could fit in King Chocolate's front pocket. Sometimes he carried it with him. He never knew when there was time to kill.

Like now.

The small-fry catapult was sitting on a dining table. The ice-cream scoop was loaded with a beautifully sculpted chocolate ball (a seamless orb no bigger than a marble). The licorice spring under tension. He adjusted the angle, turned it a few degrees to the left. When he flicked the switch, the catapult convulsed.

The ice-cream scoop sprang.

The chocolate ball went airborne.

King Chocolate leaned back and watched it arc toward the vaulted ceiling, through the fudge-dipped chandelier, reaching a crescendo and pausing before giving way to gravity. Falling like a flawless planet toward the gaping black maw full of brown teeth and a chocolate-coated tongue.

It landed in his mouth with perfect accuracy. No touch of the teeth or rattle in the throat. The lovely ball of chocolate settled on the king's swollen tongue. Melting. Painting the inside of his cheeks. Sliding down his throat with an angelic feeling of wellness and goodness. And *ahhhhhh.*

"The kitchen wants to know if you want another snack," Jelly said.

The king choked on the perfect moment. If he had been holding something, anything, he would have thrown it. He sat up and swallowed the soft lump before it completely melted.

"I told you—" He coughed into his fist. "I told you not to interrupt."

"You know how you get when you're hungry. Anything else?"

"Yeah. Like, uhhhh..." He threw his hands at the empty table. "I'm waiting, Jelly Roll. I'm the king. I don't wait."

"Give the boy a tick. This is new. I don't think he's hungry."

"What's hungry got to do with anything?" The king was serious. He never understood why others waited until they were hungry to eat. "So what—I just sit here and wait till he's *hungry*?"

He hung air quotes.

Jelly waddled closer. Reached over the table and loaded the catapult. When she launched the weapon, King Chocolate swatted the chocolate ball away. It bounced behind an antique jukebox playing a song the boy would know. At least, Jelly thought so.

"Get the eye," the king demanded. "And pick that up."

He wasn't going to let good chocolate go to waste. He'd made his point.

A few ticks later, a large orb was put in place of the catapult. It could be mistaken for a bowling ball. It was heavy and smooth with a swirling pattern of browns and grays on the surface. There were no finger holes because it was not used for sport.

Spying was what it did.

It was a receiver. A looking glass. *An eye.*

The king waved his hands around it (he did that whenever he used it; it wasn't necessary to start the thing up) and leaned closer. Jelly waited for him to finish his magic hand signals, then activated the transmission. A room appeared inside the globe. A boy by a window. The Mousequeen next to him.

It looked like magic. If you asked the king, that was what he would say. It totally was not magic.

It was science.

Tiny cameras the size of pollen were all over the castle. You couldn't blow your nose without shooting a few hundred into a hanky. It was Santa technology. Technically, it was elf technology. Santa got the credit. It was what he used to decide the naughty or nice children. At least, that was what the king said. Jelly let him think that.

The king didn't understand science. He liked magic.

His breath fogged the glass. He wiped it with his sleeve and smudged it with chocolate. The more he rubbed, the worse it got. There wasn't much to see or hear. The boy and the queen were talking about feelings. The boy didn't really want to be here. The queen asked him to describe what his emotions felt like.

"What does she want from him?" the king wondered.

"It's called active listening," Jelly answered. "She's quite good at it."

The king turned his head like a bird listening for the worm. The boy had closed his eyes now and was describing the tightness in his chest. The tension in his forehead. The king frowned. Not because he was gravely bored or because of what Jelly said or the tone with which she said it (he didn't hear a word she said).

"I'm going to punish Sweet Tooth," the king declared. "If she hadn't kidnapped the boy, I wouldn't be *WAITING!*"

"Look at it this way," Jelly said. "He trusts her."

"How does that help me?"

"I don't know. What do you want?"

"What do you mean, what do I want? I want the boy in this room! I've made that pretty clear."

"I'm talking big picture. What do you want with the boy?"

"I want him to do his thing."

"And what's that?"

"To do what I want."

"And what do you want him to do? Big picture—"

"Yeah, I get what big picture means. Right now I want you to shut up."

"Humor me. What's the end game? What do you want more than anything else?"

"I want to win!" The king didn't have to think about that. His yellowed eyes grew round. "What else is there?"

"That's right. You want to win. And the boy is here. And he's here because of *her*. Not you. He wasn't going to come with you. He came *here* because of her. You need the queen because you need him to win."

He could argue that if Sweet Tooth hadn't kidnapped the boy, he would've come straight here without the queen. The king grumbled but didn't say that. It started somewhere inside his throat. His fingers curled into his palms. Puffs of steam seeped out of his ears. Jelly could feel the heat from where she was standing. The king didn't like the queen much. He liked the truth even less. Jelly was right, and he did not like it.

The king knocked on the eye. It rattled with static, then gave up a squeal of feedback.

"Dinner's getting cold." The king spoke into the eye. "*Now*."

To the boy, the king's voice sounded like it came out of thin air. The queen was used to his announcements. She didn't flinch. She was cold, that one. The king called her a NINO and called her that often. *Naughty in Name Only*. It was obvious. But she was cold when she needed to be. Usually when he was around.

He was going to heat her up.

KING CHOCOLATE'S quiet fury cooled when Art the Fart walked into the dining hall.

The boy was taking in the wonder of the place, holding the purring furball against his chest. The king could see how he looked around, lips parted, eyes big and greedy. The boy appreciated what the king had, that was obvious. Had the king kept the eye on, he would've heard the queen coaching the boy how to act. It was her little secret on how to soften up his excellency. *Be amazed and awed,* she had said. *Even if you aren't.*

"Welcome!" King Chocolate threw his arms wide. The hoversuit hummed into overdrive, lifting him out of his throne. "Take your time, my boy. Let it soak in."

There was a three-tier fountain that spilled silky streams of milk chocolate. The decadent chocolate chandelier. The life-size statue of yours truly in the corner, sculpted from a block of virgin chocolate by an artistic ant colony (a very famous colony, the Triad assured him). It was all very expensive. And they did it for free. They liked the king that much.

Candy dispensers on the wall. A milkshake machine, too.

Chocolate chip pancakes stacked as high as a refrigerator.

Chocolate-dipped strawberries.

Chocolate flake cereal drowning in chocolate milk.

Chocolate cake. Chocolate pie. Chocolate donuts. Chocolate pudding. And brownies.

"It's all about the cocoa bean, my boy," the king crooned. "The flavor profile is affected by the weather and the soil, the harvesting techniques, and the genetic profile. All very complicated stuff my growers monitor closely. I don't want to bore you."

The king couldn't bore him because he didn't know any more than that.

"Besides being delicious, chocolate is the most versatile food ever grown. Breakfast, lunch, dinner, dessert. We drink it, we eat it, we smell it, we wear it. There are over eight hundred flavor notes in a bite of the dark stuff, you know. Eight *hundred.*"

The boy nodded with extreme interest. The king felt a tickle in his belly. He began peeling the wrapper from a chocolate bar off a stack of them.

"Try this. It's brand new. I'll be releasing it after Christmas. It's a dark red chili bar. You're going to love it."

He offered it to the boy. Art leaned forward and sniffed it. Wrinkled his nose. The pang of rejection was a fastball to the king's chest. He resisted digging through his pile for something else, something the boy would like.

Jelly gestured. *Relax.*

The king took a deep breath. A little more time and the chocolate fumes would do their thing. The boy wouldn't resist for long. No one could. No one except the Ice Queen.

"Figurines?" the queen said. "Really, Casey?"

She was admiring the delicately carved display. Each with a remarkable resemblance to the king. "How'd those get in here?" the king said. "Come, come. Sit, please. You're my guests. No more flattery, please. This table was cut from Two-Face Mountain. I had it polished for this occasion. No big deal. Pull up a chair."

The king ran his fingers over the smooth, marbled surface, his rings making long metallic sounds. The boy looked confused. The queen picked up on it, too. Then she explained what Two-Face Mountain was. "The big one," she said. "Half-light, half dark."

"The one on the border?" the boy said.

"That's the one," the king added. *Duh.* "You're a smart boy, I can tell. I'll bet you're funny, too. He looks funny, don't you think, Jel?"

Jel? He'd never called her that before. Jelly shook her head. He was trying too hard. That made him feel stupid. He took a long, deep breath. Pointed at two empty chairs.

"Sit," he said. It was more of a command.

They did. They sat. Even the cat sat on the boy's lap. The king was pleased.

"There's a bowl of chocolate wafers right there," the king said. "If you don't like those, try the chocolate-covered peanuts. Oh, oh, there are—"

"Cheese, please," the queen said. "And a glass of milk."

The king warmed a few degrees. Jelly waited for him to nod. It was slight. Barely visible. It was all he could do without having a meltdown. She knew what he was doing, waving all these chocolates under the boy's nose. And she was going to stink up the place.

"Would cheddar be all right, Lady Mouserinks?" Jelly asked.

"Lovely, Jelly. Thank you."

"And for the boy?"

He shook his head. Said he wasn't hungry. Jelly went to fetch the queen her snack of cheese and milk. At least she didn't ask for blue cheese. He would've stopped that. First of all, gross. Second, the stink of that moldy stuff got into everything—clothes, hair, skin. Name it and blue cheese ruined it.

They sat there awkwardly. Waiting for the elf to return. The king drumming his fingers on the polished table. He nudged a bowl of chocolate donut holes toward the boy.

Nothing.

Like he wasn't even tempted.

"She told you she doesn't eat the chocolate, didn't she?" The king's shine dimmed a few degrees. "It's bad for you, she tell you that?"

He scoffed. It was wet and phlegmy.

"It contains antioxidants, did you know that? That's going to lower your blood pressure. Reduces risk of strokes. Increases blood circulation. She tell you that? Makes your heart healthy. Yeah, it does that, too. Makes a good heart. Strong heart. It prevents liver damage, also. It makes you smarter, too. Boosts those things that make you think, you know what I mean? The *genius snack* is what they call it. She didn't tell you, did she."

Pretty obvious she didn't.

The boy *wanted* to eat it. The king saw that, too.

The king took a thin wafer from the big bowl. He rubbed it lightly between his finger and thumb. "Appreciate chocolate. Coax the flavor out with a little massage. Feel the texture on your fingertips. Admire the sheen it radiates."

He held it up.

With two hands, he delicately broke the wafer in half, holding it to his ear when he did so. It gave a sharp snap.

"Hear that? The sound of *perfection*," he whispered. "Bask in it before placing it on your tongue and allowing it to melt slowly—oh so slowly."

He stuck out his tongue. Gently, he laid the chocolate on the fat piece of purple meat sticking out of his mouth. He closed his eyes. When it turned to sludge and slipped into his flabby jowls, he said: "Taste the beginning and the end. They're different, my boy. Sometimes fruity. Sometimes floral or earthy."

He clicked his tongue and swallowed.

"Most of all, chocolate *feels* good."

When he opened his eyes, the boy was staring down at the table. This didn't hurt the king. Not at all. He could see the longing. The hook was set. It was just a matter of time. Even with the queen at his side, the boy wasn't going to hold out forever. And once he gave in to the sweet side, he would be in the king's command.

Winning.

A PLATTER OF CHEESE ARRIVED. All the queen's favorites: thin triangles of cheddar and muenster and mascarpone and the dreaded gorgonzola. An odor of wet gym socks soaked in swamp water hovered over the tray and tainted his chocolate. Any other day and he'd throw the platter out the window. This day was a special day.

The king smiled a dark smile. Forced as it was, but still a smile.

"Great jingle bells, look at the size of that monster," the king said. He jabbed a bloated finger at Daryl. "An animal after my heart, he is. What is it? A cat? Oh, that's a fine animal. What's the thing's name?"

"Daryl," the boy said.

More importantly, the boy said it with affection. Not intended for the king, but affection, nonetheless. It was a crack the king would exploit.

"Jelly says it likes to scratch things. Posts and whatnot. We'll have a dozen in your room, just for him. Just for Daryl. How do you like that?"

The boy smiled, just a little. The king's heart added a beat.

"Daryl crossed with Arthur," the queen said. "They're familiars."

It took all the king's effort to maintain his smile. As stiff as it was,

he turned those greedy eyes on his royal partner just as she nibbled
the corner off a hunk of gouda. The odor drew tears into the corners
of his eyes. She smiled back. Even winked.

He maintained. Until a wad of hair floated by. As light as a cloud
and just as soft, it drifted across the table. Undoubtedly on its way to
ruin a bowl of wafers. He could imagine it getting stuck in his mouth.
Like cotton candy that didn't melt.

"Cats are fun," he said. Then back to the boy: "Do you like your
room? It's nothing permanent, of course. Just a little something while
you're here. No pressure."

"A lot of games in that room, Casey," the queen said. "Barely space
for him to lie down."

"Well, yeah. You're boring."

The boy's smile grew a little bit. Just a little and the king liked it.
Oh yes, he did. And not so subtly he nudged a bowl of malted chocolate bombs toward him. The boy noticed.

Oh yes, he did.

"So, we're having a Christmas Eve concert," the king said. "Would
you like to guess who's the guest of honor?"

The king walked his fingers in the boy's direction.

"That's why we brought you here, after all. To the Naughty Side. It
was to honor you, young man. Your courage. Your curiosity. You're
not like fuddy-duddy here, sitting around huffing fragrant candles
and playing with rats. You're fun. And that's exactly what this party is
going to be. *Lit!*" He chuckled, unsure if he used that word right. The
boy didn't laugh at him. "There will be games and stuff and a hard-
rocking show. Oh, I almost forgot!"

The king attempted to snap his fingers.

"The Big Bad Wolf. Heard of him? He'll be there, won't he, Jelly.
He's going to want to see your piggy shirt, for sure. Love on that, son.
Especially when he hears you nicked it from the three little oinkers.
That's what I heard, you snatched it right off their clothesline. Up
high."

The king offered a high five.

The boy patted his hand with less enthusiasm than the king had hoped for. But he hit it. Oh yes, he did. *Baby steps.*

"Anyways, we're going to change up the concert this year. Just for you, Artie. I'll be taking over for Santa."

"I think that's a wonderful idea," the queen said.

"Okay, that's enough," the king said. When Jelly poked him in the side, a poke he barely felt but understood, the king added: "It was her idea."

"Your idea?" the boy said.

Jelly got that one right. The boy brightened when the king gave the queen the credit.

"No, no," the queen said. "It was the king and queen of the Nice Side. They proposed it. I only supported it. I think it's about time—"

"Enough about them, Lady Mouserinks," the king said. He used her formal name, and the boy smiled. "Those two goody-goods trapped our dear boy in the tower and planned never to let him go. Not so nice, if you ask me. I'm an expert on naughty. If this fat cat hadn't tricked you into jumping out the window, you'd still be up there."

The king hammered the table with a meaty fist. Then elbowed a tray of chocolate-dipped cherries in the boy's direction.

"Have you ever met Santa?" the king said. "Did I ask you that already? The jolly fat man is not so very nice to us, Artie. You've heard what he puts in our stockings? Fills them right up like a dirty joke. Every Christmas. It was funny the first time. Not so much anymore."

He leaned closer but didn't whisper.

"We're not all bad, Artie. Misunderstood, maybe. Heartbroken, possibly. But we ain't bad. And coal isn't making us nicer, I can tell you that. You think the jolly fat man's never made a mistake?"

The queen nibbled a cracker all proper like. She looked bored.

"You think *she's* never made a mistake?" the king shouted. "Ha!"

He mashed a fist full of candy-coated chocolates into his mouth until his cheeks were chipmunked. Then poured a gallon of chocolate milk after them. He sopped up the mess with his sleeves. His charm transformed into hot annoyance, as it usually did when it came to Queen Lady Mouserinks.

"You want to know how bad she was? I'll tell you. She didn't have to come here, Artie. She *deserved* to be here. That's how bad she was. The things she did. Opening presents before Christmas. Switching price tags at the toy store. How you like that? She would steal candy and not even eat it. Just for the thrill. Throw it in the ditch after she took it. You believe that? She *burned* all her sister's trophies or threw them in a lake. What?! She did that to her sister, Artie. Her sister. Can you imagine!"

Somehow, the queen looked more bored than before. She wasn't denying anything he said because it was all true. But the guilt and shame weren't dragging behind her anymore.

"Even her husband couldn't stand her."

Confusion contorted the boy's face. He looked at the queen. "He's not your husband?"

"Me?" King Chocolate said. "Oh, no. No, no, nooooooo. God, no."

The boy's disappointment was right there for her to see. She felt it like a ten-foot stick on the back of her legs. Even winced a little. The king tamped down the joy he felt and fanned the flames of indignity. Waved his hands at the injustice (and slapped a stack of chocolate bars in front of the boy).

"Oh, no. Her husband was another guy. He left because she was awful, Artie. Capital *A*! She sought me out when she crossed over, came straight to the castle and won my heart. One look at her and I knew she was terrible. I'd found my equal. She was the queen of the Naughty. The only one who could sit next to me and rule from her heart. Her dark, dark heart."

The king drooled with anticipation. Watching the boy devour the gossip like cocoa beans.

"But... you're not like that now," the boy said. "Why?"

"*Why?* Who cares why. She's nice, Artie. Look at her. She stinks of it. She lost her edge. What'd you say? You were tired of being you. So you changed. Admit it, Rinks. Admit to the boy you changed."

Art didn't hear a word the king said. His gaze was expecting the queen to answer. She placed the cheese she'd been nibbling on the plate, dabbed her mouth with a linen napkin, and chewed while staring at her lap. Maybe she was waiting for the boy to get the hint that she didn't want to answer. Maybe she didn't know why she changed. The king never asked why. He never cared.

Then she looked up with those creepy eyes. Glanced at the king. Then to the boy.

"From the time I was very little, I had these feelings. I couldn't explain them, couldn't tell you why I had them or what they meant. They were dark feelings. I didn't have words for them then, like guilt or shame. I just had them and didn't know why. I hated them. I hated the way they felt. And I blamed myself for having them, like they were my fault. Like I deserved them for some reason. I was a little girl, and I hated myself for having those feelings. And I hated myself for hating myself because of the feelings."

She looked down at her knobby fingers twisted into knots.

"They were heavy and loathsome. They made me feel ugly. I ran from them. I spent my life running from them, and the faster I ran, the uglier I felt. I couldn't get away from them. I didn't know what else to do. I had to get those feelings out of me. So that's what I did. I put them out into the world and made everyone feel them, too. I hurt my family and my friends. The more I hurt them, the better I felt. Well, not better. Relieved, I suppose. Hurt people hurt people, they say. I was pretty good at both. It was all I knew, Arthur."

She pushed her plate away, still playing a painful game of twisting fingers.

"Then I came here, to Candyland. All the things I'd done in my life—all the runnin', all the hurtin'—this was where I belonged. The naughties were my people. They got me. They understood what it was like living with a shadow. They knew what it felt like to be cold on the inside. I could be as naughty as I wanted here, Arthur, and no one judged me. Here, I let it all out."

A long pause grew longer. The king squirmed in his throne. Apparently, her story was over. A terrible ending. Incomplete, really. But he was glad it was over. "And then," he started to say, "you—"

"I grew tired, Arthur. It's that simple, really. Time is funny here. At times it feels like eternity. And I was tired of running for all that time. Tired of who I'd been all my life. Tired of the anger, of the bitterness and hate. I was tired of the hurt that would not heal. All I'd ever done was beat those feelings down or beat others with them. Feelings I tried to ignore or pretend weren't there. That if I could just drown them with distractions and—" She threw her arms out at the table, and the king took a little offense to that. Like it was the chocolate's fault she was so bad. "None of this helped. Because the feelings were still there."

She shook her head. Another pregnant pause on a cliffhanger ending. Maybe that was it, but the boy had to go and drag more out of her, asking what happened next. The king wasn't having any more of it.

"Change! That's what happened, I already told you. She *wanted* to change. Hit her bottom, got sick and tired of being sick and tired, blah, blah, blah. It doesn't matter. You crossers are always changing. A true Lander stays the same." He thumped his chest. It sounded like an overripe melon. "Our true colors never fade. We are who we are, forever and ever. But not crossers. You change, you grow, you shrivel and turn gross. It's disgusting. I can barely look at her."

Jelly elbowed the king hard enough for it to hurt. The more he insulted the queen, the more the boy grew distant.

"You can't trust a crosser, that's all I'm saying. I mean, I didn't say it. It's what I heard. I'm just saying, how can you trust something that changes? Am I right?"

"That's why your husband left?" The boy had not looked away from the queen. Was he even listening to the king? "Because now you're nice?"

"That's *exactly* why he left!" the king shouted. Then: "No, wait. No, he left *way* before that. Aren't you listening, son? He left because she was *awful!* Let me tell you, son, those were the good times. This one right here, Ms. Queen of the Naughty, Ms. Hurt the World, Ms. Don't Mess with Me—she was *too naughty* even for her husband. And he was a piece of work, trust me. He was a thief. A good one, too. Stole from me, he did. If I ever catch that rat, he'll be licking the bottom of Fudgy Lake with all seven heads."

The boy frowned at that. The king smiled deliciously. The boy looked slightly disgusted. *Here's an angle,* the king thought, *to make the queen seem even grosser.*

"The queen's husband, he has seven heads. You didn't know that? Imagine, a big head and then six smaller heads growing out of his neck. *That's her husband!* Picture that a tick. It's painful to watch, the way they all talked at the same time. Hideous. Hard to look at. He lost his wits, too, just like her. Started doing nice things way before she did, but he couldn't decide which side he belonged on. He was more damaged than Grimjoy, and you've seen those lunatics. You can't straddle the border, son. That's a rule around here. *Pick a lane or go insane.*"

Jelly nodded. She had his back on that one.

If the king had stopped there, maybe there would be a different ending to this story. Suppose you could say that about any small detail. But this was no small slip-up. The king wanted to poke the queen some more. It hurt her for Art to hear the truth. The king went digging for more hurt.

"Is S'ven still on the mountain, Rinks? If he is, he'd better not come back or—"

"S'ven's your husband?"

The boy stood up. The chair cracked on the floor. The king would ordinarily make someone pay for that. But he was more worried about the boy's fierce reaction. All at once, he felt his connection slip away from him.

"Why do you think they call him S'ven?" The king held up seven chocolate-stained fingers. *Like, duh.* "Wait, do you know him?"

"I've been looking for him. He's supposed to get me out of here!"

The king was alarmed to hear this. And alarmed was not when he did his best thinking. But this time was different. The boy's disgust for the queen suddenly morphed into affection for her. *Forgiveness.* The king realized, without Jelly having to tell him, there would be no way to change that. It didn't matter how naughty she *had been*. That wasn't who she was *now*.

The king needed to win the boy's heart to get what he wanted.

The queen had already done that. But it wasn't too late.

"He's coming to the Christmas Eve concert," the king said.

"I thought you said he couldn't come back," the boy said.

"Well, no. But this is Christmas Eve we're talking about. I know for a fact he's coming to the concert. Right, Jelly?"

"Right," she said, not skipping a beat.

"And do you know why he's coming here? So... you... can... *meet him*! If anyone can take you back home, it's going to be that seven-headed weirdo. We don't want you here, no offense. Crossers go home. Am I right, Jelly?"

"You are correct, sire."

"You didn't tell the boy S'ven was coming?" the king asked the queen. "Maybe you are naughty."

The king laughed for real. It was loud and obnoxious and right in her stunned, cheese-stinking face. Talk about checkmate. She had nothing to say because she didn't know where her thieving husband had gone off to. Last King Chocolate heard, he'd gone up Two-Face Mountain and never came down. Maybe he did go back home. All the king knew for sure was the boy wasn't going home. Not if he could help it.

"Let's celebrate!" the king cheered. "To home!"

He bit off the end of a chocolate bar and handed the rest to the boy. With a smile of relief (and without thinking of the queen), the boy took it from him. He sat down with a stunned look, imagining what home was like. And then he did it.

He took a bite.

He chewed it. He swallowed it.

And he smiled brighter than ever. Because chocolate felt good. Chocolate made all the problems go away.

"Have you ever met Santa?" the king asked.

❄

"LADY MOUSERINKS," King Chocolate said, "can we talk?"

He said it with exaggerated sweetness. He didn't want to upset the boy, who had a fistful of chocolate wafers and a pocketful of malted choco-balls. Jelly would make sure a mudslide soda was waiting in his room to wash all that yumminess down.

The queen whispered something to the boy (something about a toothbrush, no doubt) on his way out. Jelly escorted him out of the room. The queen returned to the table, where the plate of expensive cheese wasn't even half eaten. She reached for her chair.

"Don't bother. I'll keep it short."

The king leaned all the way back in his throne and squeezed a tube of chocolate frosting into his gaping mouth. Put a little swirl on the top. He swished it under his tongue and over his teeth, between his cheeks and gums and savored every flavor.

He'd been a powerful king in his time. Undefeated as far as he could remember. The conquests. The intimidation. The fear his name invoked was thrilling. At first. You get used to it after a while. It becomes normal. When a child cried at the sight of him, he used to feel powerful. Now he felt nothing. When a resident quivered in fear, now it was just another day.

But this. *Oh this.*

He wanted this so bad. So, so bad it hurt his bones. When the boy refused to get in the carriage, he'd felt a lightning strike of rage and cold shiver of fear. He was the king of the Naughty. He could do anything he wanted this side of the border. But this boy was another level of power. He could feel it.

And he savored it.

"Casey—"

King Chocolate had forgotten the queen was there. So surprised, he inhaled the melting frosting. It jammed into the wrong pipe. He swung his fist onto his chest. It thudded like a wooden mallet on a dusty mattress. Again and again. His face turned a rotting shade of purple. The queen got behind him and swatted the back of his head. That didn't seem like the right move on someone choking, but she did it again. Harder this time.

He painted the table with frosting, wheezing great, gurgling breaths.

Eyes bulging from fleshy pockets, he leaned forward. A string of drool danced off his lip. His heavy arm slammed the table and set off the candy catapult. The mechanical arm circled around and fired a blob of chocolate. It stuck between his eyes with a thwap. His head jerked back.

He spat at the catapult. Then battered the thing into splinters with his bare hands. He slumped in the throne like a sack of gooey lard, heaving like a pig forced to run a marathon. He aimed a finger at the queen.

"What... do you... *want*?" he said.

"You asked me to stay, Casey."

He shook his head. That seemed like forever ago. Swallowing acrid saliva that pooled under his tongue, he fell back into a more comfortable position. He wiped the sweat and food off his face with the sleeve of his jacket. Then fixed a stare on her, one that would turn a Lander into a puddle. But she didn't flinch. *Crosser arrogance.*

"Why are you *here*, with the boy? You're up to something. I can smell it."

"He asked me to come."

"Don't give me that. I know you, the way you work. Making your little magic spells, putting your thoughts into his head." He wiggled his fingers, made ghost noises. "Why do you even care about him? What do you *want*?"

"He's frightened, Casey. And alone."

"That's why you're here? Because your heart grew ten sizes?" He stuck out his tongue. "Don't you mess this up for me."

"I'm here to help."

"Good."

He didn't believe her, but he had no choice. She had no idea how much he needed her right now. The situation was delicate. Jelly was right. Without her, the boy would rebel and be useless if he stayed.

"You need to guide this boy," he said with the right amount of force. "He'll listen to you."

"Maybe he'll listen to you."

"I'm too much man for him. Besides, you're a crosser. You think like one. That's what's wrong with you. And him. We need to get this right. You and me, we'll change Candyland with him."

"Change is what I seek."

"Don't give me that. You leave the changing up to me. There's a reason I'm the king and you're not."

She took that well. Actually, too well. Breathing calmly, no tension between her brows or in her shoulders. Back in the day, when she first arrived in Candyland, her rage could blow the hair off his face. She had been a bottled storm that wiped villages off maps. He sort of missed that.

She knows something, he thought. "What is it? Tell, what is it about the boy you aren't saying? He's a mess, ain't he? Is that what you're hiding? The boy is all loose in the bucket, and now he's a pile of screws, is that it?"

"It's not easy crossing over."

What was it she did when he complained, rubbed her finger and thumb together? *World's tiniest fiddle.* And what did she say when he had an excuse, no matter how rock solid it was?

"Gimme a break," he said with a country accent. "You ain't special, darling. You think it's easy running the Naughty Side? Making sure production's on track so no one goes without their chocolate? Keeping the Nice Side from winning? I got pressure, lady! Real pressure! What's a crosser know about that? He's a kid!"

He activated the hoversuit and floated above the table. Last thing he needed to hear was how hard it was growing up on another world. *This is Candyland! There's no leaving. That's the hard truth.*

"It's not easy growing up," she said. "Not knowing where you fit in, what you're supposed to be like. You don't know, Casey. Landers don't *grow up.* You're just here, whatever this place is." She nodded with a calmness that crawled under his skin. She looked up and said, almost defiantly: "But he'll find his way."

"Find his way? What's that supposed to—" The king lurched

forward. "You didn't tell him he *can't* leave, did you. You didn't tell him he's here for good."

"He's here for a reason," she said. "He's the one."

This, strangely enough, struck the king violently funny. He began chuckling at first. It built into a laughing fit that burst from his throat in long breathless howls. He wiped tears away and let the medicine flow. It felt so good to laugh at someone. Washed all the bad feelings away and reminded him of what victory tasted like.

She remained calm.

Even that didn't bother him.

"He's 'the One.'" He splashed air quotes and let loose another howl. "Oh, dear Santa. This ain't a movie, Mouserinks. *The one.* Oh, that's good. That's rich. Anyway, just make sure he does what I want him to do and we'll be cool. Now go. Bye."

"What do you want him to do?"

The king scooped pudding from a bowl with two fingers and painted his lips. He smiled a chocolatey smile and ordered her to get out. Jelly opened the door. She got the hint. The king wanted to bask in the future glory. The game was about to be over. It was just a matter of time.

But time was a funny thing.

16

Art couldn't remember lying down. He had no idea how long he'd slept. There were no clocks on the wall. No sun in the sky. He woke surrounded by pillows on a giant bed, staring at a vaulted ceiling painted with glowing stars. He sank in the soft mattress, searching for the constellations. Nothing he recognized. Yet so familiar. It didn't feel like a dream anymore.

He crawled a mile to the edge of the bed with a head full of bees and syrup in his veins.

The room was deep and long. Big enough to host a basketball tournament and cluttered with things. Like a department store for teenage boys.

In front of him, displayed on a curving table, was a banquet of desserts. Dishes of chocolate wafers, bowls of chocolate drops, trays of chocolate cookies. Glasses of chocolate milk, scoops of chocolate ice cream on chocolate-dipped sugar cones.

Art's chest felt heavy. Legs shaky.

Fear gnawed his stomach like termites on a damp log.

He wasn't hungry. Without standing, he grabbed a chocolate bar off the table. He held it to his ear to hear the crisp snap when he broke it. Waved it under his nose to let the earthy, nutty aroma fill his nostrils. A single bite released a flood of endorphins. It melted under his tongue and went through him on a rising tide. It washed away Fear, cleared his head and opened his heart.

He breathed into an easy smile. The world came into focus.

All it took was one bite.

HE WANDERED the room (he'd come to think of it as a gymnasium). It would be the only time he explored this wonderland of teenage trappings. There were banks of video games and rows of carnival games. Darts to throw and golf balls to putt and bowling balls to roll. Remote-controlled cars to drive, a platoon of drones to fly. Footballs and baseballs and Frisbees. There was no one to throw to. It all smelled new and plastic.

He touched none of it. Not a single thing.

There was also an art station. More of a studio on a raised platform. Art climbed the steps and walked among stacks of blank canvases. Empty easels. Tubes of paint lined up on a bench. Brushes with clean bristles in a rack. There were tubs of clay to mold and wheels to spin it on. An oven to fire it in. There were boxes of pencils and trays of markers.

It had everything. Every possible medium an artist could desire. *Everything.*

One easel was loaded with a canvas. Its eggshell surface blank. A photo was pinned in the corner. It was a Christmas tree brightly lit with a thousand colors.

There was only one thing that spoke to him. Art went back to the bed and the table of chocolate. A recliner was positioned in front of a window that overlooked the dim country of the Naughty Side. He grabbed a bowl of chocolate-covered almonds and went sailing into a sea of mild euphoria beneath a chocolate haze.

Fudgy Lake surrounded the castle. It was black as an oil reservoir. Birds glided over it like dark smudges. Not a single firefly spotted the darkness. He thought how nice it would be to fish in it. To bait a hook and lounge on the shore with his shoes off and earphones playing something sharp and noisy. That was something he loved to do, once upon a time. Or so he thought. With his fingers grazing the bowl, he drifted into another dreamless slumber.

Content and comfortably numb.

HE WOKE SOMETIME LATER. Impossible to say how long.

This time it took three chocolate pieces to clear the cobwebs from his head. Fudgy Lake was still an oil stain. Birds still lugged themselves over it. Nothing had changed. Still, he watched from the comfort of the recliner. Fingers swimming in a bowl of chocolate-covered raisins.

He hated raisins.

Whenever boredom pressed down, he would reach for the table. It was always stocked (he never bothered wondering how), and the next bowl of chocolate took him to the bottom of the warm and loving ocean.

THE QUEEN WOULD COME SIT with him. Sometimes she was there when he woke. Looking at him with kind, human eyes.

They would look out the window without talking. It was a boring program, but she didn't seem to mind. Sitting there drinking her tea while he nibbled chocolate-dipped pretzels with a pint of chocolate soda. He asked her when he was going to leave the castle. She never answered him, but that was okay. He didn't really mean it. He only asked because he felt he should. He wanted things to be different. Just didn't know how to make it happen.

When the window got boring: there was chocolate.

When his body ached: more chocolate.

When emotions grew heavy: chocolate.

There was only one answer.

※

THE QUEEN ENCOURAGED him to walk about. He only did so because she wanted him to. He could not care less about the pointless toys. Thankfully she didn't want him to strap on a baseball mitt. They never slowed down. It was more of a stretch-your-legs sort of walk. To clear his head, get the blood pumping. He needed that. His heart had been thudding like a steam engine pushing sludge through narrow pipes.

Beneath it lurked the poison fingerprints of Guilt and Shame. They were inseparable, those two. When they came knocking, he ate more chocolate. When they called out his name, more chocolate. Each time required more to quiet them down. Each time they returned louder and more obnoxious. He couldn't keep doing it alone. Thankfully the queen was there.

"I really want you to see this," she said.

Of everything in the room, the art studio was the only place he liked. The supplies glistened in their wrappers. She admired the colors, asked him what he liked most. She stopped at the canvas on the easel. The one with the picture pinned in the corner. The Christmas tree of a thousand lights. She looked rather sullen in her observation.

"The king would like you to create this," she said.

"With what?"

"Whatever you like. Just when you do, envision it. Build the image in your mind before you create it. See every detail first; then let it flow onto the canvas."

She waved her hand, sweeping it back and forth like a leaf falling in autumn. She offered a kind smile and stepped back. Art considered the supplies—the endless tubes and bottles and wells. He chose a sharpened pencil with soft lead. Licked the tip of it as he stepped forward.

With dashing strokes, he scribbled on the virgin canvas.

When he was done, he dropped the pencil on the floor. Went

back to the recliner to watch another episode of Fudgy Lake and the tired birds.

The queen sat next to him. She didn't say anything.

He closed his eyes and drifted into a familiar place of unfeeling. The shadows of Guilt and Shame falling over him, he muttered something he wouldn't remember. Something the queen had once said.

"I belong here," he said.

She took his hand. She held it through the long dark night.

17

If the boy was sleeping, he wouldn't feel the cold iceberg floating over him.

His sprawling form lay in a pile of pillows. His open mouth pulling air through his dry throat. The bedsheet had come off two corners. The comforter was on the floor.

The boy didn't know or care what hovered over him.

King Chocolate bobbed over the bed. Jelly stood like a child holding the string to a human balloon. The king stared with muddy eyes smooshed in a field of doughy skin. Lips thin and grim.

He spun around and floated toward the playground. He'd become quite good with the hoversuit, maneuvering down narrow aisles and leaning into tight turns. He didn't bother pretending with his legs anymore, certain the time would come when they would simply fall off like flower petals that had served their purpose.

The playground.

Jelly promised these things would keep a crosser happy. Especially a boy. The king wanted the boy to forget the world outside the castle. Everything he could ever want or need was inside these walls. The king was living proof he didn't have to leave.

King Chocolate was afraid the playground would be too good,

that it would distract the boy from his true calling. The queen had said it wouldn't work. The king had dug his heels in when he heard her say that. Doubled down on Jelly's investment and made it even bigger than originally planned.

And nothing had moved. Nothing at all.

The king ignored the queen, naturally. And when she had told him *why* the playground wasn't working (just like she said it wouldn't), he shouted, "Why didn't you say something earlier?" And then blamed her for everything.

The art studio, however, was different.

The king was happy to see this. As he drifted closer to the canvas and read the words scribbled on it with a sharp pencil, his hopes withered. The boy was taunting him with the king's own words.

This is not going as planned.

The boy had gotten a taste of the dark stuff. Once someone experienced the healing power of chocolate, they needed more of it. That was how it worked. The king intended it that way. There was only one place to get chocolate and only one king to give it. *He needs me.*

King Chocolate ripped the photo of the beautiful Christmas tree off the canvas. All he'd asked for was a tree. The boy couldn't even do that. Time was running out. He needed some proof the boy could do what everyone said he could do. Drawing a tree was child's play!

"Cut him down to one wafer," the king said. "The boy is chocolate-brained."

"Yep," said Jelly.

Jelly snowplowed the stacks of chocolate bars and containers of chocolate drops off the table. They fell into a loose bag. Little balls of gold foil—having been peeled off the chocolate coins and rolled like giant boogers—littered the floor. Jelly squashed them with her extra-wide feet, and it made an awful sound.

The boy stirred.

He could feel the dark and heavy shadow over him. The boy climbed out of the stupor of sleep and backed away from the king, running his hand through tangled hair. He saw Jelly ransacking his stash. Chocolate lines had crusted around the boy's lips.

"You need to pace yourself," the king announced. "There'll come a time when you can eat all you want. But too much will soak your brain. No one likes a soggy brain, boy."

The king didn't care for the look on the boy. A hideous look. The kind that smelled bad and felt worse. The king descended until his twiggy legs lay across the pillows. Knobby knees buckling.

"What is it you want? I've put everything in this room, and all you do is lie there. I give you everything, and you give me *nothing*. Is that fair, boy? Nothing's free, not on this side of the border. You need to—"

He caught sight of Jelly giving him the stop sign. He was coming on a little heavy. The boy was crabwalking away from the king. There was a reason he'd been watching the boy on remote instead of coming into the room. His temper was as thin as a wafer and as brittle as the good stuff. But he'd grown tired of waiting for something to happen. The queen was letting the boy crash through rock bottom after rock bottom. The king didn't want the boy to crash-land.

King Chocolate wanted him to dance.

He spun away. The boy looked disgusted with King Chocolate. Well, the king was disgusted with him times ten. *Times a thousand.*

Jelly said from the corner of her mouth: "Should we call her in?"

"Hard no."

Enough hand-holding. To carve a statue, you need a chisel and hammer. The king rose until he was ten feet off the floor and looking down on the boy. He grimaced and growled. The boy looked more confused than scared. Maybe a little nervous.

"I thought you were an artist. I made sure every brush, every pencil and piece of paper was just right. Brand new and all yours. Everything you could want... *and you give me THIS?*"

He pointed at the art studio, the canvas where the boy had written two words with a pencil.

BLAH. BLAH.

Jelly chuckled. It wasn't funny. Not a cent. Maybe ironic—definitely ironic—but not funny.

"It's not hard, what I want. I told you *exactly* what it is." He shook the picture. "A pretty Christmas tree, see? That's all. You think

Christmas is boring, is that it? Not worth your time. I got news, Arty Farty. That's all we do here is Christmas, so you'd better get used to it and *draw!* It doesn't have to be merry, merry or blah-blah. It's just got to look like this, you see? You envision it, see it in your head, then put it on that canvas. *LOOK!*"

He waved the photo at him. The boy had to see it. Really see it. More than that, he had to *want* to make that Christmas tree *his* Christmas tree. Recreate it with his thoughts and let it flow through his hands. That was when the magic would happen. Supposedly.

It'd better.

"Time is short, son." The king softened his tone. "We're counting on you. All of us. The entire Naughty Side. You do this for us, and you'll get what you want, I promise. Because I know what you want. You want to go home."

The boy sat up. Oh yeah. That was what he wanted. Like waving a bone over a dog's nose. The king knew the power of a promise. Anyone who didn't believe magic was real never observed a promise in action. The king was a master. He wielded promises like weapons. They didn't have to mean anything and certainly didn't have to be true to work. Promises were just words. The magic was in the hands of the wizard who weaved the spell. Because he had to believe in the promise no matter how much of a fib it was.

"Listen." The king descended to eye level. His frail legs folded beneath him. "The Naughty Side isn't bad. It's not. It's the truth is what it is. The cold hard truth. It's looking at life the way it is, not the way you *want* it to be. You got to have mettle to be naughty. Ain't no sugarcoating over here. This is real life, son. Real, real life. You can't be soft, and you can't be weak. Life will blend you down and slurp you up. I see the steel in you, boy."

King Chocolate nodded with fatherly pride. Probably the best he'd ever done. He believed in this boy. Most of what he said was utter nonsense, but not that. He believed this boy had steel.

"Life isn't easy. Over here, we know exactly how hard it is. Then we do something about it."

The king delivered the speech of his life. His tone dead center. An award-winning look of empathy. It wasn't hard to do because he meant it. It was all hogwash, but he believed it. Even Jelly looked misty.

And that, ladies and gentlemen, is how you sell a promise.

"You got six rings to finish this. Or the chocolate river dries up."

He threw the photo on the bed. That part was true.

KING CHOCOLATE DROVE the throne like an electric go-cart.

He'd shed the hoversuit. It smelled strangely sweet and was starting to chafe. Jelly took it to the basement to get it refreshed. Whatever that meant. The king wasn't listening. His brain still replaying the events with the boy.

When he arrived in the theater room, he plowed through the empty seats and spun the throne to face the screen. King Chocolate flipped open the snack drawer in the armrest. A crinkly bag of chocolate-frosted popcorn was stuffed in the bottom. He ripped it open and pushed a handful into his mouth. Salty and sweet. The perfect combo for a movie.

Since the king left, the boy had moved to the edge of his bed, slumped over, hand running through his hair. Now he got up, counted the chocolates on the table (ten wafers and three malted) and went to the window. He was the artist type, all right. Sullen, introspective. Wishful. A cauldron of simmering emotions.

He's thinking.

The king knew a thinking face when he saw one. In fact, the king knew—that very moment—things were going to work out. Call it energy, call it verve or Christmas spirit. The king knew exactly what would happen.

The boy is going to draw.

"MISS ANYTHING?"

Jelly picked up a bench, straightened the bent leg, and sat next to the king. She held out her hand. He rained chocolate popcorn on it, not taking his eyes off the screen. Jelly had been in and out of the room half a dozen times since the king had arrived. *The worst movie ever,* she declared.

Not to the king.

He studied the subtleties, the small gestures. He sampled the emotions boiling inside the boy, felt them transform and shift. Change his thoughts. Crossers were ruled by their emotions. Especially young ones. No control over what they felt. A ship without an anchor. He was rudderless without a sail.

"Genius move, bt-dub," Jelly said with a mouthful. "What you did in there. The boy needed tough love. You gave it. Just when I think you're clumsy and awkward with no people skills, there you go—"

The king's hand went up.

He leaned forward. The look on the boy's face changed. It was microscopic. The king waved at the screen. The image zoomed on the boy's face. "Closer," he called. "*CLOSER!*"

"There. There it is," he whispered.

A speck of light.

The queen was right. The king was witnessing it in real time. There was no way he'd admit it to her. But he whispered it out loud.

"He *is* the one."

The boy's eyes flickered across the room. The queen had a soft touch with him. Nurturing. It was the support he needed. Strengthened his bow.

"Get the queen," the king said. "I want her to see this. Go!"

Jelly sighed. She shuffled toward the door. Picked up the pace when the king hurled the bag of popcorn at her and told her to hurry. He teetered on the edge of the throne, trembling with anticipation.

The boy leaned against the wall. Arms crossed. *Thinking.*

Jelly and the queen were outside the theater, gossiping in the hall. The king slammed his fist on the armrest.

"Get in here!"

They looked inside. He drove the throne straight at them, circled behind them, and herded them inside. Careful not to run over the queen's tail, he nudged them into the middle of the room. They leaned into each other, watching the king. Drool running from the corner of his mouth. Chins fluttering with excitement.

He lifted a trembling hand.

"Look at that," he said.

18

oredom.

Art wore it like an itchy blanket. It clung to him uncomfortably. The moment the king left (or flew out of the room; *was he really flying?*), he felt boredom wrap around him. Beneath its scratchy embrace were the jitters and the shakes—the footprints of Guilt and Shame urging him to escape, to crawl out of his skin.

He sat on the bed. Time didn't move. When it did, it sped past him. It was one long blur of eating and sleeping and wallowing. He wanted to move but couldn't. Wanted to scream, tear his clothes off, get these feelings out. He was a prisoner.

In the castle. And otherwise.

The king wasn't going to let him go. Not out of the castle. Maybe not out of the room. This wasn't a playground. It was a cell.

There is a way to escape, the queen had said. He recalled her counseling him by the window. *It'll set you free.*

She didn't elaborate. She never did. Her advice was sometimes cryptic, as if she couldn't quite say it. Not here. It didn't matter. Art knew what she was saying. He went to the window to think on it. To catch some fresh air. Gaze on the dark blemish of Fudgy Lake and the lethargic birds pecking Swedish fish from the bank. He was there for quite some time. Then he did what the queen wanted him to do.

Guilt and Shame followed him to the art studio.

HE DRAGGED his fingers over tubes of paint, the soft-bristled brushes. Drank the vivid colors with his eyes, inhaled the newness of it all—the unbroken seals, the freshly sharpened pencils. The fragrance of shaved wood and powdery graphite. He circled the open studio, surveying the supplies, the stacked canvases, and pads of papers. Drawers of glue and rags and sponges and markers. Masking tape, spray adhesive, clay. Nothing was missing, not a thing.

He sorted through the rack of pencils.

Found one he liked. The lead soft. The wood light and balanced in his hand. It fit between his fingers. He held it like a conducting baton, swung it around, carving the air with his eyes closed. Hearing music in his head and turning in a circle.

When he opened his eyes, he faced a blank canvas. The picture of a Christmas tree attached to the corner.

He didn't question the why of it. He'd stopped doing that since arriving. The why and the how. It was time to *do*. This was where Art gave Guilt and Shame the slip.

The work began.

THE CREATIVE FLOW was rough and choppy.

At times, the pencil was nothing more than a stick of wood. A stranger. Stubborn.

The first attempt was not good. It went on the floor. The second draft was no better. The third was even worse.

The mistakes piled up around him. Broken frames and crumpled canvases.

He kept going. The current carried him forward. He didn't look back on what went wrong. His stomach churned and folded. He twitched and buckled. It wasn't working. He was fighting the current. Trying to *make* something fit.

Again.

Another.

Another.

Thirty canvases were on the floor when something clicked. He felt it. The gates opened and washed him away. It took that long to let the process take over. He was a canoe gliding on glassy water. Silent and still. Effortless.

He stroked the canvas.

The tip of lead roaring on the surface.

The resistance in his hand as light as a feather.

Eyes darting from the photo to contrasting lines. No time for thoughts.

There was no pain or pleasure. No observer. He was the pencil and the canvas. He was the tree. He held it in his mind, felt its feathery branches, tasted the bright colors, smelled the gleaming lights.

The distinct odor of xylene filled his nostrils. He held a cap in one hand. A color marker in the other. He grabbed them by the handfuls, held them in his mouth, put them behind his ears. Bleeding colors across a white landscape. Blending and leaking and layering, the image of the tree gushed onto the canvas.

Something else happened.

The flow took him somewhere. Into another space. While his hands did the work, he was an observer of events unrelated to the here and now.

The creative flow unlocked a secret room inside him.

"Stunning."

The queen wiped a tear. She stood in front of Art's work. Art had paced around the room, sat on the bed. Paced some more. He had felt full and satisfied when he'd finished. But then the emptiness settled in. Guilt and Shame reintroduced themselves. He sat on the edge of the bed. Foot bouncing.

The chocolate was gone.

He'd eaten the last piece not long after he finished. It would be a few chimes before the next ration arrived. That was what Jelly had said. *Ration.* If he had any doubts about being a prisoner, they were gone now.

"What does he want with this?" Art said.

Jelly had delivered the new photo. It was a sleigh with rockets attached to the sides. Something Santa Claus would use if he were flying to the moon.

"He believes it'll help him," the queen said.

"Help him? How is that going to help him?"

She didn't answer that. Sat next to him while he stared at the picture of a rocket sleigh, aching to get back to the art studio to forget the chocolate itch and start outpacing the bad company in his head. To forget himself.

"Where are you at right now?" the queen asked.

He knew what she was asking. *What am I feeling? Where's my head at?*

Right now his head was full of bingo balls and barbed wire. He got up and paced, kept the machine moving. Twisting his fingers in knots. The queen sat on the bed, hands folded on her lap. A rock in the storm.

He ran his hand through his hair.

Her gaze was open and inviting. He could say anything to her, and she wouldn't judge him. That was what moved him to finally speak. To tell her where his head was at.

"When I was... making the tree." He pointed at the studio, teetering on second thoughts. Then said: "In the middle of it, I, uh..." He swallowed. "Something happened."

Her whiskers twitched. She nodded like she already knew this.

He'd disappeared, he told her. Not actually, as far as he knew. He had been using the markers when the tree changed. It wasn't on the canvas anymore. It was in the corner of the room. Not this room. Another room. An open room with skylights in the ceiling and hardwood on the floor. A fireplace burning.

There were others talking and laughing while Christmas music played. The smell of something sweet cooking in the next room. And people playing a card game. They'd just gotten back from a ride where they sat in the back of a pickup truck to see lights in a neighborhood. The ones with candles in sacks lining the street. What were those called? *Luminaries.*

There were presents under the tree.

Old ornaments on the limbs. Special ornaments. Ones with memories attached.

He couldn't see their faces. They were wispy forms making merry sounds. He tried to say something.

"And then the tree was done." His eyes were stinging. "I was back here."

He swallowed hard and ran his fingers through his hair. Maybe it was the markers, he thought. A hallucination. But it wasn't the markers. It took every bit of strength to say what he said next. The foundation on which he stood was brittle. Below it a salty ocean. But he said it to the queen. He said it to her because he knew she'd *hear* him. She'd understand.

"Was that a *memory*?"

He collapsed on the bed and leaned into her. She didn't have to answer, and he didn't need her to. He just had to say it out loud, to hear himself say it. Maybe it was a memory; maybe it wasn't. It didn't matter. It *felt* like a memory, a special one he held close to his heart. The creative flow had opened a channel to it.

The queen put her hand on his chest.

Her fingers long and knobby, twisted with arthritis. Warmth seeped from it. Penetrated his heart and spread to his back.

"No one can give you the answer you seek," she said. "It is for *you* to see."

She asked him to close his eyes. He did, grateful she kept her hand on him. Then asked him to breathe slowly. A long breath in. A long one out. They did this for a while. At some point, he stopped shaking.

"You may see a light," she said. "Inner wisdom, some call it. Here in Candyland, it is the Christmas spirit. The true gift Santa delivers." She chuckled warmly. "Always with you."

In and out they breathed.

Until thoughts fell away. And he was just here.

JELLY ARRIVED WITH THE RATIONS.

Art barely tasted it. He wolfed them down, chasing them with long chugs of warm cocoa. The queen didn't stop him or scold him. She understood the beauty that followed a chocolate binge.

The elation. The relief.

Jelly went to the art studio. She stood in front of the canvas, much like the queen. With emotion slurring the edges of her voice, she said the king was pretty happy. Art didn't know why the king was pretty happy since he hadn't come to visit.

But he didn't care.

He sat at the window with the breeze in his face, licking his fingers and feeling delight pump through him. If only he'd looked down where Fudgy Lake blighted the landscape. Something shimmered on its blackened depths. Balls of light reflected off the surface. There in the middle of an oily lake was an island where an island had not been.

And on that island a Christmas tree appeared.

19

The room was quiet. Except for mechanical thrumming and the occasional gooey drip. *Gloo-ip* when a drip broke from the ceiling. *Gloo-op* when it hit the floor.

A massive mound of flesh was piled in the back. Rolling pins caused the folds of sweaty skin to undulate. And the king to moan.

The steam was sticky sweet. It condensed on the ceiling in caramel drops. Streaked down the walls like exhausted slugs. Dark puddles formed on the tiled floor.

King Chocolate rested on a bed of waffles with a buttery pillow beneath his head. The rolling pins kneaded his body like a mountain of dough squishing and squashing in all directions. Two slices of jellied toast covered his eyes. Yet still he knew when maple syrup had condensed above him, and an amber droplet began to bulge. It clung and shimmered with weight. Glistening with sugar. Until it was too heavy to hold and stretched away, losing its grip, falling in a bubbling mass.

Gloo-op.

A fresh cloud of boiled syrup was released. He relished the privacy. The ecstasy. The saturation of sweets. Then it was wrecked by a droning voice.

"Decent in there?"

The king didn't bother to answer. His lower half was covered with enough cloth to sew a tent. The fashionistas had designed it with mini marshmallows hot-glued on a pink swatch of taffy. It was a bit snug, a little binding. If the paparazzi caught him coming out of the steam bath, he wanted to present well. Jelly assured him they would be watching. And he would approve the snaps before they released them.

Jelly wandered through the saccharine fog. Rubber boots mashing thick puddles. Drips falling on her raincoat and rubber hat. Her attire was atrocious (fashionistas had taught him that word: *you don't want atrocious*). Her clothes were useless, anyway. Steam penetrated everything.

"Ah!" she said. Relieved to see the marshmallow towel. "Don't stay here too much longer or you'll melt. You already look lighter."

He grimaced because she wasn't wrong. He thought he'd imagined it while getting undressed. That he'd lost a few pounds. He'd spun in front of the mirror, thought he looked slimmer and blamed the mirror. Now Jelly said it. Joking or not, he didn't like that.

Not a bit.

He groaned. Just when the rolling pins were getting to knots in his middle parts. A winch unspooled from the ceiling. He lifted his arms, let the bands wind around his wrists and pull him into a sitting position. He slumped against the wall like melting wax.

The rolling pins repositioned, kneading the lumpy knobs on his shoulders.

"Take that silly rainsuit off and have a seat," he said, slurring his words.

"I'm good."

"Nonsense. It's good for the pores, Jelly Roll."

"Well, well, someone is in a *good* mood."

The king convulsed like he'd been struck with the blunt end of a stick. "Upbeat, maybe. But never good, you silly goose. Never *good*."

As the king of the Naughty Side, he swore never to be associated with that word. Even in his current state of elation. And why not? The boy was in the groove. Or, as the queen called it, the *flow state*. Groove sounded much better. Cooler. The fashionistas agreed.

The boy was making things. All sorts of things.

He would get right to work when he woke. Stayed until he was done. Sometimes he collapsed from exhaustion and napped on the floor. Woke up and kept going. The sheets on the bed needed washing from the sweaty naps and salty tears. He had a habit of crying after finishing a painting or drawing. It was sad and sweet. The perfect combo.

The king didn't know what to make of it. The queen said to allow the boy space, let him grieve. King Chocolate had no idea what that meant, but listened to her this time. He wanted nothing to do with emotions. Maybe that was the life of an artist.

True, the boy wasn't always making what the king requested. Like that rusty robot he drew. Or that floaty rock creature wearing a helmet. Or the bull with braces on its teeth. Weird stuff was now roaming Fudgy Lake.

The king was patient, though.

Let the artist do art. Get out of his way and let him groove.

Until the boy kept ignoring the king's requests. Then he had to be reminded why he was there. *Stick to the photos, son. You'll be home in no time.*

"Do you really think I'm getting skinny?" the king said.

"What answer do you want? I'm open."

"Just shut up. Why are you here, besides ruining my sauna with *atrocious* clothing?"

"Ah, there he is, old Naughty St. Nick. You're not answering calls, so I stopped in to tell you the sleigh is working just like you said it would."

"Of course it is." He wiped a gooey slick off his forehead and sucked his finger. "Never doubt me."

"Never, ever, sire. It's on the way to the festival."

"Fab." Another fashionista word. It was short for something. "Fabby," the king said. Although that didn't sound right.

Doodling his fingers in a puddle of the good stuff, he moaned.

The taste of winning was sweeter than this entire room. He wanted to distill this feeling, roll in it till every crease on his body was filled. Eat it till there was no more room in his belly. It was the most delicious, intoxicating thing ever. He'd gain the weight back and more.

"It's good to be a Lander," he groaned.

"Okay," Jelly said.

"We know who we are," the king said. "What we're made of. We're reliable. We're *this* every day, Jelly Roll." He flexed his porky fingers with a look of disgust. "Can you imagine, Jelly, *changing*? Who needs it? Who wants it? Look at the queen. Now that's what I'm talking about. She was a sweet tart when she crossed over, amma right? A few bells later and she's sprouting gray hairs as crooked as a cane tree root."

"That's crooked," Jelly agreed.

"Blech." The king dug a chocolate chip out of the waffle bed. "She quit chocolate, Jelly. Who does that?"

"Well, not all of her ideas were bad."

"What's that?"

"I mean, she takes care of the naughties in need. Feeds them, makes them clothes. That sort of thing."

"Yeah, but... *why*?"

Jelly shrugged. "I mean, it's just..." *Nice.* She was going to say nice. "It's the right thing to do. She's gentle and kind and—"

A wad of syrup-soaked waffle hit her face. "Whoa. Whoa, whoa, whoa, whoa, whoa. It's sounds like you *like* her. Is that what I'm hearing, Jelly Roll? You like the queen?"

"She is my queen." Jelly wiped her face. "*Your* queen."

"She's not my queen. She's the queen of something, but she ain't my queen. You know what, out. Get out. Go, now, before I throw you in the fudge factory." He buried his face in the waffle bed. "You make me sick. Beat it."

"My pleasure."

Jelly turned to leave, her boots peeling off the floor like they'd been glued down. She was careful not to move too fast or the boots would pull right off her enormous feet. And if those paddles got stuck in the syrup, it would take an army to pull her out.

The king laughed at that thought.

A chocolate chip shot from his nostril. Followed by flatulence from the other end.

He laughed harder. Aftershocks rippled across his exposed belly. Jelly had almost vanished in the steam. Those rubber boots squealing on the sticky tile.

"Oh. Almost forgot why I came in here. The boy is awake."

"What?"

"He woke up a couple of chimes ago. Went straight to the studio."

King Chocolate choked on his words. The next thing out of his mouth was not funny. "You were to tell me that *immediately!*"

This was followed by a scoop of melted butter on the wall just above Jelly's head.

"We tried. You weren't answering calls. Remember?"

The king didn't exactly sleep. It was more like fading out. He didn't really know how long he'd been in the sauna, but the washboard pruning on his fingers and toes said it had been more than a few chimes. He threw more waffle at Jelly and called for a monitor. It lit up the wall, smudgy and streaked. He leaned closer, nearly tumbling off the waffle bench, to see.

The boy was already at work. At the canvas, he was. There were colors and shapes on it. Lots of them, in fact.

"What's he doing? Is he making it? Is he doing it?"

"I can't see."

The king grabbed her by the lapels of her overcoat and pressed her face into the monitor. She squirmed out of his grip. If the king wanted to see what the boy was making, then they needed to get to the theater. The sauna was like hanging out in a stomach.

But the king didn't want to miss a tick.

He grabbed the collar of her overcoat. She twisted and tried to slither out. The king came away with an empty sleeve. Worse, he teetered forward. Jelly got out of the way just before he squished onto the floor. Tiny legs fluttered like rubbery appendages. Jelly's instinct was to get away.

It wasn't quick enough.

"No, you don't." The king pulled at her boot.

She bounced like an overinflated beach ball. King Chocolate tried to use her to push himself back onto the bench. The monitor was too high on the wall to see. There was nothing to grab onto. They were like baby deer on black ice, grabbing at each other, slapping each other. Goop in their eyes and up their noses. They were lathered in the sweetest, stickiest, gooiest sauna ever invented.

Exhausted, out of breath, the king shouted, "Get help!"

"How?"

He put both hands on her backside and shoved. She went sliding into the steam cloud. It sounded like a rubber kickball on the far wall. She came rebounding out of the mist, ricocheting off the king like a cue ball. His marshmallow suit ripped. He held it with one hand and reached out with the other. Jelly went zooming past, careening out of the corner. He'd snatch her this time, then throw her at the door somewhere on the other side of the room.

A tremor shook the walls.

It sounded like someone was rearranging the furniture on the floor above.

It happened again. They were showered in droplets from the ceiling that fell all at once. Jelly was choking. Droplets were in her ears and eyes. She wiped her face, furious. The last thing she'd wanted to do was come inside this disgusting room. It smelled like rotten eggs boiled in corn syrup. That was why she'd dressed head to toe in rain gear, and now look at her. *A total sweet roll.*

"Look at what you—"

"Shush it." The king smooshed his slimy hand against her lips.

His eyes darted back and forth. Nostrils twitched.

He scrambled for the waffle bench. At first, he was swimming in place, but slowly he rocked himself forward like a walrus on beefy flippers. He climbed halfway into the seat, gasping. Eyes bulging at the monitor.

The boy had stepped back from his work.

They could see it now. It was a blurry form, but enough to recognize the photo the king had given him. What he wanted the boy to create. It was a large circle with a curving line through the middle of it. One side light. The other side dark.

"He did it," Jelly said. "I think he did it."

"Shut it."

Expectations were future resentments, the king had learned. He had to make sure what he was seeing was what he was seeing. That this was what he thought it was. And that wasn't furniture scraping the floor.

"Go! Go!" The king plopped on the floor and pushed Jelly like a hockey puck. "Get me out of here!"

Jelly went sliding into the fog. This time she didn't bounce back.

The king didn't wait. He crawled after her at worm speed. The molasses was getting thick and tacky. He was finding traction but still going as fast as a beetle on a hot sidewalk. The anticipation burned his lungs like ciders. He screamed a guttural cry, releasing frustration and potential joy. He had to know. Had to know NOW!

He was halfway there when a rope slapped him in the face.

He grabbed it with both hands.

A heave and a ho, one after another, and he was dragged out of the morass. Jelly was there with three assistants. She held out the hoversuit. He didn't even have to ask. He wanted to kiss her disgusting face.

They worked him into the hoversuit, rolling him across the hall to get it latched.

He powered up, nearly flying into the ceiling like a bobber held under water.

Hair plastered to his forehead. Nostrils glued shut, a massive mound of nudity soaring down the corridor. The marshmallow suit somewhere in the sauna. He shouted a warning to those who might be around corners to find cover or get run over.

He hit the open doorway of the theater at full throttle. Barreled through the seats like they were bowling pins. He bounced off one wall and then a second. When the stars cleared from his vision, he was on his back. The monitor upside down. The boy was mixing paint in the studio.

"Border!" the king cried. "Show me the border!"

The channel changed. It was a bird's view of Candyland. All of it. The king didn't care about the shape of it. He wanted to see where dark and light met at the border. Too impatient to right himself, he screamed at the monitor to zoom on the meeting hall—where he'd met his king brother, Macey, and his (lovely) queen, Lydia.

It did just that.

There was the little outhouse. Half in the dark. Half in the light.

But if you looked closer and knew what you were looking for, you would see exactly what the king was seeing.

"He did it," he murmured. Then louder, "He did it! He did it!" Louder still: "*I* DID IT!"

After all, it was the king's idea to give the picture to the boy. Therefore, ergo, credit goes to the king.

All of it.

The joy bouncing inside him was about to break his ribs. He'd never contained this much excitement. It came out of him in groans and cries and laughter and tears and just a little bit of gas.

Jelly came in with a blanket and covered the king. He was oblivious to his nudity. Jelly wasn't. And neither were the twenty or so employees he'd passed in the hallway.

She looked up at the monitor. She knew what to look for. And she saw it, too.

"He did it," she said.

"*I* did it!" the king said.

"*You* did it!" Jelly said.

She leaped on the king. They hugged and rolled and laughed. He fired up the hoversuit and flew around the room. Glistening tears cut down his sticky cheeks. It didn't matter who did it. It had been done.

❄

KING CHOCOLATE WAS post-sauna clean with a fresh coating of powdered sugar. Adjustments to the hoversuit had been made. The fashionistas said if he lost any more weight, they'd have to fabricate a new one. If they needed more food to be eaten, they were asking the right man.

At the moment, though, the king was banging his fists on the dining table. The plates and utensils danced. Instruments blared from speakers throughout the room, driving a beat with heavy guitars and a speedy rhythm that made the king's pulse beat as fiercely as the drums. He banged his foppish head.

"Silent Night!"

Boom!

"SILENT!"

Boom-boom-boom!

"NIIII—stop!" He waved his arms. The music stopped. "What if instead of 'Silent Night' we go 'Naughty Time'? Huh? Try it again. From the top."

The king had no idea how to play an instrument. Even fake ones. He waved his arms like an octopus being electrocuted. Rust-color sweat streaked his sugar-powdered cheeks. He tossed his head like a volleyball, not hearing the door open. Not seeing anyone enter.

Not until they were next to him.

The music abruptly stopped. The king was startled and squealed like a child spooked by a ghost. He sopped the sweat from his forehead with his sleeve.

"I was going over the set list," he said. "Needed a bit more *verve!*"

"It sounds a little dark," the queen said.

The king looked at Jelly. She shook her head. He had to do all the heavy lifting. A king's work was never done. Especially the dirty kind. Although he looked forward to this chore. "You might want to have a seat for this," he said to the queen. "On second thought, let's just rip the bandage off. You're fired."

It took a few winks to sink in. It started as bewilderment and pretty much stayed that way. "What do you mean fired?"

"It means you're fired. What else would it mean?" He glanced at

Jelly, back to the queen. She was waiting for more. "It means you're not the queen anymore."

"I don't want to be the queen."

"Good. Because—wait. I see what you're trying to do." He wagged a porky finger. "You didn't quit. I fired you, admit it. Burns a little, doesn't it."

"I haven't wanted to be queen for quite some time, Casey."

"Give me the crown. Give it, give it!" He reached for it. "GIVE IT, NOW!"

She took the crown from the nest of wiry hair on her head. She'd pried the jewels from it, made it look like a recycled aluminum tambourine without the metal zills. Probably hid the jewels on that rat-infested island. He'd find them. Even if he had to turn the island upside down, he'd find them. Without the jewels, her crown was a cheap hoop.

He whacked it on the table. It hurt his hand. He did it again, harder this time. Did it a third time, then a fourth. Not a dent, not a scratch. Just a bruise on his hand. He flung the stupid thing. It rolled down the table like a loose wagon wheel.

"You're fired! You hear me? FIRED!"

"I understand, Casey."

"You're just... *aahhhhh!*" He grabbed his cheeks. This was supposed to make him happy, but all he wanted to do was stuff his ears inside his head. "You want to know why you're fired? Because I don't need you anymore. You want to know why I don't need you anymore?"

She knew why. A little thrill ran up his spine.

"Oh, you know," he said. "But I want to show you."

An old-fashioned silver screen lowered from the ceiling. King Chocolate stared at the haggard gray rat while it came down. He didn't blink or twitch. Jelly was uncomfortable in the awkward quiet.

The queen was calm.

Ordinarily, her demeanor would make him pull his greasy hair. Not this time. He savored it this time. *Let her act like it doesn't bother her. I want to see her crack when she sees this.* He laughed at his own thoughts and sucked a deep draught of pudding from the pudding tube.

"Ooookay." He sighed. "Let's see what I have for you. Something a little—oh! There it is. What's that?" When she didn't answer, he said, "That was a real question. What are you looking at?"

"Candyland."

"Be more specific."

"The border."

It was a bird's-eye view of beloved Candyland. Half in the dark, half in the light. As normal as usual. If you weren't looking at it closely. Which she wasn't.

"Notice anything?"

She nodded slowly. Or maybe she was looking closely. A smile slithered across his face.

"Say it, then. Say it out loud," he whispered. "I want to hear it."

"You don't want to do this."

"Say it! What's different about the border? What did I do? SAY IT!"

"Casey, it won't do what you think—"

"If you don't say it right now, I'll turn your island into a sewage pile. You'll be the queen of the dump if you don't say it. I'm counting down." He held up three swollen fingers. "Three. Two. One." Long pause. A brief staring contest. Then: "All right. Jelly, have the—"

"He moved the border," she said.

"What was that? I can't hear you."

She grimaced. He cocked his hand to his ear. She mumbled something. This was exhausting. That was the thing with her: it took an army to move her an inch. He'd had enough. A win was a win. He walloped his hands together.

"Ring a belly, Jelly! Ring it out loud and give this vermin a prize." He threw a fudgesicle in front of her. "She is one hundred on the bull's eye. *I moved the Naughty Side!*"

"Arthur moved it," she corrected.

"He did. I did. What's it matter? We win, Lady Mouserinks. I guess it's just Mouserinks now. Or is it just Rinks? I never liked that name, bt-dub. It sounds made up."

"This isn't about winning."

"How is this not about winning? Winning is all there is. All there ever was! Us against them. Nice versus naughty, dark versus light. And guess who's winning now? Guess. Come on, take a guess."

She turned away so he wouldn't see her tremble with anger or fear or some other useless emotion. *Crossers. So weak and vulnerable.* He should've kept her as a pet, not made her queen.

"Go back to your island and play with the rats," he said. "Leave this to the professionals."

His laughter was raucous and mean. He leaned his head back, took a deep breath, and let it rip. It felt good. Justified. Like hitting a nail square on the head. *Just right.* He was about to call up the "Silent Night" song (or "Naughty Time" song, he hadn't decided if he should change it) when she grabbed a silver platter off the table. He cringed as she raised it.

"How old are you?" she said.

"Rude."

"You don't age," she continued. "I've been here so many bells I've lost count. I've got more gray hairs than the Christmas Wood. You haven't changed a lick. Neither of you. You look exactly the same."

"I already made that point. Now put down the platter."

"You were never young, and you'll never grow old. You were never born, and you'll never die. This place is an eternal moment."

"Why are you holding a platter?" the king said. "Why is she holding the platter?"

"The border has always been where it is. Naughty on one side, nice on the other. It's never moved. It's never changed." She put donuts on the platter, one on each side. Her hand was under the middle of the teetering platter. "Just like you."

"Cool trick." The king rolled his eyes. "Show's over. Put the—"

She added a third donut to one side. It tipped over and crashed on the table. Made a mess. King Chocolate thought about insisting she clean it up. But he was getting tired of her. The thrill of firing her was over.

But he understood her point. Her high-minded, smarty-pants point. She couldn't just come out and say it. Had to turn it into a party trick to prove she was a smarty.

"Balance, I get it," he groused. "I hope you feel better that someone has to clean up your mess. You know something, you're no better than me. You're not smarter, and you sure ain't prettier. I know it's mean, but I'm going to say it. It's what everyone is thinking. *You're gross.* Sorry, but not sorry. It's the truth. Leave, will you? And don't drag your gross tail on the floor. Go!" He threw another fudgesicle. This one stuck to the front of her long coat. "Go back to your island. You're not invited to the festival. You can watch it on your crystal ball. GO!"

She nodded to him. It was long and heartfelt. Genuine.

Then she turned and walked toward the exit.

A part of the king felt the sting of her leaving. He wanted her out of his life but couldn't imagine her gone. It was a terrible feeling. She was a habit he couldn't quit.

"You're not saying bye to the boy, either! He doesn't need you. He's got me and chocolate. Bye, loser! Bye."

Jelly looked deflated. She went after the queen. Which only twisted the king's confounding heartache. He leaned into it and, just before the doors closed behind them, shouted: "It's Naughty Time!"

A drum solo followed. King Chocolate beat the air drums until he was soaked with sweat. Then did it again from the beginning.

After that, he stuffed his face with eclairs.

20

Sweet Tooth rumbled away from the castle, looking like a tiny clown on the dim dirt road. She stopped at the edge of Fudgy Lake to scoop a handful of sludge off the shore, impervious to the gaggle of sooty birds nipping at her heels.

Art couldn't hear her from that far up, but imagined her *yumming* at the dirty birds. He was peeling paint from his fingers—grays and browns and blacks—like dead skin. Thinking of the memory unlocked in the last work he'd finished. A time he was sick on Christmas Eve with feverish dreams that lasted through the night and the restless excitement blunted by a sore throat. He'd lain on the couch Christmas morning beneath a comforter, opening presents he was too weak to sit up for.

It was not the best Christmas to remember.

The last painting he didn't like, but he was drawn to it. It was familiar. Like a comforting blanket that was cold and suffocating. *Darkness Encroaching* he'd titled that piece. It was a circle of dark, swirling clouds that mesmerized him. So deep in the creative flow, he hadn't felt the earthquake. A few things had fallen off shelves and tables.

All he'd done was paint and sleep.

He wasn't eating as much chocolate. Only when he found himself staring out the window did Guilt and Shame whisper in his ear. They were persistent and stubborn and wouldn't leave until he'd eaten all the chocolate Jelly had left for him.

He'd come to think of creating as work. He didn't mind it, most of the time. It kept his head empty and heart open. He mostly painted and sculpted and drew. Mostly slept.

Avoided the time in between as best he could.

"MERRY, MERRY!" Jelly announced. "Or blah-blah. Take your pick. Your chocolate delivery has arrived. An extra dose from the king, a reward for a fine painting."

She came bouncing into the room on those extra-large feet. Reminded him of her twin sister from the Nice Side as she laid the platter on the table. Chocolate wafers were stacked like casino chips.

"Fine painting?" Art didn't see the fine in what the king wanted him to paint. Only the allure.

"Beauty and the eye of the beholder and all that." Jelly went to the studio where *Darkness Encroaching* was on the easel. "We're leaving for the festival in a few chimes. You're going to be a star, kid. The buzz. The king's jealous, too. I can tell."

She bounced around the studio tables, admiring the drawings and paintings, the clay sculptures and toothpick models he'd experimented with. She stopped to admire *Darkness Encroaching*.

"Do you want to take any of these with you?" she asked.

"Take them where?"

"To the festival. They're inspiring. Everyone on both sides of the Land would agree." She took the painting off the easel and began stacking it with the other works, muttering to herself as she did it.

Art broke off a piece of chocolate, admired the aroma and smooth texture before nibbling the corner. "I'm not going home, am I, Jelly?"

She rolled loose sketches and gently placed them in a bag. For a moment, she considered lying to him. Art expected her to. But she stopped what she was doing and looked at him. Her eyes as dark as the sky.

"Probably not, kid," she said.

"Probably?"

"I don't know how it works. How you cross over here or why. No one seems to think you can go back home, though. But I don't know." She shook her head. "Maybe you can."

"He was lying, then. The king was lying."

"Don't take it personally. He lies to everyone."

Art wore acceptance like a vintage coat. *I may never leave. This could be my new home.* He didn't hate Candyland. Remembering where he came from made it hurt. Even if the memories were delusions. He didn't want to forget them. He held the pain and pleasure in both hands.

Jelly had all the drawings in a box. Even the doodles. The clay sculptures would stay behind, she said. Better they didn't get squished. But the paintings were coming. Especially the last one.

Sweet Tooth was farther up the road. The dirty birds beating her with their wings.

"Is the queen coming?" Art asked.

"The king seems to think she won't." Jelly was packing the canvases now, tying them together with a string. "But remember, there's a reason she's the queen of the Naughty Side. She may be kind, but she's not soft."

Jelly hobbled over to him, said someone would be up to gather his things. What few things there were. "How would you like to get out of here?"

"Yeah."

"Then trust the process." She put something in his pocket. "A gift from the queen."

Then she waddled out of the room. A host of quiet waifs came in to collect the boxes and bags of his art. Art watched them carry things out. He felt the lump in his pocket.

It was a small ball.

THE CASTLE DIDN'T SO much pierce the dim sky as it dissolved into it.

Art stood at the base of it, looking up its full length. It was impossibly tall for something so narrow: a dark tooth that never stopped growing. He leaned against it. The cold sank through his palm and into his arm. It had been so long since he'd been outside. It felt like years. Maybe it had been. Or maybe just a few days (*days are called rings?*). He breathed the dank air with pleasure, relished the odors both fragrant and rank. (Fudgy Lake smelled like low tide. *Yum!*)

A boxy stagecoach waited on the cobblestone road. Bathed in a silvery beam from above. Boxes of Art's work were strapped on the back of it. One end of the stagecoach was lower than the other. Art knew who was sitting on the low end. The grumpy elf watched Art approach, scrubbing the stubble on his chin with the palm of his hand.

Art climbed one step. Peeked inside.

The throne was filled with the pile of royal flesh wearing a crown and squirting chocolate sauce from a bottle into his mouth. Jelly was on the other end, swinging her big bare feet off the edge of a chair.

"Where's the queen?" Art asked.

"Not this again." The king wiped his mouth with a blanket. It sounded like he was chewing wet leather. "She went ahead, wants to make sure everything is ready. Is that okay with you? Can we go now?"

Art sniffed. The smells inside the stagecoach would wither flowers. It was blackened marshmallows cooked over a pile of burning tires in there. The stink watered his eyes.

"I'll ride in another coach. That one over there. Jelly can come to make sure I don't escape."

King Chocolate jiggled with laughter. "Jelly couldn't stop an ant from climbing up her nose. Go on, I trust you. Watchers are watching you anyhow. You won't get far."

"So I'm a prisoner, then?"

"No. Who said that? Jelly? I'll wash her mouth out with lemon juice."

"She didn't. It's pretty obvious you don't want me to leave."

"Just because I like you, my boy, don't make you my prisoner." Chocolatey smile. "I'm just saying you must come to the festival. We already made invitations with your name and face. Big, beautiful pictures, too. Everyone is expecting you. They want to see the artist. Besides, it's a Candyland tradition. We do it every year."

"I thought this was the first one."

"The first of many." The king didn't miss a beat when it came to weaving a story. "After it's over, you can go home. Promise and wanna die, put a needle in my eye. Besides, I think you're going to have some fun. Have a little walk on the Naughty Side this Christmas, eh?"

It looked like a wink, the way one side of his face twitched.

"And wait till you see the chocolates there. I saved the best for you, my boy. Mudslides and fudgy soakers and cocoa funnels. You'll swear this is heaven."

Again, a convulsive wink and guttural laughter. Not real convincing. Art, however, was intrigued. He was already here. Might as well have a look around.

Another stagecoach pulled up. Door opened.

Art stepped over to it and hopped on the step. He held the doorframe with one hand and leaned out for one last word with the king.

"The queen will be there?" he asked.

"Why wouldn't she be? Go, go, get in. Let's not be late."

Art looked around, soaking in the sights and smells and sounds. He had the feeling he wouldn't see it again and wanted to remember it. And wanted to see if the king would snap if he diddled around much longer. There was something entertaining when the king lost his temper.

There was a Christmas tree out on Fudgy Lake. It looked just like the first picture he drew. Exactly like it. That didn't seem odd to Art. The photo he used to create that first work of art had to come from somewhere. He must not have seen it out there before.

His pocket buzzed.

"What's that?" the king shouted from the other carriage.

"I gave him a phone," Jelly answered. "In case we get separated. Go on, boy. We'll see you at the festival."

Art put his hand in his pocket and closed the door.

The gift from the queen was buzzing.

THERE WAS someone in the carriage.

Art paused half in, half out. Hand on the door. Daryl was on a bench seat with his front legs together. His purrs filled the cramped space (no space expander on this ride).

"Where have you been?" Art asked.

"Someone in there?" the king shouted. Someone was paranoid. "Is it the queen? She'd better not be in there."

"The queen isn't in here!" Art said. "Just the cat."

"Cat?"

The king had forgotten about Daryl. Jelly was explaining who the cat was when Art closed the door. He crawled into the small space before the king asked more questions, and fell onto the bench across from the obese kitty. He seemed happy to see Art, the way his tail waved at the sight of him. The sound of the purring.

You were busy, Daryl said.

"So you left me?"

I never left you. Are you going to answer that?

The buzzing grew louder. Art pulled it out of his pocket. There was nothing exceptional about it. Just a silver orb small enough to fit in his hand. It sank into his palm with a satisfying weight. The vibrations hummed up his arm.

"How do I answer it?"

Put it there.

Art dropped it where the cat was looking. It thudded on the velvet seat, and suddenly someone was sitting across from Art. It didn't make a sound; there was no *poof* or anything like that. Just one second the seat was empty, and the next a girthy bearded man was there. His knees almost touching Art's knees. He was from a calendar or a child's storybook. The red suit and black boots. White curls in a long beard. Eyes that sparkled like water on a clear day.

"Hiyyah!" cried a grumpy elf on top of the carriage.

The stagecoach jerked forward. Art was thrown back in his seat, head thumping the hollow panel behind him. The large man across from him did not move.

As trees passed the windows and bells rang from the stagecoach eaves, the two stared at each other. Art wasn't trying to win a blinking contest. There were no words to say. His brain had short-circuited and was rebooting. Art moved his mouth, but nothing came out.

Santa Claus. It's Santa Claus.

Of all the strange things that had happened since waking up in Candyland, this one pinned him with a surreal grip. Santa touched something real. Santa was someone Art had believed in once upon a time. All those Christmas Eves when he lay in bed trying to stay awake, ears tuned for a scuff on the roof or a ring of a bell or jolly laughter coming down the chimney, only to wake on Christmas morning to see the presents left behind, the bulging stockings. Milk half gone and crumbs of cookies left out.

Then Art grew up. He stopped believing.

Now the jolly fat man was here. He was sitting across from him. Close enough to touch.

Art smacked his lips. His mouth was dry. Tongue glued to the roof of his mouth. He cleared his throat and loosened a few words. Just a few. And said: "Are you real?"

"Is any of this real?" Santa answered. "The chairs we sit on. The road beneath us. You. Me."

Deep answer, that one. Santa went straight to metaphysical, and that, for some reason, sobered Art up. That and the baritone sound of his voice was sure to carry over to the one King Chocolate was riding in.

"That's not what I mean. Like... the reindeer and the presents. Are you..." He swallowed a dry lump that wouldn't go down. "Are *you* real?"

"What do you think, Arthur?"

Someone had asked him that before. When he was little. He had been suspicious and asked someone the very same question and had gotten the same answer. Then with a wink and a nod, someone said: *Don't spoil it for your sister.*

An earthquake shuddered deep inside him. Childhood memories floated like pixie dust. Tickled his brain. Warmed his heart.

Santa Claus is real.

The magic moment collapsed when the carriage hit a bump. A tray of chocolate drops scattered over the floor and bounced on Art's lap. Only they didn't do the same for Santa. They passed through his white gloves, through the fuzzy red pants, and bounced across the bench he appeared to be sitting on. They settled next to the silver orb.

He's a projection.

He slumped in his seat, looked out the window. They were passing through a dark forest. Pairs of glowing eyes looking out from blackness. Daryl tried to talk to him, but Art wasn't interested. The cat hopped on the seat and climbed onto his lap. Art let him curl up and purr. Then he ran his fingers through the soft fur.

"What do you want?" he said without looking at the jolly fat man.

"What do you need?"

"Not this," he muttered.

He refused to look at the talking projection. Soon the forest thinned, and they were in the hills. The grasslands sparkled with moondew. Two-Face Mountain was in the distance, holding steady as the landscape slowly transitioned from prairies to wetlands and back to forest.

Santa Claus didn't break the silence.

Maybe this story would be different had Art not spoken again. If he would've clammed up for the remainder of the ride, Santa wouldn't have said anything. Awkwardness bloomed in that cramped space. It was a suffocating blanket. No distractions to ignore it, it only got thicker.

"You're here to convince me, right?" Art finally blurted. "So I'll do whatever it is the king wants me to do? That's the only reason you're *here*."

Santa didn't answer that. Instead, he put his hand on his belly and laughed. It was deep and guttural and real. "Ho-ho-ho."

There was nothing funny about it, not that Art could see. But that laugh...

Art fidgeted.

Emotions fluttered from his stomach and into his chest. Memories were attached to them and projected onto the gray screen inside his head.

Ho-ho-ho.

It was the laugh that came from across the house on Christmas morning. Before the sun was up, Art lying in bed, waiting to leave his bedroom. Imagining all the presents waiting under the tree, the heavy stockings sagging from the mantel. Not moving until he heard that laugh from his parents' room.

His father going *ho-ho-ho.*

And Art would go running. He would jump on his parents' giant bed. His little sister bouncing with him. "Wake up! Wake up!" they would shout.

Mother would get up to start coffee.

Crawling under the covers with them. Closing their eyes to imagine what was out there. Mom and Dad closing their eyes, too. Hugging them. Tickling them. They hadn't cared about presents. They had everything they wanted.

The memories were getting out of control. They rose up from the deepness of his subconscious, from those dark corners where he couldn't see, and burst across his mind in oily slicks. Ever since he'd gotten to the Naughty Side, they started appearing. Since he'd started drawing and painting.

Memories that reminded him of who he was. Where he was.

Lost.

He didn't belong. Not here. Not anywhere.

He covered his face with both hands. Sobs were coming, and he couldn't stop them. He clamped his mouth shut and muffled the sounds. His insides churned. He wiped his eyes and looked out the window, ignoring the fake Santa. But he could feel him looking at him kindly.

Art didn't want the ride to end.

He wanted to stay inside the carriage as far as it would take him and stare out the glass. It was safe inside there. The world couldn't touch him.

"Tell me what you believe, Arthur."

"About what?"

"About anything."

"What I believe?" Art laughed coarsely. No one ever asked him that. "I believe you're just a story. And this is just a dream. And not a good one."

"A story. I like a good story. Do you?"

Art sniffed. Wiped his nose with the back of his hand. "I used to believe you were real. You know? I wanted it to be true and then..." He shrugged.

"You grew up."

Life got hard, he wanted to say. The magic of youth vanished. Like it was never really there in the first place. The presents got smaller, and the magic didn't last. Like when he was little and a box could be anything. Now a new phone barely moved the needle.

He wanted to go back to that time. Go back when the world was magic. And his parents were right down the hall. Their bed was warm. *Ho-ho-ho!*

Go back to what it was like when he saw everything with wonder. Believed the world was made of hugs and there was nothing his mom and dad couldn't fix. When life was an endless sleepover.

You can't go back.

"What's your story now?" Santa asked.

"My story now." He grimaced. "I'm stuck in a crazy dream with gingerbread people and fudgy lakes and kings and queens and festivals. And I'm talking to Santa Claus in a stagecoach, and you're not even real!"

"Sounds like an interesting story."

"I want it to *end*."

It hurt to say that. To know he wanted that.

They were still in the forest. The trees were getting bigger and darker. Their branches tangled over the road like knobby fingers. People and things were wandering in the ditch, a pilgrimage of toys and creatures and animals going in the same direction as the stagecoach. They kissed their fingers when the stagecoaches passed them. There were small clumps of them at first, a few here and there. The closer they got to the festival, the larger those clumps were.

"Can I ask something?" Santa said.

"What?"

"Will you close your eyes first? You don't have to do anything else. Just close your eyes."

Art resisted. But his eyes grew heavy. He leaned his head on the window.

"Good."

Santa's breathing began to slow. The absurdity of a projection breathing didn't escape Art, but he got the point. It was what the queen had taught him when they sat on the small benches. He fell into the pattern of slow inhalations through his nostrils, let it leak out even slower.

His body began to settle into place. A weighty relaxation filled him from the bottom up. Starting at his feet.

"Where is that child?" Santa asked. "The one you seek. Find him inside you. Where is he?"

Art continued breathing.

Settling.

Sensations blooming and withering. Thoughts clinging to them and letting go.

In and out.

"Find this child on Christmas Eve…"

Santa's voice was far away now. Art was still in the stagecoach, but there was space around him. It was open and endless and forgiving. Enough space for all those bodily sensations and all those random thoughts to exist. Enough space that it didn't feel cramped inside him. Enough space to see the turbulent water without being swept into its current. He could see everything.

Including childhood memories.

"There he is," Santa said from a long, long ways away.

Art could see the boy in the bed. Lying there with a swirl in his stomach. The blanket up to his chin. Hooves scuffing the shingles above him.

So curious.

The present moment joyous whether good or bad, naughty or nice.

Curious to investigate. To feel. And nowhere to go. Nowhere to be. He was already there.

He was here.

He was here.

He didn't hear Santa Claus again. Even if the jolly fat man had spoken, Art wouldn't have heard him. He was floating in an eternal moment, resting in its embrace. The universe was endless space. There was room for all things. Art was listening for the hooves on the roof.

And the ho-ho-ho down the hall.

21

The green room was literally green. The walls, the floor. Everything.

Art was nestled in an olive-green beanbag wedged in the corner and surrounded by every imaginable variation of chocolate. Syrups and shakes and bars and dollops and puddings. A table of sculptures held little carvings of King Chocolate not intended for eating. Just for looking at.

Three gorillas stood guard.

They wore overalls in pastel colors. No shirts or shoes. Tufts of black curly hair on their black chests. Protruding brows aimed at Art. They hadn't said anything since he'd arrived. Just stood like lumps of muscle. Art liked them. They didn't seem to like him.

The others were busy with plans and outfits and schedules and things. A triplet of fashion icons insisted he try the chocolate fondue. Other than that, they told him to sit in the corner. He was happy to engage in a staring contest with the gorillas. So far it was a tie.

After some time (how much time, impossible to tell, you know), others came through the room. They were more excited, less stressed. And happy to see Art. Clapping and hopping and dancing toward him. The gorillas snatched them before they got close enough to touch him.

He knew he liked them for a reason.

A yarn-haired fabric doll asked for Art's autograph. Held out a marker and wanted him to sign her arm. The gorillas ushered her out. Whenever the door would open, he heard the crowd. It was getting loud and restless. A gruff voice was amplified. There was cannon fire and cheers. Eventually, the music started.

It shook the walls and beanbag.

There was a clock with five hands and symbols instead of numbers. Art had no idea what time it was. Or if it was even a clock. It ticked like one. Maybe it was a bomb.

It helped to have Daryl on his lap, even if he was sleeping.

Art was breathing slowly. Calmly. Eyes open, taking in sights and colors. Registering who was in the room, who was coming and going. The mood. The anxiety. He was unfazed by the festivities. Something in the carriage ride there had changed him.

He wanted to be nowhere else but here.

KING CHOCOLATE GLIDED into the room. His cheeks were frosted. Eyelids, too. His lips the color of glistening mud. He glanced at Art and gave him a scrunchy wink.

"My boy."

Before he could steer in Art's direction, he was pulled aside by the fashion icons. Another set of triplets joined them. This second set was short and skinny. Sort of military like. Missing a limb or an eye. The discussion was heated, with several glances in Art's direction, and made Art a bit nervous with the attention. He wondered if his gorilla pals would throw them out if he told them to. The king drifted toward Art.

"You're not eating chocolate?"

"I'm not hungry."

"What does that have to do with it?" The king laughed. But not as loud as everyone else. They laughed like they were paid to. Except the gorillas. "Are you feeling all right? Did the trip upset your stomach? I'm gassy after long trips."

Art said he felt fine. Truth was he felt great. Whatever the Santa Claus projection had done with him had worked. It was like he'd reclaimed some lost part of his self. He was still Anxious, still Nervous and Afraid, but he wasn't controlled by them. Guilt and Shame watched from a distance but didn't interfere. Like there was space for all of them to exist.

And no appetite for chocolate.

Did the queen learn everything from Santa? he wondered. Jelly said the silver orb was a gift from her. At least, he thought that was what Jelly meant. *Maybe the gift was meeting Santa.*

"You know what to do, my boy?" The king showed him a photo.

Art nodded. He was itching to do one more painting. There was tension to be released in the creative flow. He was about to burst. The king, however, couldn't get a read on him.

"I don't like his energy," the king said to the others. "It's low. Look at everyone in the room, boy. Look at them, all gaga for you. It's nothing compared to what's out there. An entire crowd is waiting for you. They love you! Almost as much as me."

Laughter, paid for and otherwise, erupted.

"They'll want autographs. Kissing babies and stuff. All merry, merry, it's disgusting. Don't believe me? Show him. Look."

The wall behind the gorillas turned into a monitor swirling with color. Images flickered into focus. It showed a sea of people and toys and animals and things. They were listening to music. They were chocolate tub wrestling. They were on chocolate plunge rides. There were burning barrels surrounded by wolves and fights breaking out.

It didn't look real.

Even if it was, Art didn't care.

"They've been waiting for you. All this time, waiting. And you're here. You're finally here. And all you have to do is what you do. As long as it's this." He shook the photo. "Understand? Yes or no. Answer me."

"Understood."

"That's my naughty boy." He pinched Art's cheek with sticky fingers. "Now eat. You're making me nervous."

To prove his point, the king passed gas.

He floated across the room to where an entourage waited. They picked up where the previous conversation had left off. Representatives from all corners of the Naughty Side were there, including buzzing flies and one of the Lost Boys. From time to time, they looked at Art and didn't try to hide it.

Then the king snapped. His anger boiled over and steamed from his ears. Art leaned forward to watch. Daryl repositioned on his lap and went back to sleep.

"Peter!" the king shouted. "Dunk and sprinkle!"

The king pointed at the trio of slender military figures. They didn't flinch when the gorilla named Peter knuckle-walked over and swept them up. They remained stoic when he opened the door—the crowd noise filling the room—and left with them held against his bulging chest. A sugary odor wafted into the room, one Art hadn't noticed before.

An aroma he recognized.

"Terrible advice," the king announced. "Those three misfits deserve the dunk and sprinkle. Anyone else with awful ideas?"

His company heartily answered.

"The boy will change everything. And they wanted to put him in a box? A BOX?" The king shook his head in disappointment. The fashionistas shuffled to the side and positioned themselves behind one of the gorillas. The king was confused. The advisors were against the idea. It was the fashionistas who suggested it. But they came in groups of three, so he was close. Sort of. As long as someone got the dunk and sprinkle, it didn't matter.

"Give the boy a hand, you idiots. Applaud him! Cheer him! Sing his praises."

The excitement steadily grew and was quite convincing. Hoots and hollers and stamping of feet. They gave Art a standing ovation he did nothing to deserve.

"Give us a song, Jelly. Celebrate! There's a new fat man in town!"

The king took a bow and basked in his own glory. The grotesque little legs twiddling uselessly beneath him, he bobbed around his entourage and took their hands and arms and spun them about while Jelly made up words to an imaginary song.

The crosser he's the one. The one, the one, the one.

And he's going to have some fun. Some fun, some fun, some fun.

The king yee-hawed, and so did everyone else. Then he threw a pastry at Jelly. It stuck to her fancy new coat trimmed with fur. The others threw food at her, too. Donuts, cookies, and custard. The king teased Jelly, said she sounded like a wounded walrus, then squirted her with chocolate syrup when she stopped.

"More! More!"

They were all very good actors pretending to have fun. Only the king wasn't pretending.

The gorillas hadn't noticed the mouse standing in the corner. Art didn't see from where she snuck into the room. She watched the petty fun with simmering anger.

On the monitor behind the gorillas, everyone watched the live feed of Peter walking onstage where the band was playing. The slender military figures didn't squirm in his grip. They accepted their fate like soldiers. A vat lowered down from the scaffolding. Peter reached for it. It stopped its descent a few feet over a plastic baby pool.

"Quiet!" The king parked himself in front of the wall monitor. "Watch. Everyone watch."

He was drooling from all the excitement. Intoxicated with power, wiping his chin and licking his fingers. Tiny eyes bulging in their fatty pockets. His entourage gathered around, some of them noticing the large mouse watching from the corner.

Peter held the military figures up for the crowd to see. They were limp like puppies held by the scruff of the neck. The crowd roared their approval. The king's entourage squealed their excitement. The king moaned with pleasure.

Peter dunked them into the vat.

They came out the color of mud. Milk chocolate dripped from their once-shining boots. The crowd went berserk. Then Peter dropped them in the baby pool, one at a time, and rolled them like dough. They came out covered with specks of candy. Peter held them over his head.

Excitement spilled over the audience in fits of violence.

Peter put the multicolored soldiers in a clear display box hanging between two drum sets. The octopuses began playing.

"Dunked!" The king shook his fist. "And sprinkled!"

The king's entourage repeated what he said and shook their fists like he did. And laughed like he laughed. The king looked around to make sure they were as excited as he was. Or perhaps deciding on who would go for a roll next.

Because it was so much fun.

"Tonight is a ten," he bellowed. "Let's take it to a twelve!"

He started to howl. So did the others. They took a deep breath to keep it going—to take this party to a twelve—when he choked. The entourage pretended to choke. The king waved his arms at them. Blood rushed into his face. His tongue had swelled. A few of the sycophants imitated him until they turned blue and purple, waving their arms and holding their breath.

The king finally managed two words. It was enough.

"EVERYONE OUT!"

"Throw her out!" His hand shook as much as his voice. "If her giant clown is out there, and I know she is, tell her she will be BANISHED from the Naughty Side if she doesn't LEAVE NOW! Go, you apes. Get her *out of here!*"

The gorillas did what they were told to do.

They knuckle-walked toward the frail mouse in the long, patchwork overcoat. Her crown missing from her head, where sprigs of gray shot in all directions. They could toss her out the door without grunting.

The fur bristled on the nape of the queen's neck.

She inhaled long and deep. Her voice as sharp as a papercut.

"Henry! Carl! You stop right there."

They did exactly that. It was spontaneous and undeniable. The queen's voice struck a chord only a mother could find. They were trapped between the king and the queen. An unenviable place to be.

"Now!" the king roared. "I want her out now, or you'll be scraping calluses off my feet!"

The king didn't have calluses. On his feet or anywhere on his body. Still, Henry and Carl stepped toward the queen.

"Boys," the queen said as calmly as if she asked them to pass the butter.

"I'm your king!"

"I am your queen."

"No! No, she's not! I fired her yester—*ahhhh.* I'm counting to three!"

The king held up three fingers. They fell one at a time, the king's voice rising with each one. He shrieked at the end and screamed, "ZERO!"

The gorillas stutter stepped. Stopped. Looked at each other with wide eyes and fat lips. They decided without saying a word out loud it was better to follow the king. Until the queen played her trump card.

"I will talk to your mother."

They stepped aside, put their backs against the wall. No hesitation. The king could've said the same thing and it wouldn't have mattered. The queen knew their mother and knew her well. The king had nothing on her.

Without her crown, she walked across the room. Henry and Carl didn't flinch as she passed, her mousey nails clicking on the hard floor. True royalty didn't need a crown. She took the crusted remains of pastry off Jelly's coat, wiped the custard from the elf's cheek, then nodded.

Jelly bent the knee of her stubby leg.

"You may be the king of the Naughty, but you are not a child." The queen said to King Chocolate. "Jelly has been nothing but good to you. This is not how to lead."

"Lead? What do you know about leading? I KNOW HOW TO LEAD!" He slapped his chest. "I was made for this, not you. You see those animals out there? You think there's anyone in *aallllll* of Candyland who can lead *them*? They love me, you rat. I can do anything I want, and they love me more. THEY LOVE ME!"

"That's not important."

"It's the only thing that matters! They follow *me* because they love *me*."

"And where are you taking them, Casey?"

"To the winner's circle. And you're not invited. You don't get to ride in the car when they have a parade for me. And if you do not leave right now, I will open those doors and have *my fans* drag you out. You don't know *all* their mothers."

"I know most."

"You want to try me?" He floated near the ceiling. Raised his chin to mimic confidence and power, but only looked like a child imitating an adult.

Art had not moved. Not a finger.

The queen was the first to regard him. Her look thoughtful, penetrating.

"Have your fun tonight, Casey. Do as you wish. But I will stay with Arthur for the remainder of the evening. When this is finished, you will never see me again."

"I don't make deals."

"I'm not offering one."

He appeared to be an inflatable balloon about to burst. His teeth grinding like machinery in need of lubrication.

"Never?"

"As in ever, Casey."

"Aaaah, I see what you're doing. When *this* is finished? Too *vague*. You can't trick a tricker. You will leave when Christmas arrives. And not a tick later."

"Of course. This will be finished by then."

He cruised closer. "And what do you think *this* is?"

"It's a mistake."

"You haven't a clue what you're talking about."

"I know a mistake when I see one."

The king growled and flew a lap around the room. His tiny legs dribbling over the gorillas' heads. He came to a screeching halt, the hoversuit whining to hold the massive momentum in check. Seething, the king spoke to Jelly.

"Tell her that if she tries to taint the boy, there will be consequences."

"Tell the king I will do no such thing," the queen said.

The king nodded. Then laughed, mostly to himself. She was up to something. He could smell it. But what could she do? The boy had one last painting to do, and then he was done with him. Naughty Side for the win.

"She's not the queen, bt-dub. Just so everyone knows. She has no power. None. You understand, don't you?" he said to his primate security. Both of whom would be fired sooner than soon. "She's just a rat. That's all. A rat I housed and clothed. When she was a no-name, lowlife crosser, I made her someone. Me. I did. She'd be nothing without me. Tell her this is the last time, Jelly Belly. Tell her bye, Felicia."

"What does that mean?" the queen said.

"You wouldn't understand," the king said. "Take your giant clown with you. I don't want to see that monster ever again, either. Now, boys, come here."

The gorillas were too broad for him to put his arms around. He made them squeeze closer together. "Are you listening?"

They grunted.

"First of all, you're fired when this is over. No offense, but I need someone smarter than my left foot. Second, she can't talk to the boy. Like at all. Not a word. She can sit in here till the gingersnaps come home, I don't care. No talking. You got that? Repeat it back. Let me hear it."

They repeated some of it.

"Close enough. I'm going out there now."

"They're not ready for you," Jelly said. "The schedule—"

"I'M GOING ON! Get the boy ready. I'm going to get that crowd of dirty sickos wound up for his grand opening. You're going to be a star, Arty Farty. I can feel it in my delicious bones. I love you, boy. Love you like a son." The king kissed two fingers and held them up. "Peace out."

He stuck his tongue out at the queen. Snapped his fingers at Jelly.

"Let's go, Jello. Get the sled fired up."

THE QUEEN PULLED a beanbag next to Art. A purple one. It hissed when she eased into it. She coiled her tail on her lap.

Together they watched the live events play out on the wall monitor.

The dunked and sprinkled advisors stood in their plastic cage. Chocolate rained down from overhead cannons. Sparks drizzled onto the stage while fires burned near the trees.

Then King Chocolate put on a show, and everything changed.

The queen didn't say anything. Didn't ask Art to slow his breathing. Didn't reach for his hand. She was present with him. And that was all he needed.

Anxiety didn't shake him. Panic wasn't around.

Art floated in a deep well of warmth and acceptance. *Christmas spirit,* the queen had called it. *True Christmas spirit.* He had realized that all these memories that had emerged, they existed whether he remembered them or not. To possess them wasn't what he needed to do. They were real. They'd happened. Nothing could make them unhappen, even if he forgot.

That was the peace he rested in. That was all he needed.

He was here for a reason. He had to go to the bottom of the dark side before climbing out. He and the queen watched the king's grand speech.

And then Jelly came for him.

22

L*evel seven.*

The triple bass drums washed over the king like a conga line of fists. He sat stage left, just out of view of the crowd, while a pair of long-legged spider daddies loaded a fresh set of batteries into the back of the hoversuit. It was hanging a bit loose in the midsection.

"Tighten it up!" he shouted.

They were grunting and tugging, but the spider daddies proved to be useless. He wasn't in the mood for excuses, and there was no time to call the fashionistas. He needed to wash the bad taste out of his brain. He wanted to obliterate what had happened in the green room and leave no trace of the queen.

The band helped him do that. They were destroying his rendition of "Naughty Time." In a good way. A great way.

Troll, the lead singer, had flaming red hair. Literally. He'd thrown a match on the bright orange tuft halfway through the song. Blue flames licked his head. It smelled like burnt cinnamon toast.

Two octopuses, one orange and the other purple, thrashed two sets of drums. (Dual drums had been King Chocolate's idea). The double percussion sent ripples over the king's doughy skin. And then

Wire Doll chummed the mosh pit with a head-splitting guitar solo. A string of gorillas, locked arm in arm, kept the crowd from spilling onto the stage.

A gingerbread arm went flying over them and broke into pieces. Troll picked it up and took a bite. Threw the rest of it at the shame cage where the dunked and sprinkled advisors swung in their glass prison. The smell of Fudgy Lake wafted off them like volcanic fumes.

They'll make a good ornament, the king thought. He could replicate little glass cages with dunked and sprinkled misfits inside for next Christmas, crank them out by the thousands, ready to hang on trees. *Sell them by the truckload.*

The spider daddies locked up the battery compartment. An electric vibe tickled the king's funny parts, squeezed him with fresh juice. Troll was slinging sweat all over the backs of the gorillas. King Chocolate would rather skinny-dip in Fudgy Lake than feel that. Then the dwarf leaped into the crowd and bodysurfed across the mosh pit.

"Enough."

King Chocolate gave the order. Now wasn't the time for an extended version of "Naughty Time." A halo of fly messengers went out to deliver his order. The octopuses dropped their sticks. Wire Doll let go of his guitar. When the message reached the mosh pit, Troll was launched back onstage like a toxic hair ball. He bounced once, then took out one of the drum sets. The octopuses carried him off, hair still smoking.

The lights dimmed.

Word spread like a tsunami. The crowd pushed toward the stage. The gorilla line held firm. One break and the animals would wreck the stage with joy. The king licked the air, tasted the charge. It was hot and electric. *Christmas fever,* he thought. *That's what it is. Far better than Christmas spirit.*

He allowed the silence and darkness to stretch out.

Level eight.

Anticipation climbed another level. It was a beautiful stench. The king felt bubbly inside. This was it. This was everything he'd worked for. This was the precipice of victory. He was going to squeeze every drop out of it, drink it down and fill his belly.

Adrenaline spilled over the rim. Fights broke out.

A band of pirates slashed their way toward the front.

The Snow Queen turned a gaggle of bridge trolls into ice cubes.

The Big Bad Wolf howled. His posse joined him.

The king raised a finger. Wire Doll saw it and plucked a few notes on his guitar. He strung together a slow-building intro. It ignited the crowd with furious joy. Fused their chaos into one. The fighting stopped. As one they pressed forward.

Level nine.

The king could see a blue aura rippling over the sea of naughties like heat waves over sand. *The essence of the Naughty Side!* There had always been a certain quality to this side of Candyland. A vibe that was dangerous and free, an energy that singed the skin and tickled the belly. It jellied knees and liquified the weak. It was beautiful in its prime.

The king could see it. Taste it.

He was the conductor of this mad symphony.

No one else could do what he did. No one could ever bring this horde of uglies together like him. Stir them in a kettle. Bring them to a boil. Forge a new Christmas essence. One he would bottle and sell to the masses.

Christmas fever!

On his signal came a mechanical roar. Chrome pipes blatted the raw music of power. It twisted brains and tied muscles into furious knots. The hint of something large and gleaming began to lower from the scaffolding. It was long and mean. Flashes of dark beauty were highlighted in a brief shower of flames spitting from its tailpipes.

Level ten.

The king wasn't done. But if he wasn't careful, the entire show would collapse in euphoric anarchy. The Maestro of Naughty played them like instruments, sculpting expectations, massaging beliefs.

The king drank it up and let it build to a tenuous climax. The membrane of order stretched thin. The line of gorillas began to bend.

The gleaming object touched the stage. The motor hummed a dangerous tune to feed the frenzy. Only then did the king open his eyes. He skipped right over level eleven and teetered on the brink.

"Now."

The mass of his girth flew across the stage like a pillowy puppet. Greeted with thrashing guitar chords and hammering drums that pummeled the crowd with such force they were sent reeling back. For a moment, there was a gulf between the crowd and the gorillas. Then it collapsed and nearly broke the muscled dike.

A spotlight followed him around the bright and shiny sleigh with long chrome tailpipes and fire painted down the sides. Gold rails and gold bumpers. Sleek and fearsome. Loud and obnoxious.

Just like the boy had drawn it.

He went from one side to the next, soaring to the edges of the stage, long coat fluttering behind him like a cape (plans were to sell capes after the show). He paused long enough for chocolate bars to shoot from candy cannons strapped to the king's hips (the fashionistas' idea, although King Chocolate took credit for it).

Hand to his ear to hear the roar.

Hand to his other ear to make it louder.

He blew kisses. Pumped his fists. Wound them up until leaves fell from the trees.

Level twelve.

A THRONE ROLLED to center stage. King Chocolate lowered onto it. Adrenaline boiled his blood. He couldn't feel the loose hoversuit chafing his sides. He sat very still, absorbing the madness. A spectator of violence. So many of them had to be physically restrained. Some were broken. No one seemed to mind.

Especially the king.

A live close-up of him projected onto a screen. He doused the urge to smile, not wanting to appear weak. Raised his chin to show strength. He closed his eyes for a long moment, inhaling the smell of victory.

It smelled like chaos.

When the line of security began to bow, he raised his hand. That was all it took.

Quiet fell like winter snow. He kept his hand up until the crackle of distant trash fires could be heard. They were out of breath, shaking with anticipation. Ready to do whatever he said.

This is how you lead.

"Look at you," he started. His voice effortlessly carried over the crowd. "You deplorable... disgusting... filthy... ugly..."

Each word deliberate and heavy. Slow and steady. The pace picking up. The cheering followed.

"Disgraceful, shameful, inexcusable..."

The mosh pit started throwing elbows. They climbed on each other's shoulders, threw broken limbs onstage, howled into the darkness.

"Dreadful-horrid-nasty-foul... REJECTS!"

Christmas fever went through level twelve and touched thirteen. Things were getting smashed and stomped and beaten. The Wicked Witch flew over the crowd, just out of reach, turning random naughties into toads.

His hand went up.

A calm washed through the crowd and turned the storm-tossed ocean into a glassy lake.

All attention on their leader masterfully letting the silence wrap around them.

"How many Christmases have there been? Does anyone remember?"

Some shouted out answers. King Chocolate didn't know if there was a right answer. No one remembered how many Christmases there had been in Candyland. The answer was infinite.

"And how many times did you wake up to coal in your stocking? I'll bet you remember that. *Every... single... Christmas!*"

There were murmurs and shuffling. They knew what a lump of coal felt like.

"Forever! That's how many times you got coal. Eternity! That's how many Christmases there have been. And all this time the jolly fat man dumps his trash on your doorstep, then waltzes over to *that* side and DELIVERS PRESENTS!"

He pointed to the distant line in the sky, where dark met light.

"And he stacks them high, my lovelies. He stacks those boxes and bags and shiny things as high as the sky, my precious naughties. And those happy nicies grab each other's hands to dance around their mountains of gifts, singing their songs and laughing at the poor naughties with their dirty, filthy stockings filled with soot.

"And it doesn't matter how high their piles are. No. The jolly fat man will add another present. And another. And another. Because they're the nice ones. The good ones. The jolly fat man says: Do what I say and follow the rules and *I'll bring you more!*"

The king slapped his belly like a drum.

"We don't matter. None of us. Because we're the bad ones. The rotten ones. We're broken. Deplorable. Disgusting." He took a long deep breath. "WE ARE NAUGHTY!"

He took a moment to let that one cook.

"*I've* never rejected you. Not a single one of you. I've loved you for who you are. We are free over here! Free to be naughty. Free to be nice —I said it, that's right. *Nice.* If that's who you are, then you be that. But let's be honest." A wry twist on his bloated face winked on the screen. "It's not much fun to be nice, now is it."

Oh, the joy. The rowdy joy.

"Everyone is welcome, my naughties. No one is turned away from the Naughty Side." *Except the rat queen.* "We are family. I have thousands of sons and daughters and brothers and sisters. FAMILY! We are a team. We are..." He thumped his chest twice. "*Naugh*-ty."

He did it again. Same cadence.

"We are... Naugh-ty! We are... Naugh-ty!"

The band caught on. The bass drum picked up the beat. The crowd joined in. The king raised his arms.

We are (BOOM-BOOM) Naugh-ty!

The chant generated a magnetism that drew the crowd together. A bond between brother and sister materialized.

WE ARE...

A tribal anthem was forging. There was no bond more unbroken, no salve more healing for a broken nation than us versus them.

NAUGH-TY!

"Do you feel that? Feel it! Your brother to your right. Your sister to your left."

WE ARE...

"We've been fighting them forever. Merry, merry? He gives us coal. Coal! Not very nice. Not very merry!"

NAUGH-TY!

"They're phonies, and you know it. *They* know it! That's why you're here. You're part of this family because you are real. You are free. *You* are the merry ones! I feel it. I feel the Christmas fever. You are the good and the bad and the free!"

WE ARE...

"They want to make us like *them!* Do what they say, follow their rules. Get in line and you can have a mountain of presents, too. Is that what you want? To sell your truth for a box of Carrot-Top Dolls?"

NAUGH-TY!

The beat grew louder. Wire Doll joined the drums with power chords.

Fists in the air. Fists pounding chests. Wolves howled and witches laughed and sparks danced into the dark.

"We love you, King Chocolate!" a half-inflated doll shouted.

"We love you!" others joined in.

The king let the worship fall over him like warm rain on a summer night. He soaked it in. Drank it up. Let the beat go on.

Then he said: "Aren't you tired of being judged?"

"We love you!"

"Tonight is the night!" He hovered above the throne, arms out and welcoming. "This is Christmas Eve. This is when the jolly fat man comes with another bag of coal for you rejects. You scum. You misfit toys. He comes to blacken your stockings and dust your mantels while the nicies sing their songs and sit on his lap and read their lists and follow their rules. But not tonight!"

He hovered above the throne.

"Tonight we change that. Tonight the eternal war ends. Tonight their true colors will be exposed, their fakeness stripped away. Tonight the jolly fat man will stuff *their* stockings with black, sooty *COAL!*"

The rocket sleigh ignited on cue.

Flames from the tailpipes bathed Wire Doll in fire. He stepped out of the heat, the guitar melting in orange glowing hands. The crowd loved it. They ate the power from the smoking engines like breakfast cereal, waiting for weapons to unfold from the sides.

There were no weapons. Maybe next time.

The most powerful thing didn't look like a weapon. He was sitting backstage. A canvas lowered down to the stage. The crowd recognized the map of Candyland stenciled upon it. Every Lander knew it.

A curvy line down the middle.

One side dark and cloudy, the other light and cheery.

The crowd crawled over each other with expectations. When the rocket sleigh went quiet and the chant died down, a spring-loaded anticipation took hold of them. They leaned against each other, waiting for the final solution their king had promised.

He pointed at Two-Face Mountain, where the Nice Side lit half of it.

"Tonight," he said, "we make them naughty."

23

Art didn't notice the stirring confusion and mild disappointment.

His distant gaze was inwardly focused. He hardly noticed the crowd. Didn't see their twisted faces or angry taunts. Didn't see the king hold his arms out for a hug.

Art was filled with a vision.

He saw the canvas. A canvas so big that an A-frame ladder would be needed to reach the top of it. There was a rack of aerosol cans. Spray paint of every shade and color.

He'd studied the map that was already printed on the canvas. It was just like he'd imagined. What he'd been asked to do. It sounded boring. Unimaginative. But something about it was intriguing. Meaningful. Drew him in.

Paint it black, he thought. *Paint it all black.*

His hand moved on its own, selecting cans as if the decision had already been made.

While the crowd jeered, his breath was slow and steady. He was this moment. He was the flow. The essence.

I am the Christmas spirit.

There was no crowd or trees. No band, no stage. No pain or fear. No happiness.

He was none of it. He was all of it.

It made no sense to think of it that way. But in it—in that flowing spirit—there was no need to make sense. The Christmas spirit wanted him to be everything. To see all of him. What was inside him. To know who he was. Truly was. It was why he was here. To let it out.

So the world can see me.

It flowed down his arm. An aerosol hiss dampened and darkened the canvas. Fuming the air.

The spirit poured onto the canvas.

He didn't hear the gasps or feel the wonder behind him. Didn't hear the chanting. Didn't notice the stage shaking or the ground quaking. All he saw was empty canvas to fill.

This is what I came here to do.

He was no longer hiding from himself. He wanted the world to know who he was. The hard feelings he carried. The Guilt and Shame inside him. He dug deeper, opening vault doors filled with secrets, sweeping corners that stored embarrassment. As he emptied himself onto the canvas, memories of who he was stepped into the light. Of who he was, who he is, and who he will become. *This place isn't a dream*, he decided.

It's a gift. To be here is a gift.

Shake and rattle went the cans.

This is Christmas.

Spray and hiss.

I am Christmas.

THE FIRST DROP of rain streaked the swirls of grays and blacks and browns. It dripped to the bottom and clung to the edge of the canvas. Highlighted by a flash of lightning and distant thunder.

Earthquakes followed. One after another.

Things fell from the scaffolding.

Sweat ran down his cheeks and over his lips. He painted with his eyes closed, seeing what was needed clearer than anything he'd ever seen. Both hands loaded with paint, staining the canvas with his truth. The king didn't need to tell him what to do. It was already inside him.

The instruments shorted out. The band ran from the stage as a monsoon hammered down. The ground turned to mud. The fires extinguished. The king's voice no longer projected through the speakers. Everything was the sound of rain.

Art climbed the ladder.

Stood on the very top.

On his toes.

His fingers cramped. Stomach clenched. Weak and shaking, the last swipes were applied. The cans empty. The map no longer black on one side and white on the other. There was no hint of a curving line. It was all one color.

No longer Naughty and Nice.

Art was as empty as the cans he was holding. He didn't fall from the ladder. He simply couldn't hold himself up any longer. As he tipped over the side, the rain suddenly stopped. He felt the wind in his ears and waited for the hard landing below him. He wasn't afraid. He didn't clench or brace for impact because he was empty. The weight of Guilt and Shame was no longer in him. He'd become so light and empty that he was certain that he would float away instead of crash. Float into the sky and out of this dream.

Gracefully, he fell.

Instead of the unforgiving stage, he landed in a soft embrace.

The vicious roar of the crowd fell over him. The shouting, the cheering. The hungry snarl of the sleigh rockets and the heat of their engines. The stage shook and caught fire as the sleigh launched over the trees. A stampede followed its direction.

The sky so dark as far as he could see.

A pink hand wiped the hair from his eyes. Strong arms cradled him against her furry body. The queen looked down with very human eyes and smiled with kindness. She nodded and whispered, "I see you, Arthur."

He shuddered and wept. The map of Candyland was a circle of darkness. Yet there in the middle, right where the border had once been, was something he hadn't seen in his vision. Something he hadn't painted. It hadn't been there when he finished, but he could see it now.

It wasn't a trick.

A single beam of light was etched in the darkness.

24

The engines rearranged King Chocolate's innards. His organs churning into a chocolate smoothie. Violent waves rode up his neck and over his chin, reached into his tummy and gave it a good stir. He turned to the front of the sleigh, wind stretching his cheeks into a clownish grin, and shouted: "Turn off the rockets!"

"What?" Jelly said.

The king could barely hear his own words. He clutched the back of the driver's seat. "The rockets!" he shouted directly into Jelly's ear. "Turn them off!"

"I don't know how! This is just turbulence!"

"This isn't turbulence!"

"What?"

The king let go, crashing into the back of his seat. Tears streaming across his temples and wetting his knotted hair. Even if Jelly knew how to turn the rockets off (which she most certainly did, the little liar), they'd go down like a meteor. If they survived this, he would be partially deaf. And mostly numb.

It was his fault, if he were to admit it. He'd given the drawing to the boy, this grand shiny monster that purred like a predator and flew like a weapon. Of course, King Chocolate hadn't thought about the tailpipes blasting raw power next to the back seat.

He plugged his ears with two plump fingers.

There wasn't much to see this far up. Through a blur of wind-swept tears, Two-Face Mountain stuck out like an upside-down ice-cream cone. The sleigh leaned into a turn. The king felt his stomach drop into his bottom. He pulled his fingers out of his ears to hang on. They circled around the left side of the mountain. A beam of white light was spiked into the side of it and went straight up through the sky.

The boy missed that part.

He'd done a masterful job with the painting. The king had shed one chocolatey tear as the boy had done his work. The dark sky stretching further with each stroke. If only King Chocolate could have seen all those nicies when the clouds ate up their pink sky like a video game. The big phony smiles melting away on their big, dumb faces. Imagining it sent stampedes of gooseflesh over the rolling hills of his body.

Beyond the mountain, it was dark. Not a single streetlight or lamp-lit window. There was never a need for them. It was always bright on this side of the mountain. Always merry. *Until now.*

"And who's the king of the naughty?" he said.

"What?"

"Nothing!" He kicked the seat. "Just fly!"

They rumbled over the dark land. It was too dim to see the roads and homes. Too dim to see the nicies looking up at the sleigh growling through the sky. They'd think it was Santa coming to save them. The king reached into a sack under his seat. He threw chocolate coins over the side of the sleigh.

"Blah-blah, you goodies. Here's a Christmas treat you won't be able to live without."

Most of the nicies had never sampled his chocolatey goodness.

Once they got a taste, they'd line up for more. It wouldn't be long before he had *all* the money. *All of it.* He wanted everything. And he wanted everyone to know he had everything.

"Fly lower!"

"Not a good idea!" Jelly said. "I can't really see the ground."

"It wasn't a suggestion!"

He kicked the seat. The sleigh dropped suddenly. The king rose off the seat a few inches and held on to keep from soaring out. The hoversuit wasn't made to fly. When the sleigh leveled out, faint roofs appeared. He could see the roads, as well. Jelly went lower and eased up on the throttle. The engines coughed like unfed animals smelling prey.

The king could see them now. Little mad ants running around. Pointing. Gossiping.

They'd never lived under a dim sky. They weren't going to like it. Life was heavy and harsh. Sometimes mean. Optimism shriveled under it. But they'd get used to it. Or not. It wasn't really a choice.

King Chocolate was going to rename the place. Since there was no more Nice Side, there was no reason it should be called Candyland. Just make it simple.

Naughtyland. Or Naughty Town. City of Naughty? Wait! He licked his blackened lips, this thought so delicious he wanted to taste it.

"Badland."

"What?"

The king pointed at the massive shadow ahead. Castle Nice, once a shiny pillar of merry goodwill, now looked lost and hopeless. *No more lies, goodies! True colors from here on out.*

"You're welcome!"

He bombed the gawkers with a bucket of malted chocolates. He had Jelly make a lap down Gumdrop Alley to pitch his candies like it was a Christmas parade. The nicies ran for cover. Chocolate drops shattered roofing shingles and busted out windows. They knocked over bicycles and blew through awnings until the bag was almost empty.

Going to need more ammo, he thought.

He would have to return to get the boy anyway. He'd left him with the rat queen. She could do no harm now. The game was over.

"To the castle!"

❄

JELLY CIRCLED THE CASTLE. The pristine water of Rose Lake surrounded it like a slab of obsidian. Jelly brought the sleigh closer, rippling the surface. A crowd gathered along the shore, filling the open market and shabby buildings. The king grabbed Jelly's shoulder and pointed. He wanted her to land.

"It's too crowded!" Jelly shouted. "I'll go around to the—"

"They'll get out of the way."

Jelly didn't want to do it. She tried to land short of the market. The king leaned over and yanked the reins attached to the dashboard. The sleigh corkscrewed three times and nearly dumped them into an alley.

They skidded on one rail. Bounced off a candy-cane tree. Sparks flew.

The nicies scattered like bugs. All except the nutcrackers. They held their ground as the sleigh barreled toward them. The wooden soldiers didn't flinch. They sounded like bowling pins when the shiny nose of the sleigh struck them. They spun and twisted, taking out a cart of nuts and knocking over a shanty made of straw. The rails screeched over the pavers and came to a sudden stop. The king hit his head on the back of Jelly's seat.

The engines hissed and ticked. Steam sizzled from beneath the hood.

A high-pitched whine filled the king's head. He waved off the smoke, coughing. There were screams and general chaos. The sort of thing King Chocolate loved.

Feels like home.

"Everyone, go back to your homes!" someone called in a firm voice. "Go to your families. Take the week off and get some rest. All will be well soon!"

King Chocolate recognized the voice.

The hoversuit carried him out of the sleigh and over the road. Launched him higher than he'd ever been. Like he was flying. He nearly fell out the bottom of the suit. The thing hardly fit. A rank odor wafted out from beneath the hoversuit.

Good. Stink the place up and mark it like an animal.

He started laughing. It got the attention of the citizens of the (formally known as) Nice Side. They'd never heard laughter like his. Laughter that lacked joy. Laughter with an edge that could saw down a tree.

"Happy Halloween, ladies." He stuck his tongue out. A rag doll fainted.

King Chocolate floated down the middle of the brick road. His legs waved beneath him like wet lengths of yarn. He sped toward the one who was trying to calm the citizens. The one helping them pick up their belongings and ushering them to safety. His royal crown crooked on his dumb head.

Someone waddled in front of King Chocolate. A fat little elf determined not to let him pass. He could hover over her, but he was in no hurry. There was time to wallow in victory.

"Jelly, you know this one? She looks like you." King Chocolate looked back and forth. "Sort of *exactly* like you."

Jelly didn't move from the sleigh. King Chocolate snapped his fingers.

"Are you... don't tell me." He covered his mouth. "*You're Belly!* I've heard so much about you! Oh, my bells. You two have so much to catch up on. But not now. Right now, Jelly's guarding the sleigh. It's expensive, you know. Custom made. Want to know how I made it?" He whispered: "Ancient Lander secret."

He winked.

Belly didn't move. Didn't twitch. Those fat little arms crossed over her big round stomach. And a scowl as deep as a valley etched into her face.

"Ain't you supposed to be the happy one? Jelly, is she supposed to be happy? The weather got you down, sister? It has that effect. Bad news: this is permanent. Good news: you'll get used to it. But ooooooo, good times are coming, me lady. We're going to show you how to party. Now why don't you go help that old toy across the street and let the big people talk. Scram."

The formerly merry elf who once lived at the top of the castle did not move.

"I think we broke her, Jelly! She's lost that loving feeling, I can tell. I can feel the hate coming off her. It's like acid. You know, like when you put your tongue on a battery?"

The chaos died down. The citizens who hadn't taken cover or run back home stood on both sides of the market. This was their first sighting of the chocolate king. They'd seen pictures of him, sure. But in the flesh, it was mesmerizing. A wolf was wringing his hands and biting his lip. He wore a Santa hat. There was nothing *bad* about this wolf.

"The naughties will be here in a few rings!" King Chocolate called to them. "They're coming as fast as they can. Looking forward to meeting you all, I'm sure. How are you enjoying the weather. Pink getting boring, I'll bet. I never cared for it. But this." He pointed at the swirling gray ceiling. "It's got character. Makes you work for a good day."

They didn't move or twitch. Or make a sound.

The king looked down at Belly. Back to the gawkers.

"Not big talkers, huh? I thought you'd be a chatty bunch. I'll just —" He bounced off Belly, who wobbled on those giant paddle feet. King Chocolate could have mowed her down. The hoversuit had a full charge. He could push a train with it. Instead, he leaned into her. "This isn't going to end well for you, sister."

"Enough."

Macey (formerly the king of the nicies) cradled a giant purple egg wearing Bermuda shorts and sucking a pacifier. He had dirtied the knees of his royal robe. There was mud on his hands and on his face. He knelt next to Belly, who was still eyeballing King Chocolate with tiny-dog syndrome.

"Why don't you help at the hut, Belly. The queen is in the nursery." He passed the pacifier-sucking egg to the roly-poly elf. "Thank you."

Macey wiped his hands on his sleeves and stood up.

The kings looked at each other. Somewhere a baby cried. The gawking crowd waited for someone to draw a weapon.

"Well, this is a first," King Chocolate said. "Not straddling the border with your lady. Feels a little weird, right? Just a couple of *bachelors* hanging out at the market. Heh-heh. Anyway, this place is a dump. I thought it would be more, I don't know. *Nice*."

King Nice blinked slowly.

"I'm thinking the lake here will make a good skating rink. Ever been skating? How about fishing? Now there's a sport. We stocked Fudgy Lake with some fat trophies, but their gills gummed up. It was disgusting. You had to fry them in bacon fat to eat them. Now there's just Swedish fish in it. You know, the gummy kind. I don't like them, but can't stop eating them. It's weird."

Macey watched his brother in disbelief.

"You got a little something on your—"

"Why?"

"You slipped and fell? I don't know."

King Chocolate licked his thumb and wiped the dirt off Macey's cheek. His brother crossed his arms and looked away. He looked like his dog died.

"Why? What do you mean *why*? You know why! This is what we do, brother. Push, pull. Naughty, nice. You hate me, I hate you."

"I never hated you, Casey."

"That's a lie. A gold-bar lie if I ever heard one. Hear that, Jelly? He *never* hated us." He puttered down to the ground. Rubbery legs folded beneath him. "You judged us, Macey. Looked down on us. You think you're better than us. Getting warm?"

"That's what you think? That-that-that we wanted a better life for you because we *hated* you?"

"There you go." King Chocolate pointed in his face. "You see that? Right there. That look in your eye, right there. What is it? Jelly! What's the big words a dumb naughty like me don't 'member?"

"Self-righteous pity."

King Chocolate snapped his fingers. "Self-righteous pity. Right there. Disgusting, ain't it. I'd rather you kick me in the shin than look at me like that. Go on, be honest. We disgust you." He flashed chocolate-stained teeth. "We embarrass you. What, brother? What are you hiding behind that fake smile?"

"I feel sorry for the naughties."

"Because they party?"

"You make them live in darkness with you. The way you treat each other over there." He pinched the bridge of his nose. "It breaks my heart."

"Oh, dear Santa Claus," King Chocolate muttered. "The *drama*."

Worse than high school theater.

"That's what I'm talking about!" King Chocolate floated several feet off the road and turned in a circle so all the goodies could hear him. "You disgust me, all of you! You bury your faults, your dirty little secrets so deep you don't see them and then pretend they ain't there. Pretend you don't lie. Pretend you weren't going to *use that boy to wipe out the Naughty Side*. ADMIT IT!"

He stormed down on Macey.

"Admit it, just once, brother, and I swear on Santa's reindeer I'll make the boy take it all back. You can have your pink skies and be just as plastic as you were before. Just admit it. Admit you were going to use the boy on us like I did on you."

"You don't own the boy. Shame on you for making him destroy our side. He doesn't even know what he's done."

"Oh, he knows. He knows you trapped him in your castle. You had plans for him, didn't you. You were going to use him to change us into *you*! But the boy, he's too smart. He came to the dark side, brother. Then I did to you what you were going to do to us. I won, brother." He blew a kiss. "You lost."

"This isn't a game!"

"I won! Admit it!"

"You're acting like a child."

"Admit it!"

"Admit what? What do you want me to admit, Casey? That I care about you? That I want to ease your suffering? That I want you to feel the warm light on your skin and not the clammy grip of night?" He called to the sidewalks stuffed with gawkers. "I admit I care about you!"

They murmured in agreement. The idiots went along with his nonsense. They were too dim to see through the lies. King Chocolate knew a lie when he heard one. He was a master fibber. A professional deceiver. His brother was good, though. He had these dingdongs eating baloney out of his hands.

King Chocolate surveyed the nodding heads. Little Boy Blue with his trumpet (his brother played a mean guitar on the Naughty Side). Peter Pumpkin Eater sitting on an orange three-wheeler (his brother ate ghost peppers). Bo-Peep and Jack Horner and Mary with her dopey lambs.

They're sheep. All of them gullible sheep.

He measured their forgiving disposition. Kindness in their expressions. It was disgusting and weak. King Chocolate had scorched their skies and they were going to forgive him? Well, tough love had arrived on a rocket sleigh just in time to open their eyes.

"You know he's Santa, don't you?" King Chocolate pointed at his brother. "Santa doesn't fly in a sleigh or have magic reindeer. He lives in that castle. And every Christmas he glues a beard on his face and sits in that big dumb throne for you idiots to climb on his lap. All those pictures you have with Santa—*it's him*. All those presents Santa gave you?"

He nodded at Macey.

"Your king's been conning you since day one. Making you believe the stories. Well, I'm here to tell the truth."

"Casey—"

"He's pretending to be Santa because Santa ain't real! He didn't tell you that, did he. He lied to you. He lied to *all* of you. There ain't no flying reindeer, and there ain't no Santa Claus. Well, let me tell you something—telling lies ain't how we're going to live anymore. I'm in charge of this dump now. I'm the king, and the truth will be told!"

He took a long, hacky breath.

"SANTA AIN'T REAL!"

It didn't get the reaction he thought it would. He thought there would be gasps and frowning. Lots of frowning. A few boos (at Macey, not King Chocolate). And maybe, just maybe, a little appreciation. You know, for the honesty.

None of that, though. Dead silence.

They were waiting for Macey to reply. But here's the thing. When two certified liars go head-to-head, no one wins. And nothing changes.

"If Santa isn't real," Macey said, just as calmly as asking about the weather, "then who puts coal in your stockings?"

A BRILLIANT MOVE.

The kind of move some call checkmate.

"Every Christmas you complain about the coal. You print it on your banner and wave it over the castle. You beat drums with it, write songs about it. Sing anthems. *Oh, the coal. The coal, the coal. It dirties our soul, the coal. The coal.* And how lucky are we, the Nice Side. We get presents while you get coal. Because Santa hates you. That's in your dirge. *The jolly fat man dumps his coal on our poor little souls. Why, oh why?* You preach about mistreatment, use it to bind the will of the Naughty Side against us."

Macey poked a bulge of flesh on his brother's midsection.

"If it's not Santa stuffing coal in their stockings, then who?" This was bad. Never had King Chocolate struggled to find fighting words. "If you see self-righteous pity in my eyes," Macey said, "it's a reflection."

Oooooh. That was a good one. King Chocolate had to admit, that was good. The crowd agreed. This was a home crowd. If the naughties were here, it would be different. Good thing they weren't. Not yet.

"He's *not* real," King Chocolate said.

"Then how does coal get in their stockings? Someone puts it there. Who would do such a thing?"

"You do it. You-you sneak across the border and—"

"Coal comes from burning Christmas trees, Casey. We have our trees at the top of the castle. I can show you. What did you do with your Christmas trees?" Macey snapped his fingers. "You *buuuurned* them and kept the blackened remains. They're piled high in your castle, Casey. Why would you do that? Why would you keep coal in your castle?" Macey let the question hang like a dead fish. Then for the big swing: "Because *you put it in their stockings!*"

A collective gasp.

For a nice king, his brother was merciless. Surgical. He rattled his opponent, then turned the crowd. King Chocolate bobbed like a loose kite, wishing Lydia were here to reel him in. *On second thought, she would do me worse.*

"The naughties don't know it's him, either! The lies he tells are so they'll get in line. The deception he weaves is so they'll do what he wants. He puts *coal* in their stockings! He lies so often it sounds like the truth. *He puts coal in their stockings!* His only talent—his one great talent—is that he believes his own lies. HE PUTS COAL IN THEIR STOCKINGS!"

Cheers. Fists and paws and claws in the air.

They stepped into the street. Closed in around him. King Chocolate was about to signal Jelly to fire up the engines. He could fly over them to get to the sleigh, but he'd just be a pinata. A plastic cowboy with a red plastic cowboy hat was twirling a stiff lasso just in case.

"I won!" King Chocolate shouted. "This is mine now. It's all mine. I won, you lost! So from now on you *all* get coal. How do you like that? That put a merry, merry in your tighties? And this guy won't pretend to be Santa anymore, I can promise you that. He lied to you, point blank. Right in your faces. You sat on *his* lap for pictures. His lap, dressed like Santa. But that's over. You're all naughty now, like it or not."

They still weren't upset about the Santa news. Maybe they already knew and were just going along with it. *Do the naughties know*

I put coal in their stockings? He doubted it. There would've been a mutiny.

"Welcome to Badland," King Chocolate said with a grin. Oh, he liked the sound of that. "Bad. Land. Get it? Because I won and you lost. And don't act like you're any better than us. Your king's a liar. *Former* king."

"If the boy stayed with us, he would have given you light, Casey. Your people don't have to suffer. They don't have to be bad. I was going to save you." He gestured to the darkened sky. "Now we all get coal, eh, brother?"

King Chocolate nodded with a dark sparkle in his eyes. "See, now that wasn't so hard to admit, now was it."

"I just said I wanted to help you."

"No. You said you wanted to *change* us. There's a difference."

"For the better. I wanted to change you *for the better!* How is that a bad thing? We're happy; you're sad. Think about it, brother!"

"You don't get it. That's not who we are. You didn't see Artie. You didn't really *seeee* him. That boy was troubled. He had darkness. The reason your pink sky is gone is because he had to get the darkness out. He needed someone to see it in him. See *him,* Macey. That's the difference between you and me. I accept them with all the faults. All you see is what you want them to be. And that, my brother, is the naughtiest of all. You get coal this year."

"You said you'd change the sky back if I admitted it." Macey stepped toward him. "Change it back."

"Whoa-whoa-whoa. Easy, Mr. Nice Guy. What I said? That was just a figure of speech. You didn't think... you thought I was serious?"

King Chocolate laughed for real. This was hilarious. After all these bells, his brother fell for the fake-promise bit *again.* Were all the nicies like this? It was going to be so easy to rule them.

"How do you feel about bowling? Stay with me here: we bulldoze this flea market and build duplexes around an adventure bowling course. Think golfing with bowling balls. We'll work out the details. Naughties play free. Nicies pay." King Chocolate shrugged. "I don't make the rules. It's adventure bowling."

The ground quaked.

It sounded like bulldozers were on their way. Weird, because King Chocolate just made up adventure bowling on the fly. Another tremor rattled the buildings. A baby doll started crying, and the Big Good Wolf howled.

It was something heavy. Maybe the naughties were almost here and were knocking things over. *Where are they?*

"You've ruined Christmas," Macey said.

"Oh, no. Not my Christmas. No, my Christmas is always like this, brother. To be honest, it's only gotten better. Because now we don't have to hear *you* sing about it."

"If you think we're going to change just because the sky is different... *we are nice!* We will never be naughty!"

The nicies agreed with their king, the ones who were still left. That earthquake had scared off half of them.

"Give it a few." King Chocolate leaned down. "Let this sky hover over you and see if you don't feel like breaking something. It might feel bad the first time you do it, but it'll feel good, too." He winked. "Trust me."

Macey pulled his gloves off one finger at a time. He threw them on the road. The thick leather walloped the pavers. Macey sniffed and sneered.

"I'm ready to break something now."

King Chocolate hovered out of reach. *That was fast.* He figured it would be a few bells before the king of nice started throwing haymakers. King Chocolate didn't know the first thing about fighting. He got winded wrestling a bowl of pudding into his mouth. But that was the nice thing about being king: others fought your battles for you.

Then another unexpected turn.

Macey took a knee. He was bowing right there, in the middle of the road. *In front of everyone!* King Chocolate looked around to make sure he wasn't the only one seeing this. It was a Christmas miracle. He didn't want to throw dukes with his brother. He just wanted to see him bend the knee. It took almost nothing to make him do it. In fact, it was a little embarrassing. Unless, of course, Macey knew he just didn't stand a chance and figured why waste time. Just kiss the ring already.

Or maybe that adventure bowling idea was making sense.

But King Nice wasn't kneeling in deference. He was working loose a paver. A round stone about the size of a fist.

Plot twist.

It was a stone King Chocolate couldn't out-hover. The nicies started prying pavers out of the road, too. Within a few ticks, they had an arsenal of cannonballs. Jelly was too far away to help. The engines cold.

Where are the naughties?

King Chocolate realized his mistake. He'd flipped the nicies too quickly. These dyed-in-the-wool nicies had become bona fide naughties in less than a tick. King Chocolate was just too good at it and had no backup plan. There was a price to pay for being that good. He was about to pay it.

The ground shook again. It was followed by an ear-splitting crack. Like the world was cleaved in two.

It started to hail across the lake. Giant pieces that looked like ornaments came down in waves. The flashy orbs shattered on the water's surface. They popped like gunshots. The crowd at the market gasped and ducked for cover beneath the tarps and lean-tos.

Then came the trees.

Branches snapped and cracked. Puffs of needles formed mushroom clouds above the water's surface, then flittered like confetti. Trees fell from the sky like an invisible twister was unloading them from a faraway land. Bright lights fell like glowing orbs that kerplunked into the dark water. King Chocolate looked closer and knew where they'd come from. Stars floated among the branches.

There were screams for real this time. And those who weren't screaming were frozen. Their gazes tilted toward the sky. King Chocolate looked up in time to see the unthinkable.

At least they're not throwing stones at me.

Who ever said King Chocolate couldn't see the positive?

THE ROYAL CASTLE no longer touched the sky.

A third of it was missing along a diagonal fracture. As if a sword had sliced through cheese. The top of it slid along its length and toppled over the side. It fell in slow motion, remaining upright on its way out of the sky.

And they watched it like a movie. As if it weren't happening. As if none of this were real.

Until it hit Rose Lake.

The sound was utterly devastating. An extraordinary volume of water jettisoned in a plume of frothy tea. An overpowering fragrance of rose petals blew the crowd off balance.

Then came the tidal wave.

King Chocolate lurched high above the street. The crashing wave rushed beneath him. It swept many of the gawkers off their feet or wheels or stilts and carried them off. Most clung to buildings and each other, holding on until the surge dissipated. They had dropped their stones and, for the moment, had forgotten about the obese tyrant who ruined the sky.

Macey was already helping them to their feet, carrying the weak to higher ground. The castle still rumbled. Aftershocks loosened chunks from the walls that tumbled like dice. How deep was the lake? Deep enough to swallow everything whole. And more. Another fracture split through the middle third of the remaining castle.

King Chocolate couldn't look away. He had one thought. A natural thought for someone like him. Because he'd wished he'd thought of it first.

Sabotage.

Macey was destroying everything. Pretty solid move, really. King Chocolate would have done the same. If Macey had won the war and flipped the Naughty Side skyline into bubble gum, King Chocolate would've detonated his own castle before he ever turned it over. Better to watch it burn than turn. He just didn't think his brother had the sand to do it. He was too nice. He was fake, sure. But too nice to destroy his home.

Bo Peep slogged through the flood to retrieve her sheep. Gingerbread men climbed onto roofs to keep from dissolving.

"Start the engines!" King Chocolate shouted.

Jelly couldn't hear him over the chaos. The cannon-fire breaks of the castle were about to release a second tidal wave. King Chocolate's hoversuit was already running low on juice. He was only a few feet above the road. His flimsy legs dragging in the water.

"Excuse me. Pardon me." He barreled over a harried cobbler. "Save yourself."

A sorry lot of soggy nicies were still in the market, waiting for the castle to give up another piece of itself, despite the pleas from King Nice to flee and seek shelter. The Big Good Wolf was helping a family of colorful eggs wearing cutoff shorts and suspenders onto the roof of a brick building solid enough to withstand the onslaught of water that was washing contents out the door. The wolf was dripping wet and shaking. On his hind legs, he could reach the roof, gently placing the last egg into her mother's arms. Just as he let go, the wolf disappeared.

Vanished. Gone.

King Chocolate didn't think anything of it. There were already so many things that had gone wrong to wonder why or how the wolf disappeared. Macey had something to do with it, he was sure of it.

Jelly was in the sleigh, hunched over and busy. It looked like she was bailing out water, although she didn't have a bucket. *Oh no,* the king thought. *It broke down. It flooded. I'll never get out of here. Where are the naughties?!*

He flew into the sleigh and bounced like a beach ball. Tumbled head over legs like a kickball at recess. He got upright and regained control.

"Jelly! He's sabotaging the spoils. Just when I—"

"The castle came down." Jelly popped up with the announcement. Several flies orbited her head. She looked devastated. Shocked. Just like the nicies.

"Yeah, I got eyes. Don't tell me the sled won't start. This place sucks. Get word to the naughties to go back home. Send the flies with the message. I want to be home before—"

"There is no home."

"What? Don't say that." King Chocolate looked around. The middle part of the castle was beginning to slide. "You're freaking me out, Jelly Roll. Will this thing start or—"

"It's gone. All of it. The castle back home. It fell into Fudgy Lake. The chocolate trees are falling down the mountain."

The king looked like a bird in a cage.

The explosion in the distance... my castle! How could his brother destroy King Chocolate's castle?

"Nonsense," he muttered.

"It's true," the flies whispered in his ear. "We saw it. The naughties escaped and are coming. They're not going to make it. Something's wrong."

"Wrong? What's wrong?"

"Please! Please take us with you!" A shabby shoemaker grabbed King Chocolate. But it was a purple muskrat perched in the curly locks on his head who spoke. "We have gold. Lots of it. Lots of gold. We don't need much room, just—"

Screams and panic.

The second part of the castle tipped off and began tumbling down the length of the jagged pedestal that remained. The impact wasn't as loud as the first, but the wave was just as big. King Chocolate shoved the old shoemaker into the oncoming current. He had just enough juice to hover over it. The sleigh rocked back and forth but didn't get caught in the tide.

"Start it!" King Chocolate shouted.

Jelly pushed a big yellow button. "I think it's wet."

"*Really?* You think it's wet?"

King Chocolate wasn't going to drown watching someone push a button. He turned away from the sleigh and floated toward the market. "Where you going?" Jelly shouted. "We have to leave. This isn't going to—"

"He's going to confess! I'll make him. He destroyed everything, and THAT'S NOT VERY NICE! The phony, the fake. I won fair and square, and he's going to take his ball and go home? I'm going to drag him through this mess and make him eat it!"

Jelly was begging him to turn around. The sleigh was going to start, she promised. The rest of the castle was going to fall just like it did on the Naughty Side. King Chocolate could feel the hoversuit slowing down. His useless legs dragged in the water like reeds. He was heading straight for his brother.

Belly saw him.

She stood on high ground with one of the stones in her hand.

King Chocolate didn't slow down. He leaned in like a snowplow about to clear the street.

Jelly raced past him. Her oversized feet hydroplaning over the water. King Chocolate pulled up and watched her go. *Go get her, Jelly! Tell your sister—*

And then she was gone. Jelly was gone. Her sister, too.

The identical elves, both loyal to their kings, vanished without sound or warning. Tiny waves trickled over the water where Jelly last tread.

"Jelly? Jelly, where are you? This isn't funny! Jelly Bean?"

"Belly?" Macey had shed his royal coat. "What have you done with her? You maniac! You self-centered glutton. All you think about is you! All I wanted to do was help, and you've ruined everything! YOU RUINED CHRISTMAS!"

"Don't you point at me! You did this. This is your fault. All you had to do was kiss the ring and we would've been playing adventure bowling by next Christmas but noooooo! You couldn't have it your way, so you're destroying it all."

"What are you talking about?"

"You blew up my castle! You did *that* to my castle!" King Chocolate jabbed at the remains of the castle that was slowly sinking into Rose Lake. "You're such a phony! Such a sore-losing phony!"

The confrontation came to blows. More like slaps. Weak slaps from two kings who had never been in a fight. They swatted and kicked. King Chocolate's little legs whipped at Macey. Macey could hardly reach over King Chocolate's girth.

"Where's my Jelly Bean?"

"Where's my Belly Bean?"

A rogue wave pushed them onto the sidewalk and through a crooked doorway. The smell of wet fur was on them. Feathers stuck to their cheeks. Open cages fell from shelves and into the swirling current. The kings could taste animal food in the water.

They coughed and choked. Got tangled in boxes and cages and loose leashes.

Macey threw eggs at King Chocolate, who wore an open cage like a helmet. There were more screams outside. Water gushed into the room and swept King Chocolate into a dark corner. His stupid brother waded against the current to escape.

"Get back here!" King Chocolate gurgled.

Macey didn't care about his brother anymore. It was over. Any wishes he had for him—good or bad—had vanished with Jelly and Belly. King Chocolate mattered not at all. And that hurt just a little.

King Chocolate pulled himself out of the wreckage.

The lower third of the castle had slumped halfway into the water like a broken tooth in quicksand. Rose Lake had swelled its banks. The road was gushing. King Chocolate pushed through it, squeezing the hoversuit for every drop of fizzy energy. He skipped over the water like a flat stone. No one was in the street.

He reached the sleigh without having to knock anyone over. The hoversuit died as he rolled into it. He pressed the big yellow button.

Waaa-uh. Waaa-uh. Waaa-uh.

Branches from Christmas trees that once lived at the top of the castle floated past.

Waaa-uh. Waaa-uh.

A pig wearing a white tank top swam past.

Waaa-uh.

Two more pigs followed.

The castle remains groaned like a listing ship. Its cry echoed off the dark sky. The rush of tea water battered the side of the sleigh. It tipped to one side. The open edge was inches away from taking the oncoming tide into the compartment when—

Budda-budda-budda-whap-WHAPWHAP!

The sleigh jiggled, then shook. Water shot from the tailpipes. The deafening roar drowned out the quickening flood. King Chocolate yanked the reins built into the dashboard. The sleigh lurched. Sputtered. Went quiet and began to float in the current.

Then exploded like a rocket.

It went straight off the ground and into the dark night. Had the reins not tangled around King Chocolate's wrists, he would've been expelled like trash. Instead, he dangled over the side of the runaway rocket like a weather balloon. Slamming against both sides. Bouncing like a paddle ball swung by a sugared-up boy on Christmas morning.

He was a rogue firework. His screams swallowed by the clouds.

In the gray squall, moisture collected on his face. The frigid wind scoured his cheeks and stole his breath. A trail of loneliness followed. Jelly was gone. She wasn't coming back. He could feel it.

If King Chocolate was crying (and he totally was), no one heard it.

25

ells. Tiny silver bells. Art opened his eyes as they faded
away.

He wasn't in bed with the sheets pulled up to his chin,
listening for hooves on the roof. He was on his back. The stage was
hard beneath him and littered with things—napkins and plastic
cups, torn T-shirts (*I ♡ King Choco*) and empty wrappers. The drum
sets lay on their sides. Holes punched through the bass drums. High
hats bent in half.

The sky was different. *Are those stars?*

He couldn't remember stars on either side of the border. The
skies were always perfect. Airbrushed. But the dim sky was studded
with tiny diamonds and swirls of muted color. Occasionally, one
would streak across the fabric and burn out before it touched the
horizon.

There's beauty in darkness.

He rolled onto his side, looked across a muddy field littered with
things not wanted. Holes stomped into the ground by big feet and
small feet, hooves and tentacles and wheels and such. Far away something rumbled. Trees fell into each other. A domino effect shattered
candy-cane trunks and splintered cinnamon-stick limbs.

Art was alone. And even though he was alone, he couldn't remember feeling so comfortable. As if this moment, bruised and chaotic, was imperfectly perfect. Exactly where he needed to be: on a broken stage overlooking an abused field. He wasn't bound up inside. Not trying to be something else

Free.

He didn't know what he was free from. Only the quality of the moment felt free. It contained the beauty of being. Of existing. Of knowing this breath. This space. This sky and those stars, the chill in the air.

Something rubbed against him.

He was startled by the softness of the tail. Daryl arched his back and stretched his front legs, clawing at the stage. His belly dragging across it.

"Where have you been?" Art said.

Daryl didn't answer. Only purred when Art put his arm out. The XXL cat rubbed his ears into Art's hand, then walked around a small gift on the stage. There were no other gifts. Only this little box wrapped in shiny red paper. Art studied the crisp corners and curly ribbon. The perfectly cut tape.

A card on top. *Arthur,* it read. *Merry, merry.*

Daryl curled on Art's lap, completely uninterested in what was in it. The tag didn't say who the gift was from. The queen had probably left it. Art wondered where she was off to. *I see you,* she had said. Art thought he'd wept after that.

He chuckled, then laughed out loud. Daryl looked annoyed. Art wiped his eyes and ripped the gift open, crumpled the wrapping paper in a ball and opened the box. There was an object inside. He lifted it out by an open paper clip. A polyurethane skateboard wheel spun on a fishing line. It was decorated with glitter. His name graffitied in colorful letters.

He remembered this. Sort of.

"Hello? Anyone here?"

Art guessed everyone was far away where the noises were coming from. Somewhere on the other side of the mountain. It was dark over there, too. The Nice Side was in shadows. *Maybe this happens on Christmas*, he wondered. *It all goes dark.*

But he knew this wasn't normal.

As if hearing his thoughts, Daryl climbed off his lap and strutted around crumbled towers of scaffolding that had fallen from above and crushed the band's equipment. Left a crater in the stage. Everything was dented and snapped. Except for the painting. The big canvas was still there. The ladder in front of it. Tubes of paint in the rack. Brushes and palette knives in their canisters. Not a scratch on the painting.

It wasn't a pretty painting. A swirl of yellows and grays and browns and blacks. *This is what the crowd watched me paint? This? It looks like a big, round bruise.*

Art got to his knees. He stretched and groaned. Listened to the distant cannon fire and explosions. Felt the tremor beneath his feet. It was time to get off the stage before it collapsed. He climbed over the scaffolding. Stooped in front of the easel to scoop the fat cat into his arms.

Stopped and stared.

Up close, something about the painting changed. Something didn't *look* familiar. It *felt* familiar. Like a dull fist in his stomach. A weight on his shoulders. Something about it he hated and feared. Something he wanted to bury. And there it was on the easel.

It wasn't scary. Ugly, maybe. But not repulsive. Curious, he dragged his fingers over it.

The paint had already dried. There were tracks in it from the rain. Patterns that ran like tears. The painting felt like armor. *A shield,* he thought. *A dark muddy shield.* And now it was there, on the canvas. Like he'd put down the shield—put it there—because he didn't need it anymore.

Candyland didn't frighten him anymore. It wasn't a strange land. "How long have I been here?" he said.

Since the beginning, Daryl answered.

"Beginning of what?"

Daryl rolled in his arms so Art could scratch his belly. *Time is funny here.*

It didn't matter how long he'd been there. He was there for a reason. *Was it this? To do this painting?*

He wondered.

SOMETHING WAS BURNING. It smelled like a campfire. Where the wood was dry and fragrant.

Art followed his nose. Everything was damp from the rain. There was no smoke, not that he could see. But he could hear the crackling. And there was music.

Christmas music.

People laughing. The kind of laughter that took your breath and kicked you in the belly. Made you slap a table and wipe away tears.

"Hello?"

Art went to the back of the stage. Stepped over a broken snare drum, looked down a hole made by an iron beam. The carriage he'd arrived in was out back, the doors open. The grumpy stagecoach driver missing from his post.

Art couldn't hear the music or smell the fire back there.

When he got back to the stage, the laughter returned. It was louder now. Voices were singing a silly song. He stopped and listened. Put his ear against the canvas. Jerked his head back and scowled. He *felt* the music that time. Felt it against his ear. Like it was coming through a keyhole.

There was a speck in the middle of all the dark colors. A pinprick of white. To a keen observer, it was simply a spot he'd missed with the brushes and knives. But when he stood in front of it, when he got the angle just right, a thread of light passed over his eye. He turned his head and tried again.

He stepped to the side. Put his thumb on it.

The laughter dimmed and music stopped. He pulled it away, and they returned. This was some sort of trick canvas. He looked behind it. Searched for hidden wires or imbedded speakers. There was nothing of the sort. It wasn't plugged in. Just a tiny white dot that grew brighter.

And the voices from it louder.

With Daryl napping in his arms, he leaned over to peer through it like a knothole in the neighbor's fence. His eye ached, and he pulled away. Ghostly brightness remained like a solar eclipse. He put his lips to the speck of light.

"Hello?"

It felt foolish shouting into a painting. If he was being punked, now was the time to laugh in his face. But the opposite happened.

"Arthur!"

It came from the painting.

More specifically, the little white dot. A dot no bigger than a period at the end of a sentence. He took a step and looked around. Investigated the back of the canvas one more time. Came around the front and held still, very still.

There was a party.

He put his finger on the white speck and pressed. The canvas tore rather easily. More light spilled out, and the music grew louder. There was the smell of food now. Sticky buns and fried chicken. Cherry pie and bean dip. Popcorn. Eggnog.

He hooked his finger in the hole.

The canvas ripped. Warmth flooded over him. His head rang like a wineglass struck with a silver spoon. A summer day was shining through the bitter cold of winter.

He grabbed a handful of canvas. Golden white light swallowed the stage and the trees around it. It punched holes through the night. It wrapped its loving arms around him.

And pulled him inside.

HE STOOD at the front door like a stranger.

A Christmas tree blinked. The lights were white. They were always white. The gifts beneath it in piles.

The living room he knew. The arrangement of the furniture. The fireplace on the far side, logs stacked next to it, a fire blazing. The metal curtain was open (always open). Art could feel the heat from across the room. There were two dogs curled up in front of it. A tan one and a brindle. Twitching in their sleep.

The coffee table was buried in candy wrappers and half-empty soda bottles and big bowls of popcorn and kettle corn and caramel corn. The couches occupied by kids. Some in pajamas. All on their phones, faces washed with screen glow while *New Elf City* played on the television. The same movie every Christmas. The one about a blue elf named Jack. They could quote it backwards.

The only thing louder than the television was the Christmas music. And the ruckus was right around the corner in the kitchen, where cheers and laughter roared. There were groans and slaps on the back and then a song. They were all singing it.

Goodbye, Lexi! Goodbye, Lexi! Goodbye, Lexi, we hate to see you go —*thhhpt!*

More laughter. More clapping.

Then Lexi plopped onto the couch between her cousins. She got out her phone and picked at the caramel corn stuck in her braces. It was impossible for her to care less about losing the game they were playing in the kitchen.

Cards were shuffled and passed around. Flipped over to moans and groans and cheers. Again and again until the singing started. The song began with laughter. Always laughter. This time Uncle Bobby wandered into the living room. He stood in front of the television, sipping from a beer bottle nestled in a coozy. Smiling at the movie he'd seen too many times. He glanced at the door.

Art's heart ran a lap.

Uncle Bobby fell back into television's trance. As if he thought he heard someone knock. But no one was there.

Art was trembling.

This memory was different than the others. Those were just

thoughts. Vivid thoughts. He wasn't there. In those he was only looking at them from a fond distance.

I'm here.

White light hovered near the ceiling like a poltergeist. It shifted into the corners and the recesses of the skylights like fog. Art knew where he was. He knew these people. He knew what they were doing. Because they did it every year.

But something was not quite right. There was a shaky foundation, something slightly off. A façade of thin paper that might tear if he moved. He just wanted to stand there and watch and listen. He wanted to believe he was there this time. *Actually there.* Eventually, the game would be over, and they'd all come into the front room. They would pull up chairs or stand in front of the fire, pet the dogs, and tell stories and jokes. Or simply bathe in the vibe of good company and Christmas spirit.

The white cloud spread like wisps of dry ice. It nibbled at the bay window overlooking the backyard. Crept down the chimney to dissolve one of the pictures on the mantel. Impatience thrummed inside it like flashes of summer lightning. No one noticed it.

No one except Art.

The song started again. This time Grandpa Bean was sung out of the game. Art recognized the sound of his dry hands clapping along with the others. He didn't retire to the losers' den with Lexi and Uncle Bobby when it was finished, though. He stayed at the table where the fun was.

Art took a step.

His leg was cold. He couldn't feel his foot on the floor. The joints in his fingers ached. He paused before taking another step. Uncle Bobby didn't look away from the television. The cousins didn't look up from their phones, and the dogs only flinched in their sleep.

Art made his way through the room one tiny step at a time.

He was quaking. Afraid his legs would dissolve like a sandcastle in an incoming tide. His heart threw front kicks. Ten of them were around the kitchen table. Each person had pennies in front of them.

One or two or three. Grandpa Bean had none. A card was dealt to each person except him.

The Christmas Game.

No one else called it that, but they did. A card was passed from one person to the next, each pausing to look at it before keeping it or passing it on. When it got to the end, everyone flipped their cards. They looked around for the lowest one. They pointed at the loser. She had a scarf around her neck. One she knitted. She threw it over her shoulder with an exaggerated frown and pushed her penny into the middle. The man next to her—wearing a baseball cap—put his arm around her.

Grandpa Bean began the clapping. The others joined in.

Goodbye, Annie! Goodbye, Annie! Goodbye, Annie, we hate to see you go—thhhpt!

It ended with a raspberry and hugs and high fives. The shuffling of cards and another round.

"Arthur!"

Art shook like he'd been poked with a stick. The dogs looked up and wagged their tails. Ears rotating like radar dishes.

The woman slung the scarf over her shoulder and pushed her way around the table. She came at him in hugging formation. Wrapped him in strong arms that hadn't missed a workout in twenty years. She smelled like cookie dough and shampoo.

"Oh, my Arthur," she whispered. "It's so good to see you."

He didn't want to move. If he did, this might all go away. She could hold him like that until the white cloud gobbled everything up for all he cared.

And that was when he knew.

He knew what this was. It was the moment he'd realized why he was in Candyland.

You're here for a reason.

"Your mom's mad at me." Art's dad winked.

"He gave me all the low cards," she said.

There was a long moment where they looked at each other. The way they always looked at each other. The game went on without them, and no one seemed to notice. Not the cousins. Not Uncle Bobby or Grandpa Bean. Or any of the other family or friends who were there for Christmas. Except for one.

A young woman ignored the card in front of her. She stepped between her parents. Leaned her head on her mom's shoulder. She looked at Art with that same fascination possessing his parents. In the merry chaos, they didn't move.

Then his sister said: "We got a seat for you at the table."

The cloud wrapped its misty limbs around the room. It writhed across the kitchen counter. Shimmied up the refrigerator. Aunt Maureen shuffled a new deck, and cards spilled onto the floor. A few slipped into the smoky white tendril crawling along the baseboard and disappeared. She didn't notice.

"Yeah," Art said. The word was thick. "But I..."

He couldn't say the rest. Didn't want to say it. The truth was gobbling up the walls and windows.

Art's parents stood with his sister between them, arms around each other. Proud grins. Cheerful ones. Smiles that were just grateful to see him. While Eric from down the street passed his card to Grandma Glynn, who yelped and passed it over to Maggy (Eric's wife), who screamed and passed it to Shawn from next door, the white mist crept under the kitchen table.

Art swallowed hard. "I have to go back."

He wiped his eyes.

Mom put her arms around him and squeezed him hard, so hard. She whispered in his ear, "It's all right, Arthur. You go back now. You're all right."

Art hugged her back hard. So hard.

A sob slipped out. He tried to hold it in.

The merriment around the table faded. The cheers and jeers slipped into the hungry grip of the misty whiteness. His dad, blurred in Art's vision, put his powerful arms around him and his mom. He said in a raspy voice: "We got your back, son."

His sister clamped onto him. The four of them stood together in the warmth of the fire, fighting off the cool embrace of the white cloud that came for him and this. The Christmas tree twinkled in the fog.

Art closed his eyes.

Distant hollers and faraway voices began to sing.

The white cloud grew brighter and hotter. He could feel his family's presence still with him. Their arms around him. He didn't want to let go, but he didn't want to take them with him. They belonged here, in this room, around the kitchen table. Singing songs in fits of laughter.

He relaxed his grip. Felt them slide from him.

Their forms faded. Even though he could still feel their touch. Their warmth.

Then there was light. Only light.

Then there was nothingness. Not even him. Only the warmth.

Art thought that was it. This was the end, and he would go to sleep now. He wouldn't mind that. Curling up with the love he felt. But it wasn't over.

In the mist, lights began to flash.

26

Hot air blew on the king's cheek. Like exhaust from a grass thresher.

It was noisy. Sloppy.

Wet lips smacked in his ear. Teeth grinding like hard stones. Then another blow of humid air in his face. The touch of a damp nostril on his cheek—

King Chocolate woke up.

He opened his eyes to white pain in his shoulder. His back was as crooked as a witch's broom. He clawed at the rocky ground and groaned. A shadow passed over him.

A cloven hoof fell in front of him.

King Chocolate rolled over. The hoversuit sputtered and died. He opened his mouth, tried to call for help, felt the jagged ground on his belly and elbows. His useless legs fluttered behind him.

The rocket sleigh was upside down and steaming. The beautiful tailpipes were dented puzzle pieces. He couldn't stand the sight of it, threw his weight onto his back. The dark sky roiled above him—a ceiling of dingy fluff almost in reach. He could almost touch it. His breath was frosty in the cold metal air. He rolled away from the clouds. Then rolled again.

Again.

When you're the shape of a boulder, momentum is not your friend on a hillside.

King Chocolate was steamrolling toward a rocky ledge. He didn't know what was beyond it (probably not good), but each snapshot brought him closer to finding out. Something snagged his royal overcoat.

A firm grip yanked the king to a sudden stop, knocking the wind and senses out of an abrupt exhale. King Chocolate wheezed, his eyes closed, uncertain if he was teetering on the edge of a steep drop. His brain spinning.

The ledge a rotation away.

He dared not move. If a single pebble slipped, he would make that final turn. And then, well... he didn't find out. He closed his eyes and kept them closed. Lower lip popping in and out as chocolate tears stained his cheeks.

Gravel crunched nearby. He let out a whimper and clutched his tummy. If only Jelly were here. She would know what to do. Just then a hand landed on his shoulder. A large hand with a firm grip pushed him toward the cliff. The king flailed.

"No! No, no, no—"

He was stopped facedown in a pokey clump of weeds. The ledge a half turn closer. He could feel the cool air racing over the jagged lip. Whoever had grabbed him held onto the king's shoulder and with their other hand pulled up the back of his royal jacket. Whoever it was began poking around the hoversuit in search of a wallet or bag of gold.

"I have chocolate! Back home, though, I have it all. I'll give you three—awk!"

Something snapped into the hoversuit and sent a charge through his spine.

"As much chocolate as you want! I swear it, you can have it all. I'm king of everything now. Just don't hurt—"

The hoversuit hummed.

It hugged against him and began to rise.

The king seized control of it and lurched away from the ledge. The one who had pinned him to the ground ducked, and the king went flying over him, overcompensating his escape and slamming into a blue-gray boulder. He lost control then, scuttering along a grassy path like a beach ball caught in a sandstorm. He bounced back and forth, catching glimpses of strong furry legs and wide bony racks.

He came to rest in a stone trench. It was a divot that went the length of the rocky slope.

King Chocolate lay staring at the heavy clouds. They were close enough to spit on. He knew where he was. The steep terrain. The clouds. He wasn't a genius, but he'd stared at this mountain all his life.

The gutter where he rested was once the border between naughty and nice.

Now it was all naughty. A reluctant smile crept into one of his cheeks. *Because I won.*

His joy was brief.

A LONG HEAD and a dangerous rack of antlers appeared over him.

Flakes of blue-green lichen were caught between black lips. Molars grinding. Deep black eyes staring. And humid exhaust shooting from wide nostrils onto the king's face.

King Chocolate scooted up the trench and out of the way. The top of his head touched the gray ceiling. Someone was watching him. His black boot hiked on the golden rail of a long, dirty sleigh. He was dipping a chocolate chip cookie into a glass of milk.

"Hello, Casey," said Santa Claus.

The king looked around. Perhaps he did fall off that cliff. Because there was no way the jolly fat man could be up here. King Chocolate had destroyed the device that projected him. But this Santa looked different. He looked dirtier. And exhausted.

And what's up with the reindeer? he thought. Because they'd never been in the projection King Chocolate talked to. Like ever.

The king hovered closer. A large sack was stuffed into the back seat of the sleigh (not the rocket sleigh, still upside down and shooting steam). Long, leather reins lay out front with bells sewn to the straps. Santa slurped the glass—milk dripping from his white curly mustache—and watched the king drift closer. King Chocolate could smell the sweat coming off the jolly fat man. The smoky soot from fireplaces. The king wasn't satisfied, though, and swung one of his limp legs. It bounced off Santa's knee.

King Chocolate pinched the bridge of his nose. "Are you serious?"

Santa Claus did not answer. He'd seen this show before: a nonbeliever confronted with the real deal. Everyone handled the truth differently. Some fainted; some cried. Some jumped with joy and hugged him.

Not King Chocolate.

He looked up with pain in his eyes. "What are you doing up here?"

Santa finished his cookie, swatted the crumbs off his hands. He chugged the last swallow of milk, then said: "Waiting for you."

The king turned in a circle. The rocket sleigh was destroyed. Even if it wasn't, where would he go? Candyland was covered in puffs of smoke and dust. Trees were falling like termite-infested pillars. Now Santa Claus was waiting for him. Which could only mean one thing.

A lecture was coming.

One of the reindeer wandered over. It was the one who woke him up. The big one. Chewing up lichen and staring at the king with an unkindly look. A growl began grinding in the beast's throat. He let out a howl that turned the king's spine into jelly.

"It's okay, boy." Santa went over to the slobbering beast and stroked the wet muzzle, then said to the king: "It's the end of a long night."

"Tell me about it."

"He gets a bit edgy toward the end."

"He doesn't like me."

"He's a protector is all. Wouldn't hurt a fly. Unprovoked. Would you, Ronin?"

Unprovoked. Ronin bristled at the qualifier. The oversized reindeer pawed the terrain, looking for a reason to swat the king off the mountain like a volleyball.

"So, you're real," the king said. "You. The flying moose." Santa didn't answer. Fed a cube of something grassy to the reindeer. "Those are presents in the sack, I take it. You're delivering them to us."

"Not that kind of stop, I'm afraid."

"Coal, then?"

Santa didn't answer. He didn't have to. King Chocolate knew who delivered the coal to the naughties on Christmas. It wasn't Santa. Besides, even if he was bringing presents, where was he going to deliver them? The castles were gone. Most of Candyland looked like a cinder fire. It was, like, game over. If the king had known what winning would bring him, he would've just stayed home.

"I didn't do anything wrong, you know. That wasn't my fault down there. Macey blew up the castles."

"Your brother didn't do it."

"Well, don't look at me. All I did was win. The boy was here for a reason. You said so yourself." Santa didn't argue the fake news. He'd never met the king, so how could he have said that? "Macey would have done the same thing. He admitted it. I was playing the game, that's all. And this is what I get? You got to admit, that ain't fair." The king shook his head. "What kind of Christmas is *this*?"

"You did nothing wrong, Casey."

"Yeah, well, you know and I know that—*what*?"

Santa folded his hands over his belly. "You did nothing wrong."

"All right. That's what I'm talking about. Yeah. So. You're here to make everything right, then."

"In a way."

"I like the sound of that. Merry, merry, my good sir. Merry, merry. Listen, um." The king hovered closer. Ronin grunted. "I'm not so sure about Macey. My brother, he's sneaky. They're nicies and all, but they were going to throw rocks at me. You know that, right?"

"I saw."

"That ain't nice."

"No. It's not."

This was going King Chocolate's way. It was unexpected. But it was fair. Santa Claus was a fair man. He was there to make things right and merry, merry and all that good stuff. King Chocolate hovered back to give the jolly fat man some space to work his magic. The king puffed up and tried to stick his chest out and hold his chin up. It was the power stance. When things got back to normal, he'd double down on snack time and get his size back up. His clothes hung on him like blankets. *Who wants a skinny king?*

"So?" An awkward silence settled between them. "What are you waiting for? Make the castles come back. Just like they were. Both of them. They're both mine."

Santa fed the reindeer (who was eyeballing the king) another cube and looked down the mountain. Then shuffled over to the sleigh. Heavy boots clunking the ground. The king thought he was going for a magic wand or something. But the jolly fat man began untangling the reindeer harnesses.

"I knew it," the king muttered. "What do you want, a confession? Is that it? Fine. I did the coal. I burned up the Christmas trees and then stuffed coal in stockings and blamed it on you. I did it every Christmas. Is that what you want to hear?" King Chocolate cupped his hands and shouted: "I PUT COAL IN YOUR STOCKINGS!"

His voice echoed into the mist settling on the side of the mountain.

"Sue me. You don't know what it's like to rule the Naughty Side. They don't listen. You got to be firm, or they'll run you over. You got to trick them. Try walking a block in my shoes, you'll see."

Santa chuckled. The irony of the king walking anywhere was not lost.

"So I lied, so what? I got it done, didn't I? The only thing we sugar-coat on the Naughty Side is donuts. We tell it like it is. You don't like it, then you don't belong. That's it. I'd like to see you do better."

"I don't think I can, Casey."

"That's right. Now. Are you going to fix things or not?"

"That's not why I'm here."

"Then what are you here for? I mean, we ain't seen you like *ever*, and now you stop by when everything is falling apart? You think you could have stopped to say hi? Would've been nice. Macey was pretending to be you, did you know that?"

"I'm always here."

The king burst out laughing. He laughed so hard his ribs hurt. Santa watched him.

"You're serious?" The king rolled his eyes. Ronin didn't like it. "Oh, that's perfect. You're worse than me. You know that, right? *You're never here!*"

Unperturbed, Santa checked the buckles and tightened the straps. He went to the sleigh and pulled out a plate of cookies. Double fudge, chocolate chip. When he dropped the plate on the hard ground, it multiplied into two dozen plates of double fudgies. Then those doubled. *Four dozen!*

He went back to the sleigh for another plate, this one stacked with oatmeal raisin (gross). He kept doing this like a cookie factory was in the glove box. Santa pulled out sugar sprinkles, no bakes, snowballs, peanut butter balls, snickerdoodles, gingerbreads. The varieties were endless. Dozens and dozens of each kind.

"What's all this?" the king said.

Santa took off his glove and stuck his fingers in his mouth to let out an ear-splitting whistle. The reindeer lifted their heads and started back to the sleigh, avoiding stepping on the cookie smorgasbord. Enough to feed a village. Not just a village. *All of Candyland!*

The reindeer took their places in front of the sleigh. Two by two, they stood. The big one, the scary one, the one with the mean eyes, planted his enormous hooves in front. Santa lifted the harnesses and began to buckle them in.

"No!" King Chocolate shouted up at Santa Claus, who, somehow, seemed to have grown a foot taller. "You can fix this. You can fix anything. We need you!"

The king glanced down at the mess he'd created. The white mist had spread across the mountain and was creeping over the land like a flood of white vapor. Candyland was a colorless mass. Once upon a time it had been the land of Naughty and Nice. Now it was lifeless.

"What do you want? I get it, all right? I totally get it now. Candyland is Naughty *and* Nice." He weighed his empty hands. "We were fighting each other, and I won, and now Candyland looks like that. I get it. I get it! But no one told me *that* was going to happen. No one told me *not* to win. You didn't, that's for sure. You could've, but you didn't. If you would've stopped by just one time and said, 'Hey, Casey. If you win, then Candyland is over. Merry, merry. Blah-blah.' Or something like that. *Anything!* But you didn't say nothing. You just let me win, and now it's all my fault."

The king huffed.

"This isn't fair, and you know it. But I learned my lesson. For sure. So can we just, you know... can you put it back together? I won't win again."

That wasn't true, and the king knew it. Even if Santa waved his hand and everything went back to normal, like this was all a bad dream, the king would eventually get bored. He'd forget this ever happened. *And winning was just so sweet.*

All the reindeer were buckled in except for one. Santa scratched Ronin's chin and kissed the reindeer on the nose. King Chocolate zoomed toward him to beg and plead. How was he supposed to know if Candyland lost its balance, everything would fall apart?

The queen was right. With her stupid tray-of-donuts example, she was right. There. He said it. He'd gladly say it to her face if the jolly fat man would lend a hand.

Ronin bent at the knees. Santa backed up. The reindeer leaped like a cannonball shot from a catapult. Hooves pedaled through the cloud and were gone. The shockwaves of the departure sent King Chocolate tumbling down the grassy path and miraculously touched not one plate of cookies. He landed against a boulder, condensation from the clouds streaking down its side. The king righted himself and brushed debris off his coat.

His sleeves hung over his hands. He rattled inside the hoversuit.

"Where's he going?" he said. "You can't leave me up here. I don't have anything. How long are these cookies going to last me?"

Santa tightened the laces on his boots. He touched his toes and stretched his back. He put his hand to his brow and searched the misty mountain below. The reindeer turned their heads, ears rotating in that direction. Santa looked at his furry team, and as if an unspoken word passed between them, the reindeer scuffed at the ground.

A tiny, yellow light floated up through the mist.

It was bright for only a wink. A tick later, it flashed again. King Chocolate watched it float up the hill. Then it landed on the boulder next to him. Wings folded closed.

Merry, merry, the firefly whispered.

Then it was off, rising into the clouds just out of King Chocolate's reach.

Santa went to the sack in the back of the sleigh. The reindeer felt like mythical titans. King Chocolate looked down at the fading wasteland evaporating like dry ice. More fireflies were floating toward him. Loose gravel fell from below.

From the gathering mist, two figures emerged.

THEY WERE THIN AND ROUND. Beige and crispy on the edges.

Heads down and stubby legs working, a gingerbread couple navigated the terrain with the efficiency of mountain goats. All the while surrounded by fireflies whispering encouraging words.

"Hey! Hey, you, uh..." King Chocolate had never seen these nicies. "What's your names? I'm ki—" He decided not to tell them who he was. Maybe they had been at the market when everything went sideways. "Thank Claus you made it. I need help. I need to—"

Another pair of gingerbread cookies were behind them. This couple the king knew. They were chipped and smudged. One of them was missing an arm (King Chocolate was pretty sure it had been thrown onstage during the festival). They were right behind the nice gingerbread couple. All of them walked around the king like he was a bush in the path. They stooped for a cookie (sugar cookie with green sprinkles) and went on their way.

Cookies eating cookies, King Chocolate thought. *Huh.*

Santa Claus waved to them. They waved back like he was nothing more than a mailman delivering presents by way of magic reindeer.

"Merry, merry!" the gingerbreaders said. One couple said it more sweetly than the others (you can guess which one). And then up the path and into the clouds they vanished. Right where the fireflies were flying. King Chocolate waited for them to return. Or something to make sense. Neither happened.

"What's going on here?"

Santa was digging in the sack again. Humming a merry tune as he did. King Chocolate's voice felt small. It was higher than normal. Another couple came up the mountain. They were covered in gray fur. One of them wore wire-rimmed spectacles and carried a book under his arm. The other stalked the path on all fours and slobbered.

"Hey!" King Chocolate levitated the hoversuit as high as it would go. He was eye level with the Big Bad Wolf. "Over here. Whoa, stop. I order you to—"

The Big Bad Wolf leaped over the king. The Big Good Wolf simply went around him. They argued over a plate of jelly dollops. Big Good Wolf slapped his paw. Big Bad Wolf bared his teeth.

They were about to settle it nature-style when pink porky pigs bounced past the king, carrying suitcases and wearing different hats. There were six of them. Two wore hardhats. Two wore cowboy hats. Two wore teacups on their heads. The king knew three of them. They were the muddy ones wearing *I* ♥ *King Choco* shirts. The other three had backpacks filled with books.

The half dozen pigs joined the argument over jelly dollops. The king blinked heavily. Santa was oblivious to what was happening. Take two hungry wolves and add six fat pigs and, well... *nature happens.* A jelly dollop fell off a plate and landed on one of the teacup hats.

There was a pause. A gasp. King Chocolate closed his eyes, then peeked between his fingers.

Violent laughter erupted from the side of the mountain. The Big Bad Wolf doubled over. The Big Good Wolf curled up on his side. The pigs hopped around like wind-up toys bleating laughter like lambs. When it settled, the wolves got up and wiped their eyes. They stuffed their mouths with treats. All of them went up the path, arm in arm—each wolf with three pigs—and vanished in the cloud.

"I'm losing my mind," the king muttered.

Grim and Joy (*the Border Oracles*, Jelly once called them) came up hand in hand and swinging their arms. Then Poko, that sad little puppet who brought the king his chocolate samples, skipped along with a puppet just like him. Their wooden joints rattling.

The half-horse brothers came next. There were four of them. Even King Chocolate would admit they were a bit nightmarish. The fashionistas, the Conflict Advisors (three of them still dipped and sprinkled), flies and gnats. Lost Boys on their beams.

More were coming.

He could feel them on their way up the mountain. Bo Peep, skipping with her sheep, curtsied to the king before munching on a coconut puff ball. Bo Pop with her rams threw up a peace sign. Miss Tuffet with a bucket of curds and whey, her spider running behind her. Miss Fluffet's spider perched on her shoulder.

Goldilocks locked arms with three bears. Boldilocks rode on a bear's shoulders.

Red Riding Hood with a basket. Black Riding Hood had a backpack.

There were robot boxers and plastic dancers. Princes in long capes. Princesses with sparkly crowns. There were dwarves with tools and frogs with boots, cats and mice chatting about the weather.

They came in pairs, one and all. One from the land of naughty. The other was nice.

All wobbly with Christmas spirit, their faces flashing in the glow of firefly guides.

None of them stopped to ask how the king was doing, if he was hurt or needed help. None of them seemed impressed by the jolly fat man and his reindeer. They slowed down to pick up a cookie and made their way up, up, up the mountain and into the cloud. Firefly flash fading around them.

Santa sat on a boulder and watched the procession.

Far below, Candyland was sinking. *The mountain will be next*, King Chocolate thought. But something much more miraculous than mountain-swallowing quicksand. Santa leaned back, studied the king. He was looking at what was under the king. The hoversuit had gone to sleep.

The king was standing on his own.

Those two noodles wobbled like overcooked pasta. But they held him up like a newborn baby deer. It was a miracle.

"Merry Christmas, Casey." Santa held out a small box. It was wrapped with a bow.

"For me?" The king pointed at the smoldering remains of what was once Candyland. "But I, uh... is it coal?"

Santa laughed. The moment didn't feel funny. Candyland was in ruins, and King Chocolate was to blame. And now he had a present to open? This made not a lick of sense.

"But... *why?*"

He had to know. Everything was gone, and everyone was so joyful. And he got a present.

Santa stood with a groan. All the bones cracked in his back when he stretched his arms. He climbed into his sleigh, checked the monitors on the dash, then gripped the reins. He looked at the king in his saggy clothes, holding the gift with both hands. A tired grin rose from his lips to his eyes.

"Arthur needed to see. And only you could help him do that."

"But..." The king shook his head. "I didn't help him. I just, you know..." He gestured downhill. "I don't get it."

Santa gazed at the pilgrimage vanishing in the cloud. "You will, Casey."

❄

"On Dasher, on Dancer..." Santa started.

Each time he called a name, a reindeer cocked his or her legs like a slingshot at full tension. Muscles rippled beneath the hide. The slow-moving pilgrimage veered away from them. Even King Chocolate moved. It looked like the reindeer were going whether he was in front of them or not. Getting run over by magic reindeer was not how he wanted this to end. And he still had a present to open.

But the reindeer didn't need a runway. They shot from the mountain like a spring-loaded pistol. A train of reindeer soared into the rising mist, hooves pedaling swirls in the white vapor. It swung around like a roller coaster on an invisible track. Santa waved from the caboose. The Landers who had not yet climbed into the cloud stopped to wave back.

"Ho-ho-ho!"

And then the reindeer express hit another gear. A warp drive that split space and time. They jittered like static on an old television. An electric pulse crackled from the sleigh and then—

Poof.

The Landers cheered. They clapped and hugged. Stuffed their faces with cookies. And then on their way they went. Up into the cloud.

"Casey!"

Two elves as round as berries and dressed like twins stepped out of the line. One was not terribly happy to see the king. The other was hobbling in his direction with arms wide.

"Jelly!"

The king suddenly forgot everything that had happened since he'd crashed the rocket sleigh. He powered the hoversuit in that happy elf's direction as fast as it would carry him. With less weight to carry, the hoversuit threw the king at the elf. They collided like rubber kickballs and bounced in opposite directions. They tumbled backwards, stopped, and tried again. The king had never hugged Jelly. In fact, he'd never hugged anyone.

I'm not made for hugging, the king would say.

Body or mind, Jelly would add.

Their arms barely reached each other. But it didn't stop them from trying. Jelly hopped madly on those giant flipper-feet. The king was weeping. Chocolate tears dribbled off his chin, staining his jacket. All the stress of watching Candyland dry up like a rotten plum. And then crashing the rocket sleigh and Santa leaving.

But there was only one reason he was crying.

"I thought I lost you," he blubbered. "You were at the rocket sleigh one wink, and the next you were gone. And then I had to fly it by myself, and it went too fast, and then I wrecked it. It's over there. I'm not hurt. Well, a little. But I don't care. You're back. You're back, you're back, you're back. Never leave me again."

"I didn't go anywhere."

"I don't care. Promise you won't leave me."

"I didn't leave you."

"Promise!"

Jelly promised. The king didn't bother asking what she meant by that. Because clearly she had left. He'd seen it with his own beady eyes. The loneliness he'd felt when he realized she was gone was bottomless and howling. He clutched her shoulders, wiped the tears on his sleeve. Then hugged her again.

"You dropped something." Belly was tapping her foot.

"Huh?"

Belly could not look more bored. She walked over to pick up the present. The king had chucked it on the ground when he saw Jelly. He almost didn't care about it. Almost.

"That's..." He sniffed. "That's mine. Santa gave it to me."

"Figures."

The king held it with both hands. It felt heavy now. Normally, when he got a present, he'd have the paper shredded in half a wink.

"Where's everyone going?" the king said.

"We're going up," Jelly said.

"But why?"

"It's why we're here."

"What?"

The twin elves shrugged. They smiled when they did it. Like they knew a secret but weren't telling.

"I'm going with you," the king said.

"You can't," Jelly said. "Not yet."

"What? Wh-why?"

Jelly and Belly looked around. Looked at each other. Shrugged without smiling this time. Jelly took his hand.

"I want to see what you got, first."

The king didn't feel like opening his present. But if it kept her from leaving, he'd do it. He'd never unwrapped a gift so slowly in his life. It was like he was planning to reuse the paper. First one end. Then the other. Belly tapped her foot. The king went even slower.

It was a plain box. Charcoal in color. *If it's coal...* he thought.

"Well?" Belly said.

The king lifted the lid. He looked inside. Jelly looked inside. Belly stood on her toes and frowned. Jelly began to giggle. Then she whispered in her sister's ear.

"Those don't really come from coal," Belly answered. "That's just a myth."

"What doesn't come from coal?" The king stared at what was nestled in a bed of cotton. "This?"

The elven sisters were crying laughter now. They fell over each other, mouthing words the king couldn't understand. What was in the box wasn't funny. It was beautiful. And they were laughing at it. *At him.*

"We're not laughing at you," Jelly said between breaths. "It's just... it doesn't matter where it came from. It's perfect. It's so perfect."

The king was feeling a little hurt being left out of the joke. Worse: he was the butt of it. This was a present from Santa, after all.

Then he heard a familiar voice call his name.

❄

THE COOKIE PLATES were nearly empty.

The pilgrimage had thinned with only a few fireflies to guide them. Two chubby chefs walked step for step, singing a merry tune and sloshing mugs of sparkly cider on their tunics. For a time, there was no one after them. The king began to wonder if he imagined his name called out. Then a figure emerged from the mist. The last in a long line that journeyed from below.

He carried a weary smile. His feet heavy clods on the unforgiving mountain. He stood just outside the mist's reach. The smile widened. His pace picked up, and he closed the gap, crushing King Chocolate in a bear-hugging grip. The gift was trapped between them.

"Merry, merry, brother." Macey held the king at arm's length. "Finally."

Macey should be mad. Furious, really. King Chocolate would have been. But his brother only laughed and nodded at the clouds, where all the Landers had gone. *What does* finally *mean?* the king thought. *Does everyone know what's happening here?* That was apparently the case. Because they marched without a care while Candyland turned to mush. They skipped and danced and sang, and the king didn't have a clue.

"It's beautiful." Macey wiped a tear.

The king thought his brother had spied the crumpled gift he was clutching. He told him Santa had been waiting for him when he crashed the rocket sleigh. "That's what he said. He said, *I'm waiting for you.*"

"He did?"

"I mean, something like that. He, uh..." The king sighed. His brother was smiling. It was a told-you-so smile. He wasn't about to dance and rub King Chocolate's nose in it. It was a happy-to-see-you smile. And that made King Chocolate say: "You were right. He's real. He was here. I saw him. I touched him. Talked to him. The reindeer ate green stuff off the rocks. Look, the prints. You can see them. And the one in front—giant horns, like, out to here." The king spread his hands as far as they would go. "He was not happy to see me."

"Ronin?"

"You know him?"

Macey shook his head. They laughed. The king liked the way his brother laid his hand on his shoulder. It felt good. He held up the gift. "He gave me this."

Macey looked inside. Tilted his head. Looked up at the king and back at what was inside the gift. Giddiness galloped through the king. It was the way his brother looked at him.

"May I?"

His brother reached inside the box. A silver chain rattled over his thumb. He held it up. King Chocolate bowed his head, and Macey looped the necklace around his neck. He stepped back and eyed the teardrop jewel attached to it. It was as big as a sugarplum.

"I thought these came from coal," King Chocolate said. "You know, like, after a long time under pressure, they just..." The king shrugged. "Belly said they don't. But, I mean, even if they don't—"

"It's beautiful."

The king thought so, too. Although he couldn't imagine why Santa would give him such a thing. It had to be worth a fortune. And, really, why give *anything* to King Chocolate? Wasn't he the last one in Candyland to deserve a gift?

"But let's pretend it does," Macey said. "Coal is a young diamond. I like that."

"Yeah."

Macey put his arm over the king's shoulder. The mist crept up the mountain like ghostly fingers. Candyland had transformed into a white blanket. King Chocolate would have thought ash covered the land by now, but he liked to believe that was snow down there. A pristine canvas of snow.

"We were kings," King Chocolate said.

"We were kings." Macey looked at the cloudy ceiling above them. "But we're more than that."

Macey cupped his hand to his brother's ear and whispered what was beyond the clouds. King Chocolate's eyes grew. And as they grew, he began to glow. Infected with the smile his brother had brought up the mountain.

It made sense now. It all made sense.

THE MOUNTAIN RUMBLED like it was about to erupt. Or crumble into nothingness. Rocks broke loose and bounced past them and disappeared below where a leviathan was lurking. A massive form rising in the mist. A shadow that grew darker as it neared. Casey squeaked just a little (it sounded like a mouse, but he wouldn't admit that) and grabbed his brother.

And then he heard it. A single word echoed off the mountain.

"Yum!"

And then another one that went: *"Yum!"*

It was in stereo. One from the left and another from the right. Back and forth until not one, but two Sweet Tooths plundered their way out of the mist. Big and bare feet crushing rocks into powder and splitting the earth where they stepped. Hand in hand, they came up. Swinging their laced fingers like a wrecking ball. Big teeth and bigger smiles. The only difference was the colors of their nails.

They leaped over Casey and Macey and triggered a minor avalanche. Boulders broke loose, some splitting in half, and boomed down the mountain, vanishing into complete silence.

The Sweet Tooths plodded a course upward, *yumming* their way into the cloud.

It was quiet again. The rockslide had settled. The encroaching mist was licking the ground where the reindeer prints were. It felt like nothingness creeping toward them. There was nothing to see beyond it. Candyland didn't even look like a blanket of snow.

"It's gone, isn't it?" King Chocolate said. "Candyland is totally gone."

"It moved on, Casey. But there's more." Macey nodded. "Shall we?"

Casey held the tear-shaped diamond swinging against his chest. You might think he considered apologizing to his brother after all the things he'd done, and you wouldn't be wrong. King Chocolate, in fact, did feel sorry. Truly sorry. He felt it in his heart, which had swelled in size. And his brother felt his sorrow, too. He looked at Macey with tiny eyes, a trace of remorse swimming inside them.

Macey patted the king's hand. He didn't need to hear it. It was plain to see.

There were two cookies left. An apple fritter and a double fudge chocolate chip. You know which one Casey took. The brothers held them up, clinked them together, and took a bite. Crumbs cascaded down their tunics. With cookies in hand, they turned to make the final steps of their journey.

Macey admired the jewel in the palm of King Chocolate's hand. The way it glittered and shined. The flawless weight of it. Maybe diamonds didn't start off as coal. But some things did.

And Arthur needed to see where he was, the king thought, *to become who he is.*

27

Fireflies flashed random patterns. They hung like tiny lanterns, fading to dull pinpoints in the distance.

The fog was heavy and wet. Dew collected on lichen and clumps of wildflowers and on boulders strewn on a steep slope—some the size of automobiles in a field that quickly vanished in the humidity.

Laughter was out there. Far away.

Behind Art, the ground sloped into a swirling dense cloud. He took three steps and was swallowed by white mist. He waved his hand without seeing it, felt cool moisture cling to his cheeks. The ground beneath him softened like clay. He was quickly disoriented. Only the vague sprinkle of fireflies guided him back out.

He had a sense of where he was, but not how he got there. He'd learned not to question things in Candyland. Things happened for a reason, and when they did, it was best to float downstream with them. The fireflies were drifting toward the sound of voices, luring Art to follow. The swirling cloud dampened his neck and arms—an impenetrable fog gently nudging him to get going.

He took the hint.

The rocks were wet and mossy with just enough grit for traction.

He hopscotched his way to the biggest boulder in sight and scaled it on all fours. When he reached the top of it, the wind picked up, gusting noisily in his ears, blowing the damp hair from his eyes. The fireflies swirled like lights on an incoming storm, rising higher in the distance.

He continued the hike, taking pleasure in the focus it required to keep from slipping, searching for the best location to place his foot, the right grip to pull himself over the next rock. There were times his hand slipped. He'd fallen awkwardly more than once, cut his arm on a sharp edge, felt the trickle of blood and the sticky aftermath. But his thoughts were few and uncluttered.

Each time he looked up, the wind blew harder, and the fireflies higher.

After a time, the fog began to thin.

He could see farther. The boulders were bigger and stacked on top of each other. The wind occasionally knocked him off balance. Sometimes it sang in the hollows between stones, long mournful cries that rose and fell. If there was someone else out there, he couldn't hear them. It was only when he stopped to rest or survey a way around an impossible route did he recall the memory of Christmas at home. Those details, though, were already getting fuzzy. As if seeing them through veils.

The trail of fireflies had moved above him at some point. The boulders gave way to a cliff. He stood at the bottom of it, looking up into the streaming mist. In the gray whiteness, there were patches of color. Far above, seemingly out of reach, a pink sky peeked through.

Art considered turning around. Climbing over boulders was one thing, but free soloing a cliff was entirely different. There were ledges to rest on and fractures to wedge a hand or foot inside, but it was so high.

The swirling cloud had followed him. It was only a few feet behind him and impervious to the wind. He stepped into it and, just as before, was engulfed. The boulders gave beneath him. His boots sank in softening rocks like they were dissolving. And he had only taken one step.

He went back to the cliff, leaned his head against it, and stared up at the rising cloud of fireflies. They looked like sparks over a campfire. Aches and pains started to surface. His ribs were bruised. Part of his foot strangely numb. He closed his eyes and sank back into the memories of the card game on Christmas. Only to find the details had vanished.

The faces and places were generic. He couldn't remember the shapes of them or the color of their hair. The sound of laughter and song was absent. Their names! He couldn't remember their names. The feelings, though, remained. The shared experience of laughter and love was still warm.

The essence of those moments was real.

They were a part of him that could never be removed. Sewn into the fabric that made him who he was. He sat at the bottom of an impossible climb and rested in the beauty of those feelings. He didn't have to go any farther.

"Need a hand?"

ART OPENED his eyes and stared a moment. "King Chocolate?"

"You like?"

The king turned in a circle, arms out. Smile stretching into saggy cheeks. The big surprise was below the belt. The king was standing on legs, not soggy string beans. Short, stocky legs with knobby knees and bony ankles. The king did another turn, leaped up, and clicked his heels.

"Huh? Huh?" the king begged. "Legs all day, legs all night. Come on, give it up."

He started dancing, trying to watch his legs go. His belly was half the size compared to the last time Art had seen him. He was a deflating weather balloon. He finished with a flare, out of breath with his arms out. Waiting for applause.

Surprise and confusion kept Art still. He looked around. "Where did you come from?"

"Oh, yes. That." The king cleared his throat. Disappointment lingered on Art's lack of excitement for the new legs. "I crashed the rocket. You know, the one you... never mind. Then Santa Claus—"

"We've always been here, Arthur."

Another king was suddenly there. Although he wasn't wearing a crown, he felt like a king. And he looked like King Chocolate if King Chocolate occasionally ate vegetables.

"Artie, this is my brother. Brother, Artie," Casey muttered.

"Macey." He offered a short bow. "King of the Nice. I'm so very sorry we didn't meet, Arthur. Merry, merry and a pleasure to be here. How may we be of service?"

Art didn't know what any of that meant. He scrambled to his feet, feeling the wires of exhaustion begin to pull. The wind snapped the kings' long coats like towels on a clothesline. It must have been their voices he'd heard earlier. King Chocolate reached out to put a hand on Art's shoulder. Even in the wind, the bitter smell of cacao was strong.

"Help with what?" Art said.

"Help with what," King Chocolate repeated and chuckled. "What do you think?" When Art didn't understand, he said, "How about the giant wall behind you."

"What my brother is trying to say is that we're here to help you climb."

The wall so tall and straight and high. Like, absurdly so. And these two were going to help him climb it?

"I know what you're thinking," King Chocolate said. "About us. About you, maybe. But let me tell you something, my boy. A journey of a thousand miles starts with one fat king and his brother. So when you're ready, let's get to it."

Art laughed, sort of. The king's grit and confidence were as convincing as they were hilarious. King Chocolate wasn't smiling, though. Neither was Macey. Art sobered up.

"I can't climb that."

"That's what you think," King Chocolate said.

"Yeah. That's exactly what I think. Look at it."

The royal brothers (were they twins?) nodded at each other. Then squatted down and picked Art up by the legs. For a couple of unimpressive kings, they hoisted him onto their shoulders like gravity didn't exist.

"It doesn't matter what you think," King Chocolate grunted.

Even on their shoulders, Art was short of the nearest ledge by more than an arm's length. They grabbed his ankles and lifted him over their heads. Art waved his arms to keep from tipping over. The wind gusted into him. The kingly brothers shuffled to keep him upright. This idea was getting worse.

"We're proud of you!" Macey shouted. "Never forget that!"

Art leaned against the wall, his fingers brushing the ledge. The wind howled along the cliff. He started to tilt. The royal brothers faltered. Art's knees buckled. He was going to come down, and it was going to be hard and awkward. A fall that would net more than a scuffed knee.

Two pairs of hands nabbed his wrists. One pair was dainty. The other pair hairy.

They hauled him up and over the ledge. Art fell on his face, rolled onto his back. The Border Oracles looked down on him. One bright and smiling. The other quite grim (as you know).

"Ha. Still the *mess,* kid!"

Grim hauled Art off the ground with surprising strength. Art was yanked off his feet and teetered on the edge. Joy brushed the grit off Art.

"You look fabulous, darling."

"That's a bit *much.*" Grim pulled his drawings from her white tank top still stained with mustard, fanned them out like playing cards. "I got the best ones," she whispered to him. "Just wanted you to know. Do you have any more?"

"No time to dally, darling. How do you want to do this? Saddle-style, or... okay. Yeah, just..."

Grim already had Art's shirt. Joy took his legs. They were pulling in opposite directions with Grim breathing into Art's face. It smelled like hot sauce and expired shrimp. Art couldn't look away from the little crawly things in her teeth.

"Take a *picture!*" she shouted.

Before Art could say anything, the sisters threw him on their shoulders. A beat later he was on their raised hands, hugging the wall and stretching for the next ledge. He was pulled up, just like before. Once safely on the ledge, Art sprang to his feet. Meg and Gandy were gritty like sand and smelled nothing like shrimp. They hugged him. He came away with white icing on his shirt.

"Careful. You skin yourself, sugar?" Meg shouted over the wind. She touched his arm where blood had dried.

"The boy's all right," Gandy said. "Rub a little cinnamon on it. Look at him. So different now. Ain't time funny, son?"

While they were admiring the boy who had crossed over into their home, another couple watched from the crowded space on the ledge. Another flat, cookie-shaped couple. Gusts of wind threatened to pull them off the cliff like kites.

"My manners," Meg said. "This is Clovey and Dandy. They were from the other side."

By the way they were frowning, the way their arms were crossed, Art figured they called the Naughty Side home. Gandy rubbed something on Art's scratched elbow (it was cinnamon, and it burned).

"Time to go," Meg said. "Upsie-daisy."

"I don't know if that's a good idea," Art said. "I don't want to—"

"You won't break us, son," Gandy said. "We've been out of the oven a long time. Clovey, Dandy, take that side. You grab his leg, love. On three."

Up and away he went to the next step, which he couldn't reach on his own, and someone reached down to haul him up. He fell on his back this time, staring at the stirring clouds, the wind pulling them apart like cotton fibers. Fireflies dancing in their depths. And far above them a sky as pink as a flamingo.

Two faces looked down at him. Both round and fleshy with pointy ears. Each with a single braid of silver hair. One of them hugged his leg.

"So strong," Belly said. "And warm."

"He's a warmblood," Jelly said, "for sure."

"And taller. My Artie's gotten taller. You think he's taller, Jelly Bean? Aren't you going to hug him?"

"I don't think so," Jelly said.

"Come on, hug him. The queen would want you to."

"The queen already hugged him. Come on, off you go." She pried her sister's grip from Art's leg. Belly backed up with affection all over her. She dove in for another hug, but her sister intercepted her.

"We talked about this."

The sister elves argued. Art looked over the edge. His gut twisted at how high he'd already climbed. He couldn't see the ground, though. Which helped. The kings were somewhere down there, deep in the dense fog. The gingerbreads, however, he could still see. They waved when he saw them. Well, two of them waved.

Belly clamped onto his leg. "Last one," she said. "Jelly, say something."

"Thank you for the company."

"Thank you for the company?" Belly said. "That's all you have to say?"

"I'm not good with words."

"Try again!"

"It's okay," Art said. "She doesn't have to—"

"Merry, merry," Jelly said. No hug, though. "Off you go."

Belly reluctantly let go, kissing Art on the knee before she did. The two elves latched onto his legs. The next ledge was a long way up. The elves wouldn't come close enough for someone to grab him from above. Art searched for handholds.

"You ready?" Belly asked.

"I don't think I can—"

The elves sprang onto their toes with the velocity of a catapult. With feet that were nearly three feet long, that translated into more than enough force. If Art had to do this over, he would suggest they tell him he was going to be launched in the general direction of the next ledge.

He swung his arms and started to yell. The wind stole the words out of his mouth. He was falling short and blowing off course. His belly was turning inside out when his brain informed his body it was in for a very long fall.

"Now!"

The tiny words came from behind him. Art had reached the zenith of his launch and was on the brink of reversing course when a thick knotted vine hit his hand. He thought it lucky to catch it. If he hadn't grabbed it, it was goodnight.

"Give us a kick, crossa!"

Art kicked off the cliff and clenched the vine until his fingers hurt. It sounded like it was stretching. He closed his eyes. Then he was slowly hauled up.

"The boys will take ya from here."

Art peeked through the slits of his eyelids. General Fly landed on his white knuckles and saluted. The Lost Boys pulled him to safety. They were all there. Two dozen of them crowded on the shelf. Beams strapped to their backs. That was more Lost Boys than he remembered. But then the others must have been from the other side. Rude Boy was in front, arms crossed.

"Jolly shirt," he hollered over the gale. "Nick it from the squealers?"

There was laughter. Another Lost Boy leaned in and said: "Ee no Lander, sure. Too thick in the rock and pointy knees and all. Wouldn't last, aye wager."

A few disagreed. There was pushing and shoving with no room for it. Art's heels were at the edge. He still had the vine in case he went over, but Rude Boy grabbed him. "Still owe me a beamer, dirty crossuh, you. Make it up next one."

More arguments ended with Art being pulled into the middle of the pack, which smelled like a funky sour mosh pit. He held his breath. They pushed him up and passed him around. Art crowd-surfed over them. The Lost Boys began climbing onto each other, building a pyramid. They swayed in the gusting wind, laughing as they passed Art up the human ladder. He didn't think it was funny and wanted down to try something else.

"Old steel!" they told him.

Art had no idea what that meant and surrendered. Whatever was supposed to happen would happen. There was no way he was getting up the cliff without them, and they all seemed to know what they were doing. Of course, he made it. Wolves were there to pull him up. Big Bad and Big Good introduced themselves. The next ledge was gorillas (Henry and Carl from the green room; the others he didn't know). Three pigs plus three more were next. Art tried to give their shirt back. They said no and merry, merry.

There were more ledges. Lots more. Bo Peep and her sheep. Puppets and Miss Tuffets. Goldilockses and bears. Riding Hoods and robots and princes with long capes. Frogs and mice and everything naughty and nice helped him. The half-horse brothers, too.

Art eventually relaxed and trusted the process. A few steps were a bit sketchy. And every time he landed and looked down, the clouds were following. He couldn't see those who helped him up or how far down it was, but he could feel them down there.

The top of the cliff was in clear sight now. Fireflies were pouring up and over a sharp edge against a sky growing pinker and richer. The clouds were fading. The few wispy clouds raced in the wind. He could smell bubble gum, taste watermelon with a hint of peppermint. The air was thicker. Made his fingers stick together. His eyelids gummy.

A cat was on the last ledge.

Daryl didn't do anything to help him climb up. He stood in a little alcove, protected from the wind, swishing his tail around. Art rolled onto his back to catch his breath. He was exhausted. Aches and pains and bruises on bruises. Fireflies fought to stay near the top, signaling where he had to go. It was too far to reach. And a cat wasn't going to get him there.

"Wasn't hard getting up here, I'll bet," Art said. "Not for you."

It never is for cats.

Daryl arched his back, rubbed against Art.

Art peeked over the ledge. A profound sense of sadness filled him. He wasn't going to see them anymore. Any of them. Like, ever. It seemed like he just got to Candyland. He felt a little weepy thinking about it.

They'll always be there.

Art wasn't sure what that meant. Seeing as he was on his way to the top and they were down there, and Candyland did not appear to even exist anymore. But Daryl seemed to know things.

"What's up there?"

Impossible to say.

"Okay." There were no handholds between where they were and the top. Even if he weren't gassed, there was no jumping that far. He was stuck on the last step.

"Tell me you're going to teleport me." Art looked at Daryl. "That's why you're up here."

You wish. All cats looked bored. If you heard them talk, they sounded bored, too. *Wait for it.*

Art was happy to lie there and taste the pink sky. The ground tacky against his back. His nostrils sticking shut. He closed his eyes and opened his mouth, imagined the sky was a sheet of bubble gum and he would chew his way through it. What a way to end this climb.

The aroma shifted towards burnt sugar.

Before he recognized it, an earthquake shook the world. Art was grateful he was sticking to the ground, or he might have vibrated over the edge. He stuck his arms out for maximum contact. He could hear rocks falling and shattering into smaller pieces below. The cliff exploded near him. The smell of burnt sugar was overpowering.

You might want to look to your left.

Art opened his eyes to see two purple lips and one giant tooth. Sweet Tooth had punched holes into solid rocks. Her pumpkin face smiled down on him. And then he heard from the other side another, "*Yum!*"

Two of them!

Both as merry as giant clowns could be, scaling up a cliff. They leaned closer and sniffed Art like dogs saying hello. Daryl backed into his little alcove. Wrapped his tail around his body. The Sweet Tooth sisters put their hands out for Art to climb on.

"You coming?"

Not yet, Daryl said. *I'll catch up.*

Art was happy to not climb the last leg. He was gently lifted in the pink sky, which was wet and resistant, coating him with sweet humidity. The fireflies swirled in the vortex like the exhaust of a jet engine. Art wanted to shout merry, merry to the Sweet Tooths and anyone who could hear him below, but the wind was fierce, and his throat dry.

Sweet Tooth grabbed the top ledge. Her sister lifted Art over it.

He was hiding his face from the storm when they did. He covered his ears from the awful whistling of the wind. He held his breath to keep from choking on the candied air. It felt like he was being pushed through a keyhole. Art couldn't tolerate any more of it. It was tight and uncomfortable and frightening. He was about to scream out to take him back down.

And then everything was silent.

A RINGING in his ears slowly faded.

He heard nothing. Nothing at all. Perfect silence broken only by the rustle of his own clothing on the ground. He was balled up on his side. Knees to his chest, hands over his head. What some would call a fetal position. It felt good. It felt safe.

His eyes were closed, and he was imagining where he might be. He'd scaled that cliff—that impossibly high cliff—into a violent windstorm, where the clouds grew damp and the sky was pink and sticky. All of that was gone. There was nothing but coolness on his cheeks and perfect silence in the air. It was another world. A moment untouched. He could be anywhere... until he opened his eyes.

When he dared to peek, gritty stone was beneath him. The mountain continued. A huge letdown. Until he rolled over. His movements loud and lonely, he witnessed thousands of fireflies above him, flashing their phosphorescent abdomens to each other. Beyond them... well. There was nothing he could say about that. Words would only spoil what he saw.

The universe.

Art had seen a night sky before. There were times it struck awe, especially on rural roads nowhere near a city, where it looked like God had parked all the stars in the backyard. Even if you took the most amazing sky ever seen and multiplied it by a hundred, it wouldn't touch this.

This was everything.

This was a star-dusted sky spread before him and around him like he'd been swallowed by the universe and floated in its belly. He'd forgotten the mountain under him and around him. There were just stars. Billions and trillions of stars like Christmas lights on black fabric.

Majestic and eternal.

A theater of unimaginable depth and meaning.

So big and endless. So vast.

Its splendor filled him with unarguable truth, one that could not be denied. An elementary truth. That nothing ever dies. As plain and simple as that. Right there in front of him. The grand mystery unveiled. He couldn't explain how he knew it. There was no way to tell someone if they asked. It just was this, and this was so obvious.

There is beauty in darkness.

Tears streamed down his face. He wore a gobsmacked smile and let them flow, watching the fireflies drift up and away and into space. Flashing their lights, streaking like shooting stars.

Art was unburdened. For the first time, he was free.

HE BRUSHED HIMSELF OFF. The aches and bruises still very present. Stiffness setting in. The mountain didn't go much higher. A narrow path went to the top. He didn't plan on climbing it, but something was up there.

It wasn't far.

A bonsai tree grew from a crack. The evergreen needles were short and twisted. Ornaments the size of acorns hung from the branches. A string of lights wrapped around them.

A bamboo mat lay next to it with two meditation benches facing each other. Like a blanket spread out for a midnight picnic. They were the benches the queen had had on her island, where she'd folded her legs beneath. In between were three teacups. Two of them held a small bit of tea. The third was full.

It was warm.

There was no need to look around. Everything was exposed. There was nowhere to hide. Art didn't need to see the footsteps of the couple who had sat here to share tea. And afterwards, they had danced under the cool belly of the universe.

Sometimes I imagine my husband sitting across from me, the queen had said. *We would share a cup of tea and watch the fireflies. And then dance like we did when we were young.*

Art wished he had been there to witness the reunion. Instead, he raised the cup, closed his eyes to savor the aroma, and drank the tea they'd left behind for him.

The little lights twinkled on the tree. Art pulled the polyurethane wheel out from his pocket—the gift he'd found on the stage—spun on a fishing line in one direction and then the other, his glittery name on the side of it. He stepped over the bamboo mat and tied it on the bonsai tree. The branch sagged under the weight. It seemed like a good place for it.

A present was below the tree. It was flat and narrow and wrapped in plain, brown paper. No bow or ribbon. A piece of twine, however, was tied around it. Art picked it up, plucked a folded piece of paper from beneath the twine. He sat down on one of the benches, pulled his legs under him. He took his time with the tea, resting in the silence between sips and gazing up. Sometimes losing himself in the view.

When he finished the tea, he opened the letter.

DEAR ARTHUR,

I wish I could tell you what Candyland is. Or was. By now it's returned to the source. I wish I could tell you why it existed in the first place and why crossers like us ended up there. Landers would tell you what they believe it was. Even crossers will claim to know. The truth is no one knows. Not me or S'ven or anyone else. And even if we knew, we wouldn't find the words any more than you can find words for what you see above you right now. But I can tell you this much, and this much is true: this is the true essence of Christmas. It is all things naughty and all things nice. It is not always what you want, but always what you need.

This place is a gift, Arthur. And you are part of it.

It has been an honor to have shared it with you, as brief as it may seem. Your journey has not always been easy. Journeys worthwhile rarely are. You once asked why I was still here. Initially, I never desired to leave because I felt I belonged in Candyland. I had done so much wrong in my life that I didn't deserve to leave.

My husband often said life is suffering. The real question, he would say, was if all the suffering we endure was to help one person, only one, would the hardship be worth it? That's why I never left, Arthur. I didn't know it at the time, but looking back, I believe I was waiting to help one person.

Some believe this place is a story. Some of those stories are epic journeys with timeless adventures that go on and on. Some stories are short and as bright as the sun. Their worth can be equally measured in the joy they bring. Whether long or short, stories never truly end. They just move on.

As you know, time here is funny. It is eternal, yet passes in a wink of an eye. To be here when you arrived and to have shared your story has been a privilege, Arthur.

And, yes. It was worth it.

Merry, merry, Arthur. Perhaps we will meet in another story.

Truly, Lady Mouserinks.

ART READ IT AGAIN. He didn't know why he was crying.

Maybe because he wished she were there to say those things instead of writing them in a note. She had seen him for who he truly was. She understood him. She saw him. If she were here, he'd have a chance to say how grateful he was she stayed. What would have happened without her?

He wiped his eyes and folded the note, tucked it into his back pocket. Then searched for something to blow his nose into, used one of the napkins on the bamboo mat. He was still holding the present. He almost didn't want to open it. He pried the string off and unwrapped the generic paper, the crinkling so loud in the silence. Lifted the lid on an ordinary box. A small card lay inside.

Create your next adventure.

What looked like a crooked stick was nestled in shredded paper. It was knobby and nearly a foot long. Something a wizard would wave. He swung it around, cutting the silence and still air, pointed it at the sky. Sparks didn't fly out. No pixie dust, either. A ballpoint tip was embedded at the end of it. He touched it to his finger; it left a spot of ink. An odd gift. But then there was nothing normal about this place. That was when something snorted. Almost in agreement with that thought.

Art swung the crooked pen like a sword or a magic wand (just in case it did do magic). The ballpoint end was aimed at the horned beast. It was so big, so massive, Art didn't recognize the animal for what it was. It stood over him with antlers spanning the average width of a bedroom. Eyes as black as coal yet shined like jewels. It pawed the rocks, scraping the dust away, and snorted again.

Breath humid on Art's cheeks. Grassy in his nose.

A reindeer.

That was what it was. Plain and simple, but not by the looks of it. Unless it was ripped from a storybook, reindeer didn't come super-sized like that. Not with heads the length of dinner tables and hooves the size of catcher mitts. But a reindeer no less.

Art felt the raw power of the thing, enough to send living crea-tures for cover. But underneath it was the warmth of love and protection. The promise and richness of Christmas spirit radiated in waves that stirred in Art's stomach. The reindeer kicked at the rock again and bowed his head. Held the muzzle at Art's feet.

Art reached out to touch it. Stroked the short fur running the length of his snout.

The hum of bells went through his fingers and into his arm. They rang in his head and stoked a fire in his heart. Bells, he heard. Bells, he felt. They were everywhere. So strange, the way this vast open space was suddenly as intimate as a small room. As quiet as an empty box. But all around him, bells.

Ring, ring. Ring, ring, ring.

Art smiled. Joy beamed from every pore.

The reindeer bent the knee of his front leg and then the other. When he settled on the haunches of his back legs, he slowly picked up his head. Nudged Art gently with his muzzle.

Art's boots scuffed the hard ground.

He dragged his hand down the bony antler, walked around it to look at the girth of the waiting animal. Unsure if the reindeer wanted him to climb onto him. The reindeer turned his head, the back of his antler guiding him closer.

To be clear, climbing onto an animal this size isn't as easy as it sounds. Art did it, though. He grabbed handfuls of shaggy fur and threw one leg over him. Before he could settle, the reindeer stood up. The sudden shift tossed Art into the air. He landed square on the reindeer's back. Felt the muscles flex and roll beneath him. The reindeer turned his head, careful not to rake Art off with an antler, and fixed him with one eye.

Art smiled back.

It would be hard to explain the liftoff of a flying reindeer. True, it would be hard to convince anyone reindeers could fly. But even if you made it that far, the launch would be impossible to explain. Only felt. The best words could do is imagining oneself holding a musky shag carpet. And the next second the wind is in your face.

Art ducked his head against the reindeer's powerful neck.

He felt the legs pedaling below as if the reindeer were galloping on thin air. His blood pumping hot. A steam engine firing exhaust from his nostrils. They circled the bamboo mat and tiny Christmas tree with a skateboard wheel ornament weighing down a limb. Fireflies flowed behind them like miniature comets.

Higher they went. Wider the circle.

The stars grew bigger and brighter. The one star, the North Star, flashed like a beacon. Galaxies emerged from deep space in every shape and color.

Art had never felt freedom like this. Never so unencumbered. So unburdened. The fireflies whispered their secrets, and so did the stars. The truth all around him.

Love.

There was a time in his life he would have laughed at that thought. Love was something you felt toward a new bike or a puppy. A girlfriend or newborn child. But now he knew what it really was. He felt it. *I am love.* To know this love was out there and in him and of him and there was no difference between any of those things made him weep with joy.

The essence of Christmas.

The reindeer pedaled faster. Fireflies flew in all directions now, shooting into space. The stars streaked into the darkness.

Art put his arms around the reindeer. Laid his cheek against the musky fur. He closed his eyes and held him so tightly that he didn't feel where he ended and the reindeer began. Art was the soaring, the roaring, the stretching limbs and snorting muzzle. He was the warmth. He was the protective generosity.

He stayed that way until he was no longer a name. He was just the beauty of existence.

He was flight.

He was freedom.

A beautiful beam of light shooting toward the North Star.

Where there are no endings.

28

Pinpoints of light from the neighbor's yard rotated through the window. Cal watched them run across the popcorn ceiling, over the water stain that had grown larger over the last year, thinking today was the day he'd fix the leak. Knowing he wouldn't.

The windows were open. It was chilly enough to see his breath. He huddled under the thick blanket, where it was toasty warm, and planned to stay there till the sun was up. It'd be hours before that happened. He didn't need to look at the clock. He knew what time it was. This was a nightly ritual.

Wakey-wakey, his brain said. *All aboard the Thinking Express. Toot-toot!*

And then the thoughts came marching in. Planning out the day, telling stories, making up scenarios. Most of the time they dragged memories out of the cellar and played them on a loop. Those he didn't mind so much. It was the *what-ifs* that bothered him most.

What if I'd done this, would things be different?

What-ifs were tireless and endless and no good. There was no way to prove them right or wrong. That was the thing with parenting.

You choose a direction and will never know what would have happened if you went the other way.

When the Thinking Express hit supersonic speed, he got out of bed. Feet on the cold floor, he went to the bedside chair to read. The room was mostly windows. That was what he loved about the back room. It never felt closed in. Landscape lighting made for great views all night long. Christmas time he would put red or green lenses on the lights to make it festive. Not this year, though.

He had just sat down when he noticed someone standing on the deck. He searched for his glasses to make sure. It could have been a tree, she was standing so still. He got dressed and walked through the closet to get to the main house. The back room had been added thirty years after the house was built. The closet was the only way to get there from inside the house. When the kids were little, they pretended it was a secret passage to a fantasy land.

The main bedroom was empty, the blankets thrown back. He'd sleep-divorced his wife years ago (it was her idea), and they'd never slept better. *Beds are mostly for sleeping.* She wasn't wrong.

Cal took a detour on his way to the kitchen, passed an empty bedroom on the left, and opened the door at the end of the hallway. Marlowe was home from college. He peeked into her room. It looked like her dresser had vomited. She was on the bed, buried beneath a pile of jeans. Cal snuck in and closed the laptop. *New Elf City* was still playing.

If she woke up, it might freak her out to see someone standing in her room. Watching her sleep. Remembering when he read stories to her at bedtime. Sometimes he'd make them up. Now she was writing her own stories. Full-length novels. And people were reading them.

In the kitchen, he put the kettle on and a teabag in a mug.

The only lights in the house came from the Christmas tree. There were ornaments and white lights wrapped around the branches, but it was not your normal tree. It was really a big, barren branch taken from the backyard. They stood it up in the middle of the room so that it went up into the well of the skylight. Fallen leaves were attached to it—leaves from the sycamore the kids planted when they were little that was now fifty feet tall.

The ornaments were all homemade. Things the kids made. It was tradition to take them out one at a time and tell stories about them. It was a little different this year.

He took the kettle off before it whistled. On his way around the tree, he noticed an unfamiliar ornament. It was easy for him to forget such things (he was the first to admit that), but he was pretty sure he hadn't seen this one.

The dogs followed him to the back door. Grace was outside the screened porch, on the deck, looking up at the sky. She didn't turn when the door opened or when the dogs shook their heads, ears slapping like mudflaps. She was hugging herself.

"You okay?" he asked.

She nodded. Okay was a relative word. Wrapped in a blanket with a knitted scarf around her neck under a moon so full you could read a book. He put his arm around her. She leaned into him. They stood in the lunar glow, watching the sky like a drive-in movie. A million stars were playing.

The dogs got bored and went inside.

Grace blew her nose into a secret tissue she kept tucked in her sleeve, pulling it out like a magician when she needed it. He felt her quivering and held her close. She wasn't cold. They didn't say anything. Words only cluttered these moments. But when a star streaked across the dark sky, Cal lifted his mug.

"See that?"

Grace nodded. Even chuckled before giving her nose a honk. This was where Cal would joke about Santa Claus coming to town. Not this year.

"Maybe this is a new tradition," he said. "We watch shooting stars."

"I don't want a new tradition."

Neither did he. But there they were, on the back porch in the middle of the night. He had the feeling it wasn't the last time they would do this. He asked if she wanted some tea. With a nod, they went back inside. Cal started another kettle. This was the first holiday they didn't have a mess to clean up in the morning. What he'd give to see plates stacked in the sink, cups on the tables. Candy wrappers everywhere.

Grace was at the Christmas tree. Cal handed her a mug smelling of peppermint. She was holding the ornament Cal had seen earlier: a polyurethane wheel with sparkles.

"I don't remember that one," Cal said.

Grace shook her head. "Marlowe must have done it."

"Mmm."

Marlowe was becoming the princess of card making and gift giving. Her mother was the queen. This, however, with the skateboard wheel and the glitter was good. She'd probably put it on the tree after Cal and Grace went to bed.

With tea in hand, they went back outside. This time they cuddled under a thick blanket on the couch inside the screened porch. Strobing lights from the neighbor's speckled the bare branches of the trees. They were warm beneath the blanket, holding the mugs to their chins, listening to things scurry in the dark. A small forest was beyond the fence where storm sewers emptied out. That was where the kids had played when they were little.

Grace was thinking that, too. She didn't have to say it. The look in her eyes did.

The kids had built forts out of sticks and stray lumber. They would tread through stagnant pools barefoot. And no one ever got bit by a snake. They made bows from saplings and arrows from branches. Shot at each other without anyone losing an eye. They cut giant grapevines and drank the water that leaked from them. All the things parents wouldn't let their kids do if they knew they were doing them.

The neighborhood was different now.

They were no kids playing Manhunt in the summer. No road hockey games or basketball hoops without a net. No screams of delight or cries of a skinned knee. It was quiet now. Just the stars; just the insects.

It all goes by fast, just like they say. Time is funny that way. It inches by at the speed of light.

The back door opened. Marlowe held it for the dogs to follow her out.

"What are you doing out here?" she said.

"Waiting for Santa," Cal said. "What are you doing up?"

"Dogs."

That was Cal's fault. He hadn't closed her bedroom door after he checked on her. He lifted the blanket. She crawled in between them and snuggled against her mom. The dogs whined, but there wasn't enough room. Cal put his arm around his wife and daughter. If they had to start a new tradition, he rather liked this one. It reminded him of a card someone gave them. It was propped in front of the television. Out of all the cards they'd received that year, it was his favorite.

Joy and grief can coexist, it said.

"Merry, merry," Marlowe mumbled.

"Merry, merry?" He chuckled. "Where'd you hear that?"

"I dreamed it."

He liked it. It had a ring to it. He wasn't certain, but it felt like maybe he'd dreamed it, too.

They sank into the couch. Marlowe relaxed and was breathing slower. Soon she was lightly snoring. Grace was squashed beneath her but didn't dare move. Cal's arm was numb. The sun was still hours from rising.

"What's that?" Grace whispered.

Cal didn't see what she was pointing at. Maybe another shooting star. She kept her finger aimed across the yard. Owls were usually sitting in the trees at night, but then a bright light flashed for a long second. It was different than the neighbor's lights.

"Firefly," he said.

"I didn't think they were around this time of year," she said.

They watched it hover higher and higher, periodically signaling back to them until it was just a small dot. No different than a star. Christmas would arrive on a beautifully incomplete note. Different than before. He held his family a little tighter.

"Merry, merry," he whispered.

29

A blue tent was the first on the beach that Christmas morning.

The sun was barely above the horizon, burning red ribbons on incoming waves. A man and a woman set up where the sand was soft. The tide was low that morning. It would be a long walk to where the water lapped the hardpack. But they were mostly going to sit.

They were an older couple. Older than most. Their hair was white, and they walked with patience, holding hands through the soft sand. They never came to the beach this early. It wasn't going to be crowded, not on Christmas. This was a special day. More special than most. They weren't going to miss it.

It was cool in the shade of their tent. They were bundled up, but trying to stay out of the sun. They still weren't accustomed to the brilliance and hid in the shade when they could, covering their eyes with blackout sunglasses. The sound of the ocean put the old man to sleep. His wife had a sketchbook in her lap. Pencils in her hands. She wasn't an artist (she'd be the first to admit that), but this had nothing to do with being good or bad. She just like the way the pencil sounded on the paper, the way sweeping lines could capture a moment.

Soon beachcombers came looking for treasures—seashells and sharks' teeth and such. Down by the pier, a crowd had gathered in bathing suits and swimming caps. At the sound of an air horn, the polar bear club plunged into the ocean. They came right back out and wrapped themselves in towels. Not long after that, families began migrating out of million-dollar beach homes. Not the impressive kinds of houses you would see up the coast. These were older homes where locals lived. They hung their own Christmas lights.

They came out to ride their new bikes on the beach. Fly their new kites. Try out their new wetsuits on new surfboards. The old couple watched from beneath wide-brim hats, occasionally getting up to loosen their joints, dip their toes in the frigid water, and watch the dolphins swim past.

It was sometime after lunch when a family set up next to the blue tent.

They came to this beach often and always the same spot. The waves were calmer there. There were no riptides to worry about, and rarely was someone fishing. The sand was good for castling. Especially the oozing drip castles. The old couple had studied these things from afar. They'd been planning for this day.

The family pulled their stuff out in wagons with oversized wheels. There were three coolers and five beach bags. Two tents and one baby carriage covered in netting. The kids attacked the sand with full-sized shovels. They had a trench dug and the start of a sand sculpture before the chairs were unfolded. Two of the young adults helped with the digging. Country music played on a new all-weather speaker. Soda bottles were opened, and sandwiches passed around. The two little kids were standing over the baby carriage, scratching at the netting. An adult made them stop.

The peaceful moment the older couple had arrived to had become laughing chaos. They held hands and loved every second of it.

One of the men, the oldest of the bunch (not nearly as old as the couple under the blue tent), began setting up a tripod when the tents were staked and the chairs set up. He mounted a fancy camera on it. Brand new, by the looks of it. Opened that morning. He waved a young woman to stand in front of it. She wore a long, flowing robe. Her skin as fair as the sand. Her hair as red as the sunset.

When he was done with her, he got a drone out of one of the beach bags. He fussed with the controls and got it off the ground. It sounded like a giant bug. He checked his instruments, seemed pleased. Said something to one of the women—his wife—who began rounding up the team. It took more than a few minutes to drag the kids out of the trenches and away from the surf. They stood in a semi-circle, wearing sweatshirts and ballcaps. The little ones wore T-shirts and swimsuits.

The old couple watched.

They couldn't hear the speech given. But everyone laughed. Then the young woman with sunburnt hair and a young man about her age took their place in front of the tripod. Someone handed them road flares. There were more instructions for them. Then all together everyone began to chant.

"Three! Two! One!"

The young couple twisted the flares. Instead of flames, smoke shot from the ends. Thick and bright blue smoke. Everyone cheered. Everyone leaped and hugged and kissed.

The little kids ran back to their trench and castle while the adults clinked cans. Hugs for everyone. Drinks all around. In the melee, one of the bags fell over. A red apple went rolling across the hardpacked sand. It came to rest with the stem pointing up. No one noticed. A helicopter could have landed next to them and they wouldn't have noticed.

The old couple looked at each other.

They squeezed hands. The woman pushed herself out of the chair. Her bones achy and joints stiff. She used an umbrella like a cane, pushing the tip into the sand as she walked toward the water. Her husband came with her and picked up the apple. He handed it to her and returned to his seat under the blue tent.

The family was still celebrating. The hugging had slowed, but the laughter and drinking had not. The flares were spent and smoldering. The mother of the family saw the old woman approaching.

"Oh, thank you!" She took the apple from her and said with a Southern drawl: "I'm so sorry. I hadn't realized we were spilling all over the place. We're making a fuss over here, aren't we."

"Quite all right," the old woman said. "Gave me a reason to get my steps in."

"Bless your heart." She took off her sunglasses. "You look familiar. Do I know you?"

The old woman was covered head to toe in a checkered robe, and her hat was wide enough to shade a family of meerkats from the noonday sun. Her sunglasses were round and as black as asphalt. It was the way the old woman walked she had recognized.

"We're neighbors, I believe." The old woman gave her address.

"Oh, my lord. You just moved in! Honey, come over here. It's our neighbors."

The man who set up the tripod came over. His name was Jack. Jack was the only adult wearing a T-shirt. His wife's name was Lorraine. Lorraine wore two sweatshirts. The old woman introduced herself. Pointed at her husband under the blue tent, who waved back. The coincidence of setting up right next to each other was uncanny. What were the odds?

"I love your coat," Jack said. "Aren't you hot?"

The old woman tugged on her checkered overcoat. It was thick and comfortable. "The sun is very bright. We're not used to it."

"Where'd you move from?" Lorraine asked.

"Far away. It was much darker there."

"What brings you here?"

The old woman shrugged. "Family, I suppose."

"Well, welcome. We've got everyone here, so excuse our mess."

"My husband and I rather enjoy it."

Just then one of the little sandcastle builders ran up to Lorraine and started pulling on her sleeve. She bent down, and he whispered something in her ear.

"Go ask your mom, love." When the little boy stared at the old woman, Lorraine ran her fingers through his hair.

"What's that?"

The boy pointed at the sketchpad she was holding. The old woman explained she liked to draw when she came to the beach. That she wasn't very good and that mostly she just liked to make lines. When she showed him what she'd drawn, he seemed mesmerized. It made the old woman smile.

"Go on and find your mother, now," Lorraine said.

Just then the young couple of the hour came up. The young lady with the red hair was pushing the netted baby carriage. Lorraine said it was for practice. The old woman bent over. There wasn't a baby inside the netting. "Well, look at you," she said with a smile. "All cozy in there."

"Is it weird?" Lorraine said. "He just showed up at Tommy and Ann's house, like, four months ago. No collar or chip. He's well fed, though. Look at him."

Ann, the young redhead, said they'd put signs up, and no one ever called. And the cat never left. Now he was in a carriage on the beach. The old woman put the back of her hand against the netting.

"Good to see you," the old woman said. Jack could've sworn she said *again.* A loud purring came from inside the stroller.

"He's not fond of strangers," Lorraine said, "but I think he likes you."

The cat rubbed against the old woman's hand. He strutted around the small enclosure, waving his tail and dragging his belly over the blankets. He didn't seem to mind the pampering.

"I knew a cat like this once," the old woman said. "His name was Daryl."

"Oh, my God!" Lorraine covered her mouth.

Ann grabbed Tommy's arm. Someone shrieked. Even the kids looked up from their sandcastle to see what had happened. Lorraine was shaking her hands like something bit them.

"Did you hear that, Jack?" Lorraine said. "Did you hear what she just said?"

"I'm standing right here."

"That's what Tommy named the cat. He named the cat *Daryl*!"

Tommy and Jack weren't as excited as Lorraine and Ann. It was rather odd, though. How many cats were named Daryl? And the old woman knew one, too. Almost as weird as neighbors setting up on the beach next to each other. Tommy said he'd just thought of the name. Like it came out of the blue and fit. He didn't mention how his head hurt right before he thought of it. The old woman didn't ask him if it did.

"Do you know the owner of the cat?" Ann asked.

"Once upon a time, I did."

"Of our Daryl?" Ann was a bit worried.

"That would seem unlikely, wouldn't it? I think your Daryl has a home with you. You look like family. And you're growing one, I take it?"

Lorraine explained that Ann was her and Jack's daughter. And she was pregnant. "Blue for boy," she said. "Just like your tent."

"Coincidence," the old woman said.

There was more general giddiness. Jack and Tommy faded from the conversation. Lorraine put her hand on Ann's stomach. They touched their heads together.

"Congratulations," the old woman said. "Do you have a name?"

"We have a list," Ann said. "A very long list. It's a lot harder picking one than I thought it would be."

"I'm sure you'll come up with one that fits. Just like Daryl." The old woman winked at the cat. It didn't seem all that strange when she did. Not that time. "Well, it's very nice to meet you."

"Listen, don't be a stranger. Please. You come over anytime you like. There's always room at the table."

The old woman considered it. She looked at her husband. Whether he heard it or not, he waved. "We would like that very much," the old woman said. "That's very kind of you."

As it turned out, the old couple would be neighbors for a long time. Long enough to see Tommy and Ann's boy grow up. She would give him all her art supplies, and he would show her all the things he drew and painted. The old man would have him mow their lawn. Afterwards, the boy would sit on the porch and drink sweet tea. Every Christmas, he would visit.

The old couple would never tire of the sound of his laugh. Or the brightness of his smile.

"I didn't catch your name," Ann said.

The old woman turned around. She pulled the black sunglasses over the scar on her cheek. "Rinks."

"Ms. Rinks?" Ann said. "I don't think I ever met anyone named Rinks before."

"A few have."

And she winked at the cat again.

THE CLAUS UNIVERSE

Don't stop now. The Claus Universe awaits. Catch up on all the holiday adventures.

http://bertauski.com

YOU DONATED TO A WORTHY CAUSE!

By purchasing this book, you have donated to the **Novak's House.**

10% of the profits from Candyland is annually donated to Novak's House: a recovery residence that was founded in 2020 by Brandon Novak and George Evagelou to help those struggling with the disease of addiction find a safe, sober place to call home in the early stages of recovery.

#BENISHERE